PRAISE FOR *THE RULE OF ONE*

"Ava and Mira's world is an all-too-believable mix of advanced technology and environmental collapse. In their debut, Saunders and Saunders, themselves twins, lend an authentic voice to the girls' first-person narration . . . Readers are in for a fast-paced ride, poised for a sequel, as the twins embrace their father's call, in the words of Walt Whitman, to 'resist much, obey little.'"

—*Kirkus Reviews*

"Dystopia fans will enjoy this adventure set in an all-too-plausible future America."

—*School Library Journal*

"Utilizing a sf-fantasy setting and a survival-oriented plot, the Saunders sisters are careful to promote growth and differentiation between the twins . . . There are parallels to current news stories, such as immigration, environmental resources, and an autocratic political system. Try this with fans of James Dashner's Maze Runner series, Margaret Peterson Haddix's *Double Identity*, or such clone books as Rachel Vincent's *Brave New Girl*."

—*Booklist*

"Twin storytellers Ashley and Leslie Saunders are modern-day soothsayers who beautifully spin a suspenseful tale of the not-so-distant future. Pay attention—this could be what *1984* was to 1949."

—Richard Linklater, Academy Award–nominated
screenwriter and director

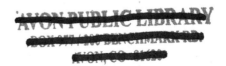

THE
RULE
O F
MANY

BOOKS BY
ASHLEY SAUNDERS &
LESLIE SAUNDERS

The Rule of One

The Rule of Many

The Rule of All (forthcoming)

THE RULE OF MANY

ASHLEY SAUNDERS
+
LESLIE SAUNDERS

SKYSCAPE

Text copyright © 2019 by Ashley Saunders and Leslie Saunders
All rights reserved.

Published by Skyscape, New York

www.apub.com

Amazon, the Amazon logo, and Skyscape are trademarks of Amazon.com, Inc., or its affiliates.

ISBN-13: 9781542043700 (hardcover)
ISBN-10: 1542043700 (hardcover)
ISBN-13: 9781542043687 (paperback)
ISBN-10: 1542043689 (paperback)

Cover design by David Curtis

Author photo by Shayan Asgharnia

Printed in the United States of America

First Edition

To Jason Kirk and Ginger Sledge,
for saying yes and leading us on our greatest adventure.

PART I

THE SEPARATION

AVA

"I'd like to go to your party, and I'll bring yellow flowers," I say to Mira. "May I come?"

My sister smiles—I've puzzled out her secret rule.

"Yes, you can come to my party, Ava."

Groans erupt around the spacious suite we share on the seventh floor of the Paramount Point Hotel. A series of massive glass windows frames an exquisite view of downtown Calgary in the waning afternoon light.

"That's not fair. You probably told her the secret with one of your twin looks or something," a snub-nosed boy disputes from the corner. He's already been refused entry to the party for bringing an inflatable shark.

Half a dozen young Common members lounge on chairs, our beds, or the floor, all of us a sort of unofficial Games Club formed with the sole purpose of keeping Mira and me occupied.

After we hijacked Governor Roth's Anniversary Gala two weeks ago and revealed our illegal twin existence to the entire Rule of One America, Emery ordered us to stay inside the hotel. The repercussions of our surprise appearance sent shock waves rippling across the United States and all the way up here to Canada.

The next morning, the powerful Texas governor proclaimed across millions of screens that Mira and I assassinated his grandson, Halton, in an attempt to obliterate the Roth family name. He coined us the "Traitorous Twins." *What great family will they come for next?* he asked the nation.

So once again Mira and I must stay hidden. For our own safety, Emery insists. We're too important to risk being kidnapped or killed by a Roth sympathizer or one of his undercover agents.

Ever since we entered the rebellion safe house, Mira and I haven't been allowed outside. Fourteen whole days and nights carefully stashed away, we're a secret just like before. Isolated and confined, with no real agency of our own.

Despite leaving everything we ever knew in Dallas to join the Common in Canada, our lives haven't really changed that much after all.

But at least we're together, Mira told me one particularly aggravating night when I felt so trapped I almost burst out the safe house doors, my safety be damned. *And not stuffed down in a basement.*

I glance out at the magnificent buildings that line the bright horizon and think of my father. *He must be in his own dark basement right now.*

"Tell me what you'll bring to my party, Pawel," Mira says. "Then I'll tell you if you can come."

Pawel exhales from across the room, his steel-blue eyes wide, eager to get it right. He runs his hand through his sandy hair, its waves dominated by an impressive cowlick. "I'd like to go to your party, and I'll bring red roses," he answers, guessing that the required item must either be coded by color or taken from nature. "May I join you?"

Mira shakes her head, her lips curling mischievously. "I'm sorry. You cannot come to my party with me, Pawel."

His shoulders sag in defeat, and he locks his disappointed eyes with mine. His cheeks flush pink; then he quickly joins the other rejected partygoers lined up in a corner. I can feel their frustration mounting.

Technology forbidden, our amusement is restricted to simple entertainment using board games, pen and paper, or our minds. Mira or I have won every single game we've played. If there's anything we're masters of, it's games. Especially ones with secret rules.

Mira started this game by announcing she's throwing a party and that she'll be bringing white paperback books. Everyone is invited, but in order to attend, you have to bring the correct gift. So far, it's a lonely party of two. Mira and me. Typical.

"Tell me what you'll bring to my party, Barend," Mira says. "Then I'll tell you if you can come."

The attention of the room shifts to Barend, who stands rigid in the open doorway. Our sentinel, dressed and ready for action at any moment, with a gun strapped to his hip. He's always refused Mira's entreaties to join our daily games.

He scans the hallway and then grunts dismissively.

Barend's somewhere in his midtwenties, with muscle roping across his exposed arms. His squared jawline and disciplined shoulders scream *soldier!* And maybe he was. Just like I was a student and a daughter before I became a rebel and a traitor.

"Let me take Barend's turn," a tall girl with a fountain of twisted braids says, stepping out from the losers' corner to face Mira. The girl seems open and friendly, but I've never spoken to her, keeping to myself the past two weeks, participating in game night but not much else. I still find it hard to socialize with people who aren't my sister. The launch of a rebellion doesn't seem like the best time to make friends.

"I'll bring a big, fat T-bone steak. Isn't that what you Texans love to eat?" The girl cradles an invisible steak in her empty hands, wafting it dramatically under Mira's nose. She lifts her eyebrows in triumph, sure the door to the party is about to be opened for her.

Mira laughs and shakes her head again, about to reject the girl's offbeat request, when Emery and her entourage suddenly storm into the room.

"Bring her confetti-filled balloons, and she'll let you into her party," Emery says with a knowing wink. She must've been listening in from the hallway. "Mira might even let you bring a guest."

Objects spelled with double letters are the secret key to the party, and Emery came with two. I'm glad she's been away the past five days, or I'd have to concede every game to her; Emery's the smartest person I've ever met.

"You're back," I say, rising from my bed. Everyone in the room stands, acknowledging Emery as leader of the Common.

She wears her signature look: an unstructured, slightly oversized yellow coat that ends at her knees. Her rich nut-brown hair is short and wild like Einstein's, but curlier, and she's taller than everyone in her small entourage. The more I've studied Emery—my mother's childhood best friend—during my stay here at the Paramount, the more I've discovered she's not the perfectly straitlaced leader I'd expected her to be. Looking closely, I can see the rough edges that hint at the woman she was before having to bear the weight of being the rebellion's leader. The leftover holes from a double eyebrow piercing above her left eye. The way she bites the inside of her cheeks when she's angry, as if withholding a fiery reaction. A poorly healed scar just below her collarbone. It all makes me like her even more.

Emery studies the room, her intent gaze passing over all the young faces eager and willing to carry out her orders, however small. We're all unified in the reason we're here with the Common, so far from our homes, and I find an unhappy comfort in the shared white-hot pain of loss. And the anger that comes with it.

"It's good to see you all again," Emery says. She nods to each of us in greeting. "May I have the room? I need to speak with Ava and Mira."

The Games Club immediately disassembles, Barend directing everyone out into the hall. He shuts the door behind them and turns on his heel, returning to his post inside our room.

Three members of Emery's inner circle remain at her side. They're all Elders, members who've been a part of the Common the longest. Their faces are hardened with world-weariness, and although I've never spoken to any of them personally, Pawel tells me they've each seen the inside of a prison cell more than once.

The door opens, and a young woman who looks a few years over twenty strides with pure confidence into the room. She stands a short distance from the group, unchallenged by Barend. She must be a new recruit, and an important one if she's included in Emery's close circle. The young woman's jet-black hair is pulled back tightly into two French braids, highlighting her dark eyes with their long, intense lashes. If the eyes truly are a window to the soul, hers has taken more than a few beatings.

Mira clasps Emery's shoulder in welcome before asking, "Did you find him this time? You're back early—did something go wrong?"

Countless missions to rescue my father have led to nothing but disappointment. Wherever Roth is hiding his former Family Planning Director, he's making damn sure he'll never be found.

All four Common Elders lower their heads. Something did go wrong. Horribly wrong.

My stomach drops like a heavy anchor cut loose into the sea.

"What happened?" I demand, stepping forward. *His execution date has been moved up. The Guard caught wind of our extraction plans and changed his location . . .*

Emery raises her head, biting the inside of her cheeks, hard. "It's with great sorrow that I have to inform you of your father's murder," she tells us straight. "I am sorry that we could not get to Darren in time."

He's dead. My father's dead. I've learned to always prepare for bad news, but I wasn't prepared for this.

Through a haze of salted tears, I lurch backward. Mira catches me, and I hold on to my sister tight—our combined strength the only thing that keeps me from shattering against the floor.

"No, no, no . . . you said Roth wouldn't kill him!" I cry. "You said he wouldn't risk turning the people to our side!"

"What about the stay of execution!" Mira says in disbelief.

"The official statement from the Governor's Mansion is that it was a suicide," Emery says. "Roth made a speech, weaving a story that Darren hanged himself with his bedsheets during the night, leaving behind a note detailing his great regret for his traitorous crimes against his country and its people."

A cold panic rushes through my body, and I feel faint. Mira shakes uncontrollably beside me. I turn to my sister, and both our green eyes scream, *Lies!*

Father would never, *never* take his own life. He would fight until the bitter end to get back to us.

"The note said his greatest shame of all was raising illegal twin daughters who turned into dangerous traitors themselves."

Roth is using our own father against us. Bile rises to my throat, and my knees falter.

Emery seizes both our shoulders, pulling us close, making sure we listen.

"We know both the suicide and the note are bullshit. We know just before sunrise, Roth entered Darren's cell and shot your father in cold blood."

I try to break free of Emery and my sister. I can't breathe. I need space for my heartache, but Emery grips my shoulder harder.

"Listen to me. We have the surveillance video. Your father's killing will not be buried. Roth's corruption will be exposed—another link in his chain of lies. Your father will continue to help the cause even in death, as your mother did."

"The video could be fake, too, just like the suicide note. He could still be alive!" I find myself pleading.

The new recruit with the French braids steps forward, shaking her head. Her eyes soften with sympathy. "I wish that were true."

She pulls something from her jacket's inner pocket and carefully opens her palm: a metal capsule the size of my fingernail.

Father's microchip.

"I was held in the same prison as your father," the young woman explains, her steady voice struggling to break through the fog of despair that separates me from everything else in the room. "While the Common arrived too late to rescue your father, they were able to rescue me."

Who is this person? Why was she imprisoned, and how did she gain access to my father's chip? *It's always a never-ending maze of questions.*

"Scan the chip," Mira says, her voice hollow.

Barend produces a microchip scanner from his duty belt—he always seems to have the necessary tool or weapon—and hands the device to Emery to scan.

Ping.

A death record pops up on the chip scanner's screen:

Name: DR. DARREN JAMES GOODWIN
Status: DECEASED
Cause of death: SUICIDE
Burial location: UNKNOWN

The only thing I have left of my father is this tiny scrap of metal with his blood still on it. *Where is his body?*

I want to scream.

"It's Darren's chip. It has been authenticated," Emery declares with full conviction. "Skye Lin has been fighting for the Common's cause for half her life. She turned a Guard at the prison, who gave her the chip and surveillance video in the midst of our rescue mission."

Skye Lin. The assassin who poisoned two states' Family Planning Directors and made an unsuccessful attempt on my own father's life. I've never seen her face; after she was arrested in Dallas five years ago, Roth banned images of the teenage murderer across all media outlets.

The governor made sure criminals in Texas never became famous—they were simply thrown in dark cells and never heard from again.

"I didn't know your dad was a member of the Common," Skye insists. "I wasn't trying to kill him. I was trying to kill his office." *The Family Planning Division.*

With that, she turns and walks out, leaving Mira and me drowning in confusion.

"I want to see the surveillance video," Mira says from beside me.

Taken aback, I turn to face my sister. "You want to watch our father's murder?"

"I have to see it for myself." She looks up at me, her eyes red and glassy with anguish. "We were raised on so many secrets, Ava. I just have to see."

I shake my head. "I can't."

As I move to leave the room—I need the open air; the hurt inside me suddenly seems too large for this crowded space—Emery holds up her hand to stop me.

"We leave for the Common's headquarters in the morning—Paramount Point Lodge. You both are needed there. I can explain more tomorrow, but for now take the time to grieve." She lowers her head in a respectful bow. "Your father was a brave man."

Chills run through my body. Rayla had said those same words.

He wants a better future for you both.

I close my eyes and remember one of Father's greatest lessons: it takes iron to sharpen iron. Metal bullets forged my father's death into a cast-iron weight that sits at the bottom of my heart. To be brave like my father, I must endure the painful process of honing. I must become so sharp that no one can touch me or mine again.

"Show me the surveillance video," Mira demands once more.

"It will not be easy to watch, but the choice is yours to make," Emery says.

Visions of my father tied helplessly to a chair, Roth standing over him with a gun, a smug smile on his lips . . .

No! I rip open my eyes and push past Emery, away from my sister. Barend gets out of my path, allowing me to throw open the door, and I stumble into the hall alone. Without any clear direction in mind, I head toward the stairwell. Anger clouds my vision; my knees are shaky, and I lean on the wall to stay standing as I move. My entire world feels upside down, spinning out of control.

Bam. My shoulder slams into someone, jolting my body back upright.

"I'm sorry," I say automatically.

But sharp-edged things don't apologize. They just cut right through. I steel myself and keep going, not looking back, continuing to drag my wobbly legs down the hallway.

"No, I'm sorry," a tentative voice says behind me. Pawel. "I'm sorry about your dad. I just heard the news." Intensity seeps into his words. "At least he died for a reason. You can be proud."

His words shoot at me like bullets, a gut shot with no exit wound, and I stop short. I wrap my arms around my waist—like that could stop the bleeding—and peer inside the room Pawel just exited.

A group of kids, no older than eleven or twelve, huddle on the floor around a tablet screen. Barend would be livid if he caught them with this smuggled technology. As I wonder fleetingly what their punishment would be for risking the Common's safety, one of the kids' heads tilts to the side, giving me a full view of the screen.

My father's face is splashed across an underground virtual newscast. The kids watch, enraptured as a computer-generated anchor with blue hair and violet eyes gives a breathless account of how the disgraced Family Planning Director shockingly took his own life out of shame.

"My brother says it's all a conspiracy," a girl with a high ponytail says. It's Ellie, Pawel's adopted sister. "A Goodwin would never give up."

Another girl spies me standing in the doorway, her breath catching in her throat. She nudges the boy sitting beside her, and the entire group turns to stare at me, their mouths slightly open in reverence.

"Our parents sacrificed themselves for Ellie and me too," Pawel says quietly. A crushing sadness marks his face at the memory. Pawel's four-person family was illegal, even if Ellie wasn't related by blood. Whatever hardships he experienced that led him to the Common will haunt him the rest of his life.

All at once my sharp edges soften with empathy.

I flick my gaze back to my own father on the newscast. They chose a photograph of him in his stately dress uniform. He looks strong and proud and so violently alive it hurts.

I scan the youthful faces of my unexpected audience. Ellie rises and holds out her forearm, fist curled into a tight ball, like Mira and I did at the end of our hijacked newscast. She's petite but fierce, her oval-shaped hazel eyes reflecting her tremendous appetite for defiance at such a young age.

Everyone around her stands and does the same.

Tattoos, drawn with identical dark ink, cover their right wrists, each one a unique emblem of their own resistance: a charging bull, two thick parallel lines, a scorpion ready to strike, a beautifully patterned sun with a face inside.

Next to me Pawel lifts his shirtsleeve, revealing his own tattoo of a tree with thick roots sheltering the letter *E*.

Our spark worked. The flame of revolution has been lit just as Rayla said it would, and now even the next generation can feel its burn.

My heart races wild inside my chest. I hold down my wrist, fist clenched.

"Resist much," I say.

"Obey little," their voices answer in unison.

I pull the hood of my jacket over my head and slip through the back door of the hotel's kitchen. The alley is narrow but clean and devoid of people or any cameras but the Common's. I take off toward an avenue lined with impressive trees, releasing a sigh of relief to be out in the open once more.

The Elders must know I left the Common's grounds—I didn't make my escape a secret. I'm finished with secrets. *Why would they just let me leave?* Sympathy? Sympathy is dangerous in wartime. Then I feel a presence at my back. *Of course.*

As I turn the corner, I sneak a glance behind me and spot Barend. My sentinel, my own personal special agent, following me, protecting me. *Look who has a babysitter now,* I hear Halton's ghost sneer.

I reach for the small of my back, checking on the pistol tucked into its leather holster. Halton's gun hasn't left my body since I pulled it from Mira's trembling hands. *You had to shoot the agent,* I assured Mira afterward. *You saved our lives.*

My pace quickens to match my heartbeat, and I pull my hood lower over my eyes. I make a series of sharp turns along the maze of downtown streets before losing myself within a crowd.

The city buzzes with a vibrant energy. The unfamiliar sounds and unexplored sights all beckon for my attention, but I can't bring myself to lift my eyes from the freshly washed pavement. I just want to keep walking aimlessly, my only companion the loud thoughts that scream for my father's revenge.

Roth is untouchable. Out of reach. You'll never be able to get close enough to deliver the silver bullet.

But our grandmother could. Rayla could find a way straight to the monster and bring back his severed head to lie at our feet in a bloody pool of justice. The one and only time we heard from her, via a secured line in the middle of the night, Rayla swore this was her overriding mission and the reason she isn't with us in Calgary.

Emery's philosophy is the opposite of heads rolling. She believes— *Whack!* Something pointy suddenly jabs into my stomach, interrupting my musings, and I draw in a quick breath. I snap my head up to find the crowd around me has changed from random pedestrians to a frenetic mob of people, signs clutched in their fists.

The muffled voices I've been blocking reach me all at once in a clear, thunderous roar. *"Send the twins back! Send the twins back!"*

Every hair on my body stands erect like tiny flags of warning. *Run!* But before I can even think to follow my burning intuition, a hand-sewn protest sign slams into my face: "Gluts!"

Angry adrenaline courses through my veins. Mira and I are still Gluts in Canada: surplus, unwanted. Not for being twins, but for being in their country at all. Everyone must stay on their side of the wall. We're American; we stay in America, no matter how horrible things get. Being part of the Common doesn't change that hard fact.

How big is the rally against us? Is it the entire city or just a small but vocal faction?

I have to get to the heart of the rally to find out.

From the corner of my eye, I catch Barend rushing toward me. He reaches out his gloved hands, shouting for me to stay put, his deep-set eyes narrowed in rescue-mission mode.

"Send the twins back! Send the twins back!"

Just before Barend can grab me, a trio of protesters wearing some kind of smart technology bandanas over their faces bulldozes their way past me and straight into my bodyguard. He's pulled into the unceasing sea of bodies.

"Aeron, stop!" I hear Barend order from behind his human barricade. Aeron Rowe, the name registered with my counterfeit microchip, now my code name for the Common.

Seizing on the protesters' unintended help, I disobey Barend's command and charge deeper into the mob, directly toward the source of the escalating chaos.

I can't see anything beyond the mass of bodies and the swell of protest signs. I need to find higher ground.

Maneuvering through the overwhelming swarm of people, I spot what looks like a giant, fifty-foot hill covered in bright-green moss and colorful flora. Water cascades serenely down its sides, pooling into a flower-shaped stone basin.

A public water fountain, used for actual drinking, not just as pompous decoration like in Governor Roth's greedy gardens. There must be some kind of filtration system, unseen pipes connected to an underground water tank. Even in my fog of grief, I'm dimly impressed. I've never seen such a display—nature in the middle of a metropolis. It's extraordinary.

I climb onto a small balcony that juts out from the hillside. Immediately two protesters wearing the same black-and-white bandanas with computer-generated patterns I saw earlier approach the lip of the fountain directly below me, refilling their bottles with the precious resource.

Resupplied, one of the demonstrators pockets his bottle as his partner scans his bandana with his tablet.

A block of jumbled text appears on the man's bright tablet screen. I covertly watch as his fingers type in some kind of password to unscramble the sentences, but he turns away before I can read the decryption.

"A cellular pod is needed around Central and Ninth," I overhear the man say. "A communications blackout by the Glut-loving bastards."

The bandanas not only preserve the protesters' identities, they carry with them hidden messages. It's how they must be secretly communicating.

And the military allows this?

I rip my eyes from this fascinating display of abundance and liberty and scan my surroundings. A rally now thousands strong stretches across a vast, artificially grassed square, ringed with colossal honeycomb-shaped towers made from what has to be engineered wood, with shiny glass facades and plant-filled balconies.

Woodscrapers.

Iron may rule Dallas, but wood clearly reigns supreme in Calgary.

Where is the military? The Scream Guns, dropping the crowd to the ground, immobilizing them with overpowering high-pitched sound? Controlling them into obedience. I've never seen a protest before—the people of Dallas were not permitted to use their voices to fight back.

I jump down from my perch and push without direction through the tangled throng of bodies, letting their anger and fear wash over me. It's better than feeling the raw anguish of my father's death.

Then suddenly a gigantic screen that scales a soaring timber-structured building pops on, projecting the impassioned protest back to all of us inside the public square, live. Thousands upon tens of thousands of virtual-reality avatars materialize on the screen, swelling the crowd to unimaginable numbers. People stand on rooftops, shouting for the Gluts to be returned; they hang from high-rise windows like monkeys swinging from trees and climb atop autonomous cars and lampposts; there's even a human pyramid as tall as the Great Pyramid of Khufu, boasting a flag at its apex declaring, "All surplus must go!"

I quickly sweep the ring of buildings surrounding me and find them demonstrator-free, the streets, though teeming with real protesters, devoid of pyramids. *The people are marching from the comfort of their own homes all across Alberta by virtue of VR.* Ingenious.

I have to tell Emery—the Common could use this to our advantage—even if right now it makes me feel like the whole world is against us.

As I wade deeper and deeper into the center of the rally, the heated call to *"Send the twins back! Send the twins back!"* intensifies to an almost unbearable fever pitch. My nerves thrum with energy, sending a shiver of warning through my body. I need to get out of here, but it's like I want to punish myself. I pop my knuckles and readjust my hood, making eye contact with no one, and continue to wander among the mob screaming for my death.

That's exactly what would happen if the protesters' wish were granted: Roth would make sure Mira and I were dead. The entire Goodwin family, gone.

After what seems like an eternity, I'm pushed through a line of people and find myself standing alone within a thin strip of no-man's-land. A divide.

It's then I see one of the greatest surprises of my life.

Hundreds of real people clad in yellow shouting, *"Save the twins, and the revolution begins!"* The unified call is loud and clear, jolting into my veins like lightning. A multitude of Albertans march down a broad boulevard and into the hostile square in support of twin girls from Texas stuck in limbo nearly two thousand miles away from home. It's so humbling. For a moment the heavy weight inside my heart is lifted, and I'm almost moved to tears.

The Common is more powerful than I thought. *I have to tell Mira.*

But when I turn to find a path back toward Paramount Point Hotel, I'm hit with the stark reality of our situation. The opposition that howls to expel Mira and me from their country outnumbers our side four to one. My eyes dart to the mega screen, and I watch as anti-twin VR protesters continue to emerge, filling every available space throughout the square. *Eight to one.*

A slender woman with a gleeful smile on her face taps my shoulder and hands me a pair of sleek glasses. "Look up." She points to the cloudless sky.

In a daze, I throw on the glasses to find giant, colorful hot-air balloons floating above the crowd, passing straight through buildings. The fabric of the gas bags is decorated with threatening slogans like "Find the Traitorous Twins!" and "If we let them in, we let them win."

I suddenly feel terrifyingly claustrophobic inside the mass of strangers, and I have an urgent need to get away, to find a quiet space where I can think.

My heart races like the frantic wings of a hummingbird, and my hands and fingers start to go numb. I feel faint, and my breath comes in fitful bursts. I need to get out of here before I lose all control. *Move. You're good at that.*

I rip off the glasses and stagger through the signs and the bodies, unable to think of anything except how the majority of the people here want us out.

We've already overstayed our welcome.

Somewhere on the edge of the metropolis, I sit on a sculpture of an endless wooden staircase that leads to nowhere. My legs dangle off the edge of the twentieth flight of stairs, nothing but still air in front of me. Quiet and alone, I gaze out at the magical colors that linger on the horizon, the fluorescent pinks and yellows not quite ready to say good night to the world.

The best view is west, to my right, but I can't tear my eyes away from what's spread out so plain in front of me: south. The direction home.

I lean back against the polished wood, close my eyes, and dream that these limitless stairs could lead me all the way up to wherever my father is now waiting.

MIRA

We're on the run again.

Ten of us, packed inside a white passenger van, "Paramount Excursions" painted on its sides. Two vans follow close behind, others traveling an alternate route somewhere farther north. All heading where?

They never tell me.

Ava and I sit in the back row, baggage stacked between us. The locks and zippers clink and jingle, mixing a maddening duet I have to fight to tune out.

I haven't spoken since we gathered our measly belongings and fled the hotel. I haven't thought much either, too busy willing my swollen eyes to dry up. I refuse to let any drops fall. To let anyone see my pain leak from me through wasted tears.

The AC blasts through the air vent, sending chills down my spine and legs. I shove the vent away, shifting the arctic current toward the row in front of me, directly at Pawel's head. He doesn't flinch or say anything. No one has said anything. They're all too afraid to even look at us.

"Mira," Ava whispers beside me.

I continue to stare straight ahead, fixated on the bursts of air that plaster Pawel's thick hair to his skull, reminding me of the way grass flattens as a drone lands.

A squeeze of panic shifts my eyes to the window. A few cottontail-shaped clouds dot the sky, the only disruption in the azure blue. No drones.

I flick my eyes down, searching the rolling slab of concrete that cuts through the forest, leading to the mountains. We've passed several military cars on the highway since we set out over an hour ago; I've counted six so far. Mounties, everyone calls them here. But none have stopped our van. To them, we're nothing more than big-city tourists looking to get away.

If only we could.

"Mira," Ava's voice pleads from the other side of the suitcase barrier. I can't see her, and I'm glad for it. Like the others, I can't bear to look at her. To see her face, her eyes, would be to see my pain reflected. And I've been avoiding mirrors all day.

Either my silence or the relentless rattle of the luggage proves too much for Ava. In one fell swoop she shoves a duffel bag and a silver suitcase into the overstuffed trunk behind us, creating a domino effect. Barely missing my head, an avalanche of trekking poles slides down my shoulder, landing hard on my thighs and feet. Backpacks shift and burst open, supplies spilling to the ground in a nerve-twisting racket. I lift my feet as steel water bottles wheel past like hell-bent cannonballs searching for targets. A hollow thud tells me one found Skye's ankles.

As the gear settles and the clanking of metal ceases, an awkward hush falls over the van. Ava gives a satisfied grunt, her goal achieved.

No one looks back to find out what caused the hubbub. Behind the wheel, Barend keeps his iron focus on the road, not trusting the GPS or autonomous system with our destination; Emery continues her relentless scrawl of thoughts in her tattered journal; Pawel, Ellie, and Skye all stare out windows. But I feel Ava's gaze on me, her hand resting in the empty space between us.

"Mira," she tries again.

Someone rolls down a window, as if to let out the tension. The rush of wind transports me to the past, to the last time I was inside a car heading north with Ava and my long-lost grandmother. Just before I walked away from my sister through a field of a thousand windmills.

I close my eyes, and I'm back in Montana. Memories come surging forward, so strong and sudden I almost can't breathe. Lingering emotions and forgotten words float unbidden to the surface. Words I thought I left behind on the other side of the wall.

"You told me it would be my fault if Father died," I barely whisper, trusting Ava to hear.

Through the twenty seconds of quiet, I know she's replaying our argument. Our heated battle of bitter jabs and low-blow accusations. I wonder if she'll use my own words against me.

I'm too tired to fight.

"It's not true," Ava says quietly, head bowed. "You know I didn't mean it." She speaks slow, her voice catching. "I didn't mean a lot of things I said that day."

I know. Me too. Why can't I tell her this? Instead, I just nod.

She moves her hand closer, but I don't take it. "The only one to blame is Roth."

Now that Halton's dead.

I shove the trekking poles from my legs, the sharpened points reminding me of the agent's knife that pierced Halton's chest. His grandfather promised we would pay for our crimes. Maybe Halton paid for his.

"We'll get Roth back for what he did." Ava's whisper is like a vow.

"For what he did," I echo.

For murdering our father. We can't say it out loud. We failed and couldn't save him.

Did he wait for us, watch for us? Did he hold on to the faintest hope, even at the very end, that we would come and he would live and all would be made right?

With numb fingers I toss off my seat belt and slide across the seat toward my sister. I tuck my hand into hers, and we both stare out the window, watching the forest whip past in a blur.

"I don't want to just get him back," I finally say. "I don't want to just get even."

The van turns a corner, revealing the mighty Canadian Rockies ahead. I marvel at the jagged peaks of the endless range that jut out from a cloudy mist. They look like the razor-edged teeth of a monster, and I'm stupefied by the mountains' sheer size, their utter dominance of this land.

I am so small. Our numbers are small. Roth and his Guard are giants. Who are we to think we can take down a mountain?

"Half an hour left before we reach Paramount Point Lodge," Emery tells us from the passenger seat.

Everyone else springs to life, stretching sleepy limbs, packing up, preparing for arrival. Ava and I stay still.

My head on Ava's shoulder, I gaze up at the Rockies and attempt to search through the dense layer of trees and thickening fog for any sign of the rebellion and its headquarters. When I find nothing, my eyes drop to my boots, soles worn and caked with dirt.

"Mira," Ava sighs, squeezing my hand.

She looks straight at me, and I know I can't avoid her question any longer. Her hair is wild, tangled from constant worry, her face ashen and young and far from innocent.

"I just want to know one thing. Was it quick?"

I wish I could erase what I saw in the grainy footage, but it will stay with me forever. I had to know. To witness. To be with my father in his last moments, even if I was too late.

"Yes," I lie, both to her and to myself. "He didn't suffer."

An elaborate iron gate bars the road ahead. Its black metal twists and curves into shapes of elk, wolves, and bighorn sheep, with a greeting in the middle:

A Place to Rest & Find Common Ground

Barend drives forward, and the gate yawns open, allowing our three-van party to enter without stopping. A forest of evergreens flanks our muddy road, so fragrant and alive, its sharp pine scent reaching through the window.

We speed on for several more miles through a thin fog before the haze suddenly lifts like a curtain, unveiling a sweeping one-story luxury lodge, a yellow door gleaming in the sunlight.

Skye lets out a sharp whistle. "Richest safe house I've ever seen. How do the towers stay up?"

I lean across Ava, craning my neck to get a better view, and catch sight of three grand towers that shoot up from the solar roof, each twenty levels tall. Reconstructed shipping crates, wrapped in spruce and lined with dazzling glass windows, are crisscrossed on top of one another like the giant wooden blocks of a Jenga tower. We spent many sleepless nights playing that simple game back in Calgary. To stave off the nightmares.

The game ends when the tower falls, I remember. Let's hope these never do.

Inside the highest block of the middle tower, behind the glare of a glass wall, I can just make out a figure staring down at us.

"That's Ciro," Pawel informs Ava and me as the van's doors slide open and everyone crawls out.

Upon hearing the name, Barend stops unloading the trunk and looks up with the rest of us. A softness rounds his downturned eyes, completely incongruous with his usual dour countenance. But the metamorphosis is fleeting, vanishing as quickly as it appeared, his face settling into an exaggerated glare as if overcompensating for his slipup.

"Ciro owns the place," Pawel continues, Ellie stretching luxuriously at his side. "Owns the Common, too, he likes to say. Some even say he leads us."

I throw Ava a side-glance. *I thought Emery led the Common.*

When I gaze back up at the center tower, Ciro is gone.

"Ten minutes before all Elders regroup in the Council Room!" Emery shouts so arriving members from every van can hear. She shrugs off her long chestnut coat, turning inside out the loose sleeves to expose the reversible yellow interior. It's too risky for any of us to wear the rebellion's color outside the safe houses. But here Emery slides back on her familiar uniform, bright and unmistakable. I can't help but think she uses it as a crutch, a bold statement that speaks volumes to every member: *I'm in charge.* Not Ciro.

Shouldering my rucksack, I linger next to Ava on the two-lane solar driveway. The panels are divided by lush grass, the kind that would make me want to run around barefoot in a bygone life. Instead, I stand still and breathe in the fresh air, taking in my surroundings.

Patches of wildflowers flourish across the impressive property, as do dozens of "guests." If, like us, they are more than they appear and all really part of the fledgling cause, our numbers are growing. *Maybe we have a chance.*

"I'm going to have a look around," Skye tells the group.

Emery lets her wander. Skye was in a prison cell for nearly two thousand days. The sun, the open land, the people. It must be a lot to take in at once.

My eyes track a group of three as they weave through the tall, bare trunks of the pines, heading toward the rushing waters of a river the color of turquoise.

"Glaciers," Ava says, pointing up at the serrated tops of a distant mountain range. Sure enough I spot gleaming white ice nestled atop the pointed peaks, ice fields that have somehow survived the heated earth.

It's magnificent, a wonderland of natural beauty. But all I can think about is how soon we can leave it.

This is the perfect place to grieve, but I don't want to soothe my pain; I don't want my wounds to heal. I want them to fester. I want them to hurt. I want them to remind me of what I've lost and the bastard who stole it all from me.

"The Secret Sisters!" a voice shouts from the front steps, causing every head to turn. A sky-high beanpole of a young man stands alone on the metal landing, the morning sun glinting off his silver suit, making him shine like platinum.

This must be Ciro.

He strides toward our small group, arms flung wide in welcome. He swings his head back and forth like a pendulum from Ava's face to mine, as everyone always does when they first see us.

"The Traitorous Twins!" His boisterous laughter echoes through the grounds, and I try my best not to cringe. My eyes dart over every stranger, finding them all captivated by our impromptu reception. I want to turn and run. I'm still a novice to this kind of attention, to being singled out and talked about in front of so many. But Ava holds my elbow firm, making me stay.

Pawel and the others, even Barend, smile and join in with Ciro's infectious laughter. Emery stands by my side, giving an encouraging nod, and I remember we're among friends. I take a breath and pop my knuckles, forcing myself to adjust and acclimate to our new role. *Suck it up. You chose this.*

Ava moves to meet our so-called leader, and I follow, our quick steps syncing in an effortless rhythm. His position of power, his confidence, the way everyone seems to look up to him, *literally*, all tell me Ciro must be well beyond his teens, but he looks even younger than I am. Cherubic face, boyish grin. A buoyant effervescence that life somehow hasn't popped.

"Ava, Mira," he says, placing a hand on each of our shoulders. "Welcome to Paramount Point Lodge. We have been waiting for you for decades."

I lift my chin and meet his gaze, but he stares for so long I have to look away.

"My apologies. I know it's rude to stare. These worldly eyes of mine have seen many twins, but none so identical as the two of you. And of course, never *American* twins."

"Thank you for letting me and my sister stay here," Ava says, offering her hand.

"Of course, of course. It's your home now too."

"Is this just another safe house, or do you have a plan?" I blurt out. "Can we actually *do* something? For weeks we've done nothing but hide." I don't know why I'm directing all my pent-up frustration at him, but my anger seems only to make him smile.

"A woman of action." He looks from Ava to me. "Twofold. We will work well together, then."

"It's been a long morning, Ciro," Emery cuts in, directing everyone with a wave of her hand to continue unloading the vans. "Let's allow Ava and Mira to settle in and find their bearings."

Ciro's smile falters, and his head drops in a bow. "Of course, what a terrible host."

He ushers us up the porch steps, Barend suddenly close by his side. They trade confidential whispers as we move through the wide front door, and I wonder where Barend's loyalty lies. With Ciro or with Emery? I hope we are all one, but the cool look Emery shoots our new host tells me it's much more tangled than that.

"Everyone, please be sure to check in at the front desk!" Ciro shouts at the steady stream of newcomers. "No exceptions!"

"Is he serious?" Ava asks pointedly, clearly finding the whole thing excessive.

"We must keep up the facade," Emery answers, appearing next to me with a stiff smile. She carries her own duffel bag and a backpack, most likely heavy with journals and maps. A leader who carries her own weight.

"Keep up the show for who?" I ask. They seem not to be concerned with either spies or turncoats, or Ciro wouldn't be so carelessly shouting out our arrival with enemy catchphrases for anyone to hear. "Traitorous Twins." The nickname makes me want to punch a wall. Or the man who coined it.

"For the Crosses. Ciro's mom and dad," Pawel chimes in behind us. "They check the books."

We stop a few feet away from the long line of guests waiting to check in and receive their room numbers. Emery leans in, lowering her sharp, lusty voice.

"Ciro's parents believe that their family wealth finances a string of successful luxury hotels all across Canada, run and managed by their only son," Emery tells us, motioning toward Ciro. "But unbeknownst to them, the Crosses are the sole benefactors of our cause."

With all that's been going on, I hadn't thought about who was funding the Common's revival. Getting it into running shape and fighting order.

"How long has Ciro been doing this? Using his Paramount hotels as a rebellion front?" Ava asks, gazing around the grand foyer, its massive corridors hinting at even grander rooms beyond.

"Are the Crosses Canadian citizens?" I ask, wondering for the fiftieth time today how plausible it would be for Ava and me to obtain political asylum and official protection. "Or are the family secret refugees?"

Our questions go unanswered.

Barend marches across the spacious room, headed straight for us, and stands at attention with a click of his shiny boots. He nods to Emery but addresses Ava, then me. "Ciro wants to see you in his room before the party."

I feel the full brunt of Emery's exhale on my shoulder. She clears her throat, asking evenly, "The party?"

"That's all he told me," Barend replies before he takes his leave. A man of brevity.

"I'm not going to any *party*," Ava whispers heatedly in my ear, echoing my thoughts. *There's nothing to celebrate.*

I want to find the Council Room, the War Room. I want to find action.

Through the large, open windows, I see the vans that took the alternate route pull up, the last batch from Calgary. Standing on the tips of my boots, I search for Ciro, but he's lost in the growing crowd.

"Ava, Mira, if you would meet me at the elevators, I will show you to Ciro's room," Emery says, scanning the enormous analog clock that decorates the entire back wall. It almost makes me smile. Hints of the Common are on display here. The Elders, like Rayla, abhor all forms of technology, no matter the inconvenience. Their paranoia of government surveillance matches even mine.

The vintage clock's numbers seem to measure the height of my five-six frame. Like a giant airplane propeller, the second hand goes round and round, making time fly. I watch the minute hand tick forward, then look down at the cracked glass of my wristwatch. The last thing my father gave to me: time. Yet it turns out there wasn't enough of it to save him.

"Ciro said everyone must check in, no exceptions," Ava reminds Emery.

"And I say you are both the exception," Emery states firmly. "Now, if you will excuse me." She moves to greet and instruct the incoming arrivals, leaving us with Pawel, Ellie, and a gaggle of strangers who pretend not to stare. Ava pulls her oversized hood low over her restless green eyes.

"We will check in for you," Pawel offers.

"Marley Townsend and Aeron Rowe," Ellie says with a cheerful wink.

I touch the smooth skin of my inner right wrist, inked with a watchful eye, the counterfeit microchip my grandmother gifted me still embedded underneath. I wonder if Rayla has heard the news. If she knows our father's dead.

"The elevators are to the left, down the hall," Pawel informs us as I adjust my rucksack and Ava nods in thanks.

We start to push our way through the spectators when suddenly Pawel adds, "Emery tells us to humor Ciro, to make him feel . . . useful. He's very important, you see."

Ava and I exchange quick glances. *The man himself is important, or his money?*

We stand before the wall of elevators, stuck behind a long line of chatty guests. Emery hasn't arrived yet.

Ava pulls her hood even lower, popping her thumbs as I avoid all eye contact, focusing on my feet. I really don't feel like being a part of a crowd right now. Not that I ever do.

Suddenly a tall man in a serious suit steps out from nowhere, cutting us off from the line. *An agent,* my mind fires wildly.

Before I can even blink, my hand is in my pocket, my fingers curled around the familiar grip of my knife, its handle wrapped in the steel rings of a knuckle duster. But as I move to attack, Ava stops me.

"He's with the Common," she whispers.

The man pulls up his tailored sleeve, exposing the cursive ink of a woman's name on his wrist. The letters are inverted and so wobbly it's like he marked himself. "Olivia," it reads. He looks me squarely in the eyes. "'Courage, for till all ceases, neither must you cease.'"

Emery appears behind me. She places a light hand on the man's arm. "Walt Whitman. A wise man."

The poet whose words inspired the Common. *"Resist much. Obey little."*

Straightening his sleeve and squaring his shoulders, the man turns and strides down the expansive hall. As swiftly as he came, he's gone, but his words are lasting. I pocket my blade. Ava pulls off her hood. *Courage. Neither must you cease.*

"Others find strength in your courage," Emery tells us. I find strength in hers. She motions Ava and me toward the elevators.

Seeing Emery, the line parts, allowing us to cut to the front. A glossy door lights up and opens, and our party of three files into the spacious elevator car.

I move to the corner in anticipation of the other guests, but no one follows us in. The door shuts, and an electronic voice pleasantly asks, "Tower and Level, please?"

A glowing panel illuminates the options: Towers One through Three, Levels One through Twenty. Instead of giving a voice command, Emery plucks a set of keys from her pocket with a metallic jingle. She slides one into a tiny keyhole I did not detect before, twists, and off we go.

"Tower Two, Level Twenty," the elevator announces. "Estimated travel time, ten seconds."

I realize we're not moving *up* like normal elevators do. Our elevator car is speeding us *left*.

"The elevator system uses electromagnetics," Emery explains. "Without the limitations of cables, the linear motors allow us to travel any direction."

Vertical, horizontal. Diagonal. I can't help but lament not having such technology inside the immense buildings of my old university.

"What's inside each level?" Ava asks, tossing back her unruly bangs. They've grown out since we've been in hiding. "Can we see them?"

"There will be time enough for tours later," Emery answers as the elevator door opens at Level Twenty onto a long, thin room that must be Ciro's private quarters. "I will see you both in the Council Room afterward. Pawel will retrieve you. There is much to discuss."

She waves us out, and Ava and I step into the heavily decorated room that seems to house everything except our host.

Releasing a drawn-out sigh, Ava moves toward a wall lined with portraits of faces I don't recognize, dragging her rucksack after her. She tosses it to the floor and collapses onto a bench. I drop my own rucksack, lightly packed with the few items I still own, and join her. With no one to watch us, analyze us, or size us up, we both allow our shoulders to slump and take a moment to breathe.

It's hard keeping up the facade. To always look like we know what we're doing, to be worth the sacrifices, the efforts, the great risks others are taking because we came out of hiding and lit the match that spread the flames of disobedience.

Always, we must look like we're strong, like Roth hasn't made us crack.

"Their numbers are overwhelming," Ava says beside me, breaking the relaxed silence. I don't have to ask who. *They, them,* all those who want us found and gone. She must have seen something in Calgary when she disappeared last night. "We can't stay here much longer," she continues softly. "I want to go back."

It's strange being homesick over a country, a home, that never wanted us. Never wanted *me.* The illegal second twin.

"I want to go back too," I say. We know we can't, of course, but it feels nice saying it out loud, a comfort of sorts. A kind of admission. Because we both know there's nothing to go back to.

The elevator door glides open, and we spring to our feet, making ourselves presentable.

"Before either of you say a thing, the party this afternoon is not for you," Ciro declares before even crossing the threshold. "I mean . . . it is, but it isn't," he adds with a sly smile.

His legs are so long he eats up the wood floor that separates us in three swift steps. He looks down at Ava and me expectantly with an extra-large smile, and I realize he seems to want our approval. He wants us to like him.

"We'd love to hear more of your plans," Ava responds politely. *Let's hope they're good.*

His smile stretches. "Please, follow me," he says, leading us into a formal sitting room. I take a seat on the L-shaped couch, Ava beside me. Encased in ornamental glass, a fire burns in the center of the room.

The flames glint off Ciro's silver suit like tiny fireflies as he perches on the chair across from us.

"If I may ask," I say carefully, "why are we not in the Council Room, meeting with the others?" I can't help but feel they are leaving us out. We had hoped to be in on the discussion, key players in planning the Common's next move. But from the look on Ciro's face, he's already made his own plans.

"The real meeting is tonight," he answers. "I wanted you both to be the first to hear the good news."

Ava slides forward to the edge of her seat. *How good? Our father is still alive? Roth is dead? Rayla has returned to us?*

"My parents will be arriving within the hour, in honor of the Paramount's little soiree." He stands, his animated hands communicating as much as his lips. "My mother and father like to check up on things, and *I* like to use things to my advantage."

Ciro's eyes swing from Ava's to mine. "They are bringing with them our most promising ally. The man with enough power to protect you from Governor Roth and his long, brutal reach."

"President Moore," Ava says before Ciro can reveal his own big surprise.

The leader of Canada.

"President Moore," Ciro confirms. He finally stands still, beaming down at the two of us like a knight in his shiny-suited armor.

A rush of blood pounds in my ears, making it hard to hear myself think. I feel light-headed, overwhelmed. Ava takes my hand and squeezes hard. If we can't go back, we must go forward. Political asylum means safety, immunity, protection from being hunted and thrown back to Texas, left to the mercy of Roth. *This is our best chance.* A chance for an entire nation, a superpower like Canada, to validate our existence and our cause.

"Does the president know we're here?" I ask.

"He only knows I have requested a private audience," Ciro says. "No one in his administration knows you two are here. They know nothing of my ties to the Common."

"And you trust him?" Ava asks bluntly.

"With my life," he answers, his voice firm, his eyes sure. A shadow crosses his face, his flashy smile gone. "He saved my family from being deported back to the States when I was a child."

"So you're American?" Ava asks.

"I'm a child of American parents. My mother and father, along with my eldest sister, only a newborn when they crossed, made the journey north as climate refugees. Ten generations of Crosses in the state of Florida. Our future swept away by Hurricane Davon."

Davon. The world's first Category 6 hurricane.

I should feel sorry for him, but I stop myself. Ciro's family seems to be doing just fine. More than fine.

"You have a sister?" Ava asks. Siblings. Blood siblings. I can see Ava's mind working through this. It's astonishing enough watching Pawel with Ellie.

"Emery told us you were an only son," I say.

"It must be difficult for your American minds to fathom this, but I am the last of four. Three exemplary older sisters." Ciro buttons up his jacket and runs his long fingers through his already perfect hair. "Thus nothing much was expected of me . . ." For a moment he's simply a youngest child desperate for validation.

I can understand that feeling.

So Ciro decided to secretly fund a rebellion for a country he's never even seen?

Deeper questions burn for my attention—*How did the Cross family make it over the border? When was their illegal status discovered? Did their money buy their freedom?*—but all my musings quickly fade away. I remember that my father is dead and nothing else matters.

"President Moore is a compassionate man," Ciro says. His smile is back. He moves closer, the red light of the fire dancing behind him. "The president is a dear friend to our family. He will save you, just as he saved me."

Save the twins! I remember the roaring chant of our allies, supporters, friends. *Maybe he will.* Maybe we can stop running.

My feet suddenly feel overused and bone tired, and I wonder how they took me this far. I draw in a deep breath, releasing a mountain of tension I didn't realize I'd been carrying. Ava leans back, resting her head against mine, and we hold each other's weight.

"Okay," Ava answers for us, popping the knuckles of her right hand. The jerky movements make the black-and-yellow curves of her infinity snake tattoo dance across her wrist. "We will go to your party."

Ciro nods, bowing formally.

Never must we cease.

Limos and luxury cars line the extensive circular driveway, stuffed with partygoers ready for the welcoming bash. Mrs. and Mr. Cross have already arrived with much fanfare from their son and his doting employees. I wonder if Ciro's sisters are here.

I hear him get on the microphone, introducing his unwitting parents onto the stage of the overflowing banquet hall, the governor of Alberta and the mayor of Calgary looking on from the front row.

Everything's falling nicely into place. If only the man of the hour would show.

I look at my watch: 7:30 p.m. He's late. Ava's knee bounces furiously, as if she can shake out her anxiety.

"He'll come," I say.

From our hideout in the corner of the foyer, shadowed and easily overlooked, we have the best seats in the house. A perfect vantage point to see and be unseen. Ava scans the budding festivities through the glass walls on our left. I keep my eyes on the glass windows straight ahead, seeing past the dazzling flares from the cars' headlights, holding out for the first glimpse of the president.

A string quartet begins to play, and an electric energy pulsates through the hotel, enlivening the party guests with a giddy exhilaration, and I can't help but feel it too. Eager, I spring to my feet. I pace up and down our tucked-away corner, checking the time, watching Emery from across the room, waiting on her signal.

"Do you hear that?" Ava asks. She stares up at the ceiling. I move beside her as we listen to the muffled roar of whirling blades slicing the air somewhere above the building.

"A helicopter," Ava says.

"He's here."

We look to Emery, who stands near the entrance, her gaze locked skyward. Guests file past as she removes a headscarf from her pocket, drapes the silk over her distinctive curls, and pulls it into a tight knot at the back of her neck. She folds her right arm over her chest, our cue to move.

I feel, rather than see, Barend steal into place behind us, our long shadow, as we push to the end of the foyer. Pawel detaches himself from the crowd and crosses our path as he follows Emery out the front door. "Lots of luck," he whispers earnestly. *Like luck has anything to do with it. It's all up to us.*

Our target is the oversized clock that consumes the entire wall alongside the vacant concierge desk. Ava stops before the number six, and we slip behind a false door and stride side by side down an empty staff hallway. Three right turns, two left, a final door, and we're outside.

There are no lights behind the hotel and no people. The night is chilly and moonless, but we find the footpath we were directed to take and make our silent way to the small grove of trees just twenty yards out.

Ten paces into the grove, Ava and I turn from the path and weave through the evergreens until we spot the narrow clearing that is to be our stage. We position ourselves in its center, shoulder to shoulder, and wait. Somewhere to our right, concealed within the trees and darkness, Barend stands guard.

When told of the plan, Emery immediately authorized the private rendezvous. She knows pleading our case face-to-face with the president is the only way. *Cameras and screens provide a barrier,* Emery said. *The media paints you solely as American rebels. Let him see how human you are.* With Pawel at her side, Emery is to meet and escort the president here, while Ciro entertains his parents and guests, keeping them safely ignorant inside the banquet hall.

The minutes tick off, and Ava starts to shiver from either the cold or nerves. *Or is that me shivering?* Ava and I brought no weapons with us, to show good faith. No guns, no knives. Just us, with our naked conviction and hope.

This could be our last stop, a final end to the endless chase. A place to plan and plot and devise our crucial counterattack.

Ava nudges me with a sharp elbow. She points to the trees in front of us. Two distinct shapes emerge, a faint silhouette floating behind.

"Ready?" I whisper needlessly. Ava tightens her jaw, and I ball my hands into white-knuckled fists. I take a big gulp of air and exhale slowly. My breath comes out in swirling smoke, reminding me of a dragon. There's a fire inside me, and suddenly I feel warm and calm. One look from Ava and I know she feels it too.

We're ready.

The outlines become faces and bodies. Emery appears first, then President Moore, with Pawel a few steps behind. I stare at Moore, transfixed, my eyes glued to the man who can grant us refuge.

He stumbles forward, as if his own eyes have not yet adjusted to the dark. I search his every feature, looking for any hint of surprise, or shock, or understanding. But his face, though startlingly attractive in the starlight, is blank. Indifferent.

"President Moore," Emery says, "this is Ava and Mira Goodwin." His round eyes squint as he moves his head from side to side, taking us both in. We all stand motionless, awaiting his response.

"You don't look identical to me," the president finally states, his thin voice magnified in the still night air. "One of you is slightly taller, the other rounder."

The leader of the free world opens with an insult. My first reaction is to defend my identicalness. Surprising, when all I've ever wanted is to be seen as different from Ava.

"Sir—" Ava and I speak at the same time.

The president laughs. "Ah, there it is." The ground spins as he turns to leave. "This conversation will be moved to a different setting. Just the twins and me."

Barend detaches from the shadows. Pawel and Emery enclose my sister and me. Ava grabs my arm, her grip tight enough to bruise.

"We do not agree to any change—" Emery starts, but Moore shouts over her.

"Security!"

Everything shatters, all plans and expectations smashed to pieces.

A gunshot rings out, then two more.

"Run!" Emery yells.

The last thing I see is Ava's face, twisted in fear and fury.

Then something covers my eyes. My mouth.

I'm thrown over a bulky shoulder, the deafening sounds of a helicopter growing louder with every footfall. With every one of my muffled screams.

I'm shoved against something solid. I reach out, arms flailing, but there's no one beside me. *Ava.*

I feel the chopper lift into the sky. Two spinning blades taking me higher and higher away from Common ground.

OWEN

"Bullshit," I scoff.

I'm keyed up and restless, bored out of my mind. It's impossible to sit still like I'm supposed to. The collared uniform the high rankers of Kismet Automotive Factory make all its lucky employees wear is itchy as hell—a getup I wouldn't be caught dead in back home.

"Well, if I *were* back home, I probably *would* be dead," I reason out loud to the girl next to me. *"Georgia,"* I whisper, and then pause to let my place of birth sink in. The wildfires, the drought, the plague of mosquitos—it's a conversation starter for sure—but my nameless coworker doesn't bat an eye.

Fifty other Programmers, or Code Cogs as I like to call us, are crammed inside the room with me, burning the midnight oil. This is my third double shift in a row, but I'm not complaining. Complaining is what my parents do if half my earnings aren't in their bank account every other Friday by six.

Like me, everyone is staring hypnotized at their overly bright screens, mindlessly sorting through millions of lines of code, looking for vulnerabilities in security. We've been at this for seven hours straight with no bathroom breaks, no outside breaks, no breaks for stretching or talking, and definitely no breaks for thinking. I swear they've started to count our blinks, and they're working out ways to accelerate that *pesky* lag in their machine.

"Bullshit," I tell the room again, a little louder. No one responds or looks up from their screens. Not even a grumble or glare is thrown my way. I check the guy on my left to see if he's even breathing.

"Hey, are you still there, or did you turn android after all?" I ask.

"Shh," the girl next to me hisses. Her eyes jump to the surveillance above the entrance doors. I turn toward her, naming her Amelia inside my head, the only one in here who seems to remember English and not just the programming language we were all trained to speak.

"It took me fourteen hours today to search one hundred twenty-four thousand fifty-three lines of code to find why a stupid period was added to the end of the output," I vent, but I think she's stopped listening. "What did you accomplish today? Something as equally life changing, I hope?"

"We're doing important work," Amelia informs me. "Complex problems require complex solutions—"

"And every found key can unlock victory," I finish the company motto for her. I smile because she's earnest and pretty and composed of warm flesh and blood and not cold zeros and ones. But she doesn't smile back.

I'm not saying what we're doing doesn't matter—we're one of five teams challenged with making an autonomous car "survive and thrive!" inside the 150-plus mph winds of a superstorm—I'm just saying I won't have anything to do with it. I'm only a back-row lackey who does what he's told. A Code Cog till I die.

All fifty screens suddenly dim in unison, blinking out a three-part pattern that signals a shift change. Well-conditioned, everyone lifts their right wrists and scans their chips to log off. Right on cue, the back doors slide open, and a wave of replacement Programmers files into the stale room like robots, wrists already extended to log on for the next graveyard shift.

One and all we rise, most of my coworkers asleep on their feet while we wait for each row's turn to exit. My fingers twitch with pent-up energy.

"The future waits for no one," I say to Amelia, knowing full well I'll never see her again. Every shift brings new faces. *This is a place of work, not a bar,* my Team Leader once told us. *Fraternize on your personal time.* What's personal time?

I break protocol and bound for the front doors, bumping through the orderly line of people on my way into the hall. My brain switches on the second I make it out.

Rambling down the wide corridor, I pass a series of doors that lead to massive data centers stuffed with machines and hundreds of what I call Code Monkeys, the people below even the Cogs, who receive and manage all the data from your Kismet autonomous cars. They're the ones who ensure you always get to your twelve-hour shift up in those gleaming high-rises safe and on time. Extra bananas for the Monkeys if you smile at the end of your riding experience. The sensors know if you're happy. Remember that.

Here it is. My favorite place on the entire 375-acre factory grounds. The room where the magic happens. I stop and press my face against the enormous glass wall. They're beautiful, the scores of autonomous cars positioned in the final line of assembly. Pale silver or jet-black, each curved like the slope of an aluminum hill, with dark one-way windows and electric-blue trim, the spiral Kismet logo on the front and rear bumpers. All that's needed is a test run in Little Detroit, and off they'll go, serving the citizens of the megalopolis by next week.

The factory floor is powered down and quiet now. The cars are getting their beauty sleep. But in the back a light blinks on—Leeland is making his midnight rounds. Stern and official-looking in his Security Guard uniform, he's much friendlier than he looks. Trust me; I've tried his patience the four years I've worked here like the annoying little brother he could never have.

I wait until I pass within his sight before I raise my hands in the air to grab his attention. When he pauses and glances at me squished up against the glass, I give him my best grin, making sure both my dimples show. I shrug my shoulders in a can-I-come-play-with-you kind of way.

Leeland seems visibly miffed for about five seconds, and if I were anybody else, I'd probably run for the basement to hide from the glare he's throwing at me. But then his serious face cracks into a smile. Or at least I think it's a smile. It comes off as more of a snarl, but I know he means well. He gives a reluctant nod toward the doors to the factory floor, and I'm in.

"You know the drill. Twenty minutes, then you're out," Leeland says beside me. "Remember, no touching."

Our friendship is forged out of the timeless bargain of "you scratch my back, and I'll scratch yours." The terms of our bimonthly meet up consist of Leeland allowing me twenty midnight minutes to walk around and drool over the cars up close in return for unlocking all the top-secret features in his favorite VR games using my custom software hacks. He's not the sharpest bullet in the ammunition box, and he'd be racing around the first levels of *Grand Virus* and *Everchase* for eternity without me.

"Yeah, yeah, yeah," I say, half listening as I stroll down the rows of switched-off cars. I know everything about them: the parts that were used to build them, how the powerful electric motors work, how their computer minds were programmed to think and communicate and anticipate. Yet I've never actually been inside a Kismet car before. Too rich for my common blood. But everyone has their dreams, right?

A bright cherry sheen catches my eye. "Well, who are *you*?" Before I can stop myself, I dart for the dozen or so red beauties parked at the very front of the line, my hand outstretched, fully recognizing how good I look next to them with my dark mahogany skin. The perfect pairing.

They're a bold paint color I've never seen on a car—it's always silver or black—and they look more expensive than a decade of my earnings could buy. This must be the new model.

"Hey—what did I say about touching?" Leeland yells.

Right as I press my fingertips against the small and agile frame at the front of the pack, I hear the eerie *thrum* of a hundred cars turning on at exactly the same moment.

"What the heck . . . ," Leeland blurts out in confusion. Every headlight in the factory flashes on at once, blinding my dim friend and me into stunned inaction.

Then the alarm starts to blare, as loud and urgent as an air-raid siren. Overhead, red lights pulse on and off, on and off. Not good. Leeland pulls out his gun.

"Um . . . that wasn't me," I insist.

Behind me, the bay doors roll open as if by magic. A blast of hot, humid air spills into the facility along with a dozen or so darkly dressed bodies. "Code Wolf," Leeland screams into his mouthpiece. "Code Wolf!"

He grabs me by the scruff of my neck, and we dive behind the gigantic orange arm of a manufacturing robot. "What the hell's a Code Wolf?" I shout over the sirens.

I peek my head around to see for myself and find a dozen Ava Goodwins—wait, that can't be right—fan out across the chaotic red-lit floor. All of them rush directly for the cars.

There are wolves in the henhouse. "It's a raid!" I cry. I can't believe it.

A volley of bullets causes me to whip back around to Leeland. "What do we do?" I ask, breathless. "We're not going to let the bastards steal the cars, right?"

Leeland shoves his shock baton into my hands. I try to shove it right back. "What am I supposed to do with this? They have *guns!*" I say. "Give me one of yours."

Leeland shakes his head. "I can't give a gun to a citizen!" he chides me. Ah, right. But who gave the raiders theirs?

"Don't worry. Their firearms are nonlethal." Leeland lifts up a discarded shell casing. "Plastic bullets—painful, not fatal," he says. "Only, don't get shot in the face," he adds, not comforting me at all.

The corridor doors fly open—the Kismet reinforcements have arrived. "Rise to your feet and shine, my friend." With that, Leeland lifts his gun and surges out into the firefight.

The *pop, pop, pop* of very real bullets firing off is mixed with the high-pitched squeals of tires peeling out. I snake around the robotic arm and see six cars stealing their way through the bay doors. In front of me, the entrance to one of the new luxury-model red cars lifts open like the wing of a falcon. A taller, bulkier version of Ava Goodwin dressed in hooded coveralls slinks into one of the ice-white premium felt lounge chairs. Through the hard-red alarm light, I see the raider spin the chair around to face the dashboard and thrust some kind of device into a port on the control panel.

On instinct I spring to my feet. Nope, that's my car. Purely in my dreams, but still. Mine.

Gripping the shock baton with sweaty fingers, I race forward without fully thinking through what I mean to do. Shock him into submission? The guy doesn't appear to have a weapon. Sure, let's try it. Maybe Kismet will give me an earnings bump for heroically saving one of its valuable assets.

With the speed of a practiced pro, the thief detaches the retractable emergency steering wheel, exposes the car's foot pedals—is he going to *drive* the car himself?!—and is on the verge of taking off when Leeland suddenly jumps in front of me, his index finger on the trigger of his gun.

"Hands up now!" he shouts at the raider. He gives him two solid seconds to comply, and when he doesn't, Leeland fires multiple rounds into the passenger seat.

What I do next happens in a blur. In what I can only imagine is a swell of protectiveness for the injured car, I whack Leeland in his lower back with the baton and then hold it there, jolting my friend onto his knees. He stares up at me, his big brown eyes round with shock. I snatch his gun, and next thing I know, I'm hurtling headfirst into the car just as the winged door snaps shut.

"I'm sorry!" I call out to Leeland at the same moment the tires screech in their frenzied struggle to accelerate from a dead stop to top speed in seconds. As we charge out the factory doors, the car swerves so hard I slam like a rag doll against one of the lounge chairs. Well, that certainly didn't feel good.

"What the hell, man!" I yell. "Do you even know how to drive?!" *Why disable the autonomous driving system if he can't even operate the damn thing?*

Once we've made it onto the open test track, I look through the rear window and see six other stolen cars immediately assembling into a V formation behind ours. I can't help but scoff. If this car is the leader, those bandits are doomed.

When we careen off the test track and into Kismet's Little Detroit, the swerving stops. The driver must've gotten his shit together. I hoist myself off the floor to properly sit in the lounge chair that I just noticed has two bullet holes in the headrest and turn to face my Goodwin-masked driver.

Up close I see that the mask is 3D printed and very illegal, but very cool. I also see that the lower half of the man's left shirtsleeve is ripped off, a section tied tight around his upper arm. "Are you wounded?!" I say, way too panicked. I clear my throat and try again. "Did you get hit?" I say, much more calm and cool.

I seem to have forgotten I'm holding a gun for the first time in my life, because the man answers by taking the thing from my hands so easily I'm embarrassed. Whoops.

I just might get shot in the face after all, Leeland, because that's exactly where the man points the barrel. Payback.

We tear through the streets of Kismet's faux megalopolis built solely to refine their autonomous cars. It's so lifelike and crazy detailed it looks like there's no way it's just ghostly facades with no buildings behind them. The real Detroit looms ahead of us, big and booming. "You're not going into the city, are you?" I blurt out. "Because that would be stupid." Wolves in a slaughterhouse.

"Shut up," the driver snaps at me. A woman, not a man.

There's a fleet of Kismet Guard cars in close pursuit. The woman might be able to beat them in a car chase—I'll give it to her, turns out she *does* know how to drive when she isn't distracted tying bandages—but I seriously doubt she'll make it past the security gates.

But I'm proven wrong. In a slick move, the woman slams our car left into an alleyway while the other cars skid off to the right, breaking up our pack. The chase cars swerve opposite, following the greater number, leaving our escape route down the replica of the famed Woodward Avenue clear and free. When we reach the eastern edge of the factory grounds, there's a section of the gate open and waiting. "Is this an inside job?" I ask, unable to stop myself. It's just all too unbelievable.

"Who are you?" the woman yells at me now that we've successfully escaped Kismet property.

"Owen Hart," I yell back. "Ma'am . . . ," I add for good measure.

"I don't care what you're called," the woman screams. "I'm asking who you are!"

"Nobody!" I scream back. "I'm just a Programmer for Kismet!" She doesn't seem to like my response and points the gun closer to my face. I'm answering to two hotheads: this crazy masked woman and the round barrel that responds in bullets.

"Why did you get in my car?" she shouts. "Why are you here?"

Huge mistake. Why the hell *did* I get in this car? "If you could just slow down, I can kind of roll out, and I'll be out of your hair," I offer.

Another wrong answer. The gun's trigger clicks with a threat not to move. Her boot still on the accelerator, the woman rips her eyes off the road, seizes both my hands with her one free claw, and the next thing I know, I'm handcuffed to the car door with a nasty-flavored rag stuffed into my mouth. How the heck did that just happen?

The woman grunts like that impressive takedown just used up a huge chunk of her life force. She's going to pass out, and we're going to die. "Just shut up and sit still," she orders. Two things I'm no good at, turns out. The rag smothers my curses, but I launch a whole vulgar list of them anyway. My best ones. And when I get to the end, I start again from the top. Saliva drips down my chin, and my throat stings with every curse I try to push out, but the masked bandit flat-out ignores me. She simply turns her creepy blank stare back to the road, rests the gun on her lap, and wraps her two fists around the steering wheel like she owns the damn thing. My curses reach a new level. When pushed, people can achieve greatness.

The car speeds up to what has to be eighty and turns a fast right. I chew and spit and cough and heave to eject the gag from my mouth, and pop, it shoots like a missile from my jaw, landing on the bamboo-wood floor. I'm about to tell her she needs to *slow the hell down or she'll burn the tires!* but my mouth just hangs open.

Silver hair falls down the woman's shoulders as she shoves the mask over her forehead and tosses it onto the dash. There's scant light, and she only shows me her profile, but still, I know that face . . . It's number two on the Wanted List. Behind only Ava and Mira Goodwin.

"Rayla," I choke out. "You're Rayla Cadwell."

All Guards in the fifty-one states are looking for this rebel woman. Every camera in this country is waiting to catch her in its sights. But she's in this car, with me, an arm's length away. And somehow, I'm the one in cuffs.

I bury my face in my armpit, mentally drop-kicking myself. What's she going to do with me now that she knows I recognize her? Why can't I keep my big mouth shut?

I rally and break out in hearty chuckles. "Pshh, of course you're not Rayla. You look nothing like Rayla. Rayla is off fighting and winning big in Canada or maybe Dallas. Why would Rayla be in *Detroit* stealing cars . . ."

"To build a Common Cavalry." Rayla looks right at me, like you do a cockroach before you squash it. Yep, I'm a goner.

I decide to stop talking. Time would be better spent devising an escape plan.

We've been driving west down pitch-black back roads for half an hour. Half an hour feels like forever in abduction time. I can't feel my hands anymore from the plastic cuffs, and I am so bored I almost miss talking with the Cogs. Rayla's icy silence has turned glacial, if that's even possible. Her quiet has gone quiet.

"I can be useful," I say. She gives no indication she heard me, just sits there stone-faced, her eyes never leaving the road. Maybe she only responds to shouting. "I can be useful!" I repeat. "I know cars!"

"You know nothing about cars," she mutters under her breath.

"Um, excuse me, did you forget where you got me? I work for *Kismet*," I say, accidentally proud of this fact.

"You sit behind screens and codes. Have you ever been behind a wheel?" She laughs at my dumb silence. "I don't need a trained government pet that can't make his own decisions."

"I'll have you know I make decisions all the time. Plenty of them. I got into this car, didn't I?"

"An idiotic decision."

If I can just get out of these restraints—was it *really* necessary to make them so tight?—I can overpower her and take control of the car. She's, what, eighty or ninety? And wounded—it's unclear if it's grave or just a nick, but either way, I can take her.

She's a former Common leader, though. She won't go down easy.

The media outlets from every side warn that this woman is armed and dangerous. Well, she is armed—*with* my *gun*, at least it was mine for the thirty seconds I had it—and there *does* seem to be a hell of a lot of danger in her. But dangerous to the public? The Common was firing off plastic bullets at the factory raid, and Rayla wasn't using a weapon of any kind, from what I saw.

I reposition my sore neck and do a once-over at "Rayla the Slayer," as every reporter and patriot has come to call her. Governor Roth of Texas tells us she's nothing but a common assassin out to murder the innocent sons and daughters of our leaders. She's the bloodline of Ava and Mira, the Traitorous Twins, and most think she's the root and reason for all hell breaking loose.

She's a threat to the life of every good and honest citizen, my own mom has determined. My dad spits every time he hears her name.

"Look, if you think you can't let me go because I'll run and tell the Guard where you are and what you're doing, you're wrong. I'm no squealer."

I'm not on the government's side or the Common's side. I'm on my own side. I make my own decisions.

Big surprise, Rayla doesn't answer.

"What are you going to do with me, then?" I ask, remembering to shout.

Rayla grimaces, and the car suddenly slows. With her right hand, she veers off the road and parks near a ditch. Without a backward glance, she opens her door, grabs her backpack, and vanishes into the dark.

Three possibilities: Rayla the Slayer is going to relieve herself; Rayla the Slayer has abandoned the car and me and is not coming back; Rayla the Slayer is off digging my grave with only her callused hands. My best guess is it's probably the latter, so I better get moving.

I hoist up my left leg and use my heel to press the small button on the tongue of my right sneaker that loosens my shoelaces. I repeat the process with my other sneaker, then haul my legs up onto the lounge chair and crouch into a squat. In a pose normally reserved for gymnasts, I stretch my right leg up to my swollen hands, which are still cuffed to the door handle. Grabbing the end of the shoelace, I slide it through the tiny gap between my wrists and the plastic cuffs. I grip the shoelace with my teeth, pull, and, in the final touch of genius, tie the laces of both my sneakers together into a strong double knot.

I'd pat myself on the back if I could.

"Okay, last step," I coach myself. "Don't get cocky."

Something moves outside the car, and I speed up my pace. I pump my legs up and down, up and down, working the cotton laces back and forth like a do-it-yourself friction saw, until bam, the plastic breaks, and I'm free. A little trick I picked up back in Georgia: *always* wear shoes with laces. You never know when you might find yourself in a bind.

Do I drive, or do I run? Rayla overrode the autonomous system and shut off the car before she disappeared. It would take too long to figure out how to manually override her hack so that I could reboot the software before she returns. Guess it'll have to be run, then.

"Son of a Glut," I curse out to the batty woman. She must have thought this was a summons, because the door opens, and there she is, back in the driver's seat, sans coveralls. She doubtless buried it as evidence of her nighttime heist, right next to the empty pit waiting for me. A baggy combat jacket, way old-school and five sizes too big, swallows her tall frame. Who knows what she could have hidden in there. *Get out of this car, you half-wit!* I scream at myself.

Too late—I don't know how to manually unlock the doors. I'm trapped. I dive-bomb for the wheel as a last-ditch option as soon as Rayla starts the motor with her device—but Rayla points the gun in my face, and there goes that.

Cowering back in my corner, I put up my hands. I present her with my most savage snarl, though, to let her understand I won't go down without a fight.

"Looks like that wasn't the first time you've been cuffed," Rayla says, almost like she's impressed. She grips the steering wheel tight, puts the pedal to the metal, and the car launches forward.

And we're off, zipping down the back roads, and I'm still alive. I'm starting to think she likes me. Maybe even gets me.

"Put your hands on the dash," Rayla orders. "And keep your mouth shut." Okay, maybe not. But her voice has lost its bite; it's now groggy and strained. Maybe she's getting tired of me. Maybe she's weakening. She might just let me go.

"My parents will be wondering where I am," I lie. "And my friends. I have lots of friends who'll be looking for me."

Rayla laughs, or more like wheezes. "How old are you? Twelve, fourteen?"

I restrain myself because I'm not in any position to be snappy. "Nineteen," I say very maturely.

She wheezes again.

"A year older than your granddaughters, right?" I venture, aiming to appeal to her matriarchal sensibilities. "For the record, I don't agree with what happened to them tonight."

"What?" Rayla shouts, caught off guard. She twists her head in my direction and tries to push the gun closer to my forehead, but she can't seem to hold it up. Her arm is shaking. Her whole body is shaking actually.

Wrong topic. She's going to shoot the messenger.

"It hasn't hit mainstream media yet, but I thought you would've known already . . . being a rebellion leader and all," I say placidly. The news broke just before my graveyard shift. "You can only get the real headlines browsing the illegal Dark Web, which, obviously, you can't find without getting past the government's firewall. And good luck doing that without a super illegal VPN—"

"The news!" Rayla interrupts my tangent. She sounds distraught.

"Right, the news is the Mounties took the twins. They've been detained by the Canadians."

The car passes a series of streetlights. Under the harsh blue beams, I get an eyeful of Rayla's deathlike complexion. Her head is bent at an awkward angle, and it looks like she's fighting to keep her eyes open. And then I see the blood.

"Um . . . you're bleeding," I point out to her. "Like, *a lot.*" The sleeve of her upper left arm is soaked with red, confirming my earlier suspicions. One of Leeland's bullets got her.

The gun drops from Rayla's slack hand, and the car swerves. Her body goes limp and collapses onto the floor between us. With only a small yelp, I spring for the driver's seat and slam the brakes, narrowly saving us from crashing into the pole of a solar streetlight.

Stabbing the button to make the car park, I sigh a long breath of relief. I'm fine. The car's fine. I make myself peer down at the woman lying beside my sneaker. *She's not fine.*

She's breathing, but it's slow. And fading.

Not good.

Dammit, now *my* hands are shaking. Her tentlike jacket slipped off her shoulders on her way down, showing me what she tried to hide and what I *really* didn't need to see: an oozing bullet hole just north of her elbow. I spot a tourniquet on her upper arm. It's made of the same ripped-off cloth from her coveralls and a stick she must have found when I thought she was out trying to dig my poor man's grave. It untwists before my very eyes and even more blood gushes out, making *me* want to faint.

Double not good.

If I take the car and leave her here on the road, she'll bleed to death. If I take off on foot and have the car drive her to a hospital, she'll get arrested and *then* die. The Guard will kill her.

"Bullshit," I curse at the night. "What am I supposed to do with an unconscious *Common* member?"

ZEE

There are no clocks in the Sleeping Barracks. But I'm one hundred percent sure it's 3:29 a.m.

No matter what Camp the Corrections Guard moves me to, my body always wakes me up one minute before Morning Call. I like to have time for myself. Even if it's only sixty seconds.

All the other seconds of my waking hours belong to Texas.

3:30 a.m.

The lights turn on. The alarm sounds off from the speakers. I've learned the loud noise comes from an instrument called a trumpet. It's good to know the name of your enemy.

Trumpet. Corrections Guards. Wardens.

When I was small at Camp 1, a Warden told me I was an enemy of the state. When I asked why, he told me to open wide, and he spit into my mouth. He said I belong to the state and him and to shut my mouth and swallow it.

I never asked questions after that.

Before my feet hit the floor, a Corrections Guard is already on the row of bunks for Inmates X–Z.

"Assessment Checkup! Assessment Checkup!" the CG orders.

CG Hale, the other Corrections Guards call her. She holds another one of my enemies. The scanner that tells us if our bodies pass or fail.

"On your feet! Move, move, move!"

In this Camp, we don't need to change. We sleep in our uniforms. *Efficiency* is a new word I learned here.

Every X, Y, and Z of my section lines up outside our bunks. All of us match in our bright-red uniforms. The kind of red you see when a CG goes too far and takes blood from you. "INMATE" is printed on the fronts and backs of our shirts in thick white letters. Inmates are easy to spot and shoot if we run.

No one runs from Camp 22.

CG Hale stops in front of the young girl who sleeps in the bed above me. Inmate Z-TX-558.

Pointed at her flat chest, the scanner beeps. Red dots of light move around the Inmate. Assessing the body for illness or injury.

Z-558 won't make it past her fifteenth year. Her arms are thin. Like twigs. She cries in her sleep.

Ninety-nine percent of Inmates fail before twenty-five, but here I am. From what I can count, my body's forty-five or fifty. The CGs call me an *old hand*.

Every Morning Call I think my time is up.

"Pass!" CG Hale shouts and moves on to me, Inmate Z-TX-11.

"Fail!" a second CG shouts somewhere down the line. There's a cut-off scream. Then nothing. The failed Inmate is dragged from the room.

I spread my arms and legs to be scanned. The red dots light up my skin and uniform. Like when chicken pox took over the Camp last year.

"Pass!" CG Hale shouts. She sounds angry about it. The big Guard gets in my face, but I don't step back. It would only make what's coming worse. I stare at the floor instead.

The Guard hits me with the strength of a wave. For one second I'm confused. I think I'm tied down in the ocean. On one of the after-hours training nights for the new Guards.

But it was just CG Hale's fist punching the air out of me. My face ends up between her boot and the hard floor of the Sleeping Barracks. Blood before 3:35 a.m. I'm too old for this.

"I hope I'm the one who takes you to the Gulf the day you fail," CG Hale spits down at me. "It'll be soon. Get ready."

She wipes the sole of her boot with my long hair. Uses my back as her path to get to the next Inmate.

CG Hale and the other Guards have targeted me this past month. It's normal for CGs to get bored with an Inmate after one week. But they never move on from me. They're going to force my body to fail soon. I'm not ready to fail.

It takes me a full minute to get back to my feet. No Inmate helps. We're not allowed to speak or touch. Inmates don't even whisper in their beds at night. Like in some of the nicer Camps. Here, surveillance sees and hears everything.

It's been three years and eighty-eight days since I last spoke out loud. I don't remember the words. *Yes, sir.* Or *No, ma'am. Goodbye* to my old bunkmates.

3:40 a.m.

Morning Meal.

The other bodies that passed Assessment Checkup file into Mess Hall. At the entrance, we grab cups filled with a dark liquid off a tray. Suck the tasteless meal down by the time we reach the exit.

We have to walk by the CGs seated around big tables, eating a hot meal. Tallying scores before their shifts. Most mornings they add up the Inmates they hurt the day before.

The CGs have a point system. One point for every bruise. Two for a broken bone. Four for a drowning in the Tank. Ten for when a CG takes an Inmate to the Gulf.

Today the talk is cats, not Inmates. Several were found in a work shed. I hear the word *litter*. One CG gets sixteen points. The CGs all laugh.

3:45 a.m.

It's Day Five of June.

Harvest season. The worst time of year for an Inmate at Camp 22.

Spotlights flood the gated grounds. Armed CGs march the X–Z bunk unit to Shift One Stations. It's hot even in the dark. Come sunup it will be worse. Sticky and sweaty. Hard to breathe at all.

The X Inmates go to the fishponds. The Y and Z Inmates continue to the saltwater fields stocked with sea-bean plants.

Since my transfer to Camp 22, I've worked every Station. I can run this facility better than the CGs. For twenty-five months I was the Attendant to a Warden in a Camp like this one. Aquafarming for biofuel.

When I was young Warden Clove taught me to read and write. She talked to me. Allowed me to talk back. She told me the importance of the Inmate's work. She told me the Inmates' lives are not wasted. We are helping Texas survive. Warden Clove told me my "excess" life is not my fault and things had to be this way.

That was a long time ago.

Camps like 22 are step one in the production of biofuel. For the military's airplanes and helicopters, Warden Clove explained. *Growing plant-based aviation fuel* and *feeding the public at the same time,* she said. *That's maximum productivity at its finest.*

Pipes pump seawater from the nearby ocean into ponds stocked with fish. The pond's runoff water fertilizes the sea-bean feedstock. The beans are next shipped off to step two in the biofuel production. Those Inmates get to work indoors. It's still hot, but there is a cover over their heads.

There is no cover for Field Two work. I wade through a middle row in rubber boots. I begin to pick, three of the towers watching my every move.

CG Hale is the lone patrol for Fields One and Two. No need for more. There is no escape, and no Inmate ever refuses to work. Even Freshmates know that to work is the only way to live.

I don't know why so much attention is on me. For seven days now. I have done nothing to earn it. I've kept quiet. Done the work. Still, a Sniper has been assigned to me.

A red dot from a rifle's laser is aimed at my forehead. Same thing when I leave the Sleeping Barracks. Mess Hall. One word from a CG and the unmanned Sniper will fire. Take me out.

I pose little threat as an old hand. If I were a trouble causer, I would never have lived this long.

I continue to pick. To work, like I have my entire life.

Ten barrels must be filled with the bean plant by the end of Shift One. A night spent inside the Tank if an Inmate fails to meet the quota. Twelve hours standing on her tiptoes, water up to her nose. If the Inmate survives, she lives to work another day. But eleven barrels will be her quota tomorrow.

"Life Must Be Earned" is the motto above our Camp gate. I'm the only Inmate who can read it.

8:45 a.m.

I know it's 8:45 a.m. because the strongest Inmates have completed their barrels. Fifteen minutes left to complete mine.

The air is different here on the coast. It's thick. Wet. Makes the work much harder than at other Camps.

Sweat covers my body. My mouth is dry. I can't swallow. Inmates only get water three times a day. I place my hand on my tenth barrel of sea beans. I'm going to faint.

"Inmate Z-TX-11, get the hell up now!" CG Hale shouts. Twenty feet away. A metal club is pulled from her belt. Ready to beat me back to work. The beating will last the remaining fifteen minutes of Shift One.

My tenth barrel will not be complete.

A night spent on my toes in the Tank. I won't last the twelve hours this time. CG Hale would like that. Four points for her.

I want to pass Shift One. I want to live. I grab two handfuls of beans, throw them into my barrel. Five more handfuls and it's complete.

CG Hale strikes her club into my back. I fall into my tenth barrel. It spills the beans into the Field.

"We've got ourselves a date tonight, Inmate," CG Hale says. "I think it will be the best one I've had in years."

I crawl to my barrel. Drag beans back inside. The club cracks into my shoulder. Pain. And anger.

CG Hale sits on my overturned barrel. "You don't want to see me tonight?" A smile on her face. "Are you scared I'll ask you to take your clothes off? Don't be shy."

No Tank. No Gulf. It ends now, 8:50 a.m. On my own time.

Five seconds before the Sniper will react.

I take hold of CG Hale's boot. Pull her down into the Field. Lunge for her neck with my hands.

A Scream Gun, not the Sniper.

It goes off somewhere by the loading docks. Every Inmate drops to their knees. I let go of CG Hale's throat. Our hands press against our ears. Trying to block out the screaming. I've learned many times nothing can keep out the noise. But I have to try.

Large vehicles break through the Camp's closed gates. Six of them. The women and men standing in the truck beds don't wear uniforms. They shout, *"Surrender!"*

They have guns. Aimed at the CGs. Two are shot dead.

The Scream Gun cuts off. A Camp siren takes over. *Stay on the ground or die.* All remaining CGs run to the gate, weapons out to fight. "Aim to kill! Aim to kill!" the Warden shouts from the front.

CG Hale aims her gun at my forehead. Not at the women and men she was ordered to kill.

"Fail—"

A bullet fires into the back of her head. She falls into the Field at my side.

I dive face-first into the bloodstained water. Cover my head with my hands. There's a ninety-eight-percent chance the Sniper can still find me. End me.

Two minutes go by.

My lungs burn. When I come up for air, the sounds of the fight have stopped. It's hard to breathe. I can't understand what I'm seeing.

The Corrections Guard of Camp 22 has failed. Killed off in 120 seconds. By the women and men with guns.

A man steps forward. He puts out his right arm to show the Inmates a symbol on his skin. "We are with the Common," he says. "We've come to liberate this Camp and every other Camp across the country."

None of us know what *liberate* means. We stay pressed to the ground.

"Stand up!" the man with the symbol shouts. "The Guard is dead. Join us or go your own way. Whatever your choice, you are free."

The young Inmates get to their feet. They move to the trucks, to the open gate. A girl wearing no uniform walks up to me. Holds out her hand. I take it. She pulls me up to stand.

"You're going to be okay," the Common girl says.

I clear my throat. No questions for more than half my life. Now feels like the time again. I have to ask the question I've asked myself every day since I can remember. "Why? Why did they put us in here?"

The girl looks at me with tears in her eyes. "You honestly don't know?"

Every Inmate in Camp 22 is outside now, laughing. Hugging.

A handful of the Inmates strip off their red uniforms. Sprint around the Fields naked. They stomp on the sea-bean plants, shout out every word they know. Because they can.

"You're a Multiple," the girl says. "Probably a twin."

"What is a twin?" I ask.

There are so many questions.

AVA

Lub-dub. Lub-dub. Lub-dub. The sound of valves closing as blood travels through a heart. I'm surrounded by it. It's soothing, life affirming. And wholly familiar.

Lub-dub. Lub—

No *dub* follows. The strong heartbeat suddenly stops. All at once I rip through a weight of blackness, screaming, "Mira!"

But when my eyes wrench open, my sister isn't beside me. No one is. I sit up on an unfamiliar twin-sized bed in a bare, seemingly doorless room. "Mira!" I cry out again, certain the heartbeat I dreamt was hers. Where is Mira now? Is she hurt? I can't feel her presence. *"Mira!"*

Calm down. Breathe and think. I remember a bag being thrown over my head and then ascending up, up, up in disorienting darkness. A helicopter, stealing me away from the Common's headquarters.

It was an ambush. The Canadian president was never going to grant Mira and me asylum. But why have they separated us? Did they capture all the Common members? I have absolutely no sense of where I am or how much time has passed since I was taken.

Then my own heart stops beating.

Have we already been deported back to Texas? Roth could walk into this room this very minute and kill me in cold blood just like he murdered Father. What if he already got to my sister? *It wasn't a dream at all.* Oh God.

"Mira! Mira!" I scream my sister's name over and over. I rise and pound uselessly against the white walls, my heartbeat racing at a dangerous speed. "Mira!"

I'm trapped, powerless and ignorant, unable to protect Mira or myself or the Common.

If we die, will the cause die with us?

I sit on the twin bed with my knees drawn protectively against my chest, arms wrapped around my ankles. Hours must have passed—maybe even an entire day. My eyes sting from lack of sleep, and my stomach grumbles from lack of food and water.

A meal tray—surprisingly decent—sits untouched on the far side of the room. It appeared through a narrow slot in the wall with a jug of water shortly after I first woke up inside the cell. I ran to the small opening and screamed for my sister again, but the slot closed as soon as it opened.

Nothing has happened since.

I've been left alone with my thoughts for hours. With each passing second, I'm more and more sure we've been betrayed.

Was it Ciro? Maybe he was always the Canadian president's man—a mole that burrowed its way to the very top of the Common's ranks. He was the one who orchestrated the secret meeting with Moore, disguising it as a ploy for Mira's and my freedom, but really he must have intended all along for us to be taken captive. For trade? Out of loyalty? A hidden hatred?

If so, Barend must've been in on it too. They seem to be a team.

Or did Roth get to Ciro? To the entire rebellion?

What if the Common itself turned its back on us? The Traitorous Twins became too unruly a face for the movement, and they needed to find a new mascot. We became too much of a liability as publicly branded murderers, diluting the justness of the cause. Mira and I have been abandoned in our hour of need. Sacrificed for the greater good.

And left alone in our own fight.

Three uneaten meals now lie in a pile against the wall. The spoiled stench permeates the stuffy room. My message to whoever holds me prisoner and whoever put me here: *Screw you.* I won't comply. Lock me in a box and throw away the key, and still I'll fight back.

A hunger strike—the only weapon I have left.

I haven't taken a single sip of water, and I feel the agonizing consequences. The body can withstand only three days without the vital liquid. I've withheld mine from it at least a night and a day—I'm unsure exactly how long I've been locked inside this cell. It's torture, and I'm inflicting it upon myself. But Roth has taken everything from me. First my family, one by one, and now my freedom. But not my free will, the very thing that makes me human. And I'll resist him at all costs. Even if the cost ends up being my life.

The walls must be screens because suddenly they all turn on, immersing me within a 360-degree view of a peaceful river winding its way through a forest. Hidden speakers reproduce a convincing natural soundscape, completely at odds with the silence I've been trapped with. The whole long wall in front of me displays a waterfall straight out of a fairy tale—its free-flowing water like a tranquil lullaby. A clear blue sky projects onto the ceiling above.

A manipulation tactic to coerce me into drinking. From my schooling at Strake, I know that the levels of feel-good brain chemicals like dopamine increase just by being around water. Stress hormones reduce, lulling a person into a sense of calm. It's called being in a "blue state of mind." I close my eyes, refusing to be sucked in. All I see is red. My rage at being in captivity and separated from my sister can never be soothed.

Your waterfall will not make me drink.

I cast my mind out, poking around with a twin's sixth sense, seeing if I can find Mira. I know she must be looking for me too. Sensing nothing except bleak emptiness, I open my eyes, and my heart breaks into jagged, aching pieces. I'm back in a digital version of Trinity Heights.

Home.

Dizzy and weak, I stumble up to the painfully detailed neighborhood greenhouse Mira and I used to tend so carefully, and I peek through its glass windows. Hundreds of black-eyed Susans grow strong and resilient inside, row after row after row of the bright-yellow flower. I'm hit with a force of longing for my home—my old life—so powerful that I can scarcely breathe.

I turn to the opposite wall of my prison cell to face the house I grew up in—the place where Mira and I were born, and where our mother died. A sustainable, modern two-story home with a rock garden out front, the vast and impressive Dallas skyline looming behind. A house of secrets and duty and strict schedules. But it was also a house filled with love.

Tears fall down my cheeks. I drop to my knees and rest my head against our silver front door and let the flood of memories wash over me.

I'm jolted back to the present when the slot in the wall suddenly opens, and in pops a giant slice of chocolate cake. *How did they know?*

Endless data has been collected on my every preference and desire since the day I was born. While we managed to keep Mira's existence hidden from surveillance, I couldn't keep my food choices private. On

more than a few ration splurges, I used my microchip—breaking my
father's strict rule of sticking to our packed lunches—to order a slice of
the dessert from the 3D-printing machine at school. It instantly made
me feel better if I was having a particularly hard day.

Father would always request that Gwen, our housekeeper, bake
a chocolate cake on any special occasion, big or small. It was our
mother's favorite, he said. We had six different housekeepers over
the course of my life; Father had to hire them to be consistent with
his high-ranking status. It would've been suspicious for him not to
take on at least one house employee. As a precaution he replaced
them every three years—but all of them handmade the sugary dessert. Gwen not only baked the best; she was also the only one who
felt more like a friend than just an employee. Gwen never knew our
truth—none of them did. Father would never have implicated anyone. But I know that even if Gwen had found out, our secret would
have been safe with her.

She must be in a Texas prison now, in a cell probably much worse
than mine. Charged with aiding a family of traitors. A traitor herself in
their eyes. She'll be ruthlessly interrogated before being shipped off to
spend the rest of her life in a work camp. Every house employee ever
employed by my father will.

Who else has Roth taken that Mira and I have touched? Our fingerprints are all over so many since fleeing Dallas. Rayla, Emery, Pawel,
Ellie—and any other loyal Common member. Lucía, our brief road
companion who saved us in the deserts of west Texas with her gun;
Kipling, the cowboy who supplied us a custom-made motorbike and
kangaroo sticks; Xavier and his son, our grandmother's friends who
offered us their car. So many people helped Mira and me on our journey
north to Canada. And what did we give them in return?

I pick up the tray of chocolate cake and launch it across the
room.

I lie in the fetal position, turned away from the meal trays and jugs of water. I must conserve my quickly fading energy. I stay very still and wait for someone to talk to me. Eventually someone will. Why else am I still alive?

There's nothing I can do to alleviate the pain that comes with severe thirst.

The cause is sustaining me, keeping me alive.

I must hold out.

"Hello again, Ms. Goodwin."

I remain still, wondering if I am hallucinating.

"I'm very sorry to hear you have not been eating or drinking. That does not help anyone, especially yourself."

It's the same thin voice I heard in the forest at Paramount Point Lodge just before the bag went over my head: President Moore. I'm still in Canada.

I flick my eyes to the speakers.

"Where's my sister?" I push out in spurts through my bone-dry throat. I don't even have saliva left to swallow.

An apathetic click of the tongue. "You need to worry about yourself right now, my dear. Will you please eat something? I can't be seen as responsible for your death. Twins come in a set, and I need you both."

President Moore is a compassionate man, Ciro promised. *He will save you.* But he's no different from Roth—he only cares about saving himself. Politicians are all the same, no matter the country.

I narrow my eyes before lying, "I'll eat something if you take me to Mira."

Silence. Then out of nowhere a gap appears in the blank white wall, and in walks the president of Canada himself. For a split second my heart lifts—an escape, a way to find Mira. I can bulldoze my way out of the opening. But just as I surge to my feet, I fall faint onto the thin mattress again. Too weak to stand, I sit at the edge of the bed and scrutinize my captor.

President Moore is the most handsome man I've ever seen—it's not just editing tricks like I had assumed whenever I saw him on-screen back home. He's dressed in a well-cut navy suit with a maple-leafed flag pinned onto his lapel. I take in his flawlessly styled chestnut hair, smooth face, and amber eyes, as striking as a lion's.

The world's most influential leader stands five feet in front of me and smiles, switching on his famous charm. The whole room suddenly feels warmer.

"You must at the very least take a few small sips, Ms. Goodwin. No one would fault you for that."

He holds out a cold glass of water, but I keep my hands clenched on my lap. The president purses his lips—it's clear he's used to people doing exactly what he says—before placing the glass on the floor next to my bed.

"For later, then," he says, confident he will change my mind.

It makes me angry how safe he feels alone with me. The door's wide open. No Mounties are here to guard him; he carries no visible weapons for his own protection. *He thinks I'm no longer a threat.* He believes I've already lost. And maybe I have.

"Where's my sister?" I choke out. My voice has no bite at all. Frustrated, I pause to gather my waning strength before attempting to rise to my feet to face the president. A power play learned from my father: make sure to be on the same level as your adversary, or they will always see you as beneath them.

But President Moore motions for me to remain seated. He sits down on the bed next to me, ignoring my feeble probe for Mira's location. I turn my fiery gaze to meet his directly—he's the very picture of infuriating calm.

"What you're doing is brave," he says with a hint of condescension. "But it's not going to work."

"Are you sure about that?" I counter, breathless but maintaining eye contact. "I'd already be in Dallas by now if the handoff to Roth was going smoothly."

President Moore and Governor Roth hate each other. While Roth has tremendous power, control, and wealth in Texas, Moore has more of it and on a country-sized scale. And to top it off, he's beloved by his people—something Roth will never be. I tremble at the ego-filled rivalry that will ignite between our countries if Governor Roth achieves his greatest desire and becomes the president of the United States. It's only a matter of time before he announces his bid.

"You hope to exploit your starved condition and the publicity it would be sure to provoke to generate public pressure on my government for your release," President Moore says evenly, "and as a result, free you and your twin to return to your traitorous activities."

That's exactly what I'm hoping. If enough supporters of the rebellion cry out against Mira's and my detainment, there's a chance President Moore will be forced to answer their call.

"A political protest is commendable. Something the citizens can really rally behind," he says. "The People's Champion, just like your father."

That apathetic click of his tongue again—I want to rip it out—then his smile extinguishes, and all his warmth vanishes.

"But what you need to understand is that no one will get your message, Ms. Goodwin. No one knows what you're doing. And frankly, no one cares," the president continues. "Everyone in this facility works for me. Your valiant hunger strike will begin and end inside these walls, without fanfare or a zero-hour rescue mission, because no one here is on your side."

My empty stomach reels like the floor's been dropped out from under me.

"You and your twin are a liability to Canada, and I will not risk further damaging my nation's relationship with the United States by harboring its famous fugitives."

Mira and I are a liability no matter where we go. We were born liabilities.

"You mean damaging your relationship with Governor Roth," I say. Even *he's* sure Roth's next in line for America's highest office.

Moore doesn't flinch.

"And so, you've signed our death warrants . . . ," I say, almost completely drained. "You're deporting us back to Texas."

All in secret. We'll simply disappear.

"You lead the most powerful country in the world. If you can't help us, no one can."

President Moore shakes his head. "Canada, though mighty, is a lifeboat that will sink if we let too many people on board," he says with certainty. "It is not my responsibility to save the world—we must all save our own."

"But there are only two of us," I say. I hate the unmistakable desperation that has taken hold of my voice.

"Yes, with the whole world waiting to storm the boat behind you," he counters. The president sits relaxed, patiently watching me. What is he looking for? The negotiations are over. He's won.

But he let Ciro in. He saved his entire family.

I square my shoulders, stretching to my full sitting height. "And the Cross family? How did they gain entry?" They had money enough to buy their own private row on the lifeboat.

A trace of the president's charming smile reappears. "Everything comes at a cost," he says. "And yours is information."

My insides twist in confusion, but I keep my face blank. All my family's secrets have already been exposed: I have an illegal twin sister, my parents were rebellion members, and my long-lost grandmother is a former Common leader and current enemy of the state. *He must want information about the Common's whereabouts or their future plans.*

"I've been locked in this cell for days. I know nothing about what the Common is doing."

"Oh, your doomed rebellion is of little consequence to me. That is Governor Roth's problem, not mine," the president dismisses with a wave of his hand. "I'm interested in Project Albatross."

I have no idea what he's talking about. I wait for him to expand.

"Your father's 'twin gene' mutation trial," he presses, eagerness clear in his voice. "We know it reached the human testing phase before his . . . untimely death."

Twin gene? *Mutation?* Father would never . . .

It's like one betrayal after the next.

"My government knows Project Albatross is already being used across Texas to prevent fertilized eggs from splitting into two, eradicating the risk of a Multiple pregnancy," the president claims, almost wide-eyed, like the cure for cancer has finally been discovered.

I can barely process his shocking statement over the heartbeat pounding in my ears. A distressed and agonizing *lub-dub! lub-dub!* that races as fast as my painful thoughts.

Father shielded me from the worst of what he did while heading the Family Planning Division. Of course Roth must have tasked him with determining why twins even exist at all. It's a biological mystery. A malformation in conception. And Father must have convinced himself that gene therapy was the humane way to enforce population control . . . by not even allowing Multiples to be born in the first place.

"Even you, an American twin, must sympathize with our planet's plight. Every year our temperatures grow warmer and our resources diminish. Population control is now an unpleasant necessity," President Moore presses. "Prosperous nations like my own must face this bold reality. I must think of the future of Canada, which is the future of the world."

Is Canada about to carry out its own Rule of One? *My God.*

"Ms. Goodwin, it is your legal duty to tell me what you know of Project Albatross."

If my father has really found that a "twin gene" exists in a person's DNA—making it much more likely that a pregnancy will result in Multiples—and then discovered a way to fix nature's error through gene therapy, Governor Roth is obligated by international law to share the results. A nation can withhold food or other forms of foreign assistance, but it cannot withhold information that could save humanity and the planet as a whole.

Roth must have broken the Treaty of World Prosperity and refused the Canadian president—kept the research hidden, intended only for the advancement of Texas.

"The power to control an excess of life," he continues, determined. "One state should not hold on to such important knowledge all for itself, keeping the rest of the world in the dark. Every country deserves access to such mercy."

Mercy. If President Moore really is about to implement a one-child policy, he must think he can execute it better than the United States did, cleaning one of the ugliest stains that comes with such a brutal law: Multiples ripped from their mothers' arms to be sent to work camps, or worse.

He wants to keep his title as Benevolent Leader.

To do that he needs to rectify America's mistake: prevent any chance of a political disaster like the Traitorous Twins from existing.

The president takes hold of my shaking hand like a friend in need.

"Give me access to your father's research," he says. "And in return I will give you your freedom."

Moore searches my face. It's painfully clear I don't know a thing about Albatross's existence. I can't even pretend; it would be useless.

He clicks his tongue in disappointment and then lets go of my hand. "You really should follow my advice and eat something," he says, rising to his feet. "You won't like what happens next if you refuse. I won't let it be said that I didn't take proper care of you while in my custody."

All my vitality is suddenly sucked out of me, and I deflate. My shoulders sag forward, the burden to continue the fight much too heavy for one person alone.

"Just drink, Ms. Goodwin," President Moore says as he places the water glass into my lifeless hands. He walks toward the open door. "There's no need for you to suffer like this."

I launch the water glass across the room, narrowly missing the president's head. The glass explodes dramatically against the blank white wall, but I get no satisfaction. I'm left feeling somehow emptier than I already was.

The president stops and drags his gaze from the pool of water on the floor to me. "Such a waste," he says before the door seals shut behind him.

Such a waste.

OWEN

"She doesn't look dangerous," Blaise observes.

The guy's a genius, a legend, the best black-hat hacker in cyber-crime. But he can't decipher people worth a damn.

That's because she's asleep! I almost point out to him, but I keep my mouth shut.

"Not anything that you can't handle," I flat-out lie, knowing full well that if Rayla ever wakes up, she can snap his scrawny neck like a discarded toothpick. Best to keep that knowledge to myself if I want to pawn her off.

"So, can I leave her here?" I ask, my conscience squeaky clean. I did my duty. I gave Rayla her best shot to live, and now I want to wash my hands of her.

I've already skipped two days of work and my parents must be calling every hour on the hour. These are fixable problems, if I act now. Even the slight wrinkles of tasering a Kismet Security Guard and hopping into a stolen car with a Common member can all be smoothed out with a little inventiveness and the right silver-tongued excuse.

"You really are just a corporate Cog," Blaise accuses me in his low, muffled voice. A black bandana covers his nose and mouth, his unsettling signature printed on its front: a wicked orange smile with teeth made of flames.

We both look up from Rayla's unconscious body, almost buried beneath the wires and tubes that are keeping her breathing. "Are you sure you're a Programmer and not the prog*rammed*?" he throws at me.

Another poor observation, bud! I want to hurl at him, but I keep my comments to myself.

Blaise_of_glory was the lone user to answer my distress call. I was careful and cryptic, but I was sure any savvy lawbreaker crawling around in the Dark Web would be able to piece together current events and know the person I was asking aid for.

Key words: *factory raid* and *slayer*. Blaise responded immediately with an address to some no-name town a mile outside the sacred waters of Lake Michigan. Past online interactions with Blaise have been limited and brief, but he was the only option, and Rayla was starting to look like a corpse.

My first time manning the wheel of a car was a bit rough, what with dodging the Michigan State Guard down back roads while transporting a dying criminal in my back seat. But I did it. I found the address of the lonely, pitch-black house where a Goodwin-masked doctor was waiting for us inside.

After Rayla was stable, the doctor split, leaving me solo to watch over the fancy high-tech monitors and wait for her to wake up. If she wakes up. But I *really* don't want to be here if or when that happens.

Blaise only just showed up this morning, making all his mudslinging put-downs a bit hasty in my opinion. I am shocked, however, that he had the moxie to turn up in person at all. Hackers usually hide behind screens and codes, so I'll give him points for that.

"You just have hideouts and anonymous doctors on standby for emergencies like this?" I ask, glancing over at the medical equipment, adding up how much it all must cost. Whatever. The guy's extorted millions from big corporations and government agencies—he can afford it.

"Miscreant Life One-Oh-One," he sighs, like he's bored of me.

"I didn't think *Blaise* would join the Common," I say, air quoting his username. "Hackers stay underground."

"The rebellion's going above ground," Blaise answers slowly, like I'm hard of learning. "It's a once-in-a-century opportunity to subvert the powers that be. The kind of thing I live for. *Obviously.*" He throws a nod at Rayla. "This woman and her family could take down the government. I'm all in. Anyone with half a brain should be."

Well, that's my cue. "Look, it's been fun," I lie again, starting my discreet shuffle toward the exit. "But it's back to the real world for me."

Blaise lets out a fiendish laugh, made all the more disturbing beneath his gaping smile of flames. I can just make out his eyes under the shadow of his hoodie; they're an imitation gold, glaring at me in a kind of challenge.

"I don't need to prove anything to you, Blaise," I say flatly. "Or whatever your real name is." I puff up my chest with pride and superiority. He's just a dark-side hacker who's jealous of the light.

"You think you're the good guy and we're the criminals, don't you?" Blaise points to himself, the notorious boy wonder of cyberextortion, then to America's second most wanted lying comatose on the bed.

Well, if we're keeping tabs . . .

I see Rayla's fingers twitch on the mattress, first her middle, then her pinky. Better speed things up.

"If I lose my position at Kismet, the government will cancel my work permit," I summarize my situation for him. "My parents and I will be expelled from the state and shipped back to Georgia, where there are no jobs for me. We'll all starve, yada yada. I won't bore you with the typical details."

"Then why," the raspy voice of a ghost whispers from the bed, "did you get in my car?"

At first I pretend not to hear. I decide not to move, thinking if I stand still, maybe she won't see me. But I can't help myself.

"It wasn't your car!" I yell. *It's* my *car,* I finish in my head.

For some reason I expect her eyes to still be closed from her weakened condition, but when I finally turn to Rayla, her green eyes are wide open, fixed in her usual determined stare.

"Where am I?" Rayla demands. She has the gall to rip off a few of the wires attached to her arms and stomach. With a hardheadedness that seems to run in her family, she sits up, completely ignoring the fact that she just came to after a gunshot wound.

Her kin all have a death wish. And I really don't intend to be around when that wish comes true.

"Where am I?" Rayla demands a second time. Her shirt is plastered with dried blood, but she doesn't notice, or doesn't care. She lifts a steady finger toward Blaise standing like a dark angel at the foot of her bed. "Who is that?"

"*That* is Blaise," I say, shuffling him closer so Rayla can get a better look at him. "Meet the guy responsible for your miraculous return to life."

While Rayla sizes up this masked newcomer, I slowly back away, hoping she's already forgotten me.

Naturally, I expect Rayla to mistrust Blaise's intentions and ply him with questions like she did on our first meeting, or at least jab him with an undercut like "What kind of a name is *Blaise*?" But all she does is hold out her hand, the yellow scales of her snake tattoo glinting with sweat.

"Thank you," she says, simple and earnest.

I scoff so loud it echoes off the four bare walls that make up this dump of a house. Rayla twists her head in my direction, the last place I want her attention aimed.

I should have sneaked out when the sneaking out was good.

"Give me my gun, and tell me where the car is."

"Really? I don't get a thank-you too?" I ask. "Thank you for not turning me in, thank you for your exceptional driving skills that got me here, thank you for risking your safety and watching over me for two days *alone*—"

"It's been two days?" Rayla cuts my speech short, her voice weak, almost scared. She looks to Blaise, who confirms this with a nod.

The mattress dips as Rayla attempts to swing her legs to the floor and escape the bed. She makes it halfway through the undertaking before she realizes this was a bad idea. With a hiss of pain, Rayla falls back and leans against the wall that serves as her headboard, her right hand gripping her sewn-up bullet hole.

"The twins," she moans. A quiver shoots down her body, and I have to look away from her vulnerability.

"You must heal before you can return to the fight," Blaise tells her.

From the corner of my eye, I see him pull the covers over Rayla and see that Rayla lets him. A bizarre pang of jealousy hits me, which I immediately shake off like a virus. *Why are you still here! Leave!*

The front door is right behind me. A few steps and I'm out, free, done with this dangerous, no-good-can-come-of-it, ill-starred saga of a mistake.

I continue inching backward, wondering if I should make a formal announcement of my imminent departure, or if I should just hightail it and run. Leeland's gun is in my back pocket, a backup in case they get any ideas to try and stop me.

"Does he have them?" Rayla demands, her old intensity stealing back into her words. I halt my retreat, startled to find Rayla looking to me. "Does Roth have Ava and Mira?"

"No," Blaise answers for me, like an annoying teacher's pet.

"Not yet," I add. "But he will." She doesn't like this blunt fact, but it *is* a fact. The governor of Texas killed Ava and Mira's father, and any day now he will get his hands on the twins and kill them too. The cause will die with them. The sooner Rayla learns this and accepts it, the more people will be saved.

Rayla the Slayer, they call her for good reason.

"Thousands are dying all over our country because they believe in an unrealistic dream you and the Common are peddling," I press on.

I register that I'm regurgitating words and thoughts I've heard my parents scream at news screens, and I question if I really agree with them, but I keep going.

"It's over, Rayla," I shout, so she will really hear me. "Tell the Common to stand down before more lives are wasted on a dead rebellion."

Rayla barely shakes her head, like I'm not worth the energy.

"Shouldn't you be running home now, Kismet puppet?" Blaise spits.

"I told you I'm no squealer," I remind Rayla with as much pride as I can muster. "If the Guard questions me, I'll tell them nothing." I can't look her in the eyes.

I do feel sorry for the woman; she has no other option. For her, it's either die fighting or die hiding. But I still have options; I can go back. She's the matriarch of this mess, and she'll go down for it. Those around her will go down too.

Suddenly panicked that I'll wind up collateral damage, I make a clean exit. No goodbyes or last looks.

With a bang I shut the door, anticipating footsteps to follow as I move down the abandoned street.

None do.

Why am I not in my car right now?

It's fine. Rayla won't be searching for where I hid the car anytime soon. She couldn't even stand up before I left.

After bolting from the hideout, I just kept walking. When I hit Lake Michigan, a stupid part of me thought I would be able to dip my toes in the water or something, but nope. There's a security gate. Valid, since the lake's the most important body of water in the country—it's the only Great Lake that's pure American from shore to shining shore, *and* it's the main source of drinking water for Midwesterners, keeping even low rankers like me alive.

New game plan: I'll stare at the rolling waves for a bit to clear my head, then go back for *my* car and drive the hell back to Kismet where I belong.

Shit. That's something one of the prog*rammed* would think, isn't it? Best not to dwell on it.

I check out a fleet of boats on the choppy water instead. It's hard to tell in the dark, but it could be Guards patrolling, or a moonlit booze cruise full of tourists, or possibly vessels shipping products from state to state. Take your pick—whatever it is, they're government. The Water Guard regulates the lake; no one gets near the priceless resource unless it's through them.

All right, enough dawdling. I turn my back on the lake and consider what might be the most interesting route to take back to the house.

I think this might be the first stroll I've ever taken in my life. I'm a net junkie; I don't go outdoors much. It's actually kind of nice. *Nope. Sightseeing is over. Go back the way you came, and get the hell out of here.*

Right. I direct my sneakers north and hustle down the crushed gravel path lining the gate, doing my best not to stroll. This is a stroll-free zone. Absolutely no eyeballing anything but the route that leads to the car.

About ten minutes into my disciplined look-at-nothing walk, I hear a loud commotion break out behind me. I look up, because hey, this distraction found *me*, and rubberneck toward the beachy-looking downtown.

I can't make out what's being said, but whoever's doing the yelling is angry, and there's a lot of them. Unable to stop myself, I backtrack my way toward the hullabaloo.

It's immediately apparent something big is happening. The main street is packed with people, most wearing their government-issued work uniforms, which makes sense given the demographics of this blue-collar town. Everyone's probably connected to the Water Guard in some way, and that means everyone's government—or knows someone who is. Best keep my head down.

Sides appear to have been taken, because two hot-tempered groups shout back and forth to each other. No one's listening, but everyone has something to say.

Devices are in every hand. The people around me have one eye glued to their screens, the other on their opponents. I force my way into the personal space of an off-duty Water Guard, trying hard to see what's going on. The first image I glimpse is of Leeland, my coworker, giving an interview on the now-empty Kismet factory floor. He's wearing a back brace and looking all victimized. "Owen Hart was a Programmer at Kismet, and I thought he was my friend, but he was in on the rebellion raid. He beat me with my own baton. He's armed and very dangerous."

Bullshit! *Well, you* did *baton shock the guy and steal his gun . . .*

But it doesn't stop there. I almost jump out of my skin when I see Rayla Cadwell's pale face pop up on dozens of the crowd's devices. She's live on national news. *Live!*

"What in the actual hell . . ."

"Cut out your microchips!" Rayla tells the nation. Her tattooed arm's held out in front of her, her sweaty fist clenched into a ball. The rebellion's salute. She then uses a knife to dig into her right wrist, removing her own microchip. *No way that's an authorized chip.*

"Disrupt the way things are run!" Rayla says. "Show those in power we won't be tracked or controlled any longer. The power is now in our hands."

Mouth open, I watch several people actually cut into their right wrists with whatever sharp object they have on them. What really has me bowled over is the sight of government employees resisting. Gluts, yeah, I get it. But people who work for the government? This is crazy.

But before they can rip out their chips, the progovernment half of the crowd rushes forward, tackling the newly minted rebels to the ground. Then the real Guard show up.

"Disperse immediately!" a Michigan State Guard orders from a voice amplifier. More soldiers swarm the main street, swiping devices from people's hands.

Despite the Guard's best efforts to censor the news, several large screens suddenly light up against building facades, all displaying Rayla's message front and center.

"The Common's gained intel Ava and Mira have been detained by the Canadian government. The twins have staged a hunger strike. Even inside a prison, my granddaughters will still not obey." Cheers erupt throughout the crowd. "And neither will we. We will *not* simply stand by, unquestioning."

Rayla pleads into the camera. "Save the twins!"

The woman is a tank—nothing can take her down. She looks like she's ready for imminent battle, not in hiding, recovering from a gunshot wound. I can't help but be impressed.

I blink, and the newscast has suddenly cut into split screen, making room for the last person I thought I'd see next to a Common leader's face. Governor Roth.

The battle lines are drawn: Rayla's on the left, Roth's on the right.

The governor's an intimidating man for sure, his military uniform stacked with a ridiculous number of medals, his cocky face a masterclass in authority. He's a man I wouldn't want as my enemy.

"A cowardly traitor such as you should be locked inside a prison cell, not broadcast on national airwaves," Governor Roth growls at Rayla. Wild shouts of joy come from half the crowd.

Unfazed, Rayla smiles. "I thought I might see you here, Howard." This is exactly what she wanted. Roth took her bait clean.

In the corner of the screen, the dapper young newscaster looks just as shocked as I am. Eyes wide, voice frozen in stunned silence. He can't believe his luck—ratings gold just fell into his lap. He simply has to sit there and let it happen.

"My daughter and my son-in-law are dead," Rayla fires off. "Next you've set your sights on my granddaughters in Canada. You've openly announced your intention to deport the twins back to Texas, where you will murder them without due process of law." Her ferocity leaps off the screen.

Rayla's anger is magnetic; the people around me hang on her every word. "Who will stop the government's bloodshed?" she demands.

The Common's side of the crowd erupts in a pissed-off, unified roar. "We will!"

"Disperse immediately!" a Guard's electronic voice cries, trying and failing to drown out the anti-Roth shouts. A tear gas grenade goes off, and I pull my collar over my nose, stinging eyes still glued to the sparring match like everyone else in this fired-up crowd. We're not going anywhere.

"My grandson is dead," the governor strikes back. "Whose son or daughter will be next? Your criminal gang is on a rampage that will soon spiral out of control. You seek to bring chaos, but I *will* bring order. I am officially announcing my bid for the presidency of the United States."

That's when things get really crazy. A gaggle of protesters wearing those seriously sinister Goodwin masks explodes into the street, shouting at the top of their mutinous lungs. *"Cut out your chips!"*

Next thing I know I'm knocked to the ground, heavy feet crushing my hands and legs. In front of me an abandoned tablet flashes a list of wanted photographs: Rayla Cadwell, Emery Jackson, Xavier King, Owen Hart . . .

"What!" I exclaim. Things just keep getting worse. But before my new fugitive status can sink in too deep, an armored truck rolls up and a legion of soldiers spits into the street, guns raised. Time to go.

"An eye for an eye will make for a blind world," I hear Rayla threaten. "But we will blind you first. We are many, and we are coming."

Then all screens cut off, and military floodlights wash the street in bright light. Chaos out in the open—there's nowhere to hide. *Get out of here now!*

A Goodwin mask falls seemingly out of the sky and onto my chest. Two split seconds of hesitation and then I put the damn thing on. *It's safer to hide your face,* I do a good job persuading myself. I jump to my feet, ready to bolt. *It's just to blend in.*

But I think I just joined the rebellion.

MIRA

I've lost track of time.

The Mounties took the wristwatch my father gave me all that time ago when he told us to run. *I wasn't fast enough, Father.* It was all for nothing. Now I can only lie here and wait for the feeding chair.

Ava and I have gone on a hunger strike before. We were sixteen and applying for college, and Strake University was our only application. Father demanded Ava go to medical school, believing if we became the future Director of the Family Planning Division, we'd always be safe. Ava didn't know what she wanted, and I certainly didn't either, but we wanted our right to choose. *We must be perfect* was always drilled into us. If we weren't, we knew we could lose everything. This left very little room for teenage rebellion. But that one day we did rebel, in our own quiet way. We managed no food or water for a full ten hours before Father entered the basement with a fast-food peace offering. That night we gathered around the fold-out dinner table in the basement, our dual protest starting a conversation.

I miss my father so much. I'd do anything he demanded of me now, anything at all to make him real again and not just a memory.

I keep my eyes perpetually closed and seal myself off from the hallucinations that have come to populate my cell since I decided to stop eating. Blurry visions of Ava appear now and then, but I've come to dread these visits. It hurts too much to watch her disappear; it's like I keep losing her again and again. Like heartbreak on a loop. *Where'd you go, Ava?*

The worst agony of my imprisonment is not knowing where she is. Or *if* she is. There's a powerful rage intensifying deep inside me where Moore and Roth cannot reach. It's dormant, but it's flammable, waiting for a torch so I can burn everything down.

If only I could move.

Exhausting the last of my energy, I open my left eye.

I'm still lying where the doctors left me—curled on the carpet in the center of the floor. They stopped bothering to drag me to the bed I refuse to sleep in, knowing I'll put up a fight and just wind up here anyway. It's a small victory, not doing what they want, just lying on the floor that smells of peroxide and vomit.

Thick wooden legs of a dining table rise directly above my dwindling frame. Two high-backed chairs sit empty on either side. A geometric bookcase stands behind them, stacked with real paper books, hundreds of them, my favorite titles prominent, just a few arm's lengths away. Tucked inside little cubbies, exquisite plants and flowers dot the four walls like lavish wallpaper. High above, imitation sunlight spills through ceiling windows, blanketing the room in a golden-hour glow that never fades.

It's all designed to make me feel like I'm not in a cell. A well-styled fabrication especially for me—a futile attempt to lull me into a tranquilized submission. When the doctors visit, they even call me a guest.

Dress it up as you like, President Moore. It's lipstick on a pig.

I'm a prisoner in a prison. A girl with no country.

A girl with nothing to lose.

Two small slits open in the wall beside the dining table, and out pop two bowls, one for each chair. My body jerks at the commotion, my own soft breathing the only sound I've heard since I lost track of time.

"Mira," a soft voice fills the room. "It's me."

I open my other eye. "Ava?" I barely breathe. I muster a reserved strength, the kind that allows fathers to lift automobiles off their children, and roll onto my back. Tilting my neck, I search the room with darting eyes, but she's nowhere. I'm alone.

"Ava, where are you?" I plead. "Are you here?"

"I can be," Ava's voice tells me from the speakers. "If only you would agree to eat, we could be together."

My mind is so muddled, my will so weak, I almost believe those words. Truth and lies seem indistinct and interchangeable. I don't know what to think anymore. I flick my blurry gaze on the two waiting bowls, one for Ava, one for me.

"Starving yourself will give us nothing, Mira. You're only keeping us apart," Ava's voice presses. "You're suffering alone by choice. It doesn't have to be this way."

But this is the only way.

There's no escape, and giving in was never an option. Dallas is our inevitable endgame, and if we're going down, I'll make sure their win isn't easy. A hunger strike is the last chance any of this could matter. Maybe people will find out what happened here; maybe it will send a message. The flame might stay alive.

"Please, eat for me, Mira," Ava's voice begs.

Ava wouldn't want me to eat. She would want me to fight.

The voice is Ava's, but they aren't her words. They aren't her truth. I know, in my very soul and with every fiber of my being, that Ava is striking too.

This is another manipulation. Another lie.

"No!" I cry out, banishing the fraud pretending to be my sister.

I brace myself for what comes next.

Four lines of a door materialize on the far wall, and in rumbles the feeding chair. My stomach drops, and a primal panic spreads through me, urging me to crawl away and cower in the nearest corner. I crush the impulse before it can take root. I steel my nerves and sharpen my resolve, knowing my willpower is my best weapon. *No fear.*

Two doctors, both wearing white surgical scrubs and no-nonsense expressions, wheel the chair toward me. The young one, the same assistant from our last session, leers down at me as she prepares the restraints. Deep-purple bruising swells below her eyes like twin crescent moons, the result of my flailing fist connecting with her nose. I almost smile.

The lead physician looms over me, not bothering to take my vitals or examine my condition. She's already made up her mind. Or someone made it up for her.

Lying stock-still on the floor, I gather all traces of residual strength.

"What you're doing breaks every international law," I protest to deaf ears. "It is my right to refuse food."

"Based on my expertise, immediate treatment is needed to ensure and preserve the life of Mira Goodwin," the doctor announces formally. *To who? Are people listening?* She takes two steps back, out of kicking distance, and nods to her bodyguard of an assistant. "Begin the medical procedure."

The assistant lunges for my arms, but I'm ready. Awakening my rage, I drive my left foot into her left kneecap quick as lightning, taking her by surprise. She topples over like a struck tree trunk, and as she falls toward me, I use gravity to bury my fist into her solar plexus, just below her sternum.

The air is knocked out of her with a satisfying wheeze, but she rebounds fast and seizes my wrists, slamming me down with her bulky weight. I thrash and writhe until my limbs are spent and I can barely breathe.

My body goes limp. I have nothing left to give.

"Good girl," the doctor says, pulling on her sterile nitrile gloves. "Allow yourself some dignity."

The assistant scoops me up like a rag doll and carries me like a child to the feeding chair. *Dignity?* All I can do is scream.

"Gluts don't have rights," she whispers in my ear. "Murderers don't have rights."

Incongruous with its purpose, the chair looks like it could belong in a president's dining hall. With its towering tapered back and cushioned armrests, luxuriously upholstered in a velvet free of any marks of leftover humiliation and torment. A pristine white, the color of purity and surrender.

The instant I'm dropped into the seat, the restraints burst out from hidden compartments, locking around my wrists, ankles, and shoulders, completely immobilizing me. The assistant straps my head into place as the final touch. My fury burns through me like an uncontrollable fire until I think it will consume me. Wet tears drip from my eyes, down my fevered temples, trying to extinguish the flames. *Stay calm. Stay calm. Don't let them break you.*

"All secure, Doctor," the assistant announces.

The lead physician approaches on my right. She sprays two quick pumps of a numbing anesthetic up my nose and positions the long plastic nasogastric tube under my flaring right nostril.

"You're not a doctor," I spit at her. Doctors treat and heal, not hurt and torture.

I was going to be a doctor once.

My father was a doctor once. *He did harm to others,* I remind myself. *How many families did he hurt executing the Rule of One?*

"It's easier if you don't struggle," the doctor tells me. *Easier for you, or me?* She inserts the feeding tube up into my nasal cavity and down my throat. I fight to jerk my head away, but even the slightest of movements wreak a violent pain all over my body. I feel the tube slide down deeper, and I start to gag. I cough uncontrollably, choking on trapped air. Still, they keep going.

"Swallow," the assistant demands, placing a metal straw between my lips. Swallowing and drinking water will help ease the tube past my oropharynx to reach my stomach, the end goal. I resist for as long as I can, but my lips involuntarily curl around the metal, and I finally obey.

The pain and choking stop. "Good girl," the doctor says. Holding a handheld X-ray scanner over my abdomen, she checks to make sure the tube didn't end up in my lungs. "Excellent positioning," she confirms flatly, and peels off her gloves.

Rough hands secure the nasogastric tube to my cheek and chest with a clear adhesive. A distasteful grin on her bloated face, the assistant steps into my fixed line of view, lifting the feeding bag so I can see. "Dinner time," she whispers, mocking my pathetic helplessness.

I can't beg or plead. Instead, I just watch while she attaches the tip of the tube to the bag and follow with teary eyes as the liquid formula flows down the thin plastic toward me. My stomach clenches, preparing for the assault.

"You need to be strong for your journey," the doctor's voice says from somewhere near the door. "You have a visitor arriving."

Oh God. Roth. Our time's up. My plan has failed.

The formula fills my stomach, and my muscles start to heave. I cough up spittle and defeat. In a last-ditch effort, I will myself to vomit, to reject the liquid and protest, but my feeble efforts are spiritless and empty.

"It's easier if you just give in," the assistant says. She drags one of the chairs from the dining table and sits directly before me, leaving me nothing to look at but her taunting face. I close my eyes.

"Just give in," she whispers.

I'm still strapped to the chair. They think I still might retch up my meal like I did after my last force-feeding. But I don't see the point.

The doctors will just order another session, and I'll have to go through it all over again.

So I simply sit and digest. Absorb my future and my fate. I wonder if they will let me see Ava before the end.

"You killed your leader's son," the bullish assistant says from her chair, sharp elbows on her knees. She looks a few years older than I am, an age I'll never reach. "You deserve whatever's waiting for you."

It's a waste of energy to argue my innocence. Her false viewpoints and inflexible judgments are cast in stone. What words could possibly be said that might reshape her way of thinking?

"Halton was his grandson, not his son" is all I say. She might as well hear the facts even if she won't listen.

This shuts her up for a bit, and I'm left alone again with my burnt-out thoughts.

Most people confuse this fact about Halton's parentage. His mother died from skin cancer when Halton was just a child, but his father—Governor Roth's son—had disappeared long before this. About a year after Halton's birth, as Father told it. No one dared to probe further as to why Roth's true son would vanish from high-ranking society and abdicate his position as the governor's heir. Ava and I suspected foul play. A transgression or scandal that we could use as blackmail if our family secret was ever discovered. But such thoughts quickly faded, knowing proof could never be found inside our censored state. Halton's father became a fuzzy recollection, then an unremembered man.

The forgotten son, Ava and I called him.

What was his name . . .

Stop thinking about the past, I chide myself. *You should think about what lies ahead.*

"I've been wondering," the assistant asks, rising from her chair, "will your country live-stream your execution?"

I can't lift my hands to plug my ears and block her threats. A song rises up in my throat, and I start to hum, trying desperately to tune her out. It's an old favorite of my mother's, one I would sing with Ava when we were little.

"I hear Texas is bloodthirsty enough to make a real show of it. The final end to the twins."

My song dies. I let my body go slack, and I give in.

"How do you think they'll do it?" she ponders, inviting images of my father's death to play inside my mind. "Whatever they choose, I hope it's not quick and easy."

Nothing ever is.

They gave me back my wristwatch. A prize for good behavior. I haven't bothered looking at the time. *Does it even matter anymore?*

I hear the door open. I have the energy now to easily turn around and see who entered, but I don't. I keep my back to the door, staring at the single pink flower of a blooming eagle's claw on the wall shelf in front of me. It's the same cactus I tried to give Halton in the greenhouse the night everything fell apart.

I don't question its presence all the way up here, in the wrong climate, the wrong setting. It's clear it's a sign. I imagine it as Halton's final message: *My family won.*

"Mira Goodwin," President Moore says behind me.

When I make no indication I've heard him, he moves toward me, his footsteps heavy despite the plush wool carpet. "Ms. Goodwin, if you would follow me," he says pleasantly. I remain seated, my legs crossed, my arms folded over my chest. "I see you have decided not to wash or change," President Moore continues, his voice tight with displeasure.

A fresh set of clothes and unused bottles of waterless-bathing gels lie next to me on the floor. I won't clean up and look pretty for the handoff. *Did they really think I would?*

"I trust you will follow me by your own volition and not make me call my officers," he says. Looking away from the cactus, I glimpse the red uniforms of two Mounties waiting by the door.

I wait a few more seconds before pushing myself up from the floor. My bangs, overgrown and oily, hang low over my eyes, blocking my view of the man who caught me. I follow him out the door.

It's a short march down the white, characterless hallway. President Moore stops beside an open doorway, motioning for me to enter first. With the two Mounties closing in behind me, there's no other choice but to move inside the small, excessively bright room. As soon as I cross the threshold, the door seals shut, locking me in.

A clear glass wall greets me, a woman in a solemn black suit seated a few feet away on the other side. I immediately recognize her as the United States Secretary of State. Any hidden spark of hope I might have still had is extinguished at the sight of her and her kitschy boots. She's a Texan, a Roth woman through and through—his rumored running mate for the upcoming presidential election.

"Both of you, take a seat," Madam Secretary demands.

Both of you?

"Ava?!" I scream. She must be locked in a room like mine somewhere close by.

Pounding erupts on the wall to my right, the sound of fists fighting to break down a barrier. I slam myself against it, a wave of fury and relief sinking me to my knees.

"Ava!" I scream again, beating my own fists against the thick wall to make sure she knows I'm here.

The secretary watches our reunion, unmoved. President Moore appears behind her, his two Mounties on either side.

"Ava and Mira Goodwin," she says, swinging her head left and right to get a good look at both of us. "I have orders from our president to take you back to New Washington."

Ava must have said something Madam Secretary didn't like. She raises her penciled-on brows and shakes her head.

"Girls, you don't have the numbers," the secretary informs Ava firmly. "The Common is nationally hated, considered a low-ranking guerilla group bent on killing the government and its people."

The Canadian president smirks, taking a seat in his velvet chair, an I-told-you-so twinkle in his hard-hearted eyes.

"Your dual hunger strike was seen as nothing but a selfish stunt. A last-gasp effort to make headlines. I am speaking with you now only to gauge your strength for travel. There is no debate; you are returning to the States."

She stands, and I stand too.

"You claim you want the killing to stop," I say, my fast breaths fogging up the glass that separates us. "And yet you take us to our murder."

"Both you and Ava will stand a fair trial and pay for your crimes as justice sees fit," she responds, turning toward President Moore. "Mr. President, we are ready for the detainee transfer."

I smash my fist against the tempered glass, oblivious to the pain. Again and again Ava punches the wall between us, trying to get to me, her wild strikes like the fervid beat of a war drum.

Then suddenly everything stops. All movement and sound ceases with the click of a gun.

"Everyone, listen and do as I say," the Mountie holding the weapon announces. "And the secretary will live."

I watch dazed as he pushes the gun between Madam Secretary's shoulder blades, shooting a warning glare at his fellow Mountie, who looks as if he's psyching himself up to charge. "Bad idea," the renegade Mountie advises. "Better move to the corner and put your hands on the wall."

Is this man with the Common? Is he here to assassinate or save us?

My eyes rake over his strong-boned features, his jet-black hair knotted at the crown of his head, his easy posture. I don't recognize him. He was never at the Paramount hotels.

"Moore, what is this?" the secretary demands.

President Moore remains seated, his arms raised helplessly. I look on in satisfaction as every inch of his body shakes with either anger or fear. He's probably never felt so powerless. *How does it feel?*

"Open the doors and release the twins," the man orders.

It takes a long five seconds for the president to respond, his voice gruff and seething. "Open rooms A and B."

The door slides open behind me, and before I can move, Ava's in my room, her arms around me. She holds my face in her palms, checking to make sure it's really me, then rests her forehead to mine. "Did they hurt you?"

"Ava, can you run?" I ask, surprised how calm I feel. There's little time to escape. *We need to move. We have to make it out.*

"If you interfere with this operation in any way," our rescuer shouts at President Moore, knowing everyone inside the facility is listening, "the Secretary of State will die, and Canada will have a real shit storm to clean up."

He pulls his hostage with him and makes his exit. Ava locks her hand with mine, and we sprint into the deserted hall, unsure where to turn. "To me!" we hear the Mountie yell before we see him. "Follow me!"

The Secretary of State appears first, her valuable, brawny frame the perfect shield for a rescue mission. The Mountie pokes his head out from behind her puffy bun, his high cheekbones flushed with exhilaration.

"Cover my back!" he shouts at Ava and me as they barrel toward us, showing no signs of stopping. *Should we trust him? What if he's just another abductor? Where will he take us?*

Ava yanks us forward behind the stocky Mountie and his gun, her grip on my hand inseverable. I dam the panic that threatens to flood my composure and fight to keep pace. I block the man's left, Ava blocks his right, making him a hard target for a taser or bullet.

Moore wouldn't shoot. He wouldn't risk harming an American, sparking international chaos . . .

Cold doubt pushes me faster, the overwhelming need to get out and break free overpowering my burning chest and legs. We race at top speed for the far door labeled "Stairwell."

Four flights down, another long hallway, and no sign of any other Mounties. The path is clear all the way to the emergency exit doors, just ten yards ahead. The loud *click, click, click* of the secretary's boots sound like a ticking bomb. A few more seconds and everything will explode.

But we make it through the double doors, the alarm piercing the still night as we plunge deeper into darkness. I can't make out where we are, but it feels remote. The silence is total, and the sky is crowded with a thousand stars.

The isolation of this facility must be its top security. *There's nowhere to run.*

"Forward!" the man yells, still holding the gun to the secretary's spine.

A drone's spotlight trails our mad flight, the narrow beam so intense I have to seal my eyes shut and sprint blind. Ava stumbles. I stumble. My legs will give out at any second; there's nothing to fuel them but the primal need to survive.

"A forest . . . ," Ava gasps between ragged breaths, ". . . twenty yards . . ."

The trees' canopy will make it difficult for the drone to track us, but what about the Mounties? Despite this renegade's threats, there's no way President Moore won't send them after us.

The red-hot light searing the back of my lids fades to black. We must have made it to the forest. The Mountie finally stops, and I open my eyes.

The first thing I see is two strangers moving toward us from behind the trunk of a tree. No, not strangers. It's like looking into a mirror. They're wearing Goodwin masks and clothes identical to ours.

I can barely stand upright. I can't catch my breath.

"What is this?" Ava pants, turning to the Mountie. She teeters beside me, her body folded forward, sweaty fists on shaky knees.

"There's no time," Madam Secretary says, her eyes wide, searching the dark. The Mountie lowers the gun, and she turns to him, giving a quick nod. They share a smile. "You did well, Kano," she tells him.

Shock prevents me from speaking, thinking, reacting. All I can do is take Ava's hand and squeeze.

As the secretary moves toward us, I wipe the saliva from my face and straighten to my full height.

"I must go back and play my part," she says, her own chest heaving. "This is where I leave you."

Ava nods, her eyes burning with the strength her body lacks.

"We will distract the search party, but you must move quickly." The secretary points to the masked pair, complete with red and blonde wigs. *Decoys.* "Go knowing that I am with you. You have many on your side."

She was in on our escape. *She's with us.*

"Resist much," the secretary says.

"Obey little," Ava and I reply in unison.

We're still in the game. We're not alone after all, not forgotten like Moore had said. My deep-seated fury returns and burns through me, making me feel strong and boundless, like an unrealized wildfire waiting for the right burst of wind.

"This way," Kano says, motioning toward a dirt road and the silhouette of a getaway vehicle. He tears off his Mountie uniform, and I catch sight of the elaborate rebellion tattoo that dominates his forearm. A massive koi fish fighting against violent waters. The symbol shines even in the darkness.

"The Common is waiting for you."

PART II

THE MISSIONS

ZEE

It's time for Lights Out on a normal night.

But tonight I'm a civilian, not an Inmate. A Common member if I want to be. I could sleep if I want. Eat if I want. Leave if I want.

Right now I choose to eat.

They took us to a building in a city they said was the old capital of Texas. Austin. The Mess Hall here is big and crowded.

Everybody sits together at round tables. I can't pick out the former prisoners.

We burned the red uniforms that labeled us "INMATES." We look like the others now.

"Hot stew!" a boy shouts.

I've never had a hot meal. My mouth waters. I step into the line forming at the back of the room.

A handful of men by the open windows stare and point at me. I'm the oldest Inmate from the Camps. I stand out.

I let my long hair fall over my face and look at the floor. It's not good to stand out. Life may be different outside the Camps, but that will still be true.

Attention is dangerous.

11:15 p.m.

What is this place?

Questions. No one will spit in my mouth now if I ask them things. I want to know where I am. What is a place if it is not for work?

The building is big and worn down. It looks like a warehouse. Much of the first floor is wasted space. Inefficient, a Camp Warden would say. Why are we here if it is empty? All buildings must have a purpose. If not, they should be leveled.

I keep walking. Open every door I pass. At the back of the first floor are big rooms filled with rows of crops. Grown by LED lights, not the sun. The sight confuses me.

The Texas government is the only producer of crops at scale. The only farms that exist are Camps. The Camps help Texas survive. That is what I was made to believe.

Does the Common run this city they call Austin? Are they the government?

I close the door and go up a flight of stairs. The second floor is used as storage. No walls, just a single open space. Packed floor to ceiling with wooden crates full of fruits and vegetables I never knew existed. Five Corrections Guards could be fed with the amount of stockpiled food.

A noise on the stairs behind me. I go rigid, prepare my body for punishment. I've found something I wasn't supposed to see. My arms, legs, and torso tighten. I exhale. The best way to take a baton hit.

Nothing comes. I turn and see the girl with straight dark hair. She helped me to my feet in the sea-bean field. She smiles at me. A different smile than CG Hale's smile.

I'm a civilian now, not an Inmate. I need to behave like one. I relax twenty percent.

"I was looking for you," the girl says. "Do you want to join the group gathering on the third floor? I'm Cleo, by the way."

No title of CG or Warden or Inmate. Just Cleo.

"Sorry, I didn't catch your name," Cleo says.

Inmate Z-TX-11 is my name.

"Just Zee," I say. My voice sounds rough, out of practice. The girl doesn't seem to mind.

Cleo holds out her hand. Why would she do that? I pull away. No touching, even if I am free to do it.

"Follow me, if you'd like," she says. She drops her hand. Doesn't make me feel like I made a false move. "The talk is about to begin."

"Where are we?" I ask.

"We're at one of the Common's safe houses," Cleo says. "Did you see the yellow door when you entered? That signals the building is a safe place for our members."

A safe house? That means the Common needs a hiding place. If they're hiding from the Texas government, the Guard, they have a zero-percent chance of living.

I still choose to follow Cleo.

She leads me up another set of steps. "I wanted to say, it's an honor to meet you."

Why? I don't ask.

We get to the third floor, and I hang back, away from the crowd. No straight lines and shut mouths like at the Warden speeches. Members stand in little groups, talking. Smiling.

Actions that would have cost me twenty strikes in the bad Camps.

The young Inmates don't have as many years to unlearn. Forget. It's hard for an old hand.

I make my way to a corner window, looking at no one. Just listening.

"A member said we have siblings."

"You belong to a family, not the Camps."

"What's a family?"

"Will they want us?"

Did my family give me up? That's a question I can't stop asking myself.

I move the cloth covering the window and look onto the street. The CGs will be here soon. Surveillance hears and sees everything.

I'm safe here. But for how long?

"Today you might have heard a lot about Ava and Mira Goodwin," a man shouts from the front. He stands on a box. He has no microphone. "The Secret Sisters of Dallas, the twins, came out of hiding a month ago and changed our future."

My height gives me a good view of the wall. The place where everybody points their attention. A line of ID portraits hangs behind the man. Not the digital holograms I'm used to. Images I could hold, made from a material I've never seen before. The portraits are all covered in glass, like they're important. Should be protected.

The speaker keeps telling the crowd about the Common, but it's hard for me to follow.

The portraits. The faces behind the glass. I go to them. The members move out of my way.

The two young girls at the top must be Ava and Mira. I feel like I'm seeing double. Like after a club strikes my head. Then I understand I'm seeing twins.

Their hair is different, one red, one blonde, but their faces are the same. An ID portrait of a silver-haired woman hangs below the twins. She has the same green eyes as they do. They must be a family.

The time I saw myself in a piece of glass, I had green eyes too.

"Roth . . ."

"Tyrant . . ."

"Darren . . ."

"Sacrifice . . ."

I don't understand any of these words.

I don't understand why so many eyes are on me. I've attracted too much attention.

I need to leave. But I don't. The Common speaker has gone quiet.

"Is that you?" my old bunkmate asks, Z-TX-558. She points to the portrait of a woman beside the twins.

I touch the glass. The face that looks like mine. A pretty, younger image of me. Smiling.

Who I could have been.

"What's it say below your face?" Z-TX-558 asks.

No member speaks for me. All wait for my answer.

The letters come into focus. I clear my throat and read the words out loud.

"Lynn Goodwin, Mother of the Rebellion."

My twin.

AVA

The Council Room, the War Room. Tower Three, Level Ten. This is where Mira and I should have gone immediately when we entered Paramount Point Lodge the first time. We never joined the Elders at the last meeting, but we should have demanded it.

We can only trust ourselves, I told my sister during the frantic drive back to the rebellion's headquarters, hidden underneath the seats of the white tourist van. Our father taught us to go where we're least expected—when we fled our home in Dallas, we ran deeper *into* the inner city, not away from it—and I can only hope that his lesson remains true, because we've returned to the location of our ambush. The Elders must be betting President Moore doesn't know the lodge is the rebellion's nerve center.

Still, we should remain at headquarters five, six hours max.

I sit inside the War Room, at the head of a long oval table next to Mira, every seat filled with a leading member of the Common: Emery, Ciro, Pawel, Skye, Kano, the three Common Elders who were there when I learned of my father's murder. Barend's here too, sitting in a chair at his usual post by the door, on guard as always. Everyone stares back at us, expectant, but all I can think is *Which one of you betrayed us?*

The expertly crafted maple tabletop is painted a striking shade of yellow, and I'm hit with the nagging notion that this color can also represent cowardice and deceit.

I open my mouth to commence the meeting, but Ciro talks over me, attempting to lead our dead-of-night emergency council. "The Elders have spoken, and we all agree there was unquestionably no treachery from within the Common's ranks," Ciro proclaims, confident. "I urge you both to understand that *the moment* President Moore acted remarkably out of character and abducted you without so much as a civil conversation, every Common member sitting at this table sounded the alarm and began plotting your recovery."

He looks shiny and bright, like he hasn't missed a wink of sleep since his plan backfired and Mira and I were tossed into a prison cell. I bet he's about to tell us that he's the one who put the pieces back together from the mess he left behind.

"Myself especially, since I am the one with the *in* to the US Secretary of State," Ciro says, running his fingers through his honey-blonde hair, a move that achieves little except to further heighten my annoyance. His tawny skin is perfectly moisturized. His whole body practically shines. *Looking perfect doesn't make you a leader.*

I can't remember the last time I've looked into a mirror. I glance at Mira to assess my current appearance. Mira and I are still identical except for her hair, which is now closer to Ciro's shade than mine. I hope one day she'll return to her roots. Fiery red.

Our time in the detention center has changed us both: we look dirty, gaunt, and empty—similar to how our father looked in his prison surveillance footage before he blinked out his coded message for us to revive the rebellion.

We did, Father. But it's taking its toll.

"Madam Secretary—she asks me to call her Danica—always stays at one of my family's Paramount hotels when she's in Canada on official business, you see," Ciro concludes buoyantly. "The safest place for any foreigner."

Does he expect me to thank him? He can try and lead by speaking the loudest and using the most words, but it's more than clear it's because of him that Mira and I now have *two* pissed-off governments that we're running from.

Emery, seated to my right and directly across from Ciro, shifts forward in her seat. She looks like she might have been staging her own strike in solidarity: thinned-out face, tired eyes, and wrinkled coat. The rebellion's leader probably hasn't rested a single moment since losing us.

"The Secretary of State made her sympathies to the Common known following Darren's nefarious execution," Emery says plainly, minimizing Ciro's role. "And after Rayla's call to action on national news earlier tonight, Madam Secretary alerted the Common of her plan to aid in Ava and Mira's escape."

Mira and I lock eyes. *Our grandmother was on national news?*

"The right hand to Governor Roth is a powerful ally for the Common's cause," Kano speaks up, his dark, deep-set eyes flashing, his low voice urgent. "Think of who else we can turn to our side because of her influence."

The man's entry into the inner circle went unchallenged by Emery. Or me. Free of his Mountie disguise, he's now dressed in tactical gear like Barend, but styled in a more laid-back manner: the first three buttons of his shirt are casually undone, and he wears black stud earrings and a warm smile. He looks to be somewhere in his midtwenties. I don't remember seeing him at the lodge when we first arrived—and I have a habit of memorizing faces. He must be a recruit from a different base who was called into action. Whatever the case, I'm thankful Kano answered the call.

"We can discuss Madam Secretary's significance in a subsequent meeting," Emery says firmly, "but right now we need to strategize which is the optimal safe house to shelter the twins."

"No, actually that will not be our next move," Mira announces beside me. "Ava and I are not going to hide behind TV screens, border walls, or safe houses anymore."

We had decided together, during our own private family meeting, that it was time for us to stop running. That we needed to take control and step into the front lines of the fight.

Mira, just like me, was locked isolated and starving in a cell. Our captors must have forgotten that we spent half our lives confined within an eighteen-by-fifteen basement with nothing but our thoughts to keep us company. It's like our minds were trained for that moment. Though they took everything from us—the worst was each other—they couldn't take our thoughts; and thoughts can be more dangerous than anything if the right person is left alone to think. Father taught us that.

And so I made myself dangerous, turning over every possible method and idea, thoroughly searching my mind for a way to bring down our adversary behind his seemingly impenetrable wall.

My mind kept coming back to the people. Together the many are powerful and can tear down walls.

But my heart kept going back to Project Albatross. I withheld the knowledge of the heartbreaking project from Mira, from everyone, to protect our father's memory. His name shouldn't be tainted because he was forced to carry out the orders of a monster.

If Canada gains access to Albatross, the "twin gene" therapy could spread and become a global pandemic, wiping out Multiples forever. *I have to shut it down.*

But I know the Elders won't let me venture back into the US for that purpose alone. The Common's cause has grown much larger than the Rule of One, yet the reason the cause was even reborn was because my family wanted Mira to live. This whole movement was started to save my twin sister. She was the spark, but the Common needs more to fan the flames.

It may seem like a secondary mission to others, but I can't let twins become extinct. I know that if I don't try to destroy Albatross, I'll carry that weight around my neck the rest of my life.

I need a big plan. Something that will help dethrone governors like Roth, who've appointed themselves kings and queens, but will also save the future of Multiples.

Alone in her cell, Mira had also been thinking. Mira told me her plan, and I told her mine, and while we devised entirely different courses of action, our end goal is the same.

Our next move means we must separate. We immediately agreed on that.

Divide, and conquer Roth.

"The Common needs more than just guns to fight Roth. The Texas Guard is too strong. We need a scandal," Mira proclaims, her voice at half its usual strength. A venous line is inserted into her left arm, delivering rejuvenating fluids. I have one in my arm, too, the infusion coursing through my veins.

"From what Emery told us, the leaked footage of Roth murdering our father wasn't enough to sway the people," Mira says. *Doctored. Fake.* That's what Roth's loyalists are peddling.

"So we need to link Roth to an action so morally and legally wrong that it will cause a public outrage. Something irrefutable," Mira continues, her voice steady and sure. "And to do that, we need to find Governor Roth's forgotten son."

"Alexander Roth," Emery says, thunderstruck.

"If there's smoke, there's fire," Mira declares. "A father doesn't cast out his only son unless he was fearful his legacy could be burned. I believe Alexander is alive, and I want to find him, wherever he's hiding. There is a scandal there, and the Common can use it as our weapon."

My face flushes, the intensity of this moment pulsating throughout my body. "And I'm going to Washington State. I'm going to flip the senator to the Common's side," I say, feeling stronger by the second.

"We need to rouse those in power to help us take the rebellion mainstream, on a national scale. I'm going back over the border."

Two birds, one stone. Washington State—one of the few places that actually planned ahead for the climate crisis—is among the most prosperous states in the country, along with Texas. Prosperity means influence, and its senator, Eli Gordon, also happens to be the former Director of his state's Family Planning Division. *He must know something about Albatross.* He was Father's greatest rival—they were likely competing to discover the gene therapy first.

I feel electric. I feel ready. Real action is about to be taken, and we're not asking permission.

Stunned silence; then everyone objects at once.

"We must stick together—"

"You only just reunited—"

"Much too risky. We've got to keep you both safe—"

Mira and I side-glance each other, resolute. "There are two of us for a reason," Mira says to our tableful of objectors.

"So that we can do two things at once," I conclude reasonably. It's been our method our entire lives. The advantage of having twins as the mascot of the rebellion: two stones, twice as many birds.

"But the US senators are simply ceremonial, relics of a dead American society," Skye declares, throwing holes into my master plan. Her hands rest empty on the smooth yellow table, but I can still see my father's bloody microchip inside her callused palm. "They hold no actual power. The central government is weak; we should be going after the governors."

"You mean assassinating them?" I ask, thinking of her crusade against the Family Planning Division that nearly killed my father. *I was trying to kill his office,* Skye had promised. Not the man.

Even in my vengeance this is not a road I wish to go down. Roth's propaganda is not true; the Common is not running around blindly killing the ruling class. It matters how we get our power. The way we rise will follow our cause—we won't be able to wipe off the blood if we compromise the message.

What about Roth? I've been thinking of his death from the moment I learned he killed my father. Does his killing somehow count as different from other murders because it's personal to *me*?

"No," Skye says, pulling me out of my complicated musings. "I'm suggesting we flip the governors. Forget the senators."

Skye stares at me from across the table, her two French braids framing her intense expression. I can't help but be drawn to her: her blunt attitude, her confidence, her dedication to the rebellion even when it was fragmented and obscure. Though she's only in her twenties, Skye's already viewed as a Common Elder, and she earned it by fighting as a lone wolf, not by simply being born a twin.

There's logic to her thinking. Governors have siphoned off most of the power from the federal government, claiming it for themselves. Along with the Senate, every year the Office of the President becomes more and more useless. That enduring American figurehead clings desperately to tradition and diplomacy for survival.

But Roth aims to change that. Before entering the War Room, Pawel told me about the Texas governor's recent presidential announcement. It's something I knew was coming—his original intention was to declare his run at the Rule of One Anniversary Gala before we crashed the party—but hearing that it's actually happening turns my blood cold. *Even a state as big as Texas can't contain Roth's vast ambition.*

"Governors are out for themselves, always. The public knows that. Citizens trust senators more than governors to represent their best interests," I say. "So if we can get the senators to openly support the Common, the people will see it as them standing up to the governors for the first time."

"It will galvanize the citizens," Mira says in support beside me.

"I agree with Ava. It should be the senators," Emery declares. She raises her hand thoughtfully to her pointed chin. "If we were able to throw the weight of dominant states like Washington, Michigan, Colorado, New York, or even North California onto the Common's side, their combined strength added to ours could be enough to tip the scale in our favor."

In the past, every state had two elected senators in Congress, but thirty years ago, it was cut down to one. The Senate rarely ever meets, and when they do, it's done virtually—the high cost of travel to New Washington simply isn't in any state's budget.

Now, the fifty-one remaining senators are nothing more than symbolic overseers of state-run aid programs and charities, spending the bulk of their time cutting ribbons and solemnly surveying the damage from their states' latest superstorms, offering little more than sympathy and prayers. Never action. *But we can change that.*

Big, small, resource dry, or rich, every state used to have an equal voice on the national stage. Divided we fell, and we can only stand up again if we do it together.

"The Common must empower the Senate, allowing our country to govern as one, like before," I insist, even more steadfast in my conviction after Emery's surprise backing. "America needs to reset our country's original foundation. It's cracked. That's why governors like Roth were able to grab hold of so much power." I pause, taking a few breaths before my final proclamation. "The Common must unite the states again."

"It's too soon," the Elder with the bristly beard argues. His furrowed brow deepens with caution. "Yes, the Common's long-range goal is to reunite the country, but the time is not right to—"

"The time is now," Mira says, cutting him off. "The rebellion has been waiting in the shadows for almost sixty years. There will never be a better time to strike than right now."

Most of the inner circle nod their heads in approval. *We're winning them over.*

The last holdouts are Barend and the bearded Elder.

Pawel thrusts his hand into the air, then speaks without waiting to be called on. "If we were successful in gathering states to our side, we could take on Roth and Texas," he says, excitement in his voice. "Just in time to sabotage his bid for the presidency."

"Yes, but how?" Barend argues, rising from his chair. "The opposition will fight against any campaign that tries to turn its own people against them. Is everyone forgetting each state has its own army called *the State Guard*, with governors at the head?"

"We keep things underground, appealing to senators in secret, face-to-face," I contend. I had plenty of time to think this through. "As the people continue to join our cause, we will amass our own army against the Guard."

"And what about Alexander?" Kano asks, turning to Mira, doubtful. "If Governor Roth truly banished his only son, he'd be squirreled away some place so dark we'd never be able to find him."

"That's what the Intelligence Room is for, isn't it?" Mira says to the group. "Members like Pawel are our searchlights."

Everyone's heads turn to Pawel. "I can certainly give it my best shot," he stammers, not used to having the light directed at him.

Mira and I nod, satisfied, knowing Pawel's best shot means it's good as done. Tracking is his greatest skill and the reason he has a seat at the leadership table.

"It's settled, then," Mira declares, her vigor returned. Both our IV bags are empty; simultaneously we withdraw the catheters from our venipuncture sites and apply pressure before fixing a clean gauze dressing onto our arms.

We rise from the table.

"You both share the number-one spot on America's Wanted List—it's even more dangerous for you now than before," Emery says, her curls bouncing as she shakes her head. She's torn. *She doesn't want to lose us again.* "And this time you won't have Rayla's coordinates *or* your father's map to guide you. I can't permit you to do this alone."

"Then who will come with us?" I ask the room.

She's right that we have no map to tell us where to go or where to find safe houses—we'll have to figure it out as we go along. She's also right that we can't do this alone. If I follow my own rationale that two is better than one, then I must admit that many is better than two. *But which members can we trust?*

To my great surprise, every single member rises to his or her feet. I look to Mira: she wasn't expecting this either. We discussed the one or two people we hoped would accompany us on our missions, but we didn't expect this many. A swell of emotion surges through my chest and up to my head, making me slightly dizzy.

"It appears it's not a matter of *who* will go with you; it's *where* each of us will go," Emery says, gripping the lapels of her yellow jacket, clearly proud to be a part of such a courageous group.

The Common is unanimously willing to follow where Mira and I lead. They are with us. *Maybe there wasn't a betrayal after all.*

Pawel steps forward. "I offer myself wholly to Ava's mission," he says formally, standing close at my side. "If you'll have me, that is." He's shivering. Is he frightened or excited? *He should be panic-stricken.*

"Crossing the border will be an extremely high-risk undertaking," I warn Pawel, turning to face him. "Even if we make it across without getting captured or killed, we could still be shot if we get anywhere close to Senator Gordon. Are you sure this is what you want to do?" *Going with me takes him away from his sister, Ellie.*

Pawel meets my eyes, his face completely open and trusting.

"I'm sure," he says. *He must be doing this for her.*

Kano and Barend advance toward the head of the table at the same time. "I offer you my protection on your mission, Mira," Kano vows to my sister. "And I offer you mine," Barend says to me, both men clasping our shoulders, pledging themselves to us.

"I offer my diplomatic skills to Ava's mission," Emery vows, gripping my shoulder. She gives me a confident wink. "I also know a thing or two about crossing border walls."

The leader of the rebellion wants to join me? I'm immediately filled with gratitude and an abrupt sense of longing. It's like having Rayla back on my team.

Ciro clears his throat, calling the room's attention back to himself. He solemnly buttons his suit jacket. "If Emery is pledged to Ava, it stands to reason that Mira's team needs a Common leader as well." It's unwelcomely clear he's about to offer himself to Mira's mission. *The moneyman is nothing but dead weight out on the field.*

Exuding self-sacrifice, Ciro glides to the front to stand beside my sister. Barend directs a heated gaze at him, and Ciro glares back, daring Barend to intervene.

What's that all about? Does Barend want Ciro to stay so he can better plot their betrayal?

"I offer my abundant connections to Mira's mission," Ciro says to the room, the very picture of gallantry. "The relationships I have spent my entire life fostering were carefully procured for a moment just like this."

Mira and I lock eyes, communicating with a glance: *There's nothing for it; he's the one funding the missions.* All Mira can do is nod.

"Who will go to North California, New York, and Michigan?" Emery asks, turning to face the remaining Common members. "We will ask Rayla Cadwell to take on Colorado—if anyone can flip that senator, she can. She knows him well; it is her adopted state."

Rayla. My heart skips a beat. *Where is she?* I half expected our grandmother to be at headquarters, waiting for us upon our return, but I know she's somewhere in the US, on an important mission of her own.

Will Rayla go to Colorado by herself, or will she have a team too? The Common has to deliver our grandmother her assignment somehow— *maybe we'll get to talk to her again before we leave.*

The remaining Elders, including the bearded naysayer, offer themselves to be sent to North California and Michigan, leaving only New York, which will be a difficult state to flip yellow. Millicent Cole, the governor of New York, is one of Roth's staunchest allies, and she rules her state with an equally iron fist, her sharpened nails just as daggerlike and deadly as his. Getting to Senator Riggs will be extremely difficult.

"I offer my services in the battle for New York," Skye announces boldly. "Governor Cole will not be a problem for me." Skye has history in New York—the state's Family Planning Director was one of her poisoned targets.

Emery grants her consent. A weighty silence follows.

I look around the room, amazed at what has happened in so short a time. Six separate missions have been formed, yet each team will fan across the continent for a common goal: to bring down Roth.

Take the head, and the rest will follow.

"We will gather our intelligence and supplies, sleep the little we can, then leave at daybreak," Emery says, closing the meeting. "We will reconvene in the Medical Room in half an hour." She proceeds quickly toward the door, Pawel following close at her heels. The leading members of the Common file out after her, until only my sister and I remain in the large room.

"It worked," I say, the enormity of what's about to happen setting in. Half in disbelief, I turn to face Mira. I clasp her shoulder, and she clasps mine. "You're ready for this."

"We both are," Mira says, her voice strong and steady. We press our foreheads together. "How far we've come, Ava."

A part of me is still torn. I don't want to separate from my sister. But we are being called to different actions, and we must answer our own call.

MIRA

I look at my watch: 2:00 a.m.

Three more hours until Ava leaves me and I leave her. It's a voluntary separation, but the truth is I'm terrified. Not for me, but for my twin. No one can watch over her like her own blood. But I have to let her go—she doesn't belong to just me anymore.

"Everyone's ready," Emery says as the elevator door slides open to Tower Three, Level Two. "We thought it right for you both to do the honors."

All nine members who offered themselves to perilous missions stand in a majestic line inside the Medical Room. Emery breaks from my side and moves to the open space held for her. In the Common salute, she holds down her right arm, fist clenched, exposing her tattooed wrist. One by one, the others do the same.

Ava and I hover outside the elevator, taking in the moment, staring at the two instrument stands, each tray filled with everything we need for the quick procedure.

Cut out your microchips, Rayla told the nation. *Show those in power we won't be controlled.*

Like Ava and me, everyone here also has counterfeit chips. Hard-earned, incredibly rare implants that have allowed all of us to evade the government and stand where we are today. *They're also an unspoken safety net.* If plans and hope collapse, if we fail, the counterfeit chips offer a last-resort option for them to return to the United States. The others could start over, form new identities to match their fake chips, conform, blend in, and live out an underground life. Knowing the safety net is there if the Common towers fall is not an easy thing to cut loose.

Eighteen years I survived without a microchip. More than fear even, I always felt envy and inadequacy. As if I had a defect because I was chipless. To contemplate a reality where people could exist unmonitored, independent of a piece of metal that tells us we belong, is almost unimaginable.

No more Guards scanning our wrists, no more tracking, no more population control. No more Rule of One.

A blind world, Rayla promised Roth. We can rebuild it in the dark.

Ava makes for the right-hand instrument tray, and I head for the left, where Ciro waits for me. He wears a plain short-sleeved undershirt, and I see his tattoo for the first time. It's small, but it's there, a skeleton key with the top shaped like a yellow diamond.

"Putting your Strake education to good use," Ciro says with a wink, draping his lower arm over the stand.

"I'm surprised you would have implanted yourself with a microchip," I say, stretching the gloves over my fingers. "Being born in Canada and all . . ."

"One must be prepared for any situation," he states with his customary charm, if a touch more restrained than usual.

I select the nearest scalpel and medical tweezers and set my concentration. Ciro turns his head away, as if he's scared of sharp objects or blood. *He better get used to them.*

I make quick work of it—six seconds and it's done. A thin incision that will leave only a trace of a scar. I seal the wound with cutting-edge surgical glue I've only read about in e-textbooks and toss the microchip into an empty bowl.

With a formal nod Ciro takes his leave, and Skye walks forward, holding out her bare wrist. Faded, indistinct lines and dots are all that remains of her tattoo. *The Guard must have removed the mark in prison.*

What made Skye go after the Directors? Did the Division take someone close from her? I'd never ask such personal questions for fear she'd ask me some in return. It's an old fear, rules from my old life. It will take years to share and let people in.

I feel her studying me as I make the cut. She doesn't flinch or say a thing. Neither do I.

Kano comes next, then an Elder, until I'm the only one left in my group. I lift the final scalpel over my right inner wrist and make the incision along the inked curve of a black-eyed Susan petal shaped like a falling tear from a watchful green eye. With the angled tip of the tweezers, I remove the chip smaller than my fingernail out of my body and add it to the pile. It's amazing how such a small thing can hold so much power.

I look up and find Ava observing me. How different this feels from the night I watched helplessly as Ava cut out her own microchip inside the kitchen of our childhood home.

That night the act was done in defeat. This time, it's for control.

The elevator opens to a narrow antechamber. I see no door, only four sheet-metal walls, lustrous and sturdy like plate armor.

"Tower Two, Level Zero. I didn't even know this room *existed*," Pawel whispers to Ava, his enthusiasm uncomplicated and pure like a child's. After all he's been through and lost, he's still able to feel joy. I admire him, but that will never be me.

From his chest pocket, Ciro produces a single key and approaches the far wall. Pausing a few breaths to heighten the anticipation, Ciro twists the lock, sending the entire steel sheet shooting upward.

"Welcome to the Offering Room," he says, watching our faces with a nervous hesitancy. I can see how badly he wants to dazzle. "Please, take whatever you can carry."

Emery flicks on the lights and steps into the climate-controlled stockroom. But calling it a room is inaccurate. It's a warehouse. Twenty-plus rows of bulk storage racks brimming with wooden packing cases and metal containers, each aisle an endless procession of supplies safeguarded for a moment like this.

Kano releases a drawn-out whistle. "A beauteous sight."

"Everything you will need for your mission is here," Emery says, pointing to the various aisles. "Disguises, foodstuffs, and general field provisions to the left. Weaponry and defense to the right."

The company parts and disperses, intent on their mission. Ava and I stay behind, reviewing the various rows, determining where to explore first. Heads together, Emery and the other Elders move for a shelf labeled "Navigation," Emery scribbling down notes on a pad of paper. Skye and Kano march for the last row on the right. I can't read the sign from here, but I'd bet it's labeled "Firearms."

I still have my gun. Ava still has hers. Concealed beneath her jacket, she carries Halton's handgun in a holster tucked inside her waistband. I keep mine, the pistol that once belonged to Halton's agent, buried at the bottom of my rucksack. I haven't touched it since the day we found the Common.

"I'll get us more ammunition," Ava says, reading my mind. I nod, my gaze following Pawel roaming the camouflage section.

"I'll find us some disguises," I say, turning back to her shock of bright-red hair. Like always, we will need to shield our faces and conceal our identities. The public doesn't know the Goodwin twins have broken out and are once again at large. As of now, both presidents have kept our newfound freedom a secret, a secret we intend to use to our advantage. Fewer eyes will be on the lookout for us. *The easier to move around.*

"Meet by the food supplies in five," Ava says. I nod again and watch her as she marches away, her carriage straight and sure.

With a glance at my watch, I set off to find Pawel. Five rows over, three columns deep, I stumble upon Ciro and Barend instead. They're quarreling, sequestered behind a stack of crates. There's a secretiveness in their manner that makes me stop and listen.

"What?" Ciro whispers hotly. "You didn't like my impromptu decision in there?"

"You know I didn't. It puts a machine gun to our plans."

"You can't always be the one who gets to leave," Ciro snaps, spinning on his heel to walk away. Barend catches him by the arm and pulls him close. "It's not too late," he urges.

Emery calls out Ciro's name somewhere across the warehouse, and the two immediately jerk back from each other. Lowering my head, I move before they spot me, and continue my way toward the camouflage aisle.

What's "not too late"? And what "plans" is Ciro ruining by leaving headquarters?

I wish I knew their full history. Emery told us Barend was once Ciro's personal bodyguard. Is he merely scared for Ciro's safety, or are they plotting something? I'm glad they're going on separate missions. Ava and I can keep a watchful eye on them.

I finally locate Pawel picking through a box of Goodwin masks. He shoves four into his already-stuffed backpack, a bashful smile tugging his bow-shaped lips. "It must be weird having others hide behind your face."

"They said we'd be the face of the rebellion," I mumble with a shrug, distracted by the urgency of what I've come to say.

Free from the crippling censorship of the US's Internet Defense Act, it was easy enough to find the forgotten son. Pawel and the Intelligence Room located Alexander in less than half an hour.

Turns out Governor Roth's skipped heir is here in Canada.

I was prepared to cross the border with Ava, then continue on with my team to search for Alexander somewhere within the States. My mission now will diverge from Ava's much sooner than we expected.

But we were right. He's hiding. Why else would he flee to a foreign land?

Dwell on this later. We embark on our missions in a matter of hours. Time is precious.

Between his thick rows of lashes, Pawel's eyes pop like a bright sapphire sky. There's a clarity there, like he knows what I've come seeking.

He understands a sibling's bond.

"I've seen you with Ellie . . . how you protect her . . . ," I say, trailing off. I clear my throat, swollen with emotion. Pawel lays his hand on my shoulder. I place a hand on his. It feels comforting.

"Ava's my entire life. Promise me, Pawel, you'll watch over her."

Pawel stares back at me with determination, his muscles tensing beneath the weight of my request. "I promise."

I nod, satisfied, and release my grip, turning to the boxes marked "Women's Wigs."

"Now, how do you think I'll look as a brunette?"

I lie on the king-sized bed inside the penthouse room of Tower One, wide-awake and fully dressed.

"What's the time?" Ava asks, twisted in the sheets next to me. She's been tossing and turning for the past hour, a fitful battle with ever-elusive sleep. With a heavy sigh, she throws back the comforter and rolls to my side of the bed.

"Four thirty," I whisper. Another half hour before we say goodbye.

We stare up at the darkness above us, the blackout glass sealing any hint of the coming dawn. I've been fantasizing that we're back in our twin bed inside our basement—that Ava and I will only be separated for the routine eight hours of a school day.

"It's only two weeks, Mira," Ava assures me. "Fourteen days and we'll be back together."

No matter the success or failure of our missions, all teams are to be in Dallas by the end of the second week. Each of us memorized the address of the designated safe house called the Last Stage. I repeat it over and over in my mind, *818 Akard Drive*, as if otherwise I'll forget where to go and Ava and I will never see each other again.

That's the plan anyway. *It will work.* Complete our missions and reunite in Texas for the final takedown of Roth.

There's so much that could happen between now and Dallas. But I can't think about that.

Think about the task at hand.

"I wish we could have found a way to talk with Rayla before we left," I say. "To let her know we're okay." I let a long beat pass. "Do you think *she's* okay?"

After the Council Room meeting, Ava and I had huddled alongside other Common members inside the Intelligence Room, watching the hours-old news footage highlighting Rayla's war of words with Roth. I exchanged anxious glances with Ava and Emery, those who know Rayla the most. No one else but us seemed to notice that my grandmother looked unwell.

Ava has no way of knowing the status of our grandmother any more than I do, but she answers anyway. "Yes," she assures me, and I believe her. I have to believe what's left of our family will make it through the coming rebellion-made storm.

I feel rather than see Ava slide her head closer to mine, sharing my soft buckwheat pillow. Loose strands of her freshly washed hair fall across my shoulder, reminding me of when my own hair was long. Pushing back my trimmed bangs, I turn to my sister, trying not to memorize her face the way our father did when we said our last goodbye.

We close our eyes and pretend to sleep until our minutes are up and my watch says 5:00 a.m.

"See you soon," Ava tells me, our traditional parting words before separating for school.

I tuck my hand into hers. She squeezes so hard it hurts my heart. *Never goodbye.*

"See you soon," I whisper back.

OWEN

A sewer rat. That's what I am right now. On my trek back to the hideout, I ran into a gaggle of State Guards and needed a place to lie low. I panicked, okay? I'm still getting used to the whole my-face-is-on-the-Wanted-List thing. So it's been the sewer life for me the past two-plus hours.

Not a very glamorous induction into the rebellion, I'll admit. But hey, at least I haven't been caught—I'm doing better than Ava and Mira. As far as I know, they're still locked up somewhere in Canada.

Speaking of the twins, I already lost my Goodwin mask. It fell into a drain and floated away down the nasty channel water, never to return. Whoops.

It feels like I've waited long enough down here. I mean, *I* think so. But then again, I've never hidden in a sewer from the Guard before.

"The future waits for no one," I jog my own memory.

I wonder what Amelia and the other Code Cogs think of my new criminal status. Are they jealous? Horrified? Enthralled?

Personally, I'm feeling a whole lot of one thing: terror.

Well, I'm back.

I should get a gold medal in power walking. Sprinting when a rebellion's on the loose is a big no-no, you see.

Two miles in under fifteen minutes. Dry heaving and guzzling air, but I'm still breathing free in the fresh, precarious hours following Rayla's late-night wake-up call.

On national. Damn. News.

No one else appears to be surveilling the house but me.

If the government knew Rayla was here—*and me,* I think with a bit too much vainglory—they wouldn't be subtle about it. Scent Hunters, UAV drones, a battalion of State Guards would all be descending on this place like vultures on a carcass.

From my lookout spot, the house appears just how I left it before sundown: quiet, dark, and, to all outside appearances, forgotten. An area of only five hundred square feet is now the most dangerous spot in the entire three-odd million square miles that make up our too-big-for-its-own-good country. It's also the safest, however, for a marked fugitive like me. Those inside could be my only allies and protection. I just have to make Rayla let me back in.

Since my wanted photo made its debut tonight—did they *have* to use the one of me in my dweeby Kismet uniform?—I figured I couldn't go running back to my parents. They've probably disowned me by now, if not publicly, then to themselves. They always wished they had a second child. Not that my mom or dad would ever say that out loud, because that would be unpatriotic. But it's obvious they think they came out losers in the breeding lottery, ending up with me. A kid who won't carry on the "Hart" family name the way they demand that I should.

Stop idling and find Rayla!

This feels like my own personal Judgment Day. My world as I knew it has ended, and it's now whether or not this bonkers old woman will forgive my desertion and take me in or leave me out here to die. I like to think I can handle myself, but the key to survival is knowing your limits. One weaponless teen against millions doesn't sound like a fun time.

I sneak out from the shed I've been hiding in—where I've also stashed *my* car—about a quarter mile from the house. Figured I should keep both my getaway *and* my selling point close: *I* have the transportation Rayla needs to get around. I'm an asset. I'm useful.

Yeah, keep telling yourself that.

It's a challenge to make my way in the dark. They've turned off all the lights, and it's an obstacle course finding a path through the rotting furniture and shells of vintage cars that make up this junkyard. For a city boy, this is the darkest place I've ever been. Seems fitting.

When my feet finally hit the cement stoop, I've written a speech in my head that I think will win Rayla over. I don't know if I believe a word of it, but I don't know what I believe about a lot of things nowadays.

I knock, wait, then knock again. For a panicked second I think they already left, then the blind rolls up, and there's Blaise's face, boogeyman bandana and all. His disturbing smile of flames almost makes me lose my footing, but I stand my ground, even take a step forward. "Aren't you going to let me in?"

Big surprise, Blaise shakes his head. I bet he's smiling wide behind his fire-toothed grin.

"You came back," Blaise says from the other side of the glass door.

"Great observation," I snap, unable to keep my thoughts to myself.

"Sarcasm is an odd choice for someone in your predicament," Blaise bites back. "Your desperation is embarrassing. Go away."

"I don't have anywhere to go."

"That sounds like a *you* problem."

I try again and nod to the thin scar on his right wrist. "I cut out mine too." I push up the tight sleeve of my uniform and show him my own wound, still oozing blood.

"You didn't cut out your chip because you wanted to. You did it because you had to."

Not a completely wrong observation. I got my hands on a sharp piece of steel and tossed my microchip into Lake Michigan the first chance I could. Now that I'm wanted, the Guard will be tracking me. Maybe they'll think I'm already swimming with the fish.

"I'm not going to grovel. Either let me in or don't."

Blaise shoves a finger under his bandana, itching a spot on his pasty cheek that probably hasn't seen the sun since . . . ever. The guy takes his privacy *very* seriously. Does he eat with it on too? Just blends up a burger and sucks it down with a straw? I'm about to ask him this vital question when Rayla appears behind him.

"Let him in," she orders. "And stop bickering."

Ha! My grin outshines his inferno smile. The door opens just enough for me to shove myself through, nearly slamming shut on my fingers. Wasting no more time on the likes of Blaise, I elbow past him to find the real boss around here. Rayla. She's disappeared somewhere into the back room.

"You better not get us caught," Blaise growls in my ear.

I spin to face him. "*I'm* the one who brought *you* in, remember? I'm not the noob here, and I'm not your enemy. I'm on your side."

He grunts and follows me into the main room. In the corner, the crusty moth-eaten rug I spent days using as a bed while Rayla healed from her gunshot is no longer there. Instead, there's a small circular door that no doubt leads to a secret basement or bunker. I help myself down the rickety ladder and descend into the dark underground of a hacker's lair.

The dim glow of computer screens provides the only light. Rayla is in the middle, bent over a long table, fiddling with equipment I can't make out from where I stand. I almost ram my head into the low ceiling but catch myself just in time, no thanks to Blaise. I have to duck in order to get to Rayla. I play it off as a bow.

"Rayla, first off, thank you for trusting me—"

She puts up a hand to stop me. "Save your speech for another time," Rayla says without looking at me. "We're in the middle of something."

I wait for her to divulge more, but of course she doesn't.

"What are we in the middle of?" I ask, including myself in the *we*.

"I'm going to the White House," Rayla says matter-of-factly. She might as well have said, *I'm going to the moon.*

"Like, *the* White House?" I question, not cushioning my skepticism. "In New Washington?"

This is a terrible plan. What did I walk back into? Then I spot the pair of VR headsets in Blaise's hands. *They mean to hack their way in virtually.*

"Blaise was able to acquire the Secretary of State's schedule," Rayla summarizes the situation quickly, "and she has an audience with the president that started exactly twelve minutes ago. I need to be in on that virtual meeting."

Finally, something I'm good at. I lean down closer to the dual monitors to check out the situation for myself.

Hundreds of unique lines of multicolored code are written across both screens, but two red error lines jump out at me in bold: **<ACCESS DENIED>**.

Blaise can't get in.

The best black-hat hacker in all the land has been shut out. He stands at Rayla's other elbow, his fiery bandana burning just a little less bright.

"Our two attempts to enter the meeting room have been rejected," Rayla says, getting testier by the moment. "And we now have only one attempt left before we're locked out of the system."

She turns in my direction, her breath catching in pain from the sudden movement. "Can you get me into the room, Owen?"

It's the first time Rayla's ever said my name. Hell, I didn't even think she remembered it. I'm oddly touched.

"I need to be in on that meeting," she repeats, doing a pretty good job masking she's leaning on the table for support. "Whichever one of you can get me into the room can join me."

The seedy basement's loaded with high-end sensors and cameras, 3D capture technology that's used to beam 360-degree holograms of people in real time anywhere. I know better than to ask how Blaise got hold of such pricey equipment. He did what hackers do best: he stole it.

But I've been a Code Cog half my life—I can compete. Even better, I can beat him into the room.

Blaise and I stare each other down for longer than is appropriate given our looming time clock; then we each lunge to a computer, and my lightning-fast fingers get to work.

I always knew I was meant for more than the corporate dungeon of Kismet Automotive Factory. But writing my way into a virtual meeting room with the president of the United States?

This is the opportunity of a Cog's lifetime.

It takes me a beat to orient myself, hopping from the cramped dark basement to the bright and sunny VR world in a matter of an eye blink. When I do, I laugh out loud.

A swarm of monarch butterflies floats through a fluffy-clouded blue sky, circling the Washington Monument. Birdsong chirps all cheerful in the background. Behind the famed pillar, I spot the US Capitol Building, and to my left stands the White House itself. *Damn.*

Rayla is a woman who gets what she wants; she demanded the White House, and there it is. A White House from a lost era, but still. *I could learn from this woman.*

Most of these monuments don't exist anymore—they couldn't be saved from the flooding that wiped out the original capital. I know all of this is made up of projections, but just to make absolutely sure, I reach down to pluck one of the many little American flags stuck in the ground. My hand goes straight through it. What a beautifully written piece of code; I have to give credit where credit is due.

"There they are" is all Rayla has to say about this dreamscape before she takes off behind me. I spin around and follow my new leader as she heads toward the Lincoln Memorial on the opposite end of the National Mall. The rendezvous point must've moved outside.

"Keep five steps back at all times, Owen," Rayla says. "And don't speak." She's really got to work on the whole "thank-you" thing.

Baby steps. At least she uses your name now.

When we stroll by the infamous Reflecting Pool on the comically perfect green lawn, I almost have to roll my eyes. Of course this virtual space is the favorite meeting place of the current prez. It's a memory of the good old days, back when his office had dignity and power. Everything the man lacks.

The only patriotic thing missing from his custom-built dream world is a bald eagle flying somewhere overhead. No sooner does that thought occur than a series of high-pitched whistling sounds causes me to mentally bite my tongue. *You've got to be kidding.*

Not one, but *two* bald eagles swoop down to land at the base of Lincoln's memorial, like they're standing guard for the president and Madam Secretary, who pace mid argument between the columns at the top of the steps. Let me tell you, those birds are *huge* in person. It's unnerving walking past the glorified raptors, but Rayla hustles up the staircase, unfazed.

Nothing seems to faze her—extinct animals, the million steps we have to climb to get to our target, the five-minute time clock we're up against before our hideout location will be traced . . .

To be honest, though, it's embarrassing a recently shot person three times my age can absolutely crush me at climbing up this staircase. Back in the basement, it's all high knees and dripping sweat just to keep up with her. I bet Rayla isn't even breathing hard beside me. *Well, you're used to sitting in front of a computer all day, and she's basically a war vet. Get over it.*

"Mr. President, you will pardon Ava and Mira Goodwin and immediately facilitate their release back into the Common's custody." Rayla comes in hot. "You will put an end to Roth's fanatical governorship before his influence spreads even further and a war between the people of the United States and their government is unavoidable."

"No, you can't be here!" The president holds up his hand, barring Rayla from taking the final step onto the pink marble floor. "Martha, lock the room down!" he shouts angrily into the sky. "Martha!"

But Martha back in New Washington can't help him—any attempt to boot us out will be automatically overwritten. I made sure of that. To show Rayla I can follow orders, I hang back the aforementioned five steps and wave to the prez, silently mouthing, *Still here.*

The president looks at Madam Secretary, totally horrified. "Governor Roth will be furious if he finds out we spoke with a leader of the rebellion!" He also looks exhausted, a defeated man with no fight left in him—his digital self can't even fake it.

I knew our prez was an ornamental weakling, but even I thought he'd have more courage than this.

"Ms. Cadwell, it appears you're behind the times," Madam Secretary says in an icy tone, ignoring the president and approaching Rayla directly. "Your granddaughters escaped Canadian custody a few hours ago. They were broken out by a rebellion member masquerading as a Mountie, and while we do not know their current location, we presume they are already back with your Common."

The woman wears a pair of cowboy boots so audacious they're cool, but other than that the read on her is "approach at your own risk." Do we trust her? Surely not. Then something passes between the women— something even smaller than a look—and I realize I don't know nearly as much as I thought I did.

Rayla blows past the secretary to stand dwarfed at the feet of President Lincoln. She draws back her head to stare at the giant statue before her words echo throughout the chamber.

"You don't deserve to be in Lincoln's presence, Mr. President," Rayla says, her voice low and solemn. "Your legacy will have no memorials, not even the smallest plaque, because you've done nothing to deserve one. You waste your time in this fantasyland while any chance at democracy our country still has is being destroyed by Roth."

The president's calmer now—all emotion seems to be sucked out of him, like he's resigned to his uselessness. He doesn't face Rayla and her accusations; instead he stares across America's front yard.

"It's true I will never be a great man like Lincoln." The guy makes the understatement of the century. "But Roth will be. He's uniting the states. It's miraculous. Northern wall to Southern wall, from sea to flooded sea."

Rayla turns to face the president, the look in her eyes more ferocious than ever. And that's saying something.

"Don't let your girls cross the wall," the president warns. "The northern governors will be waiting."

I expect a zinger from Rayla that doesn't come. Not good. That means the situation is as terrifying as it seems. But before I can think of a comeback on her behalf, the VR world cuts to black.

Back in the basement, Rayla collapses into my arms. I rip off my headset and drape her arm around my shoulder to support her weight. "A little help here, Blaise?"

Rayla's all clammy, and she struggles to cover the wound on her upper arm. Blood seeps through her jumpsuit. Double not good.

Blaise hurries over, and we place Rayla into a chair. "Should we call the doctor again?" I ask. "What if it's infected?"

Rayla overrules my concerned questioning with a guttural grunt. "Connect me with the Common's headquarters," she orders.

"Already on it," Blaise answers. He jumps to a computer screen with a secure and anonymous ghost call all set and ready. He turns the camera mounted on the screen toward Rayla. *Wow. Old-school communication.* "I just need the headquarters entrance code."

"Nine, six, eight, five," Rayla says, shooing me out of the way. "Blaise, give me your jacket."

Blaise unzips his junk-food-stained hoodie, and I'm positive Rayla got more than she bargained for, because he's wearing nothing underneath it. I don't think his chest has ever seen the sun—it's like a nightlight in the dark room.

"Behave, or you go back upstairs," Rayla snaps at me. She knows me too well. It's difficult, but I swallow the seven wisecracks that easily spring to mind.

Rayla pulls the hoodie on, wipes down the sweat on her face with its sleeve, and sits up straight, transformed into a woman who looks like she just finished a jog, not someone who should be in a hospital bed.

The video call rings and rings. Is she contacting Ava and Mira? My nerves wimp out, and I feel nervous. *Why am I still in my stupid Kismet uniform!*

Nobody answers.

"Keep trying," Rayla says. "Please."

Blaise lets it ring and ring. No answer.

This could go on all night. From the way Rayla's parked on the seat staring at the screen like my parents stare at my online bank account every other Friday, we're not going anywhere anytime soon.

"Rayla made some tea if you want it," Blaise says the exact second my lids crack open.

"Uh . . . were you watching me sleep?" I ask, full-on creeped out. "Your demon-fire face is not the *best* image to see first thing in the morning."

Blaise shrugs. "What? I happened to look at you right when you woke up." He nods to Rayla hunkered down on her office chair. "She's been at this for three hours."

The video call keeps chiming away, waiting for someone to answer.

"Still nothing about the twins' escape on the Dark Web?" I ask.

"Nothing," Blaise confirms.

Good, I slept through the boring bits, then. I yawn, rocketing from the couch to claim my tea. Sniffing myself, I confirm that yes, I smell like whatever funk I zonked out on. I'm going to have to break down and ask if Blaise has any spare shirts.

"This is some potent tea!" I choke out after taking a gulp of the searing-hot liquid. *That'll* wake you up in the morning.

Rayla doesn't move. Her lids aren't closed, but it's possible she sleeps with both eyes open like Gandalf.

Out of nowhere the ringing stops, and the twins pop up on the screen inside our little cave.

Whoa.

"Rayla! I knew we'd hear from you!" Ava exclaims. I know she's Ava from what I remember of their rousing recruiting video the night of the Gala. She's the sister who kept her red hair.

"Thank Whitman you're both safe!" Rayla shouts, springing into action. She scoots right up to the screen and touches their digital faces. She's more energetic and perky than I thought Rayla Cadwell capable of, like seeing her granddaughters is the ultimate caffeine hit, five times as strong as her bitter tea.

Ava and Mira stand shoulder to shoulder, looking way too cool and brazen considering they were just locked inside a superpower's prison cell. But what really has me bugging out is Ava's awesome and *super* illegal antisurveillance gear. Blackout Wear. You can't even find that stuff on the Black Market.

"We're about to leave for our missions," Mira announces. They seem rushed, like there's a lot going on behind their screen, vying for their attention, but all they want to do is stand there and talk to their grandma.

"Missions?" Rayla says, all serious and concerned.

"They *just* escaped. Do they ever sleep?" I remark out loud.

"Does privacy mean anything to you?" Blaise nudges me. Choice words coming from a hacker.

I stay where I am and linger behind Rayla, trying my best to be a fly on the wall that no one notices.

But Ava notices. She stares at me—more like sizes me up—giving me an enigmatic smile. She wants to know who the guy is that's with her grandmother. I get it. I'd want to know too. I puff up my chest and wave hello like an imbecile. Ava doesn't wave back.

Blaise grips me by my collar and hauls me toward the ladder. "Better go get the car, lovesick Cog."

Lovesick? I'm about to tell Blaise the only thing that makes me sick is his face, but I decide not to reason with simpletons.

"Where are we going?" I ask, climbing the steps after him.

"Don't you listen?" Blaise says from above. I have to admit, I am a bit distracted having America's top wanted practically in the same room with me.

I strain my ears to hear scraps of the family reunion, but I catch only undertones.

"We're heading for Colorado," he states nonchalantly.

"Colorado! I haven't been across a state border in over seven years."

"Thanks for your unsolicited life story," Blaise says, scrambling up onto the first floor of the house. He bends down and yells at me, "Get the car!" like I didn't hear the first time.

Buckle up, to quote the old expression.

This could be a wild ride.

MIRA

The last time I was on a railcar, I was the one being hunted. Ava and I were fleeing our home, speeding across Texas, terrified and defenseless. It's strange transforming into the hunter, the predator. The one in charge.

Across the broad aisle, Alexander sits five rows ahead, facing me. Only a smattering of standing passengers grips the handrails along the walkway, leaving me a clear view of my prey. I quickly take in his dark hair and eyes, his pompous, oval face. Yes, this is Alexander.

A Roth.

A black raincoat drapes his lanky frame—it looks expensive, and so does he. Life as a ghost has been good to him, then. His plump lips seem to curl upward in mockery both at me and at the rest of the duped world. It's a smile so like that of his son, Halton, I have to force myself not to turn away.

Why are you here? Did your father exile you? Or did you run? I want to storm over and force the answers out of him with my fists, but Kano and Ciro would stop me before I could even stand. Instead, I readjust the wavy mane of my chestnut-brown wig and wait for the planned time. Seven more stops to go.

I brush my fingers along the marked skin of my inner right wrist, outlining the single hooded eye of my tattoo. This usually soothes my restlessness, but now it only stokes my hatred. I watch as Alexander leans his head back against his cushioned seat, his long arms and legs splayed out, one man taking up the space of three. He closes his eyes, catching a nap on his commute home after a full day on the docks. He looks comfortable, relaxed. He shouldn't be.

The forgotten son has been found.

Before I left headquarters, the Common matched the face of Governor Roth's son to a Julien Wright hiding out in the open in Vancouver, Canada. The booming western coastal city saved from the rising seas by their billion-dollar flood defenses.

He's only thirty-two miles from the border wall.

My temper flares. *Did President Moore help him cross?*

Further probing told us Julien, a.k.a. Alexander, has owned and operated a profitable cargo business off the famous Port of Perennial for exactly eighteen years.

Since the precise time Alexander vanished from Texas.

So he abandoned family and country to engage in international trade? He's here to export lumber and get rich? Not likely. He's a Roth after all, even if he changed his name. And Roths want for nothing.

The railcar stops, and more commuters pile in. Every one of them wears water-resistant clothing, and every bag, purse, or fist carries an umbrella. A woman takes the seat beside me, her rain boots and raincoat zipped up tight. I look out the window and see nothing but clear skies. It's like they know something I don't.

As the railcar hurtles forward, away from the harbor and toward the suburbs, a faint twist of doubt squeezes my insides. What if this all leads to nothing? What if there are no secrets, no revelations, and Alexander was hiding nothing but himself?

No, there are secrets here.

I should go to him. Talk to him.

Let him know he's caught.

Slowly, so as not to attract my handlers' attention, I lift myself up to stand, but a firm hand lowers me back against my seat as soon as my rear feels air.

"Don't. Blow. Our cover," Kano warns in a curt whisper from the row behind me.

"It's not as if he's going anywhere," Ciro adds, loud enough for our entire section to hear. Kano must be glaring daggers at our vexatious companion, because a muted "My apologies" quickly follows.

Privately, before we left for our mission, Kano promised me he would keep Ciro by his side at all times. We both agree Ciro comes with more baggage than he's worth.

Ciro might be funding the mission, but *I'm* leading it.

I take a deep breath and calm myself. Alexander hasn't moved. He still sleeps, his body stretched out despite the crowding car. I pull down my sleeve to cover my tattoo and reach inside my pocket, slipping my fingers into the four steel rings of my knife's handle. The knife my father gave to me.

A Roth and a Goodwin, ten yards away from one another.

Six more stops to go.

"Shaughnessy Heights," the cheerful voice of the railcar announces, inciting a rush of mayhem.

Alexander is the first to pop up, already out the door and on his way to disappear on the packed platform by the time I detangle my legs from the waterproofed woman blocking my row's exit. I muscle through the commuters standing in the center aisle, trusting Kano and Ciro to follow as I push aside incoming passengers through the only open door.

Move! Hurry! I can't lose him.

Without pausing to find my bearings, I charge forward onto the platform, swiveling my head around so ferociously I nearly get whiplash.

There. Ten o'clock. Alexander's stretched, swan-like neck and shiny pitch-black waves of hair soar above the other pedestrians.

I slow my steps and quiet my thundering heartbeat. *Hush, he'll hear you.*

Alexander turns east, away from the other pedestrians, toward a serene, tree-lined street. He moves at a leisurely speed, as if emulating his surroundings, making his walk home an enjoyable stroll. Stalking is proving difficult. I want to chase and pounce. I have to force myself to preserve a sizable gap between my quarry and me.

Behind iron gates and rich, well-groomed lawns, idyllic mansions sprout from the earth, eclipsing the vast downtown skyline only a mile distant. The solar-panel walkway beneath my boots is flawless, without a single crack, unlike the pitted concrete roads that pave even the wealthiest neighborhoods back in the States. The sky is bright and free of smog, the air so clean I feel purified with every lungful.

So this is where you've been hiding? In paradise?

Clenching the handle of my knife, I quicken my pace, halving the space between us. Alexander doesn't notice or sense my presence; he's lost in his ignorance and self-importance.

"Marley," Kano cautions, calling out my alias. "Patience."

This was only supposed to be a reconnaissance mission: watch, study, form a tactical plan, then return in the morning for the abduction. There is to be no contact, no talking, no chancy behavior that could cause a scene and jeopardize our goal.

But it's like he's taunting me. His hypocrisy, his privilege. He's the son of a murderous leader, an American on forbidden soil, and yet here he is alone, unworried, like he's never known what it's like to be frightened, threatened. Hunted.

Feelings that have defined my life since the second I was born.

"Marley," Kano calls out again, this time in a friendly tone, trying to deflect attention. My eyes scour the streets and houses—there's no one around to hear. "Time to go back home."

They've caught up to me now. They're maybe five strides behind me.

"Tomorrow," Ciro says in his light manner, reminding me of the plan, hoping I'll stand down. "We don't want to be *caught* in the rain," he adds cheerily, emphasizing *caught* a bit too obviously.

But I don't see any clouds. I only see Alexander. I only see red.

Before Kano and Ciro can stop me, I shoot forward, not quite at a run, and approach Alexander's left side. I startle him, but he gazes down at me with an easy smile. I want to break his perfect teeth.

"I'm sorry," he says, genuinely apologetic. "Do I know you?" His black eyes are full of questions, but it's a breezy curiosity, not alarm. "I'm normally very good at placing faces . . ."

I can't believe it. He doesn't recognize me. He doesn't recognize that I recognize *him*. If he does, he's hiding it. *He's good at that,* I remind myself.

"You don't keep track of your family's enemies?" I say. "I very much doubt that." I tuck the rogue locks of my wig behind my ears and lift my chin, making sure there can be no misunderstanding of who I am.

Alexander doesn't bat an eye. "I'm sorry. I don't know you, but my family has no enemies." Tightening his raincoat around his frame, he crosses his elongated arms like he's bored and tired of humoring me. "Now if you'll excuse me. I'm late."

Bloated lips still pulled into a smile, he turns away, attempting to increase his speed and get rid of me. He doesn't understand my fangs are already around his neck—it's just whether or not I want to clamp down.

Three steps are all he achieves before I'm back at his side, my arm hooked around his, showing him the sharp blade of my knife.

"Just take my wallet—"

"Keep walking," I spit at him with my own smile. "You know me. And I know you." All color and confidence drains from his face, leaving behind a panicked ghost. *No, a ghost no more.*

"You're Alexander Roth, son of Governor Howard S. Roth, the long-ruling tyrant of Texas. Your father is a murderer . . . I'd say you have a few enemies."

Alexander's eyes dart wildly up and down the street, searching for help. All he finds are Kano and Ciro, weapons strapped and waiting at their hips.

"Yes, they're with me," I confirm. "You're going to talk. The question is only how difficult you want to make this."

"My name is Julien Wright . . . ," he stammers without much heart.

A thick blanket of clouds suddenly covers the sky, turning the world gray. The solar walkway instantly adapts, glowing a vibrant blue beneath our boots, lighting the path ahead for at least another quarter mile. A raindrop lands on my shoulder. Another pats the tip of my nose.

"Which one is yours?" I ask, motioning to the mansions. Headquarters wasn't able to find Alexander's address before we ran out of time and the teams set off on our missions. We only had the site of his cargo company to work with. As a result, we have no info on his personal life. *Does he live alone? Does he have a partner?* Who knows what secrets he has buried within those countless rooms.

A boy in his school blazer shuffles past, umbrella in one hand, tablet in the other. My blade against his ribcage, Alexander keeps quiet, and thankfully, the boy doesn't look up, his attention locked on his screen. Ahead, eight—no nine—more students make their way toward us, late stragglers or overachievers just now leaving school.

We need to get inside. We can't attract attention.

"Take us to your house right now, or you will never see it again," I say, the threats rolling easily off my tongue.

Alexander stiffens at my words, but his head dips into a rigid nod. "It's just up here to the right," he answers reluctantly.

From my peripheral vision, I notice Alexander's attention zeroed in on the incoming students. They're fifteen yards away now. Thirteen. *Is he going to call for help?*

I pull him closer and push us faster. Alexander's house is just after the next gate. "If you give us away, you'll be ruined too," I remind him. "I bet your neighbors don't know you're a Glut."

Alexander winces at the term. He glares down at me with such open hostility I ready myself for a scuffle. Instead, Alexander's hulking figure sags, as if all spirit has left him, and I have to almost drag him off the walkway and up the steps to his entrance. As Kano and Ciro move to block us from view of passing pedestrians, I shove Alexander toward the iris scanner beside his locked gate.

"Open it," I order. "Now."

He doesn't. Alexander keeps his eyes on me. "Which one are you?" he whispers. "Ava or Mira?"

"You won't admit to your own name. Why would I admit to mine?"

The rain starts to fall harder, dripping off the ends of my wig, soaking through my cotton clothes. I don't move for cover. I just let it wash over me.

"Are you the one who killed Halton?" Alexander asks so low I barely hear. His gaze flicks down to my knife. "Is that the blade you dug into my son's chest?" The raindrops look like tears streaking down his cheeks.

You'll get no sympathy from me. In my mind, he left his son to die when he left him with the governor.

"Dad?" someone shouts from the path behind us. I whirl around and nearly stumble backward.

Halton.

Impossible.

I steady my legs and shake my head, clearing my vision. No, not Halton. The mouth is the same, but everything else is the exact opposite: his golden-brown hair to Halton's blue black; his soft countenance to Halton's sharp, arrogant features; his round, inquisitive eyes to Halton's dark, beady stare.

The sky opens, letting loose sheets of rain. It feels like I'm under water. I can't hear. I can't see. Alexander scarcely breathes. The fine hairs on my arms stand on end, and a deep shiver runs through me. Everything feels wrong.

No one moves.

"Dad, who are these people?" the boy shouts. The umbrella slips from his hand and drops to the puddled ground, exposing his school letterman jacket to the downpour.

He looks to be my age, eighteen. A year younger than Halton . . .

Then it all clicks. I don't know whether to laugh or scream.

I turn to Alexander, my words so heated they could boil the rain. "He's a Multiple. He's Halton's brother."

That's why Alexander fled the US.

Alexander had an illegal second child. Alexander is a traitor. Like me, like my father. The only difference is he got away with it.

Bitterness and outrage hit me like a physical blow. I'm left in a daze, my anger radiating with such intensity I can almost hear it. A dull roar. I lift my knife and aim it at Alexander's throat.

"Theo, run!" Alexander yells to his son, but his pleas are drowned in the violent torrent.

Kano lunges and grabs Halton's brother, twisting his arms behind his back in a matter of seconds. Ciro snatches the fallen umbrella, throwing the canopy over his head to block the rain.

"Shall we all head inside?" Ciro asks, absurdly cordial.

With one last desperate search of the empty walkway, Alexander closes his eyes. "Have you come to finish us off, then?"

"No," I say, locking eyes with Theo. "We've just begun."

Ava

The Nighthawk Border Crossing is the least-used passage in Washington State.

That's why Emery chose it.

The area west of Nighthawk boasts the most remote patch of land along the entire northern International Boundary Wall. And with only five inhabitants living in the area, the crossing is both isolated *and* unpopulated. Exactly what we need.

The entrance point is also midway between the state's two largest metropolises, Seattle and Spokane. The senator will be in one of those cities, the honoree at some charity benefit or ribbon-cutting ceremony; we won't know which until we cross over.

If we cross over. Concealed behind a patch of trees with Emery, Barend, and Pawel about half a mile out from the twenty-five-foot galvanized steel border wall, I count five circling thermal-imaging drones.

They weren't part of the plan.

"Where's your man, Emery?" Barend asks, losing patience.

Binoculars pressed against her face, Emery searches the empty, pitted one-lane road. We've all been staring at the door of the Border Inspection Station—little more than a run-down trailer—for over an hour. But it looks like no one's home.

A narrow gate, big enough for a single car, stands wide open, taunting us to run freely through it.

My return into the United States won't come as easy as that. *Something's wrong.*

One of Emery's operatives from the Canadian Border Services Agency was supposed to meet us outside the station to safely smuggle us over the border. Was he caught? Or did he back out?

Emery pulls the binoculars away from her face and shoulders her bag. "We need to abort and move on to the backup plan. It's too dangerous to linger here."

Barend shakes his head, standing his ground. "No, what's too dangerous is the backup plan. I can shoot the drones down."

"This location has already been compromised. Taking down its drones would just cause further attention," Emery says firmly. "We move on to the backup plan."

"Certain situations require firepower to achieve the tactical objective," Barend continues to push. "This is one of them."

I wonder if Barend will battle every decision Emery makes—it's clear his allegiance lies with Ciro as the rebellion's leader, not with her. There's more to his motives in joining my mission than being my protection. What exactly those motives may be aren't clear to me yet.

"I agree with Emery. We should move on to the backup plan," Pawel says way too close beside me. He's been watching over me like a hawk since our drop-off point, and I know exactly what he's doing—I did it to Mira the whole way to Canada. But I don't need him standing guard over me. I can take care of myself.

"Any choice we make will have an element of uncertainty," Barend contends. He draws the exaggerated hood of his uniform tight over his head. "We have our antidrone camouflage—the Border Guard won't know anyone is even crossing."

The Offering Room had an entire fashion line of countersurveil-lance wear at our disposal. Ciro spared no expense—and sacrificed no sense of style. Any one of the field uniforms looked like it could be featured in some alt underground runway show. Our team chose Blackout Wear, garments that are constructed out of a silver-plated fabric that reflects thermal radiation, enabling the wearer to thwart overhead surveillance. Essentially, we're drone-proof.

Still, that open gate screams *trap* to me.

I look down at the map in my hands, my trusted anchor. It feels so good to have one in my possession again; that's all I had when I found the way through the wall the first time.

My finger traces the path to the second starred location on the crisp paper. Plan B is a three-mile hike west through wild territory and involves crossing a minefield in order to get to the border wall.

Dangerous, yes, but all plans have been thoroughly vetted and prepared—this wouldn't be our backup plan if Emery didn't think it was possible.

I fold the map and place the neat square in the inside pocket of my uniform, where it's safe and always close by.

"Plan B is the best shot we have to make it through the wall," I say to the group. "Turning back isn't an option. You all can stand here and squabble if you want, but I'm moving forward."

With that, I set off west, and if the others follow, they follow. If not, I'm still crossing over.

An hour into our trek—the team had no choice but to follow, really—we run into the Similkameen River.

"The river's only ten yards wide," Barend says after lowering his bin-oculars, seeming satisfied that he adequately scanned our surroundings for any sign of trouble. All clear. "Looks shallow enough to wade through too—maybe only waist high."

"We'll take a short ten-minute rest and then continue on," Emery says. It's odd seeing her jacketless, covered instead in a loose, full-length bodysuit, silver from top to bottom. There's not a hint of yellow on her. On any of us. I wonder if she has her signature coat stashed inside her bag, ready to slip back on when the Common unveils itself in Dallas.

"Can I borrow a pen?" I ask Emery. She's always scribbling inside a small red notebook, her hand moving so quick it's like her mind is bursting with thoughts. A part of me wants to know what she's writing—it's such a rare thing to see someone use pen and paper—but I respect her privacy too much to ask.

She lifts the flap of her metallic rucksack and pulls out a pen, handing me the antique writing instrument without question.

While Pawel passes around a water bottle, I walk downstream and take a private seat on the pebbled riverbank. A picturesque view of the Cascade Mountains fights for my attention, but I don't have time for picturesque. I reach into my pocket and pull out my map again.

I flip it over to the side that displays the entire United States. While most of the South is colored royal purple, the color adopted by Roth and his high-ranking elite, the Common is on a campaign to color the most powerful states in the North bright yellow.

Using Emery's pen, I write out the names of all the senators the Common has targeted for our missions.

Senator Riggs of New York
Senator López of North California
Senator Tate of Colorado
Senator Dalton of Michigan
Senator Gordon of Washington State

My forefinger moves down the list, stopping when I reach the final name. I circle it, focusing on that name alone. Senator Gordon.

The stream babbles soothingly all around me, and I close my eyes, allowing the "blue state of mind"—real this time—to lull me into a sense of calm.

I will turn you yellow, Eli Gordon. And I will make you help me shut down Albatross.

Each name the Common crosses off its recruitment list gives us a stronger chance to beat Roth at his own game: winning control of the country.

And I will make certain to play my parts. Both in the larger endgame, and the smaller one I'm secretly playing by myself.

I have two pieces in play, razor sharp and ruthless as my grief.

Caution: Landmines Ahead. Danger of Death.

The massive warning signs are posted every twenty yards in front of a deep antivehicle trench. Behind these two staunch secondary defenses, the border wall stretches out improbably high and imposing. This section of the wall must be fifty feet high, with a mess of barbed wire defending its top.

And I see no holes this time.

What I also don't see are drones, motion sensors, Guards, or cameras. Rayla always maintained that the Canadian border is over five thousand miles long and that every fortress has its weak points. How a field littered with hundreds of landmines is one of those weak points, I'm not sure. *Maybe the signs are just an empty threat, like the first time I crossed the wall.*

"Look," Barend says. I follow where he points and see multiple blasted holes in the earth. The blown-up carcass of some unfortunate animal lies strewn not far from where we stand. *How did the animal even get past the trench?*

The warning signs are real this time—it's not just propaganda, then. *Plan B might be too dangerous after all.*

Just as I'm about to tell Emery this, Pawel says, "I'll go first." He jumps into the trench as if he's simply diving into a pool on a hot summer's day to test the water's temperature.

"No way," I say automatically. "You're going to get yourself killed." I drop down into the ditch after him, without knowing how the hell I'm going to get back up again. "If we're going to do this, I'll go first."

I refuse to have Pawel be blown up in front of me. Too many people have already died on Mira's and my account—I can't have another. *But there will be others—the war has just gotten started.*

In response, Pawel unclasps his bag and pulls out a handheld instrument that looks just like a miniature metal detector.

Ground-penetrating radar. Of course. The sensors will be able to detect if an explosive is near, like bomb-sniffing dogs.

He lifts the device into the air, proud of his Offering Room find. "I'm not just a digital tracker, you know."

I give Pawel a second look. *There's more to this guy than I originally thought.*

A loud *thud* announces Barend's arrival in the trench. He crouches down, threads his hands together, and says to Pawel, "I'll hoist you up to the other side of the ditch."

"Much obliged," Pawel says, inserting his right foot into Barend's handmade catapult. As he's lifted up to ground level, Emery slides down.

"What happens when we get past the minefield?" I ask. "There doesn't seem to be a way through." We might be able to get ourselves across this field without dying, but there's still the seemingly impenetrable wall.

Emery gives a knowing half smile, loading her foot next into Barend's locked hands.

"Just follow me."

We walk in a tight, narrow line through the forty-yard-long minefield. Pawel's up front with his radar instrument, then Emery and me, with Barend guarding the rear. No one talks—we're all too busy holding our breath.

The worn path Pawel chose seems to be a sound one; not only are we still alive, others appear to have taken this same route safely to the wall. We use the extremely thin trail—so narrow it's clear the border crossers were wary enough to walk heel to toe—they created as our guide.

I'm careful to look straight ahead, not wishing to see any more carcasses, especially any that aren't wild animals.

Pawel stops the line when we reach the gleaming steel wall. He cranes his neck, damp with sweat. "It's so much smaller than I remember," he says, mild disappointment in his voice. "Then again, I was a child when I crossed over with Ellie. I don't remember much."

Is he looking at the same wall I am? It's twice as tall as the one I crossed with Mira.

"So what now?" Barend asks impatiently from the back. "We survived a field riddled with explosives only to have no actual way through the wall itself?"

"May I?" Emery motions for Pawel to let her pass.

Without any hesitation, Emery walks straight into the wall and passes through it, like magic.

Genius. The wall looks completely solid from where I stand, but it's just a holographic projection. The International Boundary Wall is much too long and expensive to safeguard without fault. In the most remote stretches, the Border Services Agency must use landmines to deter illegal crossings, thinking no one would actually ever risk getting close enough to the wall to find out that it isn't real.

I follow Emery through the imaginary wall, and the first thing I see when I step foot back on American soil is a shiny black Washington State Guard SUV.

It speeds directly for us, and I freeze. A wave of hot panic threatens to take over.

This is part of the plan, remember? I chide myself. *Buck up. Breathe. No time for a panic attack.*

I feel someone brush against my shoulder.

"Well, that certainly was cool," Pawel says, his words slightly muffled by a mask. I look over to find my own face staring back at me. Up ahead, Emery turns, and for a dizzying moment, I think Mira is back with me again. My heart twists.

I take courage from my sister. Mira's still with me, no matter the distance between us.

Succeed in your mission, and in two weeks you'll reunite with her in Dallas.

Divide, and conquer Roth. My new battle cry.

I throw on the Goodwin mask that Pawel hands me—to hide the fact that I'm a *real* Goodwin—just as the SUV skids to a stop in front of us. Two Guards, a woman and a man, emerge from the car, every bit as intimidating as I remember them to be. It almost feels nostalgic.

Then the Guards' harsh faces break into smiles. The woman throws Barend—the only one of our group showing his real face—an extra uniform.

"He's in Spokane," the male imposter Guard says, "giving a speech at a fundraising party."

Emery nods. "We're three hours behind. You'll have to drive with the emergency lights on." She holds out her hands to be cuffed. Pawel and I do the same.

Making sure my mask is firmly in place, I pile into the SUV—the three lawless protesters in Goodwin masks relegated to the back—and we set off south, deeper into Washington State.

I don't talk—no one must know Ava Goodwin has returned to the States. But I'm back.

And I'm headed straight for Senator Gordon.

MIRA

"Please!" Ciro shouts from the middle of Alexander's spacious living room. His valorous attempts as peaceful mediator have led us nowhere. "If we could all just sit down—"

"I told you!" Alexander screams from behind the safety of an armchair. "I won't talk to *her.*"

"And *I* told *you* I didn't kill your son!" I yell with such vehemence I feel my throat tear. "Your *firstborn,*" I add spitefully.

I pace up and down the length of his gaudy violet couch, attempting to calm myself, but I can't catch my breath. My mind races with so many questions it's difficult to grab hold of just one.

"Who is Theo?" I demand. "Does he share the same mother as Halton? Or did you have an affair?" Alexander presses his lips closed, but his panicked eyes answer for him.

"How did you evade your sterilization?" I throw at the governor's son. "Halton was born in a hospital like all Dallas citizens. I saw the press release . . . Everyone did. The Family Planning doctors would never let you leave without the postbirth procedure . . . not even you."

When I'm met with only silence, I pause my useless marching and turn toward the spiral staircase. I flick my eyes up the excessive steps, listening for Theo's muffled pleas. *Dad! . . . Don't hurt him! . . . Why are you doing this?* I imagine he's screaming.

To placate Alexander and win over his trust, Ciro agreed to keep Theo locked upstairs with Kano, well away from me, and from the truth. *Such a spoiled boy,* I think. Just like his brother.

"Does he even know what he is?" I ask, whirling around to find Alexander glowering at me, the venom behind his stare so lethal Ciro sidesteps to block him from my view.

"Don't!" Alexander's disembodied voice cries. "Theo's innocent in all of this."

"Innocent?" I seethe. "Was I deemed innocent in the eyes of your father? Was I considered an innocent to the Rule of One?"

Alexander has no answer.

"You and your second-born are traitors just like me," I whisper, my voice gruff and strained.

I take long, deep breaths, watching the last of the rainwater drip from the tips of my fingers and boots. "My parents died inside a basement and a prison cell for having a second child, and you're living in a goddamn palace."

My rage takes over, and I charge up the steps two at a time.

"Don't you touch him!" Alexander cries out, like words could stop me.

As I reach the landing, I hear Alexander barreling after me.

"Kano, let me in!" I scream, sprinting down the long corridor, twisting the handles of every door I pass.

Two rooms ahead, the knob turns, and the door swings open. Kano blockades the entrance, and I attempt to shoulder my way in, but it's like hitting a cement barrier. "Talking isn't going well?" he asks dryly.

"Who are you people?" Theo demands, his own voice stripped from his one-sided screaming match. "Someone tell me what's happening!"

I wriggle my head beneath Kano's armpit and see Theo huddled in the corner of his platform bed, his hands zip-tied to a steel leg of his marble nightstand.

"Do you really not know?" I snap. *How slow can this boy be?* My waterlogged jacket sticks to my arms like a second skin, but I manage to yank up my sleeve high enough to expose my tattoo.

Shock freezes Theo's face. "Common members?" he says slowly, as if persuading himself we're real. His utter astonishment makes me hate him even more.

I keep my voice stable so Kano will let me pass. "I'm calm" is all I need to say, and he releases his hold on me. I barge into the room, Kano on my heels, and slam the door behind us. The lock clicks, and Alexander's desperate fists pound on the door, begging to be let in.

"She won't lay a finger on him." Ciro's muted assurances reach us from the other side of the door. "Theo is what we came here for. He's the key."

I move to the foot of Theo's unmade bed, just out of kicking distance. He stares at me, a tragic fascination drawing his eyes to mine. With my right hand I reach up and rip off my ruined wig, showing him my mop of dyed blonde hair.

"Ava?" he says, confused.

Irritation pricks at my ego. For being called the wrong name, for Ava always being thought of first.

"You had a fifty-fifty shot, kid . . . ," Kano says, shaking his head.

"I'm Mira," I inform Theo, my tone as sharp as the blade inside my pocket.

"But how?" he stutters, his brain struggling to keep up with his eyes. "Why?"

I stand there, still holding the answer, reveling in his innocence and that I get to be the one to take it. I have no guilt. In fact, it feels deliriously good.

"You're a Roth," I throw at Theo, hoping it hurts. "You're a secret member of the First Family of Texas."

Theo shakes his head, but I keep going. "You're a grandson of Governor Roth, making you Halton's half brother. Heard of him?"

"That governor running for president? That's just not . . ." Theo's words die in his throat.

"If it weren't the truth, do you really think I would be here?" I say.

Doubt escalates to denial. Then fury detonates inside him, burning across his cherrywood eyes. For a moment I think he's going to upheave the bulky nightstand he's tied to and swing it at me as a weapon—his athletic build certainly looks strong enough to achieve it. But he doesn't. He simply sits there, paralyzed by the truth. His broad shoulders slump forward lower and lower, as if he wants to fold inward and disappear.

"So I'm like you?" Theo whispers. Lifting his head, he looks up at me, bare and vulnerable, a broken boy searching for glue.

You'll find no solace here.

"You're an illegal American child, yes. But I'm nothing like you."

He nods like he understands. He doesn't and he never will.

"I lived a half life underground. I didn't exist for eighteen years." I stop before I lose my temper. *You owe him no explanation. Stay in control.*

The pounding on Theo's door stops, replaced by the muted thuds of a tussle. "Theo, let me explain!" Alexander cries out from the thin gap of air below the door. The tips of his manicured fingers stab through the opening, reaching out for his son. I can see Kano's inner struggle not to step on them.

"Your stunt worked," Kano says, grinning at me. "I think he'll talk now . . ."

"Yes, yes, I'll talk!" Alexander shouts. "Just let me see my son!" His slender fingers retreat right when I believe Kano made up his mind to crunch down.

Theo turns his back to the door, his unfocused gaze on the window. The downpour has eased to a drizzle now, the view outside sodden and colorless beneath the ceiling of oppressive clouds.

"Let's see what Daddy has to say for himself," Kano taunts. He turns the lock, and the door bursts open, Alexander rushing across the room in a blur. Allowing a wide berth between him and me, he falls to his knees before Theo, gripping his bonded hands, imploring him to listen.

"Get away from me," Theo says, refusing to look at his father. He turns his vacant stare to his dresser lined with trophies. Water polo, soccer. Sports I've barely heard of.

"Does he have to be handcuffed?" Alexander pleads to Ciro.

"Seems like you should be in handcuffs too," Theo says sharply.

"Mijo, let me explain—"

Mijo? I've never heard a Roth speak Spanish before. Alexander's mother, Mrs. Roth, *does* come from a high-ranking Tejano family, but they didn't carry on the language. Halton never even took Spanish in school.

"Halton was your mijo. You had a second family." Theo doesn't say it as a question. He knows it's a hard fact. A fact his father doesn't even try to deny.

"I did it for love, Theo. I did it for love of your mother and for you."

Theo scoffs, and I roll my eyes.

"Mom's in on this too, then?"

"Where *is* your wife, Alexander?" Ciro asks, everyone suddenly fearful the woman will barge in and destroy our mission's headway.

"My personal life is of no concern to you," Alexander snaps, waving the question away.

"They're getting a divorce," Theo answers quietly. "My mom won't show up here, if that's what you're worried about."

No sympathy, I remind myself.

The entire team relaxes.

Alexander pushes himself closer to Theo and tries to force him to meet his earnest stare, but Theo bows his head, focus locked on the damp floor.

"You broke the law of your country," Theo whispers, like he's ashamed we might hear. "And then ran away like some craven sneak. My entire life is a lie."

"You wouldn't be alive if we hadn't fled," Alexander protests. Knees cracking, he lifts himself up to sit beside Theo on the bed. "My father wanted to take you from me. Are you hearing me, Theo? Your grandfather wanted to send you away. I couldn't give you up, so we ran . . ."

Governor Roth knew. Of course he did.

"And the governor just let you go?" I ask hotly, fighting to keep back the images that pop into my mind: Roth, my father, the prison cell. The nightmare sound of the shot that took him from me.

"My father despised me," Alexander answers without looking at me. "I was twenty-three when Halton was born. I'd just been expelled from Strake University—it was all very quiet, the Roth public image never tarnished—and made an officer in *his* military. I was doing everything I could to get myself out. I was undisciplined, weak willed. Too curious for the role my parents planned for me. An ill-fitted successor, the only thing I did right in their eyes was agree to the arranged marriage that gave them a grandson. An opportunity to raise a proper heir."

Then why did Governor Roth have his heir killed?

"You say you couldn't give me up, but you just abandoned him . . . ," Theo says to his sneakers. ". . . Halton," he finally names him. "You left him with a man like Governor Roth? I've hated that son of a Glut since I first heard his name in the news."

He pauses a beat, letting his reality fully sink in. "Y ahora es mi pinche pariente," Theo curses in Spanish. *And now I'm fucking related to him.*

Yes, you are, Theo Roth. And we're going to use you.

The public needs to know that Alexander and his second wife were never arrested. They should know his family wasn't marked as traitors and hunted down like mine and so many others. They should be made aware that Roths, according to their own governor, are above the law. Roth *is* the law, with enough power to bury a monstrous scandal in its infancy.

Well, I've dug it up, Governor. The old skeletons in your closet are sitting right in front of me.

"Every day I regret my decision to leave Halton behind, but it was my only choice," Alexander continues forcefully. "It was my only choice," he repeats, still convincing himself.

The parents always pick the firstborn. Rayla told me that. They never choose to keep the second child. A nasty jealousy surges through me as I watch Theo, the chosen second-born, sitting on *his* bed, in *his* room, living *his* own life.

I smother the impulse to feel sorry for myself. *Don't think of the past.* Make the future.

"If I took Halton," Alexander continues, "if I left with my father's only next-in-line, Roth would have come after us. He wouldn't have let me go. I didn't know . . . How could I have known it would end up this way . . ."

"That Halton would end up dead?" Kano interrupts Alexander's frantic appeals for absolution. "And the Common would come knocking?"

Alexander wraps his arms around Theo like a shield, pressing his lips against his son's ear, forcing him to listen. "The twins and the Common killed your brother." I hear the urgent whisper. "They're here to hurt you, mijo."

Theo lifts his head. He looks past his father, toward me. "Is that why you're here?" he asks. "To hurt me?" He doesn't seem afraid.

"We're here to take you to Dallas," I tell him bluntly. "Your existence—"

"No!" Alexander shouts, rounding on me.

Ciro steps forward, blocking Alexander's path. He flicks back his impossibly dry locks, wearing the confident smile of a closer. "Alexander—is it all right if I call you by your birth name?" He places a soothing hand on Alexander's shoulder. "Of course we would like it to be your decision to join us—"

"Never! We will never—"

"Let Mira speak!" Theo shouts at the top of his lungs, a voice like thunder, shocking the room into silence. He never takes his eyes from

mine. There's an electricity there, a wayward current that seeks to connect us.

No, he's nothing like me.

He's a Roth.

"Your existence," I resume, trying to regain my momentum, "is our
ultimate proof. Your grandfather manipulated and deceived the public,
coerced them to believe the lie that he did not murder my father. That
he did not have his own grandson killed by his agent."

I throw up my hand, stopping Alexander from his tiresome protests. "I saw both with my own eyes, yet half the country doesn't believe
it. But with you . . . ," I press, looking at Theo, meeting his open
stare, ". . . if they see you live and in person, Governor Roth will have
nothing to stand behind. Those still loyal to him will be forced to see
their leader is a deceiver. An unpardonable fraud that must be brought
down."

"We're not going *anywhere* with you," Alexander asserts.

"You don't have to go," Theo says, looking at his father for the first
time. "But I am."

"Wonderful, now that we have that settled . . ." Ciro swoops in
before Alexander can launch into another blowup. "We will be leaving
directly."

I feel exhausted and drained. I have nothing more to say. Peering
down at my hands, I realize I've twisted my wig into an unwearable
mess. Without a second glance at Theo, I move for the exit—I don't
want to be in a roomful of Roths any longer than I have to be.

Why is Theo so willing to come with us?

Why do you care? I scold myself.

We got him. That's all that matters.

"You can cut his cuffs," I tell Kano, and slam the door behind me.

ZEE

The rail is behind schedule. By thirty seconds. It's enough time for a handful of civilians in my section to look troubled.

"Is the rail ever late?" I ask Cleo.

"No," she answers. "Be ready to move fast."

A boy on the other end of the car keeps pulling down his right sleeve. Three women in hoods hide their hands in pockets, eyes on the ground.

"They cut out their microchips," Cleo says. "They must've sneaked on like us."

No problems at the other station stops. No Guards.

The capital is the next stop. Dallas. The place where my twin died. Lynn. Her body failed. She's gone. I'll never meet her. Her husband died here too. Darren.

The Common played me the video of my mother. Rayla. *Show those in power we won't be tracked or controlled . . . The power is now in our hands.*

I look down at my hands.

Who will stop the government's bloodshed? my mother had asked.

I will.

Cleo understood. She said she would take me to a safe house in Dallas. She will help me get the man they call the governor.

"Welcome to Guardian Station." An electronic voice from the speakers. The railcar slows down, then stops.

The other civilians around me are at eighty-five-percent fear. This is normal, Cleo tells me. The percentage doesn't ever go below eighty.

I'm at a hundred percent. My Camp instincts tell me something isn't right.

The doors break open, and everybody screams.

Armed Guards block the entrance. And dogs. Huge dogs with sharp teeth. Barking, biting at the leg of a small boy. Everybody screams louder.

"Line up on the platform!"

"Move, move, move!"

"Line up to be scanned!"

Nobody moves. They're all too scared to follow orders.

"Present your wrist for authorization, or you will be arrested immediately!" a Guard shouts.

The civilians form a ball. Thinking that there's protection in numbers. I've never seen women and men try to help others in danger. In the Camps you keep to yourself to survive.

It won't protect them. There are more of them than us. The back door opens.

More dogs and Guards. Pushing us out the front entrance. Onto a platform. Batons, guns. Tasers.

"Line up to be scanned!"

"Roll up your sleeves now!"

A Guard checks wrists with a scanner. Another test of pass or fail. He points right, you live. Left, you are dragged away screaming.

Two men break free, try to run. But the tasers get them. They fall to the ground, their bodies shaking. Then they stop moving.

This is no better than life inside the Camps. Dallas must be one big Camp.

"Drop to the ground," Cleo says.

I drop to the ground.

Feet step on my back, my hair. My hands. I am hardened to such abuse. Cleo cries out in pain.

We crawl to the edge of the platform. Roll off the ledge to land on the rail tracks.

But only I make it.

"Run for it!" Cleo shouts. Her voice is being dragged away, up the platform.

How do I help her? I can't.

I run.

Shouts reach me through the dark tunnel. A round of gunfire goes off. I find an exit. Marked "Emergency."

The door won't give. Anything on the other side is better than the TXRAIL.

My arms are heavy. Weak. I would one hundred percent fail Assessment Checkup. I'm so angry I scream. I've never screamed so loud. It feels good. I let out another and turn the handle.

It gives. I throw the door open, and an alarm sounds off. The alarm doesn't make me drop to the ground like it used to.

I run again.

I'm in the middle of a crowded walkway. Civilians are all around me.

Dallas. The air is thick. Dark. Loud. I can't see the sky. Tall buildings are everywhere. I don't know where to go.

My family was here. None of them are here now.

A second siren sounds off. Everybody stops.

"Make way!" a voice shouts. "Make way, immediately!"

A military vehicle drives from the gates of the tallest building I've ever seen. The top is a glass ball. I listen to the whispers around me.

"Guardian Tower."

"Prison."

"I hear it's full to capacity."

"Common members."

Cleo.

The vehicle moves down the empty street, the crowd jumping out of its way. They wave small bits of cloth, red, white, and blue. A single star.

"General Pierce . . . he's headed for the Governor's Mansion. Something's happening," a woman whispers to a young man next to her.

I look at their shirtsleeves. Blood spots give them away. They cut out their microchips like my mother told them to.

I follow the vehicle down the road.

It's good to know the name of your enemy. After all this time I finally know my true enemy's name.

Governor Howard S. Roth.

Being this close to him feels like a second freeing.

OWEN

We must've sped through four states by now. It's pathetic, but I couldn't even tell you which—I've never thought much about them before. They all start with the letter *I* . . . I think.

My butt's numb, and my brain is mush. We haven't stopped in over six hours, and Rayla the Leadfoot hasn't said a word. The woman's a driving machine. It's like she's storing up all her energy and focus for Denver. *Or her bullet wound is slowly sapping all her strength* . . . but this conclusion makes me uncomfortable, and I shift my thoughts elsewhere.

There's nothing to look at. It's the same monotonous view mile after never-ending mile, so I dust the cobwebs off my memories from school before my parents and the government pulled me out to work. There was this one teacher I actually liked who tried to teach us punk kids a catchy, cheesy song to memorize all fifty-one states in alphabetical order. I was the only student who could do it, and naturally I thought I was a genius. Let's see if I still am. The tune comes back to me no problem; it's the words that are a bit fuzzy.

> *It takes fifty-one states*
> *to make a country great.*
> *Fifty-one, we are one,*
> *the United States of America* . . .

I skip over the hand-holding kid lyrics that are complete bullshit and hum my way to the main event.

Alabama, Alaska, Arizona, Arkansas, California,
Colorado, Connecticut . . .

Son of a Glut. I know there's a *D* in there somewhere. I rack my brain for five minutes, then give up. Who cares about the state that starts with a *D* that no one ever remembers?

"Delaware," Rayla says.

I jump in my seat. I guess I was singing out loud—I'm not what you would call a songster, but I'm not completely mortified. Blaise didn't hear; he's still passed out in the back seat. That guy sleeps like the dead. Which I hope we all aren't soon.

"Delaware." I sit with the word for a bit, thinking on where exactly the state is on the map. "Listen, I'm just a fledgling, but from what I can tell, with *Operation Flip the Freakin' Senators* . . . the Common wants to unite the states." Rayla doesn't contradict me, so I keep going. "That all sounds well and good, but how will they . . . *we* . . . get people from the South or the West Coast to give two shits about people in *Delaware*?"

Rayla smiles. "It's written in our people's DNA," she explains patiently. "We are still the *United* States. We just have to remind the people of that."

When Rayla says it, it seems so simple. *Wake the people up.*

Sleep starts to pull me under, and I try to fight it. I'm not sure why, but it's always felt like a point of weakness to get caught sleeping in public—a baby who needs his nap. Blaise doesn't have a problem with it—he's snoring like one of those bulldogs people used to own.

I'm just going to rest my eyes, I tell myself. Next thing I know I rouse with a start. Chunks of time must have passed. I'm drooling.

I pick up the conversation like I never left it.

"Ava and Mira share DNA." I say the first thing that pops into my mind. *It's written in our people's DNA.*

No response.

"Did you really not know?" I ask Rayla. "Did you really not know Ava had a twin?" She probably won't answer, but I give it a go anyway. People tend to be more open to spilling their guts when they're sleep deprived.

"No," she says, her smile gone. "I learned the truth only days before the world did."

"But you helped get them to Canada," I continue, sitting up in my seat.

"I got them to Montana," Rayla corrects me. "They got themselves the rest of the way."

"What are they like?" I try not to sound too interested. I shrug. "I mean, was it crazy seeing twins for the first time?"

Rayla grimaces. She plays it off as pain from her wound, but I can tell there's something more there. A deeper pain she doesn't want to show me. I look away, pretending I didn't notice. It's like I saw her naked.

"I had seen twins before that day."

What? There are more? It's impossible for me to downplay my shock. "Did you and the Common hide another set of twins?"

"No."

At first I think that's all she'll reveal, but she continues. "I made a choice I've regretted every second of my days."

I make myself look at her while she shares her pain.

"If only I'd been braver," Rayla finishes, her firm voice breaking.

I have no idea what she's talking about; she's the bravest person I've ever met. "If *you're* not brave, then the word doesn't exist."

Taking her eyes off the road, Rayla the Slayer stares at me raw and unguarded. I suddenly feel very adult.

"I gave up my daughter. I let the government take my second-born."

Is she telling me *she* had twins? That must have been back in the early decades of the Rule of One. Back when the main job description of the Family Planning Director was to track down and "take care of" illegal children. Gluts.

My mind is blown. Ava and Mira's mother was a twin. Twins having twins. Not even the deepest pits of the Dark Web hide any trace of this truth.

Rayla doesn't seem to require a response from me, which is good, because I'm clueless what to say. I mean, how does someone respond to that? *I'm sorry* just doesn't seem to cut it. Rather than offer up useless apologies for an evil someone else did, I decide to trade hurts.

"I didn't get to tell my parents goodbye," I say. "I left them in Detroit, and now the Guard is probably on them because of what I'm doing. I don't think they'll survive without me." I keep going. It just spills out. "My mom and dad don't need me, only my Kismet earnings. They couldn't care less about their *actual* flesh-and-blood kid. I'm only worth what I can give them . . . You know what? I don't think they ever once told me they love me."

It's the first time I've admitted this. Rayla nods, telling me she heard me. I feel lighter.

Rayla wipes at her eyes with her shoulder. I pretend not to notice. "My daughter Lynn was a songbird." Her smile's back. "So are Ava and Mira."

Ava's face flares up in my mind, the image seared there like a photograph. I'd like to hear her sing.

. . . *I hope I didn't say that out loud.*

"Finish your song?" Rayla asks me.

"Sure." Clearing my throat, I resume the cornball tune, really getting into it.

Delaware, Florida, Georgia, Hawaii . . .

A few states trip me up, but Rayla helps with the tricky ones. She even joins in, drumming out the rhythm on the wheel. Rayla's pretty good. Awesome actually. She sounds like she was in a band once. The idea of drumsticks in Rayla's hands rather than a gun is an entertaining one for sure.

When the song's done, I start again from the top. I nail it on my second try, all fifty-one divided territories of the United States.

"Wake up, Rayla," I shout from the dusty front porch of our Colorado safe house northeast of Denver. "Your Cavalry has arrived."

What must be thirty cars, all definitely stolen, charge through the wrought-iron gate of Legendary Ranch, the tires sending a sandstorm of dirt whipping into the air in their wake.

They came. Before we left our hideout in Michigan this morning, Rayla sent out a message, and here they are.

A driver at each emergency wheel, the cars glide to a dramatic stop in front of the ranch house. Two perfect rows are on display like it's a private auto show, with high-rises from the distant capital as the backdrop.

What an entrance.

Rayla jumps to her feet. It took a hell of a lot of insisting, but I finally managed to convince her she needed rest—she drove the entire fourteen hours to get us here, and it showed. True to form, she flat-out refused to let me take the wheel or to use the autonomous driving system at all. But I felt a sense of honor when she closed her eyes next to me on the porch swing and fell asleep, leaving me to stand lookout alone.

She's finally starting to trust me. *Why does that matter to me so much?* Half the time I'm still trying to convince myself that I have it in me to become a rebellion member. That I didn't just hitch along for the ride because I had no better offers.

"Stay on the porch," Rayla says, resting her hand on my shoulder. I think she's using me as a support railing to help her stand, but then I feel a tiny squeeze before she lets her hand drop, heading for the stairs.

Blaise crops up from the house—he's been in there since we got here, doing whatever it is that Blaise does in his downtime. Which is probably just pace around with twitchy fingers—Rayla made him leave all his fancy tech toys behind.

"Whoa," he says, staring at the fresh reinforcements gathered in front of the house.

"Yeah, I know," I say, moving to stand beside him at the top of the porch's steps. "Six of those cars, the sleek silver and black ones with the electric-blue trim, are Kismet models, from the auto factory I used to work at. I helped program the autonomous system." Kind of.

"Okay, I see you, Code Cog."

I can't see his face underneath the bandana of flames, but his voice tells me he's impressed.

Did we just have our first bonding moment?

Who knew that all it took to gain friends was to get yourself caught up in a rebellion?

Halfway to the line of cars—I spot several inferior models from rival automotive factories—Rayla stops. Is she in pain? Does she have to catch her breath? No way the veteran leader of the rebellion would want to show any sign of weakness in front of her troops. I should be out there with her, but she told me to stay put.

Sorry, not going to happen.

The instant I step down the rickety wooden staircase to run to her aid, I abort, realizing my services are not required after all. A muscular middle-aged man emerges from the winged door of a white luxury sports car, a gun holstered at his waist. He's the most Herculean person I've ever laid eyes on—it's like Rayla ordered him straight out of my favorite childhood virtual game, *Warrior King*. A hologram lieutenant, just for show.

"Xavier," Rayla says, her arms open wide in greeting.

The man smiles and strides over to her, his hulking arms outstretched, and they embrace. To be more specific, he picks her up into a bear hug, thankfully avoiding her wounded arm, and doesn't let go for an entire fifteen seconds.

Nope, he's very much real.

He places Rayla back on her feet. "You had us all worried, my old friend, going dark after the Kismet raid," Xavier says. "Are you well and whole? I was relieved when your message came through."

"How's your son?" Rayla asks, skirting his concerns.

"Troublesome as ever," Xavier says with a grin.

"Your raid was successful, then?" Rayla inquires, back to business. "We got what we needed?"

A teenager who looks like a mini version of Xavier exits the passenger seat of the sports car, carrying two huge black duffel bags on his shoulders. He stands beside his father. "Hello again, Rayla."

Rayla nods in greeting. "It's good to have you here with us, Malik." She moves to unzip one of the bags. Even from the porch steps, I can see what's inside.

Guns. Lots of them.

The winged doors of the remaining twenty-nine other cars now swing open, each passenger with their own black duffel bag in tow.

"We've *all* been busy, I see," Rayla says, pleased. "Very good." She beckons to the freshly arrived Common members—there must be at least fifty in total—and turns to face the ranch house.

"Come inside. There's much to discuss."

Blaise and I are in luck.

Malik, Xavier's son, is a prodigy in the underground art of tattooing. How he came to discover such an illicit ability, let alone foster those skills, I don't ask. I'm too busy trying to overhear the conversation in the living room.

"Have you thought of what you want inked yet?" Malik questions me again, pausing from his work on Blaise's inner right wrist. One guess what Blaise chose. Yep, flames. I have to hand it to him—the guy really knows how to stay on brand.

Malik recognized me right off from all the news outlets transmitting my wanted photo. He called me Rayla's sidekick. He also immediately called me out on my virgin-skinned wrist.

You're one of the most famous Common members now; you have *to be marked,* Malik insisted. So he has set up shop on a fold-out table in the corner, while Rayla and his father and the other leaders discuss the plan for flipping Colorado's senator to the Common's side. Seeing their heads together, whispering in hushed voices without me, I feel like I'm stuck at the kids' table.

I used to be in the passenger's seat, right next to Rayla.

"Come on," Blaise presses. "Or are you scared it will hurt?" He turns his flaming smile in my direction. Even in a safe house, surrounded by friends, his bandana remains on.

I'm supposed to choose something meaningful for my tattoo, an image or a word that's a symbol of my own resistance. But I don't have anything like that. I haven't earned the mark of the Common yet.

I've spent most of my life coasting, not caring about anything—fighting for no one and nothing. What is an emblem for someone who just goes where the wind blows him?

A low, constant rumbling sound suddenly reaches me, saving me from having to answer. It gets louder and louder. This can't be good.

I rise from my folding chair and look to Rayla across the room.

"Rayla, do you hear that?" I shout.

Everybody stops, listens, then scrambles outside to the porch, necks craned up to the bright night sky. "Oh shit," Blaise breathes beside me.

Oh shit is right. The dark outlines of massive airplanes—military cargo aircraft—cover the sky as far as the eye can see, all flying toward Denver.

Night vision binoculars. I hotfoot it to the house. Vaulting over the couch, I dive for the trunk I was snooping around in earlier and snatch a pair of beat-up field glasses. Stumbling back out into the yard, I slam the eyepiece to my face and focus.

My jaw drops when every plane's cargo bed unleashes paratroopers, military jeeps, tanks, and boxes of equipment—no doubt stuffed with weapons—into the air.

It's a full-on invasion.

No one says a word. It feels unreal, like we're in a virtual game.

Who in the world could this be? Russia, Canada?

The planes thunder past our safe house, and I spot my worst fear on the right side of each tail wing. Even without binoculars I can see the unmistakable flag: blocks of red, white, and blue with a five-pointed Lone Star.

This is an inside job.

"It's the Texas State Guard!" I shout over the whirlwind.

"Impossible," Xavier says, still refusing to believe what he sees. "How does Governor Roth have enough biofuel to power such a fleet?"

If Roth's goal was to display Texas's military might against the Common, he's succeeded.

We don't have a chance in hell.

"Is Governor Roth trying to occupy Colorado?" Blaise asks me, confused.

"He's already done it!" Rayla yells.

I can't stop zooming in on the paratroopers. A cluster of them are level with the high-rises now. Another few seconds and their feet will touch the ground.

They'll take Denver in no time. *What does this mean? How can a governor get away with this?*

I bet the Texas Guard has already sealed the borders.

"We're trapped, aren't we?" I ask, ripping my focus off the sky, looking once again to Rayla.

Everyone is.

In answer, she shoves a gun into my hands. It's the Kismet Security Guard's, the same one she took from me the night we made each other's violent acquaintance.

"We're going to have to fight our way out."

AVA

I look like a lady, but I'm not.

I've played this game before. Dress up for fancy parties—this time I have on a white silk one-piece suit with a matching headscarf—and act the part of the child of someone important. Smile, and be agreeable. I don't know that girl anymore.

The makeup on my face is irritating. I know it's necessary for my disguise to blend in, but I keep scratching at it. I reach up once more—did I really have to wear false eyelashes?—but Pawel grabs my hand, tucking my arm into his elbow.

Pawel is my attentive date for the evening. He wears a ritzy tuxedo and looks appropriately dapper enough to be on the guest list of the charity dinner we crashed for the Washington State Heart Association. Heart disease is still America's number-one killer, followed closely by natural disasters and suicide. All the richest Washingtonians are in attendance.

And so is Senator Gordon. The guest of honor and our VIP target.

Senators don't demand nearly as much security as governors do—it was easy to slip into the event without a microchip scan. Barend, clad in his Washington State Guard dress blues, escorted us in, no questions asked. It's Mira's and my survival tactic from our school days: people see what they expect to see. We look like we belong here, so we belong.

Emery stands in front of a great stone clock tower, her elegant gown matching the steeple's rusted red shingles. She's stunning, and every person at the party sees it too. A swarm of polished men and women buzz around her like honeybees returned from extinction. Emery breaks out a Rubik's Cube from her bag, her shield against having to mingle. She twists and turns the colored blocks, solving the puzzle in under five seconds without even looking at it. Her real focus is on finding the senator.

Arm in arm, Pawel and I pass by her without acknowledgment, but I can't help but covertly smile at Emery's firm rebuffs. *No time for flirtations. She's a woman on a mission.*

The other two local Common members, still dressed in Guard uniforms, wait back at the SUV, engine running. The plan is to get Senator Gordon alone and then for Emery and me to convince him to leave with us on his own free will. If that doesn't happen, we'll move on to the backup plan: taking him by force, and convincing him later.

As Pawel and I stroll past the antique Looff Carrousel that's lit up magically in the balmy summer evening, I spot the senator on the bank of the Spokane River. He wears a cream tuxedo jacket with black slacks and bowtie, and the first thing I notice is his belly spilling over his matching off-white cummerbund. He's lived a comfortable life. *That's about to change.*

Standing alone—*where are his agents?*—the senator has his eyes glued to a tablet screen. He mouths words to himself, his free hand slicing through the air with emphasis, like he's memorizing something of grave importance. His predinner speech? He takes his nonjob that seriously?

"Ten o'clock," I say under my breath to Pawel.

We bypass the numerous circular white-clothed tables set with elaborate flowered centerpieces and head for the riverbank. Emery moves away from the clock tower, following ten yards behind. It's only when I get closer to the senator I realize how uncomfortable the man looks.

He's sweating and fidgety and appears almost as uneasy as I feel in my own suit.

I scan the riverbank one more time—still no agents. The perfect time for us to make our move; we might not get so clear a chance again. I double-check my headscarf, making sure it still conceals my telltale red hair.

My look tonight reminds me of an old-school movie star, glamorous red lips and all. It's the antithesis of who I have become: a girl with a gun strapped to her ankle, refusing to take direction from anyone.

I squeeze Pawel's hand. *Action.*

"Aeron, are you seeing this?" Pawel says softly beside me, calling me by my code name. He slows down and nods behind us at six o'clock. I follow his line of sight and discover two Washington State Guards—real ones—hurriedly setting up camera equipment in front of the small stage that's been constructed between the gardens and the circular tables.

Why would a senator's boring charity dinner speech be broadcast to the state's citizens? And why is the Guard in charge of the newscast? I've only ever seen them point tasers and guns at people—what is going on?

Then Pawel, Emery, and I freeze in unison. An additional half dozen State Guards fan out across the dinner party, guns held aggressively in their hands like they're expecting the dolled-up charity guests to fight back. *With what, their steak knives?* I snap my head back around to see two of the Guards escort Senator Gordon to the stage, practically at gunpoint.

A woman wearing a strapless pale-pink ball gown patterned in watercolor floral walks up to the podium on the stage. If the armed Guard's sudden presence has thrown her, she doesn't show it.

"Without further ado, I give you Washington State's own Senator Gordon," she intros to a round of what sounds like forced applause. The dinner guests are taking in the unforeseen development of the Guard's appearance like we are: with confusion and wariness.

The woman, who must be the director of the charity, is all but shoved off the stage by two agents in dark suits. A heavy, tension-filled silence follows as Senator Gordon is placed in front of the microphone, surrounded on all sides by his two agents and two State Guards.

Is the man about to make a coerced public confession?

Whatever happens, we need to adapt, fast. Pawel and I close ranks, moving closer to Emery.

Only pull out your gun if absolutely necessary, I remind myself. There are cameras now. The nation is watching.

Keep to the plan and don't break character.

"Good evening, ladies and gentlemen," Senator Gordon begins in a taut, toneless voice. He speaks directly to the camera, not to the in-person crowd gathered around the tables. "What a beautiful night here at Riverfront Park."

He pauses, as if savoring one last moment of peace. For a second, I don't think he's going to continue, but then the Guard on his left takes a threatening step closer. A warning. The senator takes a deep breath and grips the wooden podium, tight.

"While I'm here tonight to help raise money for the Washington State Heart Association, a very important cause impacting millions of Washingtonians' lives, Governor Elsen, our head of state, has asked me to read a prepared statement, which I will now do."

In concert all throughout the dinner party, tablets light up like mechanical fireflies, notifications flickering incessantly. Attention now glued to their screens, most of the dinner guests wear expressions of shock on their blue-lit faces.

What the hell is going on?

I try to move closer to steal a glance at a tablet, but Emery holds me back. She directs my attention once more to the senator, and I see that Barend has managed to slip his way onto the stage, one body away from our target. He's playing his part of Guard perfectly.

"Our country is under attack by a radical terrorist group," the senator continues with the governor's prepared statement. "State by state, the traitors are attempting to infiltrate the government by turning senators against their own country. They seek to divide us. We cannot let that happen. In direct response, Governor Roth of Texas has declared a state of emergency."

Our mission has been exposed. Instead of panic, the only emotion I feel is fury. My instincts held up a red flag of alert after Mira's and my capture at the Common's headquarters. Left alone in a cell, my inner voice spoke loud and clear. *Someone betrayed us!* But I didn't listen. I let myself be persuaded there was no betrayer among our own.

And now they betrayed us again.

My hands curl into fists.

"With the full approval of Governor Elsen, Governor Roth of Texas has taken temporary control of Washington State. The Texas Guard has come not only to our aid but to the aid of our fellow border states that are in grave crisis during this uncertain hour in our nation's history. Rest assured that you and your First Families are being protected."

Roth just made a power move I can't even begin to counter.

We're too late. Roth has already taken control of the country before he's officially been elected president.

My nails dig deep into my palms, a paltry attempt to keep my rage under control. How can I take down a monster whose tendrils just spread to almost half of the northern United States and in doing so has grown his power to a size nearly twice that of Texas?

You cut out its heart in Dallas.

I'm coming for you, Roth, and I want you to know it.

I think of the first word of protest I ever heard back in Dallas after a Guard arrested a woman over a stolen bottle of water. I stayed quiet then, conditioned into silence, but I won't now.

"Enough!" I shout at the senator. I pull off my silk headscarf and step into plain sight.

Gasps, from the party guests, from Pawel. Senator Gordon suspends his obligatory speech, and every head turns in my direction. Emery steps in front of me, blocking my famous face from view. But the spotlight's already on me. This is my moment; there's no more hiding.

"Stop being the mouthpiece of the governor, and start being the voice of the people," I demand of Senator Gordon.

Exclamations of "It's *her*," "It's one of the Goodwin twins," "Arrest her," spread into a chorus of hysteria. I feel a dozen gun barrels pointed at my chest. Barend has his gun out, too, but he can't protect me. No one truly can. The murder of my father—my greatest protector—taught me that.

The camera aims its eye directly at my exposed face. Live, for the people to see. For Roth to see.

Emery and Pawel place their hands on my shoulders, to show that they are with me. My vision is focused on the senator, but at the blurry edges I see bodies moving to stand around me. *The people are with me too.*

Shoot her! Roth must be screaming. But the choice isn't his to make—right now it's Senator Gordon's.

I've forced his hand: arrest me, shoot me, or join with us.

The senator stands on the stage, completely still, gripping hold of the podium like a lifeline, indecision clear on his face. His two agents ask him again and again for his orders.

One of the State Guards breaks rank and charges in my direction, her baton out and ready.

"Stand down!" Senator Gordon shouts into the microphone, his choice of rebellion echoing throughout Riverfront Park and beyond.

Those two words trigger a chain reaction: the two agents exchange bullets with the Guard now loyal to Roth, Barend grabs the senator and flees with him off stage, and Emery, Pawel, and I are all but carried into our getaway car by those dinner guests who just became rebellion members.

When I surge into the back seat of the shiny black State Guard SUV, our undercover driver finally understands whom she picked up at the border. "Holy crap, you're Ava Goodwin," she says, straightening up her uniform, staring at me wide-eyed from the rearview mirror. I wipe off my red lipstick with the back of my hand.

"Yes, I am," I say, proud of the fact.

Out of breath, Barend piles into the car along with our target, Senator Gordon, who sits in the front seat. "Drive!" Barend shouts.

As the car barrels into the night, Senator Gordon switches on the emergency lights and siren, warning everyone to *move out of our way*.

The senator of Washington State has just publicly joined the Common's side.

He has become one of the many.

MIRA

Whether I close my eyes or open them, it's completely dark. Pitch-black emptiness that makes me feel disoriented. Bodiless. A severed soul floating adrift in the endless void. The old nightmarish visions of hands gripping and pulling me take hold of my panicked mind. Cold fingers clamp down onto my right wrist, but before I cry out, I remember. It's Theo.

"Are you all right?" Theo's whispered voice reaches me in the dark.

I nod, realizing he can't see me. "Yes," I breathe.

No, I want to say. But I would never admit it, especially to him.

Ava messed up the plan. She revealed herself, and therefore exposed *me*. Now every Guard and traitor-hunter citizen will be on the lookout for the second sister. We're worth twice as much together. The reward for our capture is in the millions and rising by the day.

What was Ava thinking? Did she consider me at all? The odds that my team and I would successfully cross back into America were already monumentally low. Now it feels like a suicide mission.

I want to go back, turn around, and regroup. But it's too late.

We're already out at sea.

After Roth's unprecedented occupation of seven states and counting, we had to move fast. Ciro couldn't assemble his "abundant connections" in time, so our new plan was hastily made and heavily reliant on Alexander. He has the cargo ship, the contacts, the money, but he has zero of my trust. Why should we follow the designs of the spawn of Governor Roth, a twenty-first-century invader? But the decision was left to a vote, and I was outnumbered three to two.

Theo voted for me. That was unexpected. So was the quiet pull it gave my heart.

Stop it, I scold myself. Since our last meeting on dry land, I've made sure to send Theo numerous glares to let him—*and me*—understand just how I really feel about a Roth boy.

Alexander—of course. But Ciro and Kano voting against me? That stung like a slap in the face. Thinking everyone must do as I wish is governor-like and childish. Still, the sting has spread, burrowing deep into my memory, to be used later.

Someone leaked the Common's plan . . .

I make myself breathe and pop all ten of my knuckles.

My only assurance that Alexander won't betray us is my certainty that he would never put his son Theo into harm's way.

Keep your enemies close. A phrase to survive by. I'll never let Theo leave my side; if I'm placed in danger, Theo will be in danger. A fact Alexander must understand and loathe. He has no choice but to help see our mission through.

I readjust the pressure-point bands strapped to both my wrists. Three fingers down on my forearm, I locate the P6, the acupressure point, and make certain the bands are positioned just right to avoid seasickness. I feel sick anyway, from the toxic combination of worry and anger, and my inability to do anything about it. I'm trapped in a box, and the best thing I can do is stay quiet.

Of the whole crew, only the captain knows of our presence on the ship, the five of us smuggled below deck, concealed inside containers stuffed with illegal goods. Goods bound for the Black Market in the States.

I can't hear anything going on outside this coffin of a box. So I figure there's no way they could pick up a few brief whisperings inside here. I can't be left alone with my thoughts any longer. They keep drifting to Ava.

For the second time this week, I have no idea where she is. *If* she is. She's so selfish. *Don't go there,* I think.

Shifting my head, I feel Theo's breath on the tip of my nose. His mouth is inches from mine, which he must realize is too small a distance for us both, because his head whips upward to face the ceiling of our hidden compartment.

"Sorry," Theo murmurs. His left knee knocks against my ankle. He mutters another sorry, then goes still.

Do all Canadians apologize this much?

There's very little extra space to move around in here. His six-foot frame must be folded up in his desperation not to touch me. He must be miserable. *Good.*

"Did you know your father dealt in the Black Market?" I whisper, my tone a fraction harsher than I meant for it to be.

"No. I obviously didn't know my dad at all."

I remember some primary school lesson about glass houses and stones. My father kept an entire world from me. I know what it feels like to be shattered.

"What goods do you think are packed in here with us?" I whisper. "Fish?" I think of Canada's melted icecaps and their booming fishing industry. My mouth waters.

"If it were fish, we would most definitely smell it."

All I smell is the rich, woody vanilla of Theo's leftover cologne. I turn my head and let the conversation fall away.

I spend some time imagining that it's bottles of my favorite illegal whisky stacked above us. Japanese Nikka. The image brings back a wave of memories, flooding my mind with flashbacks of Ava and Strake and home.

I could use a drink. Hangover be damned.

"What's it like in America?" Theo interrupts my reverie, his soft breath tickling my ear like an annoying fly. "You know, since it's my birthplace . . . I figured I should start learning."

I shrug my shoulders, forgetting he can't see me. "You'll find out for yourself." No words can help him learn. He has to experience it to understand.

"Hey . . . ," Theo starts, but no words follow. A few minutes pass, and I think he fell asleep. But he stirs, his hot breath back on my skin. "I'm sorry for what my family did to yours."

"Okay" is all I say. I know he had nothing to do with the death of my mother and father, the fact that my sister and I were chased and exiled from our own country. But he's guilty by association. By blood.

With no warning at all, a loud *bang* sounds off above us, and my heart skips a beat.

"Mierda!" Theo curses under his breath in Spanish.

Our container suddenly lifts into the air, and so does my spirit. *It's happening. It's working.*

Calm down, I caution myself. *There's still plenty that could go wrong.*

"Halfway there," Theo whispers shakily, either to comfort me or himself.

"Do you always swear in Spanish?" I ask to keep my mind occupied.

"It's a habit I picked up when I was young," Theo answers. I hear the smile in his voice, like he has a thousand stories behind it.

"Does anyone even speak the language in Canada anymore?" I whisper.

"No. But my dad taught me anyway. Guess that should have been my first clue something was off . . ."

I didn't even feel the ship stop, but we must have arrived at our drop-off point. Somewhere out in the rough, open sea with no eyes to witness this clandestine trade.

If what *should* be happening *is* happening, then our containers of illegal wares are being transported to a second vessel.

A ship belonging to the Washington State Border Guard.

Corrupt Guards. My unlikely deliverers.

My stomach flips. My palms start sweating. I barely breathe, worried our Black Market buyers will hear me.

I try not to think about the crane, or whatever machine is transferring us, suddenly malfunctioning or purposely letting go its steel grip and releasing us into the ocean. I clench my fists, hold my breath—*like that would help*—and wait for the drop.

No, if they know I'm in here, that won't be how it ends. *They wouldn't waste such valuable goods.*

Slowly, I feel us being lowered and placed onto a firm surface. I anticipate shouts, our roof ripped off, guns pointing. But nothing happens. I let out my breath.

Theo's lips press against my ear. "It worked," he whispers. "We're moving."

A rush of adrenaline surges through me.

We're on our way toward American soil.

"How long do you think we've been in here?" Theo asks, the first time he's spoken in hours.

It feels like it's been days. I lift my watch directly against my face, trying to make out the time, but I can't see anything.

"Too long," I finally answer. I'm way past stir-crazy.

I wonder where we are. We're supposed to be in a warehouse on the outskirts of the port city of Tacoma, Washington. All I know for certain is the patrol ship docked, and we were unloaded onto a high-speed transport of some kind and finally dumped onto solid ground where we have remained stationary and quiet for an unknown amount of time.

"It's time to leave," I whisper, hoping I sound more calm and confident than I am.

I have to get out. My bladder stings, my stomach growls like a subterranean monster, and my patience has utterly snapped. My bones scream to move, to be let free from this claustrophobic box.

I try and breathe away my rising panic, but I'm filled with a sudden terror we've used up all the air.

"I have to get out," I say, more like shout.

We have to bust out of this coffin and deal with whoever or *whatever* is on the other side.

As I start to search out the best way how, the roof of our hiding space quivers and slides open. A burst of incandescent light forces my eyes shut in white-hot blindness. My hand dives for the gun inside my rucksack—*why don't I carry it on me?*—but before I can unholster the pistol, a familiar voice stops me.

"Good to know I'm not your only bodyguard," Kano says cheerily.

Peeling open my eyes, I see two thick arms shielding my face and chest. Theo quickly jerks his limbs back to his side of the box and pops up to stand before I can look at him, before I can remind him, *Hey,* I'm *the guard. I'm guarding* you.

"Easy, mijo. Go slow," Alexander says, appearing at his son's side. "You've had a long journey."

I scoff and get to my feet. *Try walking through the Texas desert.*

With wobbly legs, I climb from the box and shuffle out of the shipping container and into the cavernous warehouse. The large space is empty except for three other steel containers that make up our criminal cargo.

"Well, that was certainly an experience," Ciro says behind me. "Most uncomfortable." He stretches dramatically, walking like a day-old giraffe.

"At least you had your own box," I say. "That's first class in my view."

Shouldering my rucksack, I scan the walls for an exit.

"There are no washrooms in the building. I've already checked," Ciro says, appalled, misreading my desire for privacy. I roll my eyes. *This is going to be a very long journey for him.*

"We use the great outdoors," I inform him, looking at my watch. "Ten minutes before departure. We don't want to be here when the buyers show up."

"Let's get a move on!" Kano shouts, rallying the team.

It hurts to turn my neck, my muscles are too stiff, and I have to swivel my entire body to check up on the others. They're already repacking the crates, making it look like we were never here. I'm tempted to see if we had been traveling with whisky all along, but I don't. We can't linger.

The second I'm through the door, I think of Ava.

She's out here somewhere. We're in the same state. She could be only miles from me. I could try and find her. Save her from the Guard if I have to.

I've done it before with worse odds.

I stop my feet, which have unconsciously led me away from the warehouse. Away from my group and my mission, out toward wherever Ava might be.

No, I tell myself.

No matter what, we meet in Dallas. That's the plan. It's our best chance to find each other.

I can only hope the other teams have all turned south toward Texas. Our mission timeline was cut grievously short, but every hour, Roth gains more power to his side. It will soon become impossible to steal through state borders and execute our plan.

But we have to. We have to get to Dallas before Roth unites the country under his Lone Star.

Why did you do this to us, Ava? Was there really no other way? You've ruined our surprise attack, and now we're on the defensive. Like always.

It's overwhelming, knowing my sister is so near and might be in danger and I just have to let her go.

But my mission is too important to abandon. Theo is too important. *The people have to know.*

"I'll see you soon, Ava," I say aloud. It feels better to voice it. More real, like a renewed promise.

"We had the same idea," Theo says, startling me. "Finding some fresh air, I mean."

I didn't hear him approach. *I need to be more alert.*

"Stay inside," I tell Theo. It comes out like a command. "Your grandfather knows a Goodwin is in the area. Guards and Scent Hunters will be everywhere."

Maybe even his Texas State Guard.

"You're considered a Glut here. You'll be arrested on the spot."

"Oh. Right," Theo says. He backs closer to the door.

Tossing him my scent-eliminating spray, I throw up my hood and set off to find some privacy.

"Welcome to America."

OWEN

"Are we there yet?" I ask Blaise, my designated navigator. He has a ginormous paper map stretched out in front of him, the roads and towns of Colorado taking up half the car's windshield.

"No!" Blaise snaps. He's really on edge. "You asked me three minutes ago, and the answer is still no! You would fully know it if we crossed the border."

"Let's hope that's not true," Malik says from the back seat. "We *could* just cruise on through. I mean, this isn't even a real road. Why would the Guard waste resources way out here?"

"Because *way out here* is where you find people who don't want to be found," I say.

Let's hope I'm wrong. Whatever Blaise says—or doesn't say—we're close to Oklahoma. We have to be. The line of cars is speeding up.

On our dash south to the Colorado border, we've accumulated ten more vehicles, and I don't even know how many people. We form one long, single-file line, Rayla driving at the head, me at the tail. *The Common Cavalry.* It does have a nice zing to it.

Our operation's changed: It's Dallas or bust.

It's Operation Save the Rebellion.

Back at the safe house, Rayla asked who would follow her into Texas and protect the Common. Every one of us shouted, *I will!*

A top-secret mission is about to go down. We don't know the details yet, but I bet it involves Roth and the twins.

Yes, I could have stayed behind at the house and let others do the dirty work. But Rayla said the mission will change the country's future and every single American's life. Bullshit if I don't want a part in *that*. Owen Hart: a Cog in a broken machine no more.

Hey, I'm no Cadwell or Goodwin, but a Hart has to start somewhere.

I was lost for words—*and that's saying something*—when I watched the footage of Ava in Washington State. I was jealous—jealous of her renegade audacity, jealous of the spindly kid on her arm who got to be by her side while she told the nation enough is enough. I finally broke down and asked Rayla the guy's name. Pawel.

I'll give it to him: the guy looked good in a tux. I've never even worn one of those before. Whatever. Bet Pawel doesn't have a car like I do. Sure, I didn't *pay* for the luxury vehicle, but still.

Xavier flashes his brake lights in the car ahead of us. It's the signal to go dark. Whoops. *Focus, man.* I stab a button next to the steering wheel and cut my headlights.

"The border line is coming up," Blaise informs the car, voice muffled behind his bandana.

"You *think*?" I say.

It's a full moon and a clear night. The Guard can still see us if they're looking.

"Uh, guys, what's that?" Malik says, pointing to a speck in the dark sky. "It's coming at us crazy fast."

No need to take my eyes off the road to look; the car will look for me while I drive. "Duke, activate Identification Mode. Identify object approaching the vehicle's northwest, two hundred feet up."

Rayla isn't here to supervise—she wouldn't approve of us "awakening" the car to a few of its insanely awesome capabilities—but together

Blaise and I were able to program Duke to be untrackable. She'd approve of team building, right?

Beside me Blaise drops the map into his lap. "I don't need a car to tell me that we're in trouble," he says in a tone I don't care for.

"What do you mean, man?" I press, but he's turned mute, thoroughly spooked.

"Unable to identify object," Duke says in the low, gruff voice I programmed for him, styled after the classic John Wayne character. More than appropriate, I must say, given that we're riding through the Wild West just like he did in the old-time movies. Except we have cars, not horses. And our bad guys have Scream Guns.

"What the hell?" I say, frustrated. A Kismet car that's passed inspection should never fail an identification command.

What's worse, when I whip my head to the passenger's seat, I find Blaise in full-on freak-out mode. Well, *that's* an emotional response I've never seen from him before. Not good.

"Blaise, what is it?" I find myself shouting, rattled by the Prince of Flames losing his nerve.

"That's a Killer Drone!"

"What?!"

One of the vehicles in the front shines a spotlight that's attached to their roof on the flying object, now only fifty feet away.

Yep. It's a drone all right. A fully autonomous weapon that hunts down targets and kills them without any human supervision required. They're supposed to be illegal, but it's crystal damn clear that rules don't apply to Roth.

Using its six propeller motors to deftly position itself above the head of our Cavalry, it opens fire.

"Fuuuuuuuck!" Blaise and Malik scream at the same time.

Bullets light up the night sky like firecrackers. The autonomous gun targets all forty-plus cars in one fell swoop—its three-axis gimbal stabilizer making sure the killer robot's aim is dead accurate despite the fact that Rayla has led the Cavalry into driving a zigzag pattern. I weave right then left, following the car captained by Xavier in front of me.

Bam, bam, bam! A round of gunfire blasts the roof of our car. "Don't worry!" I shout at my screaming passengers. "Duke's bulletproof!"

Duke is one of Kismet's elite models that hasn't hit the market yet. Fully armored, made for extremely wealthy and robbery-prone business CEOs who can afford its four-hundred-thousand-dollar price tag. It looks like an average luxury vehicle, but it's really a mobile fortress. Loaded with bullet-resistant tinted glass windows and a six-piece, high-strength steel body, fastened with heavy-duty run-flat tires, the car was designed to withstand the high-velocity incendiary bullets that we're being attacked with right now. Hell, Duke could survive a thirty-three-pound TNT explosion. We've got this.

But not all the Cavalry has such protection.

The Killer Drone rips into the older-model cars, busting through windows and blowing out tires. One of them spins out of control in a plume of smoke—I see it all happen in slow motion—and I have to swerve quickly to avoid a collision. *Are we taking casualties?*

Shit just got very real.

"That was *way* too close!" Blaise howls beside me.

A truck in the middle of our pack skids into a hard U-turn—the designated medic to help retrieve fallen members.

Half the Common has already begun to return fire, but the drone is still winning. It's bulletproof, just like Duke. *So how do we take the thing down?*

In answer, Xavier pops out of his car window—someone else must have taken the wheel. He shoots what looks like an extra-large pistol into the air, and a wide net launches from the barrel. The snare almost wraps around the drone but narrowly misses.

My stomach drops.

Blaise places the gun Rayla gave me into my lap. "We have to join the fight," he says, dramatically cocking his own gun. "There has to be a weak point somewhere."

But Duke's gone into Lockdown Mode, making all windows and doors inoperable. I'm on the verge of informing Blaise of this hiccup in his heroic plan when Malik yells from the back seat.

"There's another one coming from behind!"

From the rearview mirror I see a second Killer Drone approach, twice the size of the first. *This one's loaded with bombs.*

"Malik, how many more net guns does your dad have?" I shout, trying hard to remain calm.

"One . . . He gave the third to me," Malik answers.

Okay, so we can't miss again. Great odds.

A loud *bang* yanks my attention back to the front—Xavier has fired off his second net gun. Blaise grabs hold of my arm, and all three of us watch in gut-wrenching silence as the snare rockets through the black sky and wraps itself around the drone, entangling its six propeller blades. For a horrifying moment, it looks like the killer robot will soldier on, but then it sputters and crashes to the ground.

"Yeah, Dad!" Malik whoops.

Blaise lets go of me and fist pumps in victory. I dance my palms across the steering wheel.

Our celebrations are short-lived because the second drone just unloaded a bomb from its belly, obliterating the road a quarter of a mile ahead.

The Common's line breaks, splitting off into two opposite directions to cut around the massive hole blasted into the earth. I make a quick, tight left turn and drive full throttle into the dried-up field, hoping to stay within sight of Xavier's car ahead of us, but tornadoes of dirt kicked up by speeding tires makes that wishful thinking. I can't see a thing. *Well, this is dangerous.*

"Duke, activate Clarity Windshield Mode," I say.

Instantly, the entire front window projects what the laser imaging camera at the front of the car sees: a clear path. Flames, fog, dust, this model can see through it all. Even at night.

At least that *feature still works.*

"All right, that's cool," Malik says in awe from the back seat.

Then in one of the greatest pee-my-pants moments of my life, a graphic of a skull that wears a pilot's cap and goggles and has two black pits for eyes grins horrifyingly at us across every inch of the five-by-three windshield. Its teeth are painted the red, white, and blue of the Lone Star flag of Texas.

"Ahhhh!" we all scream our heads off.

The car's camera adjusts, zooms out, and regains focus, revealing the whole body of the Killer Drone. The skull is just a sticker on its front, put there by a sadistic Guard to mess with us. *It's working!*

The drone flies backward as we race forward, staring us down like we're in a standoff.

The autonomous gun draws first.

Bam, bam, bam! A volley of bullets ricochets off the front of the car. Then another round, and another, penetrating all four tires.

"We've got to take it down!" Blaise yells over the racket. "We have the last net gun."

Surprising myself, I know exactly what to do. But can we pull it off? *Put up or shut up, noob.*

"Okay, buckle up, *now!*" I call out, snapping my own into place.

Here's to hoping for the best.

I slam on the brake pedal, and it bucks wildly under my foot. *Don't let go. That just means the brakes are doing their job.* To stabilize my body, I brace my left foot against the footrest—just like the Internet told me to do when I searched "how to drive a car"—and gently turn the wheel to keep us from spinning out of control. As the car's speed tapers off, I ease the brakes.

Ninety-five miles per hour to a full stop in three seconds.

I don't think I've ever felt more alive.

"Duke, initiate Power-Down Mode," I say, euphoria pumping through my body.

The car shuts down completely—a crazy gamble we have to take to get the locked-down sky roof open.

"Blaise and I will cover you, Malik!" I say, double-quick.

I point to the roof. They nod, understanding my plan.

The dust settles, and it's go time.

Gripping the cold metal of my gun, I cock it just like I saw Blaise do and then manually slide open the roof's glass window. Together, the three of us burst out, screaming bloody murder.

Blaise and I open fire, standing on our seats, defending Malik's flanks, unsure which direction the drone will attack from. *Does the thing have an invisibility mode or what?*

And then I see it.

Thwap! Thwap! Thwap! Needles hail down from the sky, stabbing into the roof of the car all around us. *Tranquilizers.*

The drone's changed tactics. It's not shooting to kill. It's shooting to take us prisoner.

That somehow feels even more terrifying.

"Malik, eleven o'clock! Shoot!" I shout, but he's not beside me anymore. *Where the hell did he go?*

He's fallen back into the car with a dart hanging from his neck. The net gun rests useless on his passed-out face.

Not good.

"Keep shooting!" I scream to Blaise, diving for the gun. It's heavy, and I have no idea how to use it, but it's try or die.

Stop shaking! I yell at my hands. Right when I pop my head out the sky roof, Blaise shouts, "On your left, *get it!*"

There's no time to hesitate. I aim and fire. The net unfurls like a spiderweb, blasting into the night sky with a force that knocks me backward. *That felt good.* My adrenaline's through the roof, and I watch supercharged as the Killer Drone's ten propeller blades are trapped inside the netting. It struggles like a caught fly, then plummets into the field, where it goes dark.

Did that just happen?

Blaise lets out an incoherent holler, and we both jump into a midair hug. It's kind of like hugging a lukewarm corpse, but I roll with it—emotions are high. Then we remember our friendship is contingent on us despising one another, so we drop back into the car and into our seats like nothing happened.

I turn the car back on and hit the accelerator, gunning east, where I last saw the Cavalry. Punching on my car's low beams, I weave expertly around random plant things and pesky pits in the ground without sacrificing any speed.

Eventually the road finds us. We veer south again, Blaise and I not saying a word until we see the string of dusty red taillights of our rebel troop.

My heart actually leaps when I pull back into position behind Xavier's car. For a moment there, I thought I'd be stranded with Blaise and a zonked-out Malik. We kicked ass back there, sure, but who knows what else is waiting for us. Monsters relish the dark.

"How's Malik?" I ask, unwilling to take my sights off the road.

"Breathing," Blaise answers, sparing a glance behind him. He seems reluctant to take his eyes from the windows too.

Up ahead, a beat-up retroreflective sign tells us, "Welcome to Oklahoma." Blaise reads the tiny print below. "Labor conquers all things."

"Is that state motto supposed to be encouraging?" I ask, dumbfounded. True, labor has conquered the American spirit. Work or die, basically. But to advertise that?

"It was meant to make migrants believe human labor can overpower anything," Blaise says, suddenly insightful.

We stare at the uncultivated, unpopulated land.

"Doesn't seem to have worked."

The only thing that's been conquered here is people.

But not us, I give myself a little pep talk. A short stint through the Oklahoma panhandle, and then we're into the panhandle of Texas.

"We'll be in Texas in forty-five minutes," Blaise calculates from the map.

"Okay," I say. "Okay, we're okay. The run-flat tires will hold out."

Another pep talk.

Blaise secures his seat belt, then swivels his chair to face the rear windshield. He's the new watchman.

"Nothing?" I ask.

"Nothing."

I strap myself in as well. Forty-four minutes to prepare for the next border crossing. I'll need every second to recover my wits.

Of course, what little Zen I had going gets blown to bits.

"Headlights!" Blaise yells.

I give three quick flashes to warn the others, and then I kill my own car lights. The Cavalry charges forward, hitting eighty miles per hour on the shoddy dirt road.

"How long until they're on us?" I say.

"Holy devil, they're coming up quick!" Blaise shrieks at me. He gets his gun ready. "Tell me again why we offered to be the tail car?"

What do we do? What do we do? We only have one shooter and one driver. Against what?

"It's definitely a Texas Guard SUV," Blaise confirms.

"Malik!" I shout, reaching back to shake his knee. "Malik, now's a good time to wake up, man! We need you!"

Nothing.

Yep, we're going to be the sacrificial lamb for slaughter.

Just when I think it's over for us, I hear the roar of a motorcycle.

"Rayla!" I shout. Straddling an antique Triumph, Rayla zooms past our car, straight for the incoming SUV. She doesn't wear a helmet; the motorcycle's headlamp is aimed toward the handlebars, lighting up her face.

She wants the Guard to know it's her. America's top wanted. She's luring them to chase her, and not her Cavalry.

"No!" I yell, easing off the gas. "We have to help her!"

"No!" Blaise screams back at me, grabbing hold of my arm, making sure I don't turn the wheel. "Never veer from the mission! Rayla knows what she's doing!"

I look through my mirrors. She's almost on them—she's so small, a tiny firefly about to be swallowed by a nighthawk.

There's no way I'll let her face them on her own.

Before I can take action, Blaise lunges for the controls and punches on the autonomous system.

"Rayla told me not to let you do anything stupid!"

I try to fight him off, but he has twenty pounds on me.

He also has a tranquilizer in his hand. *Where the hell did he get that?! Backstabber!* Literally.

The needle pokes into my upper back, and it *stings*. "Sorry, not sorry," Blaise jeers.

"Bullshit—" is the last word I think before it's . . .

Lights out.

ZEE

That's what a screen on a tall building says. The sky is still so dark I can't tell the time. Does the sun ever make it through the buildings here? Skyscrapers, somebody called them.

Civilians in the capital work early and late. Just like Inmates at the Camps. I blend in with ease, walking the paths. Looking for a way in.

I've been at this for twelve hours. Up and down the walkways on every side of the mansion. Nothing to show for my work.

Governor Roth's house is bigger than every Camp Warden's house times two. A twenty-foot wall circles it like the gates I'm used to. His is see-through. Made from a material I've never come across. It doesn't look like a Common vehicle could break it open.

The general is still in there. General Pierce.

Guards are everywhere. Guns. Drones.

"No stopping!" an electronic voice shouts. "No stopping! Move, move!"

There are more voices coming from the skyscrapers. From the screens, videos playing announcements. Citizens cheer. A woman next to me spits on the ground.

I try to listen. Understand. Learn anything new.

"Presidential nominee Governor Howard Roth hailed as the nation's savior—"

". . . inspires citizens everywhere to stand up against the greatest threat to the US since the Great Water Wars—"

". . . Texas leads the fight to save the country—"

The Wardens told us that Texas was the country. There are more states? How many? Are they all on Governor Roth's side?

One voice on a screen says Ava's back inside the US. She could be headed here. Mira isn't with her; the twins have separated. I don't like that. It feels wrong.

I was separated from my twin. Why?

Governor Roth.

He's outside. General Pierce is with him. They walk a path ten feet from his mansion. Thirty feet from his wall.

"He's come out to greet us!" a man shouts. A handful of civilians run to the wall. They wave. Scream, *"President Roth!"*

"Stay back!" a Guard shouts.

Two shots go off. It comes from the crowd. They're aimed for Roth, but the bullets bounce off the see-through wall. They land in the backs of two Guards.

Roth didn't cower even for one second. He keeps walking. He feels safe. No one can touch him.

The Guards respond with their own gunfire. The screams cover up the voices on the skyscrapers.

We will all receive punishment for those two bullets. That's the way it works. Even on the outside.

We have to be taught a lesson.

"On the ground, now! Wrists up!" the Guards shout.

Canisters are thrown into the air, chemicals spread across walkways. Women and men fall to the ground, coughing. They protect their faces with hands and shirts.

"I can't breathe!"

"Present your wrists to be scanned!"

The chemicals burn my eyes and throat. But I've felt this pain before. I run.

Behind me, the Guard charges into the civilians. Fully geared. Guns firing. I hear them arrest every civilian in their path.

5:16 a.m.

I get to the back of the mansion. The screams have followed me. The Guards will get many points this morning.

Find a way in. The time is now.

I see a woman on the other side of the see-through wall a short distance away. A small bag hangs from her arm. She wears strange clothes, as many Dallas women do. Shoes with pointed heels. A long black shirt to her knees. It fits tight against her body. How can she run in that?

She can't. She drops to the ground. Crawls to the wall. She's scared.

I watch her make it to the base of the barrier. She presses her hand against the wall. A small hole opens.

A way in. I step forward.

But the entrance closes on the woman's legs. She's trapped. She gives cries of pain and continues to struggle. She wants out.

Who is this woman? An Inmate escaping a prison?

The woman in black fights herself free.

She runs into the capital's streets, barefoot. She holds on to a hat that hides her face.

The hole closed up again. I need the woman to open it.

It takes me three minutes to find her. Fear is making her move quick. But she's surrounded. In the middle of a main street. Not by Guards, but civilians. Angry civilians.

"It's the First Lady!"

"Mrs. Roth! Get her!"

The First Lady of Texas? This must be Governor Roth's wife.

I need to get to her first. I push my way to the front of the circle. The First Lady is on her knees.

A woman my age steps forward. Slaps the First Lady's hat from her head. "You should be mourning for our country, not your dead grandson!" She lifts her right shirtsleeve. A tattoo. The Common's mark.

"See this? The Common is taking over Dallas. You don't rule here anymore." The woman kicks the First Lady in the chest. She falls to the ground.

Claps. More shouts of "Get her!"

Three civilians grab her arms and neck. Bring her to her feet. I give her an eighty-five-percent chance of dying before I can get to her.

"Take my jewelry!" the First Lady begs. "Take my jewelry and let me go, please . . ." She can't break free of their hold.

Begging never saved Inmates in the Camps.

It doesn't on the outside either. The civilians laugh.

"Your money will not save you," a man says. He takes the jewelry and throws it into the street. He pulls out a knife.

A percentage of me wants to help the First Lady. She cries like an Inmate about to be sent to the Gulf.

But this woman is with Governor Roth. The Roths are the Wardens of Texas. The Camps stay open because of them. They let women and men die. Break up families.

This woman had the power to stop it. But she chose not to.

"The First Lady is mine," I say. I charge forward. Stop when an electronic voice shouts from speakers overhead. All across the capital. As loud as a Scream Gun.

"Mandatory curfew! Return immediately to your residence, or you will be arrested!"

Half the civilians take off. The First Lady uses the distraction to free her arm and tear open her bag. She takes out a gun. A Guard's gun. She came prepared.

"Stay away, or I'll shoot!" she says. Her grip is firm. This is not her first time holding a weapon.

The First Lady turns a full circle, pointing the gun at everybody. Stops on me. "Get away from me!" she shouts. She pushes her hair out of her face.

Up close, she looks nothing like her portraits. Now she looks worn. Sad.

Desperate.

She smells like she hasn't bathed in days.

The gun clicks.

"Get away!" she shouts. "Get away from me!"

The rest of the crowd breaks up, runs from danger.

I don't run.

It's the First Lady and me, alone on the street.

"Don't make me shoot you . . . I'll do it," Mrs. Roth says. She's begging again. I pull off my hood, put up my hands.

Pretend to submit.

"Mandatory curfew! Return immediately to your residence, or you will be arrested!"

We both stand where we are. She looks me over.

The First Lady's eyes go wide.

"Lynn . . . ?" she whispers. "Lynn . . . you're alive?"

The gun drops to her side.

My twin. She knew her?

"Yes," I lie. It doesn't come easy. CGs knew if you lied.

"Darren hid you too?" the First Lady asks.

"Yes," I lie again.

She looks scared. Shakes like the starved cats that would sometimes find their way into the Camps. Before the CGs got points out of them.

She breaks down and cries. I feel nothing for her.

The kittens always die. It's the way life has to be.

But I need her to get to the governor. I will keep her alive.

A siren sounds. The Guard is coming.

"I can't go back there," Mrs. Roth cries. "I don't know what to do . . . He took them . . . He took them all."

"Who did he take?" I ask.

"Halton . . . Alexander."

Two names I don't recognize. Who are they?

"I know where to hide," I say. A safe house. Cleo told me to find a yellow door. "Come with me."

She follows Lynn.

She has no idea I'm a twin. An enemy of the state. Her state.

But she will.

AVA

I wake with a start, the harsh cry of an albatross screaming in my mind. My head slams back against the wall, and instead of seeing stars, I see long-winged birds in flight.

Tucked away in my corner refuge on the cement floor, my map draped across my chest, I open my eyes to see nothing has changed inside the safe house cellar since I finally lost the battle against sleep. I fought it as long as I could, but my body demanded rest, and the long hours we've spent waiting for our plane to arrive have been maddeningly endless and uneventful.

With no communication out or in, I can do nothing but sit tight and think while the repercussions of my actions unfold without me.

Mira, please be safe. Mira, I'm sorry if I was too reckless this time. I'm just so angry, sister.

Nobody on my team trusts me anymore. They won't say it to my face, but when I scan the room—Emery, Barend, Senator Gordon, even Pawel—none of them can look me in the eye. No one has spoken to me either since we entered our underground hideout well over twelve hours ago. I'm being shunned.

> Ah! well a-day! what evil looks
> Had I from old and young!

> Instead of the cross, the Albatross
> About my neck was hung.

The verse pops into my head unbidden. Then my heart begins to race. *Project Albatross.*

Why didn't I remember this before? Father reading aloud "The Rime of the Ancient Mariner" every night in the basement for an entire month freshman year. It became an after-dinner family ritual. Mira practically memorized the entire epic poem.

As I look back now, it's like he was trying to tell us something. Or maybe that's around the time he began his work on the "twin gene" therapy. *Was he admitting his guilt to us?*

I filter through my memories, searching for clues or hidden meanings.

Out on the open sea, being followed by an albatross was considered a sign of good luck—an omen for fair winds ahead. But killing an albatross results in a curse. In the poem, a sailor shoots an albatross with a crossbow, cursing the ship. The crew makes the man wear the dead bird across his neck, to be carried as penance.

It's a metaphor for the burdens we all have to bear.

Were your secret twin daughters your curse, Father, and Project Albatross your penance?

Or was it the other way around?

I wish Mira were here with me. Between the two of us, she was always more of the reader. She could help me sift through the poem and comb out any meaning about our father's mysterious project. *If there is any meaning to be found.*

Mira's not here, but Senator Gordon is.

He sits across the room with Emery, their heads bent close together, strategizing in hushed voices how best to capitalize on his public induction to the Common's side. Now that Roth is invading individual states, it's paramount that our side flips as many senators as we can before Roth takes hold of the entire country.

Having Washington State's influential senator join with us is a huge get for the Common. Mira and I are the face of the rebellion to America's citizens, but Gordon will be the face of the government. *I hope he's ready.*

I completed half of my mission—Senator Gordon of Washington State is crossed off my list. Even if my team is angry with how I accomplished it, my spur-of-the-moment move got us what we came here for. Now I want the other objective *I* came here for: information.

But now is not the time. Our safe house is a tiny wine cellar stuffed with people and unspoken tension. There's no space for a private conversation. I need to wait for the right moment—I'll only have one shot.

To pass the time, I spread my map out across the cold floor. Placing my finger on the spot where I am now in eastern Washington, I trace the route to Dallas.

I close my eyes and visualize myself inside the senator's airplane, cutting across the distance at six hundred miles per hour. By then, all the teams have made it to the Last Stage safe house, and when I open the big yellow door, Mira and Rayla are there to greet me.

We're still here. Stuck in a cellar, completely useless to the Common. The senator's plane should've arrived by now—something must have gone wrong.

Senator Gordon feels it too. He's been pacing in small, anxious circles for the last hour. Branded traitors by association, his wife and teenage daughter are in danger from the Texas Guard and need the Common's protection. His agent had orders to retrieve the senator's family and bring them here.

They haven't arrived yet either.

I know he blames me. Brow furrowed, the underarms of his tuxedo shirt stained with sweat, he glares at me every so often. It was I who forced his hand; I put his family in harm's way.

And I'd do it again if I had to. Every family must make sacrifices for the cause. Mine has made plenty.

Screw it.

I've waited long enough—there is no right moment.

Senator Gordon sits on the only real chair in the cellar—the rest are metal fold outs—surrounded by cases of wine. His head leans back against the 3D-papered wall that mimics exposed red brick. He's asleep.

I rise from my corner and make my move. Scanning the room, I find everyone sleeping, except Barend. On guard, as always. Secrets don't last forever—I know that just as well as anyone—but I'd like to keep this one close as long as possible. For my father's sake.

Tread carefully.

The senator's face twists with fear, eyes moving rapidly underneath their lids. He's afraid, even in his sleep. *Dreaming of what's to come.* It seems almost like a mercy to wake him.

I sit on a wine case to his right, facing him. Calmly, I whisper near his ear, "Senator." To his credit, he wakes at once, self-possessed and ready for action. Clearly habits from his past life as a doctor.

He turns to face me. If he's surprised, he doesn't show it. I get right down to business.

"You knew my father, Darren Goodwin," I say softly. I flick my eyes over to Barend, who pretends he's not listening, but I know he is. Or at least he's trying. It's part of his job description.

The senator narrows his eyes. "I wouldn't say I knew him, no," he answers. Not a great start.

I try again, keeping my voice to a whisper. "You were the Director of the Family Planning Division for your state at the same time as my father. Did you ever consult with one another about your . . . duties?" I ask. He looks at me puzzled, as if to say, *Is this really the time to be talking about such matters?*

Just ask him what you came here for.

"Project Albatross," I say, looking him square in the eye. "What do you know about the secret gene therapy?"

The senator's confusion melts into disappointment. "Darren went through with the trial, then," he says. "You wouldn't be asking otherwise."

It's true. Roth really is researching how to stop Multiple pregnancies.

"I know my father reached the human trial phase—was it successful?" I ask. "Has the gene therapy been put into practice?" I don't want to hear the answer—I don't want my father to break what's left of my heart—but I came all this way. I have to know.

The senator places his hand over mine. There's pity in his eyes. "If the 'twin gene' therapy has already begun, it would be very difficult to stop, I'm afraid."

His words hit me like a whip of fire, and I pull back fast, sending a case of wine crashing to the floor. The noise pulls everyone in the room to their feet, and they stare at Senator Gordon and me in alarm.

You're wrong! I want to shout at him, but at that moment, the door bangs open at the top of the stairs.

"Daddy!"

A girl, maybe thirteen, barrels down the steps and into the senator's arms. She has an academy uniform on, like she was pulled out of school. A plain navy blazer and slacks, no color-coded sashes displaying rank, like at Strake. She holds on to her father tight.

I have to look away.

The senator's agent and a tall, thin woman who must be Gordon's wife rush through the door. She locks the dead bolt behind her before hastening to join her family at the base of the stairs.

Emery emerges at my side. "Any news?" she asks the agent.

The agent—he looks like he hasn't stopped moving since we left him at the charity dinner—addresses the senator, his voice quick and severe.

"Sir, the senators from Michigan, North California, and Oregon have followed your lead and have publicly backed the Common."

"And New York?" Emery presses.

"Reports say Senator Riggs and the Common's representative Skye Lin have been killed by Governor Cole's Guard. The governor just delivered a speech rallying her citizens against the traitors."

Shock breaks out across the cellar. I swallow my scream. *We all knew the risks.*

"The Texas Guard has now invaded more than just the northern border states," the agent says, extending the bad news. "North California and Colorado have been confirmed." *Rayla.*

"Is the transport plane still coming?" I ask, my throat sore from holding back my emotion.

The agent shakes his head. "The Guards loyal to Senator Gordon are working on it."

The uncertainty of our situation compounded with the happy family reunion right in front of my face is too much.

I have to get out of here. *Now.*

I change back into my Blackout Wear in the cramped bathroom, then sit down on the lid of the toilet to think.

Ever since I was a child, I've sought out bathrooms in times of crisis. At school, the stalls were a place I could find privacy, a momentary escape. At home, I used to skip out on my daily showers to lie on the bathroom floor with my eyes closed and listen to the water stream down onto the glossy porcelain tile, the room filling with steam. I realize now how incredibly privileged I was to be able to waste water like that, even if it was recycled.

There's no running water in this bathroom—I checked—but still I've managed to find a small sanctuary. It's the one place I can find almost anywhere where I can rest from all the eyes watching me. School, home, safe houses . . .

My knees pressed up tight against the sink, I open the pocket-sized notebook I found zipped in a plastic baggie floating inside the toilet's tank.

It's a list of names. Pages and pages of names.

An archive of every person who has sought shelter inside these cellar walls. *This is a station stop on the underground byway to Canada.* Like the cowboy Kipling's ranch in west Texas.

He had a notebook just like this one.

I find myself scanning the unfamiliar names, line by line, as if I might recognize one. *Lucía wasn't here. Stop being foolish.*

About halfway through page fifteen I stop. "Ariadne Black: mother of Cooper, Noah, and Ruby." There's a strange mark at the end of the entry, an interlocking triple spiral.

My heart drops. Ariadne was hiding triplets. Much, much rarer than twins. *My god.*

Was the woman still pregnant, or were her illegal Multiples already born? Either way, the Blacks never made it over the border wall—I would have seen or heard of the unusual family at the Common's headquarters. Ariadne was probably arrested, years before my time.

Anger fills the empty space inside my chest.

Multiples are not a curse. We shouldn't have to hide, and our genetics shouldn't be eradicated from humanity's DNA.

I will stop my father's "twin gene" therapy before it starts. If it's already begun, I'll reverse it. Somehow.

Hot tears fill my eyes, dripping onto the yellowed paper. I let them come, symbols of strength and love.

I flip through the notebook to find the last entry and grab the pen inside a pouch attached to the spine.

"Ava Goodwin, sister of Mira," I write in my careful, cramped handwriting, so like my father's. At the end of my entry, I draw the infinity symbol, two oblong circles forming one knot.

Mira, I hope I'm not too late.

I hope she's found what she was looking for in Alexander, because we need a secret weapon now more than ever.

MIRA

Our transport is nowhere to be seen. Technically, we're forty-eight hours *early* for our scheduled pick-up, but still. After Roth's invasions and Ava's unmasking in front of a live national audience, I figured the Common would be here.

They're not. It's just the five of us, stashed away in a safe house ten miles from Tacoma with no plausible way out.

It's too dangerous to stay. It's too dangerous to leave.

"We can't just sit here," I reason for the third time. Kano shakes his head, but I keep going. "If we linger, sooner than later, the Texas Guard will find us. They're combing the entire state, searching for Ava."

I stand, looking each of them in the eye. Alexander turns away, his brow as wrinkled as his overpriced clothes. He looks like a man who's already given up.

"But if we move," I press, "we have a chance. It's small, but it's better than waiting here for Roth to catch us."

"I vote we move," Theo says, rising from the unfinished maple farm table, resting his weight on his fists.

"You're not a Common member," Kano snaps. His usual sleek topknot hangs loose and messy on the back of his neck. Chunks of silken strands fall across his eyes, giving the normally playful warrior a surly look. "You don't get a vote. Sit down."

Theo shrinks and plops back onto the bench.

"You don't have to do what Kano tells you, mijo," Alexander asserts in his clipped tone, reaching for Theo's shoulder.

"It's fine," Theo says brusquely, shrugging his father's hand away. He throws a fleeting glance in my direction.

Theo's cheeks flush in splotches, a deep red burning across his skin. The image is so like his half brother's my stomach flips, and I'm caught in a memory. I'm trapped inside my old house, my last night in Dallas. Around our dining table are the three Roths: the governor, Mrs. Roth, and Halton. Halton's tucking me into my chair, his cheeks stained with a flush of embarrassment and unvented wrath.

It was the night fate came for me.

I blink away the flashback, but I can't shake the sense that disaster is on its way. Squeezing my palm over the steel rings of my knife's handle, I move over to the window.

"The best course of action is to stay put," Kano argues. "Rescue missions are most effective when you remain in one spot. The Common knows we're here. They will come."

With a cautious touch, I brush aside the dented blinds and press an eye to the glass.

We're on a hill. I can make out the long dirt road that snakes its way down for a quarter mile. It's clear, unlike the sky, which is heavy with the threat of rain.

According to the map, we should be able to see the soaring peak of Mount Rainier. With an elevation of over fourteen thousand feet, the mountain is invisible through the clouds.

What else is out there that I can't see?

"Others have changed our plans, and now we must adjust," I say, turning back to the table. "Our transport won't make it here. I know you believe that too. We have to keep moving."

Always, forever, move. The mantra that powered me from Texas to Canada.

"How do we move?" Kano asks, propping his elbows on the chipped tabletop. His gun has never left his hand. "The Guard has taken over the rail stations, and none of us here has the skill to hijack an autonomous car, even if there *was* one within a four-mile radius."

I step forward and open my mouth to speak, but Kano stops me with an upraised hand.

"If you're suggesting walking, we might as well skip right into the Guard's arms, because we'd have an hour tops before a drone would detect us—"

"The Blackout Wear will work!" I insist.

"And the Scent Hunters? There's too many of us to go unnoticed—"

"We can split up," I shout over him. "You take Alexander and Ciro. I'll take Theo."

The suggestion's met with a resounding no. But I hear one yes in the corner. Theo.

I rake my oily bangs from my face and rush toward my rucksack like the decision has been made. "If one of our groups makes it to Dallas, we can still complete our mission. With either Alexander or Theo, we can expose the truth and win."

Alexander pops up from the bench and throws his body against the jerry-built yellow door. The three stacked dead bolt locks seem to be the only things holding the rickety door up—the only protection between us and *them*. When I step closer I discern names carved on the decaying wood. Faded names of Gluts and runaways long gone. Alexander pulls my attention back to him.

"You will take my son over my lifeless body," he fumes, staring me down. His spittle lands on my nose. "Two kids cannot take on the Texas Guard."

"I'm not a kid!" Theo screams.

"I've done it before," I inform Alexander, my voice firm and unshakable.

Theo throws on his overstuffed backpack and storms toward me.

"Theo, *sit down!*"

"No! We're moving. We can't hide from what has to be done!"

Kano grabs Theo by his backpack and makes him sit. "There will be no rash decisions."

Like Ava's rash decision last night? No, this is different. I've thought this through. Ava didn't.

"Unless our benefactor here has a helicopter on standby that I'm unaware of . . . ," Kano says, jolting me back, prompting all our necks to turn toward Ciro for the first time in hours.

Ciro sits sunken at the head of the table, his face buried in his trembling hands. On our desperate trek to the safe house, with every mile, more and more of his spunk and superiority drained from his jaunty spirit. Fear has its claws in him.

Buck up, I want to yell at him. *You offered yourself up to this.*

Almost imperceptibly, Ciro shakes his head.

"Didn't think so," Kano continues. "And unless Ciro's money can buy us all wings . . ."—Ciro doesn't even respond to this jab—"then we are staying put."

"We're *staying,*" Alexander has the gall to reiterate.

I did what I was told for eighteen years of my life. No more.

I stand on the tips of my toes, getting as close to Alexander's face as I can. He shifts, uncomfortable with our nearness, but I won't let him turn away. I bet he can feel my pain, my strength of will. I can hear his alarm, sense his panic. I won't let it spread to me. Or Theo. Theo can't second-guess what he's doing; he needs to be prepared for what's to come. He needs to believe our plan is possible.

I need him to stay on my side.

My eyes narrow into slits, and I glare daggers into Alexander's black, rayless eyes. "I'm not scared of your father," I tell him, willing my voice not to falter.

"I'm not so sure," Alexander whispers so only I can hear. "Fear is healthy, Mira. Fear keeps you alive."

"You'd like to keep me scared, wouldn't you?"

Alexander's lips twist into a sour grimace. I turn away, unable to look at him any longer.

"Take away his soldiers and toys, and the governor's just like you or me," I snap back, loud enough for Theo and Ciro to hear. "Flesh and bone and vulnerable."

"Yes, but you have to get *through* his soldiers and armaments before you reach the mortal man," Alexander presses.

Arguing is useless. Words are useless. Actions are all that matter.

I head back to the window, looking to plot the best escape route. Theo joins me, the straps of his pack fastened over his chest like he's ready to go at my command.

"This is complete crap; we need to move," Theo whispers hotly. The way he stares at me warms my cold fear.

We can do this. We just have to get out of this house. I mentally list all the supplies in my bag, calculating if it's enough to last us until Dallas.

"Did you pack a weapon?" I ask under my breath. Ciro's watching. They're all watching.

"No," he says, embarrassed. "I didn't have something like that to bring."

Why would he? His life didn't require a blade until now.

Dipping my hand into my pocket, I grip my trusted knife and hand it to Theo. "My father gave me this. Take it," I whisper. "You'll need it."

Startled, Theo grabs it, shielding the offering from the others with his body. He slides his fingers through the four rings of the knife's handle. It's a bit small, but it will do.

"Thank you," he says softly. "What will you use?"

Swinging my rucksack over my stomach, I dig to the bottom and pull out the weapon I've avoided using since I last squeezed the trigger. I secure the handgun, fixed within its plastic holster, inside my waistband and stare out at the road.

"Do you know how to use it?" Theo asks, nodding toward where I hid the government-issued pistol beneath the double layers of my shirt and jacket.

"Yes" is all I say. *I killed your brother's agent with it.*

"Hey look," Theo says, pushing aside the curtain. A winsome smile stretches his cracked lips as he points up at the dreary sky. "A hummingbird."

Dread fills my heart. For a second it stops beating. "Kano, get out the antidrone spray!" I shout as a precaution. "Neutralize the room!"

Alexander peels himself away from the door. "Do you see something?"

I slam my forehead against the glass, my eyes scouring the clouds, the trees, the overgrown weeds. *Where are you?* What *are you?*

"It's just a bird," Theo says, confused. "There!"

His finger tracks the upward ascent of a shiny green bird, its wings fluttering so fast it appears to be levitating. It rises higher and higher, vanishing into the haze. For a moment I allow myself to think it's gone. That it was nothing.

But then I hear it. The shrill whistle of tail feathers as the hummingbird dive-bombs the house at g-force speed.

"Scent Hunter!" I manage to scream before my throat closes. I suddenly can't breathe.

That is what took down Ava.

"Use my Scent Cloaks!" Ciro cries out, springing into action. He throws me a lightweight bag, and I rip open the draw-cord closure and tear out the cloak.

Theo grabs one end; I grab the other. We conceal ourselves beneath the thin, transparent shroud, and I stand stock-still.

"Don't move," I say through stiff lips. The more I move, the more I leave a trail for the Scent Hunter to sniff out.

The whirling whiz of the hummingbird's wings reaches us from the other room. It must have come through a tiny hole in the house. It wouldn't take much—the thing's palm-sized.

"Stay calm, Theo. It doesn't know your scent," Alexander assures his son under his own Scent Cloak. He squats ten yards away, huddled with Kano.

Even if it somehow does, it's here for me.

"Can it hear us?" Theo whispers.

"No, it can only smell us," I say. Slowly, carefully, I reach for my gun.

"It's here," Ciro whispers behind me, tucked under the table, enveloped in his sheer golden blanket.

Beyond the see-through material of my cloak, I spy the drone dart into the room; then I lose sight of it. It's too fast.

I blink, and it's above us. The hummingbird dives, its long, needle-like beak sucking in the smell of the cloak atop my head.

Theo whispers so low I can't hear his words. The tireless, vibrating flutter of the drone's wings drowns everything out.

A cold sweat drips down my arms. I curl my finger around the gun's trigger. I'll only get one shot. *It's too fast.*

The bird releases a piercing trill and plunges for the floor.

I scarcely register Theo scream. "It's in the cloak! Shoot!"

A blur flashes toward me. A blur with red, beady eyes. I fire two rapid shots, and the blur drops to my feet. Its tiny body disabled, decapitated by my bullet, I kick the ruined drone across the room.

Theo yanks the cloak off our bodies, and a rush of fresh air fills my lungs. I lower my gun, realizing Kano's shaking me. "Did it shoot out a tranq? Did it get you?"

With gentle hands, Theo checks my neck and chest for any sign of wounds. "Mira, are you okay?"

"I'm fine," I insist, but he goes on searching anyway.

Ciro shuffles across the hardwood floor, gathering everyone's cloaks. He mutters intently to himself, "We're fine. We're fine. We're fine."

I turn to Kano. "Can we go *now*?"

"Hurry!" Kano shouts, waving us toward the open door.

"There's no point," Alexander says, his hulking frame filling the doorway. "They're already here."

The Guard.

"How many?" Kano yells.

"We can't outrun them," Alexander answers, eerily calm. "They're Texas soldiers." He moves to his son, a new resolve in his shadowy eyes.

"The window!" Theo cries, sliding open the glass.

Ciro appears at my side. Hands clasped together, he holds them out as a step for my boots. "Mira, you first."

I hesitate. *What is Alexander doing?* He's grabbing Theo by the arm, dragging him away from me. Toward the Guard.

"Dad, stop!" Theo yells. "Let go of me!"

"Mira, we have to go!" Kano shouts, picking me up and shoving me toward the open window.

Alexander and Theo are at the door now. I see the Guards racing up the road. In a few moments we'll be surrounded.

He's going to surrender.

Traitor. He was always a traitor.

He was always a Roth.

"No!" Theo and I shout at the same time.

Kano lets go of me and trains his gun on our double-crosser. "Get back here!"

Alexander doesn't stop. He knows we can't shoot. We need them.

We watch our mission bolt out the door.

"Mira, move!" Ciro pleads, trying desperately to push me through the back window. "You can still get out! Make for the trees!"

I can't. There's no point.

We failed.

Kano knows it too. "I'm sorry," he tells me over the roaring engines of SUVs circling the house.

"Don't shoot!" Alexander shouts from outside. "Don't shoot! I am Governor Roth's son! I am Alexander Roth!"

Through the doorway I watch helplessly as Theo tries to fight himself free, but his father is just too strong. *What is Alexander doing? He's going to get Theo arrested!*

"Get on your knees and present your wrists!" a loudspeaker hisses. Guns raised, two Texas soldiers approach the pair, scanning each of their wrists.

Inspecting their chips' information, the soldiers part, allowing Alexander and Theo to pass untouched.

How? Does Theo have a counterfeit chip?

All questions melt away. I suddenly feel like I've been thrown into fire, into the sun's very core. My skin burns. The heat is searing, excruciating, the pain unbearable.

Frantic, I look down at my hands and legs to put out the flames, but there's nothing there.

What is happening?!

I try to run, but the heat follows me. I can't escape.

Kano and Ciro let out strangled cries, crawling and writhing to get to me. I drop to my knees, then to the floor.

"Make it stop . . . ," I hear myself moan.

I'm burning alive. There will be nothing left. I close my eyes, ready to give in, when the boots of a Texas Guard enter the safe house.

"Don't worry," the Guard taunts. "You're not dying."

I curl my body into a fetal position. That somehow hurts more.

"Not yet."

OWEN

"I'll make *you* sorry, backstabber!" I come to, cursing Blaise's existence. Immediately I sense something is off because a) there's no zingy comeback from Blaise, b) I'm the only one in the car, and c) the car's lifted five feet off the ground inside a freaking cave.

"What in the actual hell . . ."

I hear a jovial chuckle from somewhere down below, and then the sound of a heavy-duty impact wrench turning on. Shoving my head out the open driver's window, all I see is a white western hat and a pair of rugged hands changing *my* car's tires.

"Hey!" I shout, proprietorship raging full force. "What do you think you're doing?" I push open the door, and the left side of the car lifts up like a bird's wing.

I jump the short distance to the dirt floor, landing face-to-face with an honest-to-God cowboy wearing dirty denim coveralls and round-tipped leather boots. He has a massive silver belt buckle and everything.

"Fancy car you've got there, son," the man admires.

"Uh . . . thanks," I mumble, noticing how flawless Duke looks. The car positively shines—the man must've waxed him on top of all the body repair. There's no hint at all the car just endured the beating of a lifetime. Kismet couldn't have done better themselves. *Who is this guy?*

The cowboy holds out his hand.

"The name's Kipling. Pleasure to meet you."

"Owen Hart," I say, giving him a firm shake. I eyeball my surroundings, mouth hanging open in awe. About a dozen cars are inside the cave—half are the Common's under repair, the other half is the man's personal collection of crazy-valuable foreign and vintage models. All the cars are stored or perched on scissor lifts under a roof loaded with thin rock formations that look like weaponized brown icicles. A baby-blue patchwork truck that must be the cowboy's "everyday" vehicle is parked by the entrance.

The man's auto shop is dark and damp and *rustic*. Totally opposite from the sterile mega factories of Detroit. It's ridiculously cool.

"Where am I?" I ask. *Am I in a dream?* Because I woke up in a cave—*what's up with that?!*—and now I'm talking to a cowboy who seems to be as much into cars as I am.

Kipling smiles. "Welcome to west Texas, the land of wide-open spaces."

His slow, twangy way of talking is straight out of a Western movie. I thought that accent had died along with all the true cowboys.

Snap out of it, fanboy!

I've got to go back for Rayla.

"Thanks for rehabilitating Duke back to all his glory, but I need my car, like right now," I say, jumping into rescue mode. I dash for the controls to lower the auto lift and scan all four tires. Ready to roll. "Sorry to wake and leave . . . It's just we left someone behind that needs my help—"

A motorcycle charging in the corner stops me cold. *No way.*

I step closer. Yep, the same expertly restored black frame, the same Triumph logo painted underneath the handlebars. It's the bike we picked up after we left the safe house in Colorado. The one Rayla was riding last night. *How?*

"'Fraid that bike's already taken," Kipling drawls. "That one's special, you see. Custom-made."

I eyeball the extended two-person seat and the skillfully crafted bird's wing kickstand. This bike's special all right. And expensive. It must've been built for someone special too.

"Custom-made for who?"

"My granddaughters," a gruff voice says behind me.

I whip around to the cave's entrance to find the woman herself: Rayla Cadwell. Alive, whole, and surly as ever. I don't think I've ever been so happy to see a person in my life.

"Rayla, you're here!" I say stupidly, but I don't care. *She's here!* I run to her and limit myself to a kind of side hug. No way Rayla does full-on hugs without prior approval. "Is this okay?" I ask. She doesn't protest; she just pats the top of my head.

"All right, all right, yes, I made it here," she says. I can tell she's happy to see me too. Somewhere deep down inside. She's just scared to let it out.

Then I remember she likes bear hugs. If Rayla Cadwell ever giggled, that's what she would have been doing when Xavier hoisted her like a boss into the air. I decide to take a chance.

The key is to maximize the cuddle factor, so I wrap my arms all the way around her rigid frame—careful to avoid her bullet wound—and squeeze tight. The whole air-lift part of Xavier's embrace might be pushing my luck too far.

Then I think the world's about to end, because instead of fighting it, Rayla lifts *me* into the air, and I swear to Whitman she *giggles*.

It's brief, but it happened.

"I heard you took down a Killer Drone," Rayla says.

"Yeah, but I don't like to brag," I lie.

When she puts me down, both of us are grinning from ear to ear.

"What'd I miss while I was zonked out?" I ask Rayla, eager to get caught up. "Which was not my fault, by the way. Blaise the fire demon practically poisoned me."

Kipling chuckles. "Blaise sure is a funny one, wearin' that mask 'n' all. But he checked in on you every hour on the hour."

"He *did*?"

"Battle bonds," Rayla says, then switches things back to business. "We're moving soon. The members are waiting."

"Already?" Kipling says, buttoning up his collar and straightening his wide, flat-brimmed hat. "We'd best be gettin' along, then."

The future waits for no one.

Whoa. The wonders of nature smack me right in the face the second I step out of the cave entrance. I'm standing inside an enormous canyon floor that's surrounded on all sides by red-and-pink rock walls as tall as high-rises. It's desolate and alive all at the same time.

It's also brighter than hellfire here.

Forced to squint, I still manage to make out the crowd gathered up ahead. When we get closer I see that Xavier's leading a demonstration on how to properly handle a gun—weapons are in every person's hands.

Battle prep.

A jumbo all-electric semitruck is parked behind him, its sleek, silver profile shaped to look like a bullet. What is *that* for?

I look to Rayla, but her eyes tell me, *Hush, you'll find out soon.*

Blaise and Malik are up front, and I move to join them while Rayla and Kipling take center stage with Xavier. Our numbers have grown while I was knocked out—there definitely weren't this many people when we left Colorado. Where did this surge come from?

"Who are all these new people?" I ask Blaise.

He takes a cautious step back, thinking I might punch him. My curiosity beats out any desire for revenge, plus I *did* need that beauty sleep. I'm more awake and energized than I've ever been.

When he sees I'm not angry, he relaxes and leans in close, all excited. "Kipling's a stop on the underground. He shelters people who've *crossed the border*. Can you believe that?"

Gluts. The word pops into my head. I've never seen one in person before. I look around and spot a group of unfamiliar faces at the back of the crowd. Is that them? They look just like every other Common member. Weary, fed up, and ready to rebel.

"I don't have much to say," Rayla encourages us, "beyond that we all have a reason to fight. Remember yours in the battle for Dallas tonight." Fingers balled into a fist, she pulls up her right sleeve and exposes her snake-tattooed wrist.

"Resist much," Rayla says.

"Obey little," I answer along with the crowd, my first time saying the Common's words out loud. I'm still tattooless—I've got to change that pronto—but I stretch out my wrist alongside my cohorts in a return salute. All around me, I hear the rebellion's cry in at least three foreign languages. Double whoa.

The full impact of what we're doing hits me. People from different countries, states, cities, backgrounds, generations, and social classes, all united together in the same fight.

It's like it's the whole world against Roth.

No way the man's not going down tonight.

I've heard it said everything's bigger in Texas, but it's a whole other deal to experience it for myself. We've driven for six hours, and that's *still* not even halfway across the state. The land stretches on to infinity.

Even the sky's too big here. It's so king-sized and overbearing it feels like I'm living in the clouds.

Not a fan.

Hey, Texas, ever hear of the phrase *too much of a good thing*? That's you.

There aren't even any people here. Our Cavalry has passed only one drifter. One! What's the point in bragging about all this land when you can't even utilize most of it?

And it's *hot*. I mean Hades kind of hot. No matter how much sunblock I smear on, I've come to accept my dark-brown skin is *still* going to burn.

"*Yech*, what is that smell?" Blaise says, crammed in the bucket seat between Rayla and me.

"Cattle manure," Kipling answers from behind the wheel. "Nothin' like it anywhere else." He breathes in the sharp, rotten odor like it's perfume.

Absolutely zilch for miles, and now there's wire fencing edging both sides of the road. "Cattle farms?" I ask, incredulous. "Those still exist here?"

"The high rankers have to have their meat." Rayla spits out the words.

Nope, can't do it. Got to block all my breathing holes *now*. I unzip the bag Kipling gave me and pull out a spare shirt, tying it around the lower half of my face. It doesn't help.

"Luxury stinks," I say, my voice muffled.

The Dallas skyline is supposed to appear southeast on the horizon. From time to time I squint my eyes in that direction, but I mostly keep my mind on anything other than our final destination. It's best not to overthink things.

I gaze out the windshield to study the large herds of cattle that cluster along the fences. They barely lift their heads to watch our metal army pass by—they just munch on the grass, their tails lazily flicking away the flies.

"I've never had grass-fed beef before," I say. No big reveal there. Who *has*? Maybe the cowboy. "Is it really that much better than lab beef?"

"Not better than my 'roo sticks," Kipling says. "But these are genetically modified cattle—heat resistant and bred for top-quality beef. You can taste the difference."

"But aren't cow emissions worse than carbon dioxide?" Blaise asks, all cranky from behind the crook of his elbow. He can't stand the smell either. "How are these farms even legal?"

He's right. Livestock emit methane, a toxic combination of farts, burps, and shit. The number-one destroyer of the environment, folks. Cow farts.

I pop another one of Kipling's tasty treats into my mouth.

"You really should monetize these kangaroo sticks, you know," I say, looking over at Kipling. "You're sitting on a gold mine."

"Glad you like 'em," Kipling says. "Ol' family recipe." He makes life sound slow and friendly when it's just not. I mean, we're racing straight into the center of a freaking *warzone*.

"We'll be comin' up on the outskirts of Dallas soon," Kipling says, the mood of the truck flipping to serious on a dime. "Get yerselves ready."

"I'm as ready as I'll ever be," I mumble. *Great pep talk.*

Don't people use this time to prep their weapons or something? I rest my hand on the gun Rayla gave me, now stored on my hip, like sharpshooter skills will somehow transfer into me by touching the thing. Rayla taught me how to use it before we hit the road, and I've got to be honest, it wasn't pretty. It's like my Killer Drone shot was a fluke. Sheer damn luck.

Here's to hoping my luck doesn't run out.

I notice Rayla has gone quiet. Not good. Her head's dipped at a low angle, her focus out the window, searching for the first hint of the capital city.

She's worried about her granddaughters. Last we heard of them, Ava was being hunted by the Guard in Washington State, and Mira? Well, who the hell knows. She went dark after setting out to find Roth's son. She could be anywhere.

What if we show up and the safe house is empty?
That won't be good for anyone.
"They'll be there," I say to Rayla, leaning over Blaise.
Rayla doesn't respond, but I know she heard me.
I just don't know if she believes me.

When we hit the Dallas suburbs, self-doubt starts to kick in. I've never seen so much glass and steel in my life, and I worked at a *car factory* in Detroit. It's just building on building on building. There's no end.

And these are only outlying cities of the *big* one.

It doesn't help I'm sweating so much it's embarrassing. The under-arms and back of my shirt are soaked through. *Come on, I was born in Georgia, right?* Shouldn't that make me heat resistant, like those cows?

"I need water," I inform the truck. "I'm dying here."

But when I comb through my pack, I discover all my water bottles are empty.

"You really need to learn how to conserve," Blaise says unhelpfully. I swear to Whitman the guy would sit and smile as I slowly died of thirst.

"Take mine," Kipling offers, handing me his bottle.

"Thank you," I say to my new best friend, Kip.

I suck down the water like it's a magical liquid that can turn me into a bulletproof warrior. But you know, I'd settle for just the bulletproof part.

"Downtown Dallas," Rayla growls.

I follow her sightline out the window. *Dang.* Still miles away, the looming mega capital is already a spectacle. It's ginormous. Guardian Tower, the Guard's HQ, stands out in the mob of high-rises. Well, that's certainly sobering.

"There's smoke," Rayla points out.

To the west, black fumes mushroom out above the distant buildings. *Fire or smoke grenades?*

Whatever it is, it's spreading.

"Our side or theirs?" I ask.

"It's in the sector where our safe house is located," Rayla says. The Last Stage, the Common's rendezvous point.

Rayla seizes her pistol and checks the witness hole of her gun's magazine, counting her bullets. She flips the safety switch to off. "Kipling, you're up," Rayla says.

"Yes, ma'am," Kipling says, veering the semi toward the main highway that leads directly into Dallas. "I'll have us there in twenty minutes," he promises.

"Fortitude, everyone," Rayla says.

Please let my courage hold.

I catch a glimpse in the truck's side-view mirror and see the other forty Common cars following our lead onto the ramp. No one's acknowledging the fact that our Common Cavalry's the only one trying to enter downtown.

This doesn't bode well.

Blaise and I exchange nervous glances.

"We got this," he says to me, all dauntless, nodding furiously like a deranged bobblehead.

"Yeah," I say, feeling a rush of adrenaline from the magic water. Bulletproof. "We got this."

The skyscrapers come up quick. *So this is where Ava and Mira lived? This is where it all began?*

And I guess this is where it all will end.

The twenty minutes go by in a wink.

Up close, things don't look promising.

"The city's on lockdown." Rayla says what we all see. The entire downtown is surrounded and blocked off by hefty concrete barriers and ten-foot barbed-wire fences.

"It looks like a scene from the Atlanta Outbreak," I say. The Georgia capital was full-on quarantined for half a year.

I guess the new epidemic is the Common.

There's no way in or out.

"Good thing we came ready," Kipling says, gripping the wheel like a weapon.

The semitruck. It's not just to hide the bike and my car until we need them. It's to ram our way through.

Rayla jerks open a small door in the back of the truck's cabin.

"See y'all on the other side," Kipling says with a tip of his hat.

"Don't die," Blaise tells me by way of goodbye.

"Same to you." I nod and disappear through the crawl space after Rayla. I worm my way across the short passage and drop into the rattling trailer of the eighteen-wheeler.

Rayla's already beside the Triumph that's strapped down by the rear roll-up door. "Hold on to something!" she shouts at me.

Oh, right, we're about to become a battering ram. *Prepare for impact.*

The truck rockets forward, and I cling to a metal bar in a casual I-do-this-all-the-time kind of death grip. I just forget to close my mouth. Right as the big rig crashes into the barricade, the force slams my head forward, and my teeth crunch down on my tongue like a steel-jaw trap.

A flash flood of blood jets down my lip.

"You're already bleeding?" Rayla chides, holding out a glossy black helmet with a tinted visor.

"Same to you," I say, pointing to the dark spots staining her upper arm. *That wound just won't heal.*

She ignores this and coils up her long hair into a ponytail before pulling on her own helmet. One sight of that silvery mane and it's all over. "Saddle up," she says, patting the seat behind her.

A last look at my car—Duke's in good hands with Kipling—and I hop on the bike, locking my arms around her ribcage.

The truck makes a series of jerky turns. I can't stand not knowing what's going on out there. I know what should be going on. In the tried-and-true tactic, the Cavalry should be fanning out in all directions, making it hard for the Guard to know which car to chase. Fingers and toes crossed they didn't target us. Kipling should be searching for a street with no surveillance. That doesn't feel promising, given this city.

"Come on!" Rayla shouts, impatient.

Kipling seems to have found a good place to park, because we halt to a screeching stop and the door rolls open. Rayla stabs a lever with the heel of her boot, the motorcycle dislodges, the loading ramp juts out, and we're off.

The city's surveillance doesn't know we don't belong here. The cameras didn't see the bike break through the barrier—we just need to blend in.

A pretty bleak undertaking considering we're the only people in sight.

"Mandatory curfew! Return immediately to your residence, or you will be arrested!" a hostile voice browbeats the deserted streets through unseen speakers.

"Are we close?!" I shout. My question's lost inside my helmet. I could scream bloody murder, and Rayla wouldn't hear me.

Then the sound of gunshots echoes across the maze of skyscrapers. That can't be good.

Rayla turns a hard left, and next thing I know, we're cutting through a heavy, shadowy fog that stings my eyes and throat.

Smoke grenades.

"We're close, *right*?!" I can't help asking when I hear more bullets fire off. "Wait, should I be holding my gun?"

That's way past a fledgling rebel's skillset.

Instead I hold on for my dear life and look out for the addresses above the doors.

Is the building actually called the Last Stage, or is it more of a metaphorical kind of thing?

"The doors!" I yell. They're all yellow. Street after street pops with the Common's mark, the paint thick and clumpy like the government keeps trying to cover it up but the color just won't go away.

Rayla crushes the throttle, and we streak across an alleyway, straight into an empty parking garage.

Lo and behold, on the back wall above the double doors, there it is, the sign for the Last Stage.

Rayla skids us to a halt under the illuminated words, then cuts the motor. I kick out the side stand, and we rip off our helmets, bolting for the safe house entrance.

We don't even have to knock. The yellow steel doors open wide for Rayla Cadwell, who promptly sticks out her tatted wrist in salute. "Resist much."

Hell yeah we just did!

The gawking sentry answers "obey little," moves aside, and we're in.

"We're *in*!" I shout, wiping the sweat from my temples. I try for a high five, but Rayla stands completely still, hands shaking at her sides.

She looks like she's seen a ghost.

ZEE

I will remember that time for the rest of my life.

Rayla. My mother. I don't know what to call her. She's ten feet from me. The woman who gave me life. Gave me away.

The Rule of One made her do that. The doctors too. The Guards. The governor. But did she want me? Was her choice easy? After forty-plus years, does she remember?

She walks to me, slow. Her eyes are full of tears. I've never looked somebody in the eyes before. I look straight into hers.

"My child?" she asks. "Haven?"

Haven? She named me.

The safe house goes quiet. All attention on us.

"Give them some privacy, people," the young man she came in with says.

My heart feels swollen. Two times too big for my broken body.

She stops in front of me. Reaches out her hand. Moves her fingers in the air over my cheeks, mouth. Doesn't touch. "Is it really you?" She falls down to her knees.

I get to my knees too. Words fail me. I don't know how to say what I feel. I let my smile speak for me. Tears fall from my eyes.

"Forgive me," she says. Asks. She looks like she's in pain. Inside and out.

"You must understand," she says. "Family Planning took you right after I gave birth to you. But I never truly let you go. Ever." She holds my hand and puts it over her chest. Her heart. It beats fast, like footsteps running to me. "You lived within me. You lived within your sister."

Lynn.

There's so much to say. So many questions.

I just ask one.

"Can I call you Mother?"

She nods. Gives a small laugh.

"May I call you Haven?" Mother asks. I also nod. Place her hand over my own heart. I feel safe. Complete. Loved.

We help each other to our feet. The young man now stands next to Mother. "Owen. It's an honor to meet you," he says. Holds out his hand.

Second time I've heard those words. The first was from Cleo. She's in Guardian Tower. With the Common. And the other prisoners.

"Hello, Owen," I say. I touch his fingers with mine. Is that the correct way to greet?

"I have something to show you . . . Mother," I say. I take her hand. It's rough. Callused. Did she have a hard life too?

We walk to a dark corner in an empty hall. The First Lady steps into the light. Arms wrapped around her thin body. Dressed in civilian clothes. A long cloth covers her head. Hiding who she is.

"Show your face," I say. The First Lady does.

"Holy hell," Owen says.

The First Lady's eyes go wide. "Rayla Cadwell! Lynn, what is this?"

"Not Lynn," I say. "My name is Haven. I was an Inmate in the Camps."

The First Lady seems to understand. She starts to shake again. Backs away.

"Camps?" Mother shouts. The First Lady tries to run, but Mother catches her. Makes her face me. "You cannot hide from your crimes," Mother says to her. "Your husband taught us that."

"You're the prisoner now," I say to the First Lady. The Warden of Texas. "How does it feel?"

I feel power for the first time in my long, hard life.

I look at Mother. Smile. She smiles back. Proud.

She makes me strong. A hundred percent ready to take on the Guards. Governors.

All our family's enemies.

MIRA

Half of me always knew if I ever returned to Dallas, it would be in handcuffs.

At least my other half is still out there. Ava. She can still be the fuel, the oxygen that keeps the rebellion's flame burning.

At least I have that. Whatever happens to me, I can carry that hope with me wherever I go.

I teeter, then fall into carefree oblivion.

The sharp jab of a baton between my shoulder blades rouses me. My eyes snap open.

"No sleeping, Glut!" a Guard shouts down at me. "Don't you want to be awake for your final hours?" With a grisly smile, she stomps back to her post beside our rail compartment's door.

I rub out the sting of sleeplessness from my eyes with my shoulder. *How much time do I have left?* My hands are cuffed to the metal pole behind my seat. I twist my arms, but I can't read my watch.

It's dark out now. The high-speed train streaks past the lighted buildings, their shining bulbs of electricity multiplying with every passing second. *We're in the Dallas city limits.*

Only five more minutes, ten at the most, before we reach Guardian Station. I dip my head and try to spot Guardian Tower, the soaring, luminous ball, the brightest star in the sky. The glass tower of the Texas Guard. I can't see it through the dense fog of pollution. *Or is that smoke?*

I wonder if Roth will be on the station's platform to greet me. Will he bother secretly hauling me to the Tower, or will he just shoot me where I sit, point-blank between the eyes like he did to my father. Shoving the grainy prison footage from my mind, I strain my neck to the left.

Through the compartment's inner doors, I check up on Ciro and Kano. *What will the governor do with them?* They're both on the floor, tied to the center handrail, two Guards looming over them. A gag ripped from his own shirt covers Ciro's mouth. Blood cakes his soiled locks and drips down his forehead into his eyes. There's nothing he can do to stop it.

Barend urged Ciro not to come.

Maybe Barend's the traitor. The thought won't leave my mind. Maybe he's the turncoat, the mole, the one who told Roth of our mission to unite the States. He could have been warning Ciro we were doomed players in a rigged game.

What if Ava's here too?

I flick my eyes to Kano and see several angry wounds from the barbs of a taser gun marking his neck and cheek.

My team didn't go down easy.

Neither will I.

Twisting my neck to the right, I look past my Guard, through the other compartment's doors. I can just make out Theo sitting alone in the back row. He's staring straight at me, his eyes bulging and red like he's been waiting unblinking for me to turn and stare back. *I'm sorry,* they say. *I didn't know.*

I turn away.

Sorry for what? That your father had a backup plan to save his own family's skin? Or did Alexander, the trickster, envision this all along? The prodigal son, the rightful heir, returned to his birthplace bearing a gift of absolution. The most damning half of the Traitorous Twins. The second child.

Alexander's finishing what his firstborn started. Delivering what Halton could not. *Me.* I'm Alexander's way back in. Governor Roth will welcome him with open arms.

Theo better not do anything stupid, like give himself away. In a last-ditch act of desperation, if he attempts to complete our mission, tries to flip the Guard, and tells a soldier his real identity, he will only end up like me. A Glut in handcuffs on our way to evanescence.

Four more minutes.

Slowly, I lift up my head and turn back to Theo. He's gripping my knife. *Does he think he can take down the soldier?*

No, don't! I almost yell. I yank uselessly against my restraints. *Not now!* But instead of lashing out on the Guard five rows away, he turns the blade on himself. On his inner right wrist.

With a clumsy swipe, he cuts his skin and digs out his counterfeit microchip. Pinching it between thumb and middle finger, he holds it up, glaring at the bloody metal capsule like a tumor just removed.

He didn't know. He never knew he was microchipped.

Alexander marches into view down the aisle. Realizing what Theo's holding, he contorts his face with horror. In one fell swoop he snatches the chip from Theo's fingers and pockets it, the Guards none the wiser.

Through the glass door, I see Alexander tug down Theo's right sleeve, covering the dangerous mark his son just gave himself. A mark that brands his son a rebel. *Do the Guards smell the blood?*

What did he just do?

Theo stands to his full height, level with his father's. His curled fist shines with the steel rings of my knife's handle.

Swinging back his arm, he punches Alexander in the stomach with a quick, brutal jab.

Alexander barely hits the floor before the oversized Guard is on Theo with his baton. The Guard from my car barrels through the doors, taser gun aimed and ready.

Theo doesn't even cower. He just glowers down at his father, his eyes saying, *You did this.*

"Stand down!" Alexander wheezes at Theo's feet, raising a commanding hand for the soldiers to stop.

Reluctantly, they listen.

Baton holstered, the stalwart Guard seizes Theo, locking his arms behind his back. The soldier exchanges a few heated words with Alexander—I try to read their lips, but I can't keep up.

Shouting something I can't hear, the second Guard points to Theo's right wrist. *She's discovered the cut. She knows he's a traitor.* Drawing a zip-tie from her duty belt, she bonds Theo's hands so tight he grimaces in agony.

Alexander attempts to maintain the stone-faced supremacy of an officer in front of his Guard, but I see the edges crack. I see him flinch.

This wasn't part of his plan. He's lost his son. *He's losing control.*

Two minutes left.

Before the Guards can do any more damage, Alexander barks an order and grabs Theo roughly by the neck. He pushes his son through the compartment and into my car, throwing him four rows behind mine.

"Stop," Alexander says to his son, leaning against a pole, still coughing and rasping from his gut punch. "Stop making things worse."

Straightening his coat and hair, Alexander marches past me, not sparing a single glance in my direction. "We are pulling into downtown as I speak," he says. "Everyone will know tonight."

What does that mean? Everyone will know *what?*

The door slides shut, and the Guard takes up her post. I turn to Theo.

"You should *not* have done that," I say.

"I've joined the Common," Theo whispers earnestly. "I'm with you, whatever happens."

"I'm with you too," I admit to Theo and to myself.

I won't let the Guard take him.

The rail slows to a gradual stop. Thirty seconds.

"Welcome to Guardian Station," the soothing voice from the speakers announces.

In less than fifteen seconds, Roth could walk through the doors in front of me, nothing but a few feet of air dividing us. The old fear grips and wrings my heart, squeezing tears from my sleepy eyes.

No, I scold myself. *You are not the same girl as when you were last here. He fears* you *now.*

Show him why.

I let no tears fall.

But it's not Governor Roth who strides through the rail doors.

"Who's that?" Theo asks, not caring if anyone hears.

"General Pierce," I respond, greeting the large, fleshy man who's always reminded me of nothing more than a bulldozer. He's lost more hair since I last saw him.

He halts at the entrance, looking me up and down appraisingly. "You came back in one piece, I see. You never should have run."

I almost spit in his face, but I decide not to waste the saliva. "How could you let Roth kill my father, your supposed *friend*!"

Tearing his gaze off me, he searches the car for Alexander. *He can't look me in the eyes.* "Your father took his own life, Mira. I know that's difficult to accept."

"You can't reason with Commoners," a woman says from the platform. She stomps past the general to get to me.

Short, but somehow all the more intimidating for it, she wears a crisp military uniform with several badges on her right breast. The center badge outshines the rest. It's the same badge my father once wore.

She's the new Director of the Texas Family Planning Division.

I recognize the woman but can't recall her name. She used to be the Director in the powerful northern state of Montana.

With a forceful claw, the Director clutches my chin and lifts my face for a better viewing experience. "The infamous twin," she says. "Very nice."

I rip my chin away from her grasp, and she turns her attention to Theo. "And who is this?"

Don't touch him.

"Nobody," Alexander says as he enters the car, saving me from head-butting the woman. The general and Director stand at attention as he comes in. "He's just more Common filth."

"Where's the governor?" Alexander asks, impatient. "Where's my father?"

"Governor Roth sends his regrets for not being here to welcome you," General Pierce responds. "There have been a few . . . incidents—"

Assassination attempts?

"—involving a small number of amateur criminals . . . The governor asked me to escort you safely to the Governor's Mansion," General Pierce finishes.

"That won't be necessary, General," Alexander answers in a haughty tone not to be questioned. "I have a gift for the city. The country's top traitor, my son's killer." His mouth cuts open in a malevolent smile. "I have planned something much grander for my homecoming." He cocks his head toward me. "For both our homecomings."

I don't dare look at Theo. I don't want him to see me crack.

Everyone will know tonight, Alexander promised me.

He's going to announce I've been caught. He's going to parade me in front of the public.

Turning his back on his second child, Alexander makes for the exit. "Take us to the Capitol building," he orders.

I crack and turn to Theo. "When you can," I mouth to him, "run." *Oh god,* I hope he understands.

Possibilities race through my mind. I yield to the worst one. *We're likely headed for my public execution.*

I lived as a secret. At least I won't die as one.

Survive. Survive for me and your mother, my father's last words scream in my head.

Father. Ava.

I tried.

AVA

My stomach drops abruptly along with the plane.

The pilot explained over the speakers that turbulence is perfectly normal and that all nervous flyers should sit in the center of the aircraft with their seat belts securely fastened. I filled in the details about atmospheric waves myself, remembering the old videos I used to watch with Mira in the basement, prepping ourselves in the unlikely event we ever got to fly.

Despite this knowledge, every time the airplane loses altitude, I think we're going down. Each bump feels like a bomb sent by the Texas Guard.

We can't hide from Roth, even in the sky.

Way too anxious to sit, I pace back and forth at the front of the cabin, close my eyes, and breathe. *Why would anyone ever want to fly? It's terrifying.*

But it's also efficient, though I can only imagine the cost—biofuel is like gold in our country.

This plane transport will get us to Dallas in three hours, making up for all the lost time we spent sitting useless in the cellar safe house. It was worth the sixteen-hour wait for our ride.

Soldiers still faithful to Senator Gordon were able to get my team and me on a small government plane, flown by an actual pilot rather than the autonomous system. The senator himself stayed behind to ignite the cause across Washington State and mobilize his citizens to our side. His task will be difficult—he's battling against both Governor Elsen's army *and* the Texas State Guard. But when we parted at the safe house, I saw the fight burning bright inside him—it's like he relished being the underdog.

He gave me the rebellion salute, and I left feeling the strength our new recruit just added to the Common.

I stop pacing and take out my map—checking on the progress our missions have made calms my nerves.

Senator Riggs of New York
~~*Senator López of North California*~~
Senator Tate of Colorado
~~*Senator Dalton of Michigan*~~
~~*Senator Gordon of Washington State*~~

We've turned three states yellow. Four, counting Oregon, a state that wasn't even on our list. *It's actually happening.*

The Common's long game of uniting the country through its senators is well underway, but we still don't know if Mira succeeded with her part in all of this.

I didn't give her mission much time to succeed. My stomach drops again, this time from guilt. Now that Governor Roth is running for president, Mira needs to have found something so significant and iron-clad there's no other outcome but for Roth to sink, drowning all his presidential hopes with him.

Just as another bout of turbulence hits, the cockpit door opens, and Barend comes into the main cabin. He crashes right into me, slamming my back against the drinks cart. My temper flares alongside my suspicion.

"What were you doing in the cockpit?" I ask. "Rerouting the plane?" *He might be leading us into another trap. This time, right into Roth's hands.*

"I don't know what you're talking about," Barend snaps. "What right do you have to question *me*? You're the one who endangered Ciro's and the others' missions." He clenches his jaw tight, attempting to regain his composure. *No, keep talking. I need to break your code of silence.*

"You mean *Mira's* mission?" I spit back. "Why did you choose to be on my mission team anyway?"

My father trained me to be a master of lies, deceiving everyone around me in order to survive. Now I want to live a life only of truth, but I hope I can use those hard-earned skills to detect another liar when I see one.

Maybe they're harder to see when they're right in front of you.

"I pledged myself to the cause," Barend says. "Your plan of action was the best strategy to win back our country from the government. I had no hidden agenda."

I'm not convinced, and he knows it. "If you have something to say, then say it," Barend demands.

"Are you Governor Roth's mole?" I ask point-blank.

Barend scoffs, then looks over to Emery, who sits in the middle of the plane. She's been writing in her notebook the entire flight, softly mouthing words like she's running through a speech. There's an olive-colored tinge to her face from motion sickness—a vomit bag rests on the seat beside her. Pawel's been an excellent aide to our leader, plying her with ginger tea and crackers. *I'm sure he's had practice from taking care of Ellie when she was sick.* I did the same for Mira.

Is Barend trying to signal Emery for help? If so, she's not giving any. She watches our squabbling with the air of a schoolmaster letting her students learn a lesson for themselves.

"Don't look to Emery," I say to Barend. "Look at me."

Roth said similar words to me when he raided our house in Trinity Heights. *He thought he could root out liars too.*

The bitter taste of arrogance and paranoia fills my mouth. I want to spit it out, but instead I double down and glare a challenge at Barend.

He squares his broad shoulders at me.

"I did my duty to guard and protect you on your mission, but I couldn't save you from your youthful inexperience. Your hotheaded actions have put the Common itself in danger, along with everyone who has given up everything we care about in order to follow you." There's a fervor in his eyes that I can only believe to be genuine—passion is a hard emotion to fake. But I can't tell what his strength of feeling is toward. His rebuke of my methods, the justness of our cause . . . Ciro?

All at once the plane drops twenty feet in the air, sending Barend and I flying against the walls. When we gather ourselves together again, Barend has sealed up all his vulnerabilities. He's a hardened soldier once more.

"We're going back to Dallas too soon," he insists. "We still don't have the numbers on our side for this assault."

Whoever our betrayer is—and I'm still not ruling Barend out completely—we can use the invasion against them.

"In case you didn't notice, half the Texas Guard is off occupying faraway states. The Common needs to use that to our advantage—we need to move fast before Roth has the entire country behind him," I say, justifying myself to Barend. And to Emery and Pawel, who are listening closely. "This is the time to strike. Dallas has never been weaker."

Roth has overreached. *Let's make him pay for his blind ambition.*

I turn from Barend and make my way down the narrow aisle to the back of the plane, using the headrests for support. The seat belt sign flashes in warning, but that means nothing—it's been on the whole flight. Another consequence of climate change: roller-coaster air travel. Increased carbon dioxide levels in the atmosphere mean severe air turbulence is the norm.

Emery braces herself against her armrests, clearly fighting off another fit of nausea. When I near her row, she manages to give me a nod as if to say, *Well done.*

I decide to take a seat beside her. "Talking helps," I say, placing the vomit bag onto her tray table. "It distracts you."

Emery smiles and closes her notebook. "What would you like to discuss?"

"My mother," I say. I suddenly crave stories about my mother that have nothing to do with the rebellion. "Will you tell me how my parents fell in love in Denver?"

Emery was Lynn's best friend. She would know details no one else could.

"'How' is not the right question when it comes to love, Ava," Emery says, briefly squeezing my hand. "No one knows the how or the why of it. But I will tell you what I know about Lynn's courtship of Darren."

My mother went after *Father*? I always thought it was the other way around. Rayla certainly made it seem that way.

Fascinated, I rest my head back against the seat and close my eyes, ready to imagine my parents young and alive with love.

Now seated at the back of the plane, I rest my forehead against the cold window, gazing down on the mighty Dallas skyline thousands of feet below.

I've seen aerial shots of the capital before, but to experience this rare perspective with my own eyes takes my breath away. The cityscape seems to go on forever, and in the distance, I make out Guardian Tower, shining like a star in the twilight.

In all the hundreds of thousands of years of modern human history, this bird's-eye view has only been seen by people for less than two centuries. But recently it was taken from the public once more, reserved only for the most elite; even a government official like my father never once enjoyed the honor of flying.

I wish Mira were here to share this moment with me. *What new experiences is she having without me?*

I hope she's down there already, waiting. *See you soon, at the Last Stage.*

"Dallas doesn't look so bad from above," Pawel says from the aisle. I turn my gaze to him. He bends over to look out my window, his cowlick keeping up its resistance to lying flat. "It almost looks peaceful."

Any question of loyalty on my end and judgments of hasty actions on his, any hard feelings we had between us, have disappeared.

"It's remarkable, isn't it?" I say, staring back out the window.

All across the metropolis, the lights from the skyscrapers burn bright like beacons of change. The last flickers of hope.

We can't let them fade out.

Without warning, the plane changes course and veers away from Dallas.

"Ladies and gentlemen, we've run into an unforeseen security defense and must make an emergency landing," the pilot shouts into the cabin speakers. "Please return to your seats immediately and fasten your seat belts."

Emery and Barend barrel toward the cockpit door.

"What the hell is going on?" I say to Pawel, rising from my seat. He's turned pale.

"There must be a virtual sky fence around Dallas that broke through our stealth shield," he says as we race for the control room together. "We have to land now, or the military will attempt to take control of the plane by hacking into our operating system. If they achieve this, they can force-land our plane on one of the Guard's runways."

Governor Roth found us.

I was right. We can't hide from him, not even in the sky.

OWEN

"Well, this view sucks," I say out loud to no one.

The roof of the Last Stage theater was supposed to give me a vantage point to scope out the battleground. Roth's got home-court advantage—we need to see what we're up against.

But nope. Mega skyscrapers hem in the old playhouse on all sides—the only thing I can see that's *not* a building is the alleyway right below. Awesome.

It's better than nothing. I take what I can get and sit on the edge of the building, posting up as watchdog.

Zero action. My mind starts to wander.

Inside the theater, Haven is here. Rayla's lost daughter. Her hard life shows on her sun-spotted face and the way she doesn't talk much. I think I'm the *first* person she's ever tried to shake hands with. Imagine it. She's lived forty-plus years as a government ward, separated from her family, kept alive just to be worked to death, and now she's with her mother again. A new chance at life. It's enough to almost make me believe in miracles. Or fate. Almost.

That family is a tough breed to kill off—and we just gained *another* one on our side. That's four for us, zero for Roth. I'm liking our odds.

I'd like them a hell of a lot better, though, if everyone would get here already. Our team was the first to arrive at the rendezvous point—no

Ava or Mira or any of the members Rayla called the Elders. Scratch that, only half our team made it here. Blaise and Kipling still haven't turned up. Neither have Xavier and Malik.

"Mandatory curfew! Return immediately to your residence, or you will be arrested!" The annoying alert will not shut up. It blasts into the streets on repeat like the citizens didn't get it the first time. Dallas is a complete ghost town, or did the Guard's camera eyes decide to take a little nap?

"Yeah, we got it!" I say aloud. Right after I say it, the electronic voice cuts out. Two seconds of silence, then an eardrum-busting siren takes its place.

"That wasn't me," I insist, covering my mouth. The last time I uttered those words after an unexpected siren went off, all hell broke loose.

I rocket up to my feet, wishing I'd learned to keep my big mouth shut.

"Mandatory public assembly! Report immediately to Capitol Square!" the new order demands. That can't be good. A public assembly means Roth has something he wants to show off.

Ava and Mira.

Double not good.

I have to tell Rayla. I tear down five flights of stairs and arrive in front of Rayla and Haven, crazy out of breath. "It's Ava . . . and Mira . . . ," I stammer.

Not helpful. *Use more of your words.* "Assembly . . ."

Somebody flips on the room's speakers. Thank Whitman. *"Mandatory public assembly! Report immediately to Capitol Square!"*

The look in Rayla's eyes tells me she knows it's the twins too. Her right hand moves for her gun. Her other hand has never left Haven's shoulder.

"Save the twins!" Rayla roars. She drowns out the government's voice. "This is our time to fight back!"

The safe house explodes in response to our leader's call to arms. They raise their guns, knives, anything that can be used as a weapon, into the air. I stand beside her, raising my own gun.

Haven pulls out a Guard's pistol from her waistband, ready to fight for her family. But Rayla stops her. "I need you to stay here and guard Mrs. Roth. She's too important to lose. So are you," she tells her daughter. "Keep out of sight and danger."

"No, I stay with you," Haven protests.

"Please," Rayla says. She moves her hand up to Haven's cheek. "I need to know at least *you* remain out of Roth's grasp."

Haven relents and goes in for a hug. It's obvious she's out of practice, because it's clumsy and she squeezes way too hard, but Rayla's a noob at physical emotion, too, so it's actually perfect. Neither wants to let go. *Is that a lump in my throat?*

I turn, giving them their well-earned privacy, and stare at the heavy foreign object in my shaky hands.

We will face Guards this time, actual humans, not just drones. They will be much harder to shoot.

Are you a Common member or just a Kismet puppet like Blaise said?

I'm about to find out.

Trial by gunfire.

MIRA

I'd never been to the Texas State Capitol before tonight. A microchip scan was always required to enter the premises. Any of my days aboveground that aligned with school field trips or invites to official events as Father's plus-one would always go to Ava.

It's even taller close up. At eighty stories, it's too high for me to see its top from where I stand on the wide landing of the grand red-granite staircase. Granite torn from the old Capitol to build the new. Somewhere up there, atop its lofty pinnacle, lording over the city, stands the Goddess of Liberty. The historic statue clutches a gilded Lone Star in one hand, a sword of justice in the other.

Crushing cheers, thousands strong, erupts from the lawn, the streets, skyscraper windows, as the Family Planning Director pushes me into the light.

"Ladies and gentlemen, fellow citizens of Dallas," Alexander's placid voice says, amplified by a microphone. He wears a uniform so perfectly tailored it's like he never took it off. Or maybe Governor Roth had it waiting, knowing he'd come back. A black armband of mourning wraps around his right sleeve for the fallen son he left behind.

For the son that I took from him. From *them*. The citizens. *Or so every single person here believes.*

"I didn't kill Halton!" I scream, but no one hears me above the tumult.

"Please excuse the late hour and the disruption to your busy schedules," Alexander says. "But I bring a most urgent announcement that can only be shared in person." He lifts his arm, presenting me formally to the rabid audience, their roar reaching a feverish intensity.

The Director drags me across the slick stone floor and ties me to a pole five yards from Alexander and the podium. She makes a show of waving a purple cloth in front of me before she gags me with it, smiling.

"It will be over soon," she coos in my ear, stroking my cheek like a reassuring parent. "I look forward to seeing more of you when you're dead."

She's going to dissect and study me. Twin research. An image flashes behind my eyes of me cold and blue on her operating table.

My blood boils, red and alive. I want to wrench my limbs free and curl my hands around her throat, but I save my energy. I won't let her weaken me. I turn my focus onto the crowd, searching hopelessly for a friendly face.

Ava, are you here?

"Many of you will recognize me," Alexander continues from center stage. "I have been gone for too long. But now I have returned. I am Alexander Roth, and I have not come empty-handed."

Drones with facial recognition cameras fly above the audience, hunting for the wanted, for insurgents that don't belong. Everywhere, Guards scour the mob of people, ripping off hats, umbrellas, sunglasses, anything that could hide a lurking Common member.

Ava, I hope you're not here. For your sake and for mine. I don't want her to see this.

"For over a century the citizens of Dallas have entrusted my family, the Roth family, to watch over our shining capital . . ."

Bold white uniforms catch my roving eyes. A pack of Strake University students occupy the first four rows behind the chain of Guards. Their royal-purple sashes sink my heart into my stomach, and bile surges to my throat, burning every part of me in its path. I try to cough up the bitter acid, but the gag makes me choke. A raven-haired girl standing closest to me laughs. Mckinley Ruiz. Halton's ex. Her wide, gaping mouth a soundless cackle in the uproar.

"But for eighteen years, a shadow hid and lived among you . . ."

Sweat drips from my temples, stinging my eyes, sticking my bangs to my forehead, obstructing my view.

Where's Theo? Ciro? Kano?

Where's Ava?

The glass facades of the skyrises light up all over Capitol Square. Ava's out-of-date wanted photo projects across every blinding screen. I barely recognize her. *Us.* Long fiery-red hair, the naive eyes of a fragile girl, outfitted in makeup and a Strake uniform.

A new word flashes across our chest: "Found."

You didn't find the girl in that photo. That girl is long dead.

The photo dissolves into a live image of me bound to the pole secured to the stone floor. The screens cut to a close-up so that each and every citizen, from the low ranking to the high, in the very back rows to the front, can all see that it's me.

Boos and cheers mix to a zenith of pandemonium.

I quell my instinct to cower, to throw down my head, to keep my eyes on my feet. Instead I lift my chin so the people can plainly see my face.

I am not ashamed. I am not scared or regretful. I am proud. I am Mira. I'm the Common. Let them see.

There's movement behind me, at the Capitol's entrance. Even Alexander pauses his speech and turns to look.

Beneath the center archway, two Texas State Guards burst out of the oak doors, carrying between them a seven-foot bulletproof-glass shield. The soldiers part, and the shield extends, creating a 180-degree angle of secured shelter.

The entire city falls eerily silent, as if the governor has the power to mute us all. The air feels thick. Even the very anticipation of his presence sucks oxygen out of the air, stifles and suppresses energy and hope.

Thousands of eyes lift toward the screens, a trained horde, holding their breath for the first glimpse of their conquering leader, their false savior.

He's just a mortal man.

But when he steps onto his dais and sits on his throne-like steel chair, my conviction abandons me.

Governor Roth has changed these past few months, as much as I have. He appears twice the size I remember. Larger than life. Deep furrows line his hollowed cheeks like scorched rivulets waiting for tears that will never fall from his two black eyes. His thin lips have all but disappeared, twisted and curled into a permanent, gruesome sneer.

He looks like the wielder of death.

Courage, for till all ceases, neither must you cease.

Snatching back my courage, I look death in the eyes.

"For over three decades . . . ," Alexander stumbles on. From the top of my vision, I see him on the giant screen displayed on the Capitol building. Fear fractures his stone-faced assertiveness. He's afraid. *He didn't expect the governor to come. Does he think Roth will turn on him?* He's captured the ultimate prize and has returned home a champion. What has he to fear?

Theo. Where's Theo?

". . . you have elected my father, Governor Howard S. Roth, to be the defender and torchbearer of our nation's beacon."

Applause explodes across the concrete grounds, bursting my eardrums. I don't flinch or blink. I don't take my eyes from the bulging vein on Governor Roth's forehead.

"Humbly, and in your name, I have brought you your traitor, Governor. I have found our city's very own *unwanted* Mira Goodwin."

"More like I found you!" I cry into my gag.

The governor moves his dark gaze to his son. The deafening zeal of the people shifts and intensifies. They're growing anxious. They want action. So does Governor Roth. I recognize it in the tightening of his jaw. He wants to taste blood.

Alexander motions toward General Pierce, who stands outside the bulletproof shield. Next to him is the Texas senator, a spineless, ineffectual woman. The governor's loyal puppet.

"Bring forward the captives," Alexander demands sharply.

At a signal from the general, the Guards from the TXRAIL appear on the steps of the granite staircase, dragging Theo, Ciro, and Kano gagged and bound to stand in a line beside me. Each Guard carries a bolt action rifle at their side.

Execution by firing squad. At least it will be quick.

But this fate for Theo? Alexander's beloved son? The son he saved all those years ago, the child he risked everything for?

No, it's too cruel. It doesn't make sense.

Theo spits and screams incoherent pleas at Alexander, his face a sweating, raging red, the veins on his neck popping like tiny ropes that could strangle him.

Does the governor recognize Theo as one of his own? He gives no clue he knows.

Theo makes for the podium, but he trips from the zip-ties binding his ankles and falls hard on his face. Like Ciro and Kano, I'm unable to help him. Theo tries to crawl to his father. To stop him.

Alexander places the microphone on the lapel of his jacket next to his medals and marches up and down his line of prisoners.

"The Common—" There's an audible gasp from the crowd. "Yes, I will say the name aloud because they do exist. And these are their faces." Alexander points to me and then to Theo. "These are the faces of the Common."

He lifts Theo off the ground and hauls him back to my side. Furiously, Theo attempts to talk to me, to force words through his gag, but I hear nothing but the crowd's violent cries for justice.

You will pay for your crimes. I can hear Governor Roth's sinister promise. I can't look at him. I won't. But he's on every skyrise, on every screen. I can't escape him.

I snap my head toward the mass, searching for only one person. *Ava, I lied. I want you here. Where are you?*

Then my heart lifts. It soars.

A single figure cuts through the press of bodies, elbowing her way to the stairs. Rayla.

Another catches my eye. A youth with a bandana made of flames.

And another. Owen, the boy from Detroit.

Emery. Pawel. *Kipling.*

They're all moving toward me.

The rebellion's here.

Alexander circles me. "Let it be remembered," he shouts, looming behind me, "that tonight, Texas showed the world how to survive."

The four State Guards march forward and stand side by side in formation, holding their rifles at attention.

I feel my bonds break. There's a hot, urgent whisper in my ear. "I got you your stage. Now deliver the truth I never could." Alexander slips my knife into my hand, slaps the microphone on my collar, and steps between the guns and me.

Ripping the gag from my mouth, I scream the truth before all of Dallas, before the Goddess of Liberty, before Governor Roth.

"If I'm a criminal, then Governor Roth is also a criminal!" I yank the cloth from Theo's mouth and cut his hands free. "The governor of Texas has an illegal second grandchild!"

"I am Theo Wright—Theo Roth—Alexander's second child," Theo proclaims, the microphone picking up his raspy cry. "Halton was my half brother. Governor Roth knew, but he let me live."

The crowd is dumbstruck. Theo's face fills the screens. The family resemblance is undeniable.

Governor Roth doesn't move. As if his kingdom isn't exploding around him, he sits stock-still, impervious to the bombshell I just released.

"If I should die," I scream in a rush of emotion, "like my father died, for defying the Rule of One, then so should Governor Roth!"

Rayla and the Common are almost up the steps. They're pushing through the Strake students. The Guard has taken notice. The soldiers lift their guns.

"Resist much!" Alexander shouts from center stage.

"Obey little!" I implore the people.

Small pockets of the crowd take up the call. "Once unquestioning obedience, once fully enslaved"—a larger group on the right—"once fully enslaved, no nation, state, city, of this earth"—in the center—"ever afterward resumes its liberty!"

Alexander raises his empty hands to the general. "Tell the Guard to stand down, General. Give the people back their liberty. It is right."

Arms and legs still bound, Ciro and Kano huddle around me, blocking me from the firing squad and the governor, making it impossible for me to see what's happening.

I dive to the floor between Theo's legs, frantic for a view of Governor Roth's next move.

A small lift of a finger. That's all it takes. Such a small action, and havoc ignites the capital.

Scream Guns pierce the sweltering midnight air. Smoke grenades fill the sky and my lungs. I can't hear. I can't breathe. I collapse onto my stomach, the stabbing shrieks intensifying with every inch I move. I see flashes of gunfire, Common members being dragged up the steps by their hair.

Theo falls to the floor next to me. With great effort I reach out my left hand and grip his.

You take one second-born, you take both.

Someone grabs my other hand. Squinting through the haze, I see the outline of my face.

"Ava!" I shout. My sister shoves earplugs into my ears, shutting out the debilitating sound that keeps me on the floor. She pulls me up, and I lift Theo after me.

"Protect the twins!" Rayla's voice commands somewhere nearby, lost in the haze of the smoke grenades.

With stinging, half-blind eyes, I scour the fleeing, indistinct shapes, willing Roth to appear.

"Roth ran!" Ava yells above the gunshots.

"We have to go after him!" I insist, turning toward the Capitol building.

"Protect the twins!"

"Let go of his hand," Ava shouts, nodding at Theo. "Grab a weapon and leave him! You have to protect yourself!" She pulls me down the steps away from the Capitol and Alexander.

"Protect the twins!" Emery repeats Rayla's command, summoning a wall of Common members to surround us.

If I let go of his hand, Theo will crumple to the ground, defenseless from the Scream Gun. He doesn't know the city. He'll never find his way out. The Guard will take him. Roth will take him.

"No one gets left behind!" I yell as a Texas State Guard with a rifle breaks through the human shield, barrel aimed at Ava.

Two shots are fired at him: one from Ava, one from Owen, who emerges from the toxic fumes just as the soldier collapses to the pavement.

There's no time to see if the Guard's dead. Someone throws a heavy bulletproof blanket over our heads, and the huddled mass pushes us across the boulevard; north, east, I can't tell.

"To the safe house!" Emery instructs the growing defense.

My racing thoughts overpower the sirens, the screams, the incessant *pop, pop, pop* of gunfire.

But my mission! Did it work?

Roth's loyalists *saw* the truth.

But is truth enough? Can truth be seen in a blind world?

I hope we made them see with new eyes.

PART III

THE MANSION

AVA

I think I killed a man. Or did Owen, Rayla's new tagalong? We fired at the exact same time—either bullet could've been the kill shot. *Push that thought aside. Save it for later.*

Mira. It's dark and loud, and I don't know where we're going, but I'm still holding her hand. I squeeze, and she squeezes back.

Why wouldn't she let go of that Roth boy's hand?

Our forward movement abruptly stops, and the sound of an engine thrums close by.

"Everyone, get in!" I hear Emery shout. "Head to the safe house!"

I rip off the bulletproof blanket to reveal a line of cars parked along a nondescript side street. Common members are piling into the getaway cars en masse.

No! We have to go back to the Capitol—Roth is still there. This time, we can't run away.

Before I can object, my grandmother steps in front of me.

"Rayla!" I cry out. She wraps her arms tight around Mira and me, and all at once I feel like I'm back home. *I am. I'm back in Dallas. I made it just in time.* Our plane landed twenty miles outside Dallas, where Pawel managed to hijack an autonomous car. After we stole ourselves into the barricaded city, we immediately heard the message to report to Capitol Square.

What I found there was my worst nightmare come to life.

I thought Mira was going to die on the Capitol steps right in front of me, her executioner Alexander Roth. First my father, and now my twin sister, both murdered by a Roth.

She's alive. She's safe. We're together again with Rayla.

My head spins, and my heart aches, and for a moment I can do nothing but cling to Rayla and my sister.

I'm pulled back to reality when I feel something wet against my arm. I let go of Rayla to find blood soaking through her shirtsleeve. *She's hurt.*

My warm bubble of safety pops. I suddenly notice all the gunfire and screaming close by.

"Rayla, you're shot?!" Mira exclaims. We both reach as one for the wound, but Rayla pulls away.

"It's nothing. It's an old injury," Rayla says, supplying more questions than answers. "There's no time to talk now. We must get back to the safe house."

I know she's in pain—her jaw is stiff; she's clamping down on her molars. But before I can question her any further, a scarlet-red car pulls up dramatically in front of us. Both sides lift open like elegant bird wings, and Owen, the guy who's been with Rayla this whole time, bursts out of the driver's seat, looking almost as worried about my grandmother as I am.

It's clear how loyal he is to Rayla—he races straight for her, attempting to escort her into the passenger's seat.

She bats him away, instead pushing Mira and me into the back seat of the car. The Roth boy Mira saved gets in after us, but Rayla holds up a hand to Alexander. Wearing his uniform, he's the spitting image of Governor Roth in his prime. The next in line. "Only five passengers in this car—make for the car up ahead," she says. "We'll meet you at the Last Stage."

Why are we taking the Roths with us? They should be in handcuffs. Anger surges through me, my desire for revenge burning hot.

My hand moves for my gun. *Hurting one of his own might make Governor Roth feel my pain.*

But then the doors seal shut, and we're racing through the back streets of Dallas, and I have to use my hands to brace myself. "Buckle up!" Owen shouts from up front. I can't believe Rayla is letting someone else drive.

Out the car windows it's all chaos and smoke. Dallas was the most law-and-order city in America—never in my wildest daydreams would I ever have imagined that the heavily regulated streets I walked down for eighteen years would turn into a warzone.

"Mandatory curfew!" a warning blasts out all across the capital. *"Return immediately to your residence, or you will be arrested!"*

But the people aren't obeying.

Citizens wearing Goodwin masks flood the streets, headed toward the Governor's Mansion or the Capitol, tearing down surveillance cameras as they go, weapons in their hands. *I'm not the only one seeking revenge.*

I glimpse boarded-up windows, those loyal to Roth hiding themselves away. I see flashes of yellow doors whip past, welcoming me home.

Rayla turns her passenger lounge chair to face Mira and me. "I'm very happy to see you both again," she says, reaching out to grab our hands, but one of Mira's is already taken. By the Roth boy.

Why is he still holding her hand? I want to tear the two of them apart, break their link. *He looks so much like Halton. How can she bear to touch him?*

Mira quickly pulls her hand away like she's been caught stealing water.

"I guess I'll formally intro myself . . . I'm Owen Hart," Owen interrupts from the driver's seat with an expectant glance in the rearview mirror.

Silence hangs in the air like jagged icicles. Halton's brother looks uneasily at my sister. She doesn't dare look in his direction. One false move and Theo's going to get cut. And Mira knows it.

The boy is living proof of Roth's hypocrisy—but we got from him what we needed, and now he needs to go.

"Oh right, yeah, Ava and Mira Goodwin don't need introductions," Owen rambles on. "And Theo just intro'd himself on stage . . ." The guy was mute the first time we saw each other, and now he can't seem to shut up.

"What is he doing here, Mira?" I demand, pointing at Theo. "Our missions were to bring Roth down, not bring one into the Common family."

"He's one of us, Ava," Mira says, gripping my hand tight. "He's on our side."

"How can you be so sure?" Rayla says, echoing my distrust.

"Just listen to me," Mira pleads. I've always known what my sister was thinking, because I was usually thinking it too. Now that we've been apart for two days, and she's been having her own experiences, I have no context for what she's about to argue next.

"You heard them yourselves back there—I didn't force Theo and his father to admit what they did," Mira insists. "They both put their own lives in danger for our cause, many times. We crossed the border in a *Guard's* ship," Mira says, astonishing me. "If it weren't for them, I would have never completed my mission."

"Well, do you speak?" Rayla turns her sharp eyes on Theo. "You sure spoke loud enough on the Capitol steps."

Theo sits up straight in a gesture of respect for our grandmother. "When Mira told me that I share Roth's blood . . . it was the worst day of my life," he answers solemnly. "But if my existence helps bring down Governor Roth, I am glad for it."

And with that, Mira and I are slammed against the car windows as Owen makes a sharp left into a garage. Rayla and Theo were the only ones who had listened to Owen's seat belt advice.

"Where did all these cars come from?" I ask in awe. There are dozens of them, all makes and models. I turn to Rayla, but it's Owen who answers.

"It's the Common Cavalry," Owen says, clearly proud of the lineup. "We've been collecting them." He expertly weaves the car between the rows of tightly packed vehicles, then parks close to the Last Stage entrance. The doors immediately swing open.

"This car's his," Rayla says before sliding out of her seat and into the garage. "He helped program it himself." *Is she bragging about him?*

I want to know more of Owen's story; he's spent as much time with my grandmother as I have, and it's obvious they share a friendship, but now's not the time. Mira just bolted from the car, screaming, "Ava, our bike!"

Sure enough, the Triumph motorcycle we named Lucía sits right in front of the safe house entrance doors. *How is that possible?* A familiar jovial chuckle causes my heart to leap.

"Didn't I always say you two were somethin' special?"

I spin around in disbelief, but there he is, the west Texas cowboy, here in Dallas. He hasn't lost that twinkle in his eye.

"Thank you for coming, Kipling," I say. We clasp shoulders just as Emery emerges from her own car, enveloped in her long yellow coat once more. "We must gather and count our numbers inside," Emery announces. She's focused and composed, ready for continued action. *We're gathering so we can strike again.*

Emery takes her place by Rayla, her old mentor, and together we all walk through the Last Stage doors.

We head straight through the wings and onto the stage, where a small crowd is busy organizing supplies. I look out onto the massive auditorium—only a quarter of the seats are full. *More will come. We're the first wave to arrive.*

The Last Stage. What a clever choice for our Dallas haven: an old three-tiered performance auditorium that was once named the Majestic

Theater. The Guard will never look here. Government defunding and the VR experience have long made theater halls forgotten relics.

Incoming Common members start to fill the threadbare seats. Many are injured, more are standing guard at every entrance, holding weapons and shouting.

There's no sign of my team. Pawel and Barend must still be out in the fight.

"Alexander!" a desperate cry reaches us from somewhere in the audience. "My son!"

I freeze, recognizing the voice.

Impossible.

MIRA

The governor's wife staggers up the stage toward us.

"De ninguna pinche manera," Theo exclaims on my left. *No fucking way.*

"Since when do Roths speak Spanish?" Ava retorts on my right. She eyes Theo from head to sneakered toe. I know exactly what she's thinking about him, because I thought the same things too.

"Theo's not like the others," I say, watching as Mrs. Roth throws her arms around a rigid Alexander. "Neither of them is."

Both Ava and Rayla scoff. I don't think Theo heard.

I want them to like him. Or at least to understand him. I have no idea why.

"Rayla, please explain how Mrs. Roth is in a Common safe house?" Ava asks, her fingers clenched, ready to throw a punch. I grab the ends of her jacket, holding her back.

"Haven—" Rayla falters, then clears her throat. "The First Lady was found outside the mansion and brought here."

"Why are you here!" Mrs. Roth screams shrilly at her son.

I barely recognize the First Lady. Her petite frame and self-worshipping pride are buried under oversized civilian clothes that I can smell from where I stand. No diamonds or gold glitter from her neck or fingers. Her feet are bare, as is her usually made-up face.

All ladylike dignity completely extinguished, Mrs. Roth stares up at her son, her sanity dancing on a knife's blade. "Say something, Alexander!" she shrieks. "You left me with no goodbye. Now after eighteen years you return, and you *still* have nothing to say?!"

Alexander glances around the auditorium, realizing he's gained an audience. He flings Mrs. Roth's arms off his chest and turns toward the wings of the stage.

"Why did you return?" Mrs. Roth blathers. "Where have you been? Why are you in your old uniform? *Say something!*"

Alexander rounds on her, shouting so loudly the cheap seats on the third balcony must be able to hear. "How could you let him kill *my son*! You were supposed to protect Halton! That was the deal, *Mother*." The word sounds like a curse.

Mrs. Roth falters, raising her hands to her face as if he had actually struck her.

Ava and I, along with every member in this building, wait for Mrs. Roth to repeat the stale lie that the Traitorous Twins murdered Halton, that the Common killed their heir.

The First Lady's sanity must have taken a plunge, because the bare truth escapes her crooked lips.

"How could I have known?! How could I have known your father would spill his own blood?"

Beside me Rayla spits on the floor. Owen follows, then Theo.

Alexander rips off his military jacket and launches it at his mother. The force nearly knocks her over. "Whatever selfish reasons you had for leaving the Governor's Mansion . . . it turned out to be a smart move on your part. I told Dallas our little family secret. Looks like you'll be needing a new home."

"How about Guardian Tower!" someone shouts from the back rows.

"I second that," Ava says, casting a baleful glare at Theo.

Mrs. Roth gazes out at the audience, fear paralyzing her body like she just got hit with a stun gun.

Common members, Dallas citizens—all intermix here as one. A buzz of unified anger permeates the theater as they press closer to the stage, closer to their First Lady than they've ever been. Hatred burns across their faces.

"I left!" she wails to her former citizens. "I left. What more do you want of me?"

Emery appears behind Rayla, a hand on her mentor's shoulder. My grandmother winces; she tries to hide her pain, but Emery and I both see it. So do Ava and Owen. We all respect her too much to say anything in this moment—Rayla would never want to show frailty in front of the enemy.

"We need Mrs. Roth for our future plans," Emery whispers. "Should we put an end to this miserable scene?"

Mrs. Roth's crazed eyes sweep the stage and land on Theo.

"Oh boy, here we go," Owen whispers.

"Theo?" Mrs. Roth wails, scrambling away from Alexander. She makes it all but five feet before Alexander catches her by her baggy linen coat.

"Theo?" Mrs. Roth says again, this time her voice as flat as her deflated hair; hair that was once as big and rich as the state of Texas. She attempts to regain her poise, extending her hand to her grandson, her last hope. "I'm your grandmother. I always prayed I'd get to meet you one day."

"Screw this," Ava seethes. "We didn't come here for a goddamn Roth reunion."

"You're nobody to me," Theo says loudly, leaving his grandmother's hand dangling awkwardly in the air. His cheeks are flushed, and his hulking figure shakes like it's taking everything he has to keep his emotions in control. Just two days ago he was Theo Wright, a Canadian. Now he's facing his foreign family that he never knew he had. "I came to Dallas to help right my family's wrongs," he proclaims. "Nunca tuve una abuela."

"What does that mean! What are you saying?" Mrs. Roth balks. *Did she really never learn Spanish?*

"He says you're not his grandmother." I step forward. "He'll never claim you as his." Mrs. Roth's eyes bulge like this is the first time she's noticed my presence. Her oily head whips from me to Theo.

The governor and First Lady always wanted a Roth-Goodwin union. Ava and Halton, the perfect pair.

With me by Theo's side, we're the Glut version.

It's clear she doesn't like it.

"He *is* mine!" Mrs. Roth screams, unhinged, lunging for Theo's arm. "You're my grandson!"

To my astonishment, Rayla steps in front of Theo, blocking him from his grandmother's reach.

"Your husband killed your only grandson," Rayla spits at Mrs. Roth. "Theo was never yours."

"The Roth family is finished." Alexander releases his grip on his mother and moves to stand beside Theo. "We're Common blood now."

"I didn't . . . ," Mrs. Roth mumbles. "How could he have killed our Halton . . ." Tears of contrition fall down the First Lady's gaunt cheeks. All her power has left her.

Now to take her husband's.

I'm on the verge of demanding Mrs. Roth admit the governor murdered my father when a single word escapes Ava's mouth. My breath catches, heart in my throat.

"Mother."

Under the glowing light of the chandelier, my mother walks up the steps to the stage. She's much older than her hologram memories, more worn down and wild and neglected than I ever thought she could be. But her eyes are the same. Green and fierce. Like every woman's in our family.

"Not your mother," Rayla says in a hoarse whisper. "This is Haven, your aunt."

Ava and I snap our heads back to Rayla. She looks at the two of us, so much suffering in her red-rimmed eyes, like she was trying to find the right way to share this revelation but just didn't know how. How could she have?

Our mother's twin is alive.

My aunt. The term is so unbelievable it doesn't penetrate.

Ava curls her fingers around mine. I can feel the goose bumps prickling her skin.

Haven stops an arm's length away. Hers is a fractured smile, a lop-sided, shaky curve that says smiles were rare in her past. *Hers was a life of hardship.*

I can never imagine what she's been through.

"You survived?" Ava says like it's still a question.

I used to talk to my mother's twin in my dreams. Asking her if she was lost, if she made it out of the void. Now she's here; she's real. I reach out and hug her.

Ava also falls into the embrace; then Rayla wraps her arms around her progeny, holding on tight. We become a circle of four broken hearts, trying to be whole together.

Emery begins a slow clap. Owen starts whooping, and soon the entire auditorium erupts in vibrant applause.

"This here is what it's all about," Kipling says, fat tears in his crinkled eyes.

Click, click, click. The sudden metallic din echoes across the building. The noise stops the cheering, and pulls my family apart.

Is that coming from the exits?

"That doesn't sound good," Owen shouts to Rayla.

It sounds like a lockdown.

OWEN

"Son of a Glut!" I curse. I wave the key fob Emery gave me in front of the smart lock and try the door handle one more time, just in extra case. Still nothing.

Yep, we're trapped.

No keys. No worries. Just scan your microchip. That's the selling point of the nationally adopted electronic lock system. *It's convenient!*

Yeah, convenience is all well and good until the government decides to seize control of your door, sealing you inside.

We've been using physical keys to swipe our way in and out of the safe house, but they mean diddly-squat during a lockdown.

I turn to deliver the bad news to Rayla and company. All eyes are on me, the Common's resident Programmer. *Shit. I'm expected to figure this out.* My slightly panicked brain fires off a hardwired Kismet lesson: *Every found key can unlock victory.*

When there are no keys, you have to hack your way out.

I open my mouth to tell the team that I've got this, except the voice of a combative government official speaks first.

"Dallas is under mandatory lockdown!" the riled-up voice yells through the giant theater speakers. "Remain inside the closest building— any person found in the streets will be arrested or shot."

The whole capital's trapped.

Whatever semblance of calm the people crammed into the theater were holding on to, it blows to absolute pieces. And rightly so. Roth authorizing a full emergency protocol is historic—an entire freaking city going on *literal* lockdown has never been done before. Ever.

What other taboo lines is the governor willing to cross? The question scares the living daylights out of me. *And this is the man that wants to have power over the whole country.*

Nope! That can't happen.

First step: Get us the hell out of here.

I turn to Rayla with a quick "I'm on it!" and rocket toward the control room. *There's got to be computers in there.*

The panicky mob of Common members isn't making my passage easy. Half are scrambling to the doors, knowing damn well they're shut, and a quarter are shouting, *"What are we going to do!"* Most simply stand smack-dab in my way, looking lost.

And to really amp up the alarm, the government's threats continue to play on repeat like a playlist made by Satan himself. "Dallas is under mandatory lockdown!" ". . . will be arrested or shot." They might as well be blasting the song "You're All Going to Die," because that's exactly how it sounds.

"Screw your lockdown!" Ava calls out from the stage. I whip around to see her raise her gun and shoot down the closest speaker.

The gunshot makes me jump.

Get it together. I only half killed a man. Ava killed the other half, and she's fine. *You're fine.*

"I'm fine!" I announce out loud, triggering way too much attention. Whoops.

I race back down the aisle to a chorus of gunshots firing around the theater—Common members following Ava's lead.

Just like that, the government has been silenced.

Yeah, for now.

I'm wondering when I'm going to give myself better pep talks when the guy who was hanging off Ava's arm on the newscast shoulders his way past me through the aisle. He's switched out his tux for rugged Blackout Wear, and his face is cut and dirty, but yep, positive it's Pawel.

He hops right up on the stage where Rayla and her family have set up shop, and Ava's face lights up with relief when she sees him. The two of them hug it out. Mira pauses in doctoring her own grandmother's wound to join in on the reuniting action.

Is this me being jealous? *Well, stop.* There are bigger things to worry about, like freeing the Common from its own safe house.

I finally make it to the back of the theater. After I barrel up the stairs to the control room, I see Blaise is on it too. He's already organized an improvised hacking station—his lightning-fast fingers are busy punching in thousands of lines of code. The guy's in the zone.

We've got something Roth's side doesn't: the best hacker in all the land. He's probably already unlocked half the doors in Dallas by now. And with my added talents, the lockdown doesn't stand a chance. We've got this.

"Huge problem," Blaise informs me without looking up from his computer screen. "There's a simultaneous information blackout happening . . ." It takes him a beat to spit out the rest. "I can't break through."

What?

"Without the Blackout Codes to shut it off," he says, "we're totally up shit creek."

Okay, new problem. Digital lockdown trumps door lockdown. We can't hack our way out with no Internet.

Side step: Get the Blackout Codes.

The entire Internet, the cyber world Blaise and I know like the backs of our hands, has gone dark. No data—photos, videos, messages, and articles that could tell the world the crimes that are happening—is able to escape Dallas, just like its citizens.

A complete block on the flow of information in and out of Dallas is the worst-case scenario for the Common. Not only does it mean that Mira's public reveal of Roth having Multiples in his own family and thus being a traitor to his country will be censored; it means Roth can do anything he wants because no one outside Dallas will see until after the fact. He could massacre tens of thousands of his own citizens and then claim the Common killed them all in the deadliest act of terrorism the country has ever seen. Roth's now in control of the narrative—because he controls the Internet. He can share or block whatever information he chooses.

To top it all off, no messages out means zero help is on the way. We're on our own.

We're sitting ducks.

First Lady Roth. Through the control panel window, I see her sitting in the front row.

She *has* to know the deactivation codes to unlock the city, right? You don't get First Lady in front of your name for nothing. I'm just not buying what the crazy lady's selling—she's more cunning than she's letting on.

The First Lady of Texas has the key to unlock victory.

But how do I get her to talk?

I decide to skirt the stage on my quest to find Theo. Best to avoid Rayla and the sisters. They might be good at a zillion things, but sweet-talking a Roth will never be a tool in their talent box.

If we don't get the Blackout Codes soon . . .

Buckets of sweat spill down my face. Does Roth control the AC too? The salt stings my eyes worse than a scourge of mosquito bites to my corneas. Blinking does nothing. I bet it looks like I'm crying.

"We're sitting ducks!" I shout out of nowhere.

People jammed inside the hallway all stare up at me slack jawed. Oh right. I rub shoulders with Rayla Cadwell. I'm at least top ten on the Wanted List. People think I'm in the inner circle.

I have to play it cool.

I cut my speed and pass out reassurances as I go. *Don't worry, we're on it . . . We'll lift the lockdown double-quick . . . Be outta here in a wink . . .*

I think they believe me.

That's good. Because I sure as hell don't.

Bypassing backstage, I get myself to the rear exit doors that would take me to the parking garage if the Guard weren't holding us hostage.

There. Found him. Theo's almost as tall as Xavier; he's hard to miss.

Looks like he's taking the heat about as well as I am—he's sweating so bad his white shirt's see-through. The guy's ripped.

But all that muscle won't break electronic locks.

Xavier and Theo's weapon of choice to pry open the steel door: metal crowbars. They're giving it all they've got, but it's just not going to happen. By the time I hotfoot it over to them, Theo's resorted to whacking at it.

"Where's Malik?" I shout at Xavier. Stupid question.

"Still. Out. There," Xavier says between his own clobbering blows. It doesn't even leave a dent.

We *really* need those codes . . .

"Hey, Theo!" I yell.

But Theo keeps hammering away like the door's Governor Roth's face.

"Hey, *Theo*!" I shout louder. Theo turns midwhack, and I duck, saving myself from decapitation.

"Sorry!" Theo cries, gulping down air. "I didn't see you there."

Up close, the family resemblance is bona fide. That should tug on Mrs. Roth's nonexistent heartstrings.

"I have a better way out," I say.

"Oh yeah?" Theo asks, tossing down his crowbar. "Anything I can do?"

"Well, yeah actually . . . I need you to talk to your estranged grannie and politely ask her for the Blackout Codes."

He screws up his face. "You think she has codes to unlock the doors?"

"I think she knows the codes that can unblock the *Internet* that can help us unlock the doors. There's not really time to explain . . ."

Ava, Mira, and the whole gang are backstage watching us like surveillance drones. I throw them an a-okay signal, even toss in a thumbs-up. Nothing to see here, Rayla, I've got this covered.

"The message has changed," Xavier says, cocking his ear to a wonky speaker above the door. The audio's weak—it's on the fritz from a direct bullet hit—but Xavier makes sense of it. "To the anarchists terrorizing Dallas, surrender is your only way out. Surrender now. Surrender now . . ."

I'm sure it keeps on going, but who has time to listen? To Theo's credit, he asks no more questions and makes a beeline for Mrs. Roth.

I catch up with him, my four steps to his one, cramming in a coaching session as we head for the auditorium.

"Why doesn't Mrs. Roth have a fresh cut on her wrist?" Theo interrupts my pep talk. "Did the Elders not take out her microchip?"

"Openly known secret—governors and their partners don't have one. Their chips are removed the second they take office. For *international security measures.*" I air quote the excuse.

Really they're all head-case overlords who don't play by the same rules.

Theo scoffs. "How can I be related to these people?"

"If you could keep that kind of *out-loud* dialogue to a minimum with the First Lady . . ."

"What should I say, then?"

"I don't know . . . let her pinch your cheeks or something? Tell her you've had a change of heart . . ."

Tell her you look forward to visiting her in prison . . .

Haven and Alexander stand over Mrs. Roth like sentinel soldiers in it for the long haul. Theo's dad tries to stop us, but Theo holds out a hand, putting a quick end to *that* potential speed bump.

"Hello, Grandmother," Theo says.

Okay, off to a good start.

"Give me the Blackout Codes."

Well, I was hoping for a bit more finesse.

I'm about to hop in and save this car crash of an inquiry when—

"I'll forgive you," Theo says.

This perks up Mrs. Roth.

"If you give me the codes, I will forgive you for expelling me and my parents."

Short and sweet, with an impactful gut punch. Mrs. Roth melts, smiling a thirty-two-watt beam. She holds out her arms, and I gently shove Theo into them.

"So do you know the codes or not?" Theo asks, wriggling free.

"Of course I know the codes, dear," she says, a new swagger to her posture.

Theo's nostrils flare at the endearment. Too soon.

She grabs Theo's hand, imparting her grannie wisdom. "Always have information to bargain with. Even when you are at your weakest, you can hold on to your power, if only by your fingertips."

Control dies hard with this family.

"Pinche idiota," Theo utters. No idea what he said, but it didn't sound pleasant.

"What does that mean?" Mrs. Roth asks Alexander.

"He said thank you for the lesson," I quickly reinterpret, "and can we please have the codes now."

"You will let the Common know I played my part?" Mrs. Roth asks. Her fingers clamp down on her grandson's hand with zero intention of ever letting go. "You look so much like my Halton."

"The codes?" Theo asks, completely smooth.

"Red, Polaris, six, ocean, amity."

Victory!

Theo yanks back his hand, wipes it on his soaked shirt, and leaves.

Haven and Alexander wave at the crowd to pipe down, and I shout the Blackout Codes so Blaise can hear. He pops his head out of the control room and gives a *Got it!* nod.

Should be done in no time.

I give myself a mental high five, feeling keyed up from my gung-ho, take-charge spirit. I'm on a roll.

"Do you have any more information?" I ask the First Lady. "Like . . . I don't know, where exactly the governor's hiding?"

One mention of her husband and her teeth start chattering. She crosses her arms like a blizzard suddenly blew through.

"The governor doesn't hide. He waits."

Well, that sounds ominous.

Shouting breaks out from all exits of the theater.

"Those are happy shouts, right?" I ask Haven and Alexander.

Blaise must've hacked open the doors!

Then the general hurrah shifts gears. They're screaming now. Row after row picks up on the hysteria, passing the message to us in a high-stakes game of telephone until finally the words make sense.

"*The Guard is coming!*" I scream to Rayla up on the stage.

Holy Whitman, the Guard is coming.

Fight or flight? One look from Rayla and I know.

We fight.

AVA

A mass of citizens pushes its way through the now-unlocked theater doors, terror on their faces.

"The Guard is coming!" they scream, seeking shelter inside the safe house that was our cage only seconds ago. Adrenaline courses through my body as the Common's leadership and I elbow our way out into the garage. *We will not run from the enemy. We will stand and face them.*

Not everyone feels as I do. One of the Common's Cavalry flees out the garage's exit, the getaway car jam-packed with people who clearly feel their chances of survival are greater out on the streets by themselves. They made a mistake. *There is strength in numbers.*

"Get back here, you bastards!" Owen shouts, racing after the car. Kipling breaks rank and hurries to protect the rest of our Cavalry's cars.

"Ciro!" Mira exclaims beside me. I look at the garage entrance and find two men scrambling in our direction, their arms over each other's shoulders in support. *Barend.* He's injured.

"Please, a medic!" Ciro calls out. He's bloodied—his blonde hair and smooth face stained red—and shaken, all semblance of his usual buoyant self shattered.

Ciro tries to carefully lay Barend on the ground. Mira and I race forward to help, our deep-rooted instinct to heal still there. Turns out our hands can heal *and* hurt. *Just like yours, Father.*

"The Scream Gun . . . he gave his earplugs to me," Ciro says, frantic, his once-bright eyes glassy with fear. He places a tender kiss onto Barend's forehead and the soldier leans into his touch.

"He'll be okay. The pain will pass," I assure Ciro. I know just how it feels to have a shockwave delivered inside your skull so loud it brings you screaming to your knees. It's almost worse watching helpless as someone you love suffers through it.

I look calmly into Barend's eyes. *He's not our betrayer.* All the questionable actions, the secretiveness. Ciro's former bodyguard must've been trying to hide his feelings for his superior. *A leftover Guard habit?*

"Ten armored SUVs . . . ," Ciro pants, "and a heat-ray gun . . . are headed to our safe house." He locks eyes with Emery, who has come up behind us. "Less than a mile away."

This triggers something in Mira; her eyes grow wide in alarm, and she wraps her arms around her body as if she can already feel the agonizing burn. *Has Mira been tortured by that weapon before?*

"Create a barrier with the cars!" Rayla commands at once, facing the Common. "Draw whatever weapons you have. Be prepared to defend yourselves!"

Barend shakily rises to his feet, bracing himself on Ciro's shoulder. *A soldier never turns down a fight.* "What are our numbers?" he asks through clenched teeth.

"There is no defending yourself—it's a weapon designed to end all defense," Alexander says in an urgent undertone.

"They're here!" Xavier shouts, exiting the final car in the makeshift blockade.

"Everyone, take shelter now!" Emery orders. "Weapons at the ready!"

I take a step toward the entrance, firmly gripping my gun, but Rayla puts a hand on my shoulder to stop me. "No, you and Mira take cover. Watch over Haven and Mrs. Roth," she says resolutely, before she moves for the garage entrance.

There's no time to argue. Mira, Theo, Pawel, and I help lead the remaining frightened Common members behind thick concrete pillars as Rayla joins Emery, Alexander, and Xavier inside Owen's car. *A perfect stake-out position.*

"Duke's bulletproof. He'll keep Rayla safe," Owen says as he returns from positioning his car in the barricade. *Duke?* He named his vehicle?

Lean and scrappy, Owen has one of those charming faces that must get him out of all kinds of trouble. His combination of dimples and cheerful, deep-set golden eyes makes *him* look like the trouble. He also has a mouth that doesn't like to stay closed. The opposite of Rayla's ideal companion. *I wonder how they met.*

"Ava, there's movement," Mira says softly, sneaking a stealth look out at the action. I shake my head clear and crouch down beside her at the edge of the pillar to steal a glance at the garage entrance.

Ten armored vehicles—outfitted with autonomous machine guns—flank an indomitable tank with a massive antenna on its roof. They're parked right outside the Common's doorstep, facing us.

Why haven't they opened fire?

"Are they waiting for us to shoot first?" Theo asks, looking over our heads.

The passenger door of the closest tinted-window SUV cracks open, and an anonymous hand appears, waving something in the smoggy Dallas air.

"What is *that*?" Owen breathes below us, stacking himself underneath Mira and me for a view.

A flowy object dangles out the door.

"It's a yellow cloth," Pawel says, practically lying on the ground below Owen, peering at the scene through a pair of binoculars. *Smart move, tracker.*

"Like a cease-fire?" Owen asks. "Aren't those supposed to be white?"

"A flag of alliance . . ." Mira formulates her thoughts out loud.

"They're trying to join with us," I finish for her. We are of the same mind again.

"It's a trick!" Pawel says from the base of our totem pole.

"My sentiments exactly," Owen agrees. "No way Rayla says yes to that."

The SUV door fully opens, and General Pierce, the Commander of the Texas State Guard, emerges. Yellow cloth in hand, he marches right up to the safe house door with all the confidence of Texas.

This man turned on our father. Mira and I both reach for our guns.

"Dad, what are you doing?!" Theo shouts, darting out from behind the pillar. Alexander has exited Owen's car and is standing at attention, ready to meet the general.

"Theo, no!" Mrs. Roth calls out. She tries to go after her grandson, but Haven holds her back.

Rayla, Emery, and Xavier also leave the safety of the car to stand shoulder to shoulder with Alexander.

Amazingly, all at once, the rest of the Common abandons their shelters to gather behind our leaders—weapons out, at the ready if needed.

The general has a squadron of soldiers armed to the teeth and a heat-ray gun backing him. It's not a fair fight.

"Alexander," General Pierce says, bowing his head formally to the governor's son. The sudden onrush of enemy combatants doesn't even make him blink. "The Texas Guard stands with you."

My god.

Did the greatest army in the country just offer to join forces with the rebellion? Or with Alexander in particular?

"I'm not the one in charge here," Alexander says, stepping aside. "Emery is the leader of the Common. Address her, not me."

Emery looks to Rayla, her former instructor and the rebellion's former leader, as if asking for her blessing. Rayla nods, and Emery steps forward.

"Why do you rebel?" she demands of General Pierce.

"Because I am a patriot," the general answers with a surprising amount of heat. "I stand by my country and my state, not by the public official. Roth no longer serves his country or his state. He serves only himself. That was made clear to me at the assembly tonight. It would be unpatriotic *not* to oppose him. I should have done so long ago."

He didn't use Roth's title. A clear sign his master's leash has been broken. *Does his alliance with us also mean he openly opposes the Rule of One?* It seems so incredible I can hardly believe it.

Guards in full riot gear, at least a hundred strong, pour out of the SUVs and stand in formation behind their general. All of them have slashes of yellow paint across their chests.

"These soldiers of Texas and I request to unite with the Common against Roth," General Pierce continues. "We pledge to assist the Common in whatever capacity it requires."

"Where did the Guard take our members?" Xavier says. "My son, Malik, is missing."

"And Cleo," Haven says, hoarse, like she's overused her voice. "The Guard took citizens at a rail station."

Who's Cleo? Does she have a friend?

The general knits his brows. "All prisoners were taken to Guardian Tower."

"Can you get them out?" Rayla interjects.

"Roth still has the Tower. His loyal soldiers control the Guard head-quarters," General Pierce says. He surveys the garage, taking in the Common multitude for the first time. Civilians, not soldiers, holding guns. Lots of them. *A sight I bet he never thought he'd see in his lifetime.*

"Unless there's a majority objection?" Emery asks the Common. There are a few grumbles from the crowd but no outright dissent. "The Common accepts your pledge," Emery says.

The Commanding General of Texas and the leader of the rebellion clasp shoulders. "Resist much," Emery and Rayla say together. "Obey little," the general finishes.

At that, Mira bolts for General Pierce. "Obey is all you've done your entire career," she fires at our father's former friend.

I follow her to stand face-to-face with the general. Even together, we don't equal his size. *But our anger can overpower him.*

"I won't let my personal prejudices against you stand in the way of getting Roth," Mira says, "but I have to hear you say it out loud. Our father did not take his own life. Roth killed him."

General Pierce meets our eyes. "I wasn't there."

"I know," Mira says, her voice tight. "I saw the video."

I reach down to grab my sister's hand.

"Your father never gave up," the general says, clearing his throat. "The video is real. Darren was shot by the governor himself." Gasps of disgust fan across the garage.

The general reaches inside his heavily medaled uniform and pulls something from his pocket.

My father's Family Planning Director badge.

Does he think it's a keepsake?

"Why would we want that?" I say, suddenly enraged. "It was just a game our father was playing. It's not who he really was." I say this so earnestly it's like I'm trying to convince myself. *What about Albatross?*

"It requires two fingerprints to open," the general says, handing me the badge.

Just like Father's journal. My heart races.

The general turns on his heel toward the Elders, giving Mira and me privacy.

I flip the badge over and see the familiar infinity symbol etched next to a small clasp. *Tied together forever.* My father's words come back to me in a rush of emotion. Just like we did in the factory in west Texas, I place my forefinger next to my sister's, we scan our prints on the lock, and it opens.

Instead of words of rebellion, a paper photograph of an illegal family hides inside. *My family.*

Father has his arm wrapped around our mother, who sits in a chair, a silver sonogram device positioned over her swollen stomach. Mira and I float above her belly in holographic blue light, astonishingly lifelike, our foreheads pressed together, our tiny fingers entwined.

The only time I've ever seen our family together, whole.

I wipe away the tears that stream down my cheeks. "Where is he?" I demand of the general, raising my voice. He turns back around to face me. "Where is Roth?"

"Hiding inside his fortress," General Pierce answers. "He's underneath the Governor's Mansion."

There's a bunker below Roth's castle. Of course.

"Take the mansion, and Guardian Tower will fall," the general says.

The citizens of Dallas come for your reckoning tonight, Roth. The mighty will fall at the hands of his own people.

The degenerates, the filth. The Common.

We're all coming for you.

OWEN

"Look who's underground *now*," I joke to Blaise. The Common's out in the open, and the government's in hiding. Literally underground.

Like, ten feet below, in fact.

Never thought I'd get to visit the notorious Governor's Mansion. The front doors might as well say, "High Rankers Only, Chumps." Looks like tonight's my lucky night.

The general of the Texas Guard signals to one of his lackeys, and a hologram map pops up in front of the concrete wall. Blaise and I scramble to get a good view.

Pawel stands next to me. The guy studies the map like he's cramming for midterms. Then he turns his baby blues on me. "Good job disabling the lockdown. I'm Pawel, by the way. I head the Intelligence Room back at HQ."

Well, that's cool. I guess. "I'm Owen. I'm with her." I throw a nod at Rayla, who stands front and center beside the general, strategizing our imminent strike. *I'm in with the grandma. Are you?* I glance over at Ava, too busy discussing the map with Mira and Haven to glance back.

Get. It. Together. We're about to lay siege to the Governor's Mansion. Focus.

The general speaks in a strictly classified tone. "We have a drone—"

"Please," Emery cuts in, "if you could speak loud enough for all to hear." This puts a constipated look on the big man's face. Generals aren't used to keeping the humble masses up to speed.

"We have a drone," the general tries again, louder this time, "positioned over the mansion." His pudgy finger points to the floating map. The awesomely detailed diagram lays out every level and room of our battlefield. Tiny red dots—hundreds of them—zoom this way and that like drunken bull's-eyes.

"Our thermal sensors have pinpointed anything with a pulse inside the mansion," the general explains.

"What makes you dead sure Governor Roth is the one in the bunker?" Rayla comes in hot.

Name tags start flashing next to the dot humans.

The Guard—the *Common's* Guard—must've taken over the NSA's microchip tracking system. Impressive.

The general and his entire unit must have cut out their chips so their former teammates would be unable to track them. Guards without chips. Mind blown.

Back to the map. The general air-circles the front left rooms of the mansion. "No bodies have been picked up by our sensors inside the Governor's Quarters." He zooms in below ground. "As you can see here, a single dot is fortified within the underground shelter. The dot has no microchip. All intelligence points to this bunker as our target."

"How do we take the bunker?" Ava asks, all gutsy and fiery, like her red hair.

"The tunnels." Alexander and the general let drop this explosive info at the exact same time.

Secret tunnels? Thank Whitman. I delete the insane image of me charging the mansion's wall, dodging bullets as I run, archaic war style. Drones go to battle. Not people.

"There are five hidden access points to the bunker," the general states. He's taken to shouting now so the back rows can appreciate his military show-and-tell. "Four access points are located half a mile from the Governor's Mansion, each connected to a network of tunnels that lead to the bunker."

Yeah, and where's the fifth?

"A closet inside the Governor's Quarters conceals the final entry point."

"The fifth tunnel entrance is closest to the bunker." Alexander takes over. "Yet it will be the most difficult by far. You have to get through the wall and into the mansion all while under heavy fire from the Guard."

"I will lead a team through the fifth tunnel," Rayla shouts.

Of course she will. I command-Z the image of bullets whizzing past my head back into existence. I guzzle down the rest of my water from my bottle. *Bulletproof*, remember?

The general nods at Rayla's rock-solid nerve. "My Guard will cover your team and take the brunt of enemy fire."

Emery steps up. "The Common will charge the mansion from all sides. We will besiege the governor's house from above and below ground—strike from every angle, ensuring the governor has nowhere to run."

Our leader raises her hand, showing her members how it's done. "I will lead the south tunnel."

"Ava and I will lead the east," Mira shouts. No surprise there.

"I will head the west tunnel," Xavier yells.

"Ciro and I will take the north," Barend calls out.

"It's decided!" Rayla concludes.

"Will you use the heat-ray gun?" Theo pipes up from the middle of the crowd. His eyes latch on to Mira's.

"Only as intimidation," Emery answers, her own eyes on General Pierce. "We do not torture. We are not like our enemy."

This gets a rousing cheer.

"We need a decisive victory." The general huddles close to the Elders. "We must move out now."

"Memorize your routes! Gather your teams!" Emery shouts to the Common. "We will storm the mansion on the hour!"

One and all, we hightail it to the cars.

"I totally got this. This is *not* our first rodeo." I jog in place, getting my motor running, then stretch my fingers, prepping them for the wheel. "It's pretty nuts we're a part of something like this," I say to anyone who's listening.

"You're not just a part anymore, Cog," Blaise answers, slapping a pair of communication devices into my hand. "No matter how much it pains me to say it, you helped make this happen."

"Kind words from *Blaise*?" I say, shoving the earpiece into my ear canal. I fit the tiny mouthpiece onto my back molar. "Guess that means you think I'm a goner."

I swear I can see a goofy grin behind his flame-toothed smile.

"You'll stay at the control room, then, and guide Rayla's team?"

"I'll be your *blazing*, guiding light," Blaise says, all dramatic.

I roll my eyes. I didn't know Blaise was punny.

"Don't die," Blaise tells me, his go-to goodbye.

Don't die is number one on my to-do list. A close second: nab Governor Roth.

MIRA

Bright beams of light from the Cavalry cars shine all around me. A cacophony of ear-splitting engines and battle cries fills the massive concrete garage. It sounds beautiful to me.

Strangers, friends, fellow citizens, and Common members all surround the inner circle, awaiting the call to make our move on the mansion.

Barend hands out bulletproof vests and weapons. Ciro passes out Goodwin masks. Half of our members already have the disguises strapped to their faces.

Thousands of Ava and Mira Goodwins come to take back our city.

One face stands out. Haven's. Will I ever be able to look at her and not think of my mother?

She moves to Ava and me, tugging off her hood. She has a long red mane like we used to have before we chopped it all off the morning we ran.

"Goodbye," Haven says.

"Not goodbye," Ava tells her. My sister hovers and hesitates, not knowing if she should go in for a hug.

It's all so new. I trust time will bridge our gaps.

"See you soon," I say, gripping Haven's shoulder.

My mother's twin smiles, an easier one this time. "See you soon," she says, and rejoins her team gathered beside Owen's car.

So many of us are still missing. Kano, Malik, half my grandmother's Colorado team.

Take the mansion, and Guardian Tower will fall, the general said.

I remember the stacked towers at the Common's headquarters. *The game ends when the tower falls.*

Yours will topple tonight, Roth. Not ours.

Ava pulls me to her side, both her hands on my cheeks. She brings her forehead to mine, slows her breathing. I try to match her rhythm, to resync my energy to hers.

"Remember how this all started. Remember why," Ava says in a hurried, private speech to me. "We're two girls Roth never thought could make it past his city's border. But we got out. And we fought our way back in." Her intensity, honed and sharp like steel, stokes the fire I've been storing inside for this moment, since the first night my father told us to run. "Now let's go and get him."

"Let's rip him from his home like he ripped us from ours," I say, every word an ardent flame burning with revenge. "Let's make Roth pay. For Mother and for Father. For Rayla and Haven."

"And for ourselves," Ava says, moving her mouth to my ear. She whispers even lower than our twinspeak. "I want to be the one who finds him. You or me, one of us takes him down."

I nod, always knowing it would end this way. An eye for an eye. Blood for blood. The Goodwin twins versus Governor Roth.

Ava and I step apart. Two siblings standing in Dallas without masks, hoods, or shrouds. Carrying no umbrellas, no microchips. Instead we carry weapons and the belief we can survive.

How far we've come.

I remember the little boy I encountered in Montana when I was alone and without hope just shy of the northern border. The lionhearted boy with the chipped tooth who told me I had to make it. I thought he meant I had to make it to Canada, make it over the border. But now I understand what he meant.

Make a place where you belong. Make your own home.

Make our future.

I look at my watch: 1:47 a.m. The city should be sleeping.

It's never been more alive.

My grandmother moves to us, and I half expect her to tell us we need to stay behind. But she doesn't. "I won't tell you to be careful, because you need to be fearless." Rayla curls her hands around Ava's and mine. She squeezes tight like she could transfer all her resilience and prowess and grit into the two of us.

I feel stronger.

"Whatever you face down there, together your strength is twofold," Rayla says. "Together you are Roth's worst fear. Prove him right."

"We will," we both say.

She nods, proudly knowing we're ready. "I'll see you when we've won the night."

I look at those around me, the mass of riotous people all ready to risk their lives and face the Guard to bring down one man. The energy is explosive. Undeniable. We could win.

Let's burn it all down.

Behind us Pawel opens the van that will take our team to the east tunnel entrance. Alexander and Theo are packing last-minute gear. Theo must feel my gaze, because he looks up, that same fire burning in his cherrywood eyes from the first time I met him. I've already told him he doesn't have to come tonight. He's fulfilled his promise. He could stay behind, away from the heart of the danger, and help Blaise and the others here.

I told you I'm with you, and I meant it, Theo said to me.

I feel more powerful than I've ever been.

A hush falls over the garage as Emery moves to the center of the circle. I see her pocket one of the small journals she's always scrawling in. Owen helps our leader onto the hood of his car so she can see each and every one of our members. We've multiplied. We're an army now.

Emery holds down her wrist in the rebellion salute, her tattoo gleaming in the headlights. "Every one of us here, we share a common bond. We feel oppressed, voiceless. Silenced. And to this I yell, enough! Yell with me. Resist with me. *Fight.* For the strength of many will forever outweigh the power of tyranny. Resist much."

Obey little.

HAVEN

I have a new name. Haven. I have a new face. My nieces'.

Ava's and Mira's. A Goodwin mask, they call it.

Everybody in the vehicle has it on. Mother, Owen, the First Lady.

Nieces. I was told that is the word for what they are to me. When I see them side by side, I think of how Lynn and I would have looked together.

Not exactly identical. Ninety-nine percent.

There are small freckles on Ava's nose, a line between her eyes. Mira's eyes have guilt in them. Like she's done something wrong. The boy Theo has the same look.

The mark of a second child.

If I saw my own reflection, I would see it too.

No time for these thoughts. We are here.

"Whoa. Look at all these people!" Owen says. He's in the driver's seat. More women and men than I ever knew were alive surround the Governor's Mansion.

Weapons out. Trying to break through the wall.

General Pierce and his Guard's vehicles stop at the main entrance. They have the heat-ray gun. They will take the front.

The Common Guard against the Texas Guard. Soldiers fighting soldiers. Is Roth leading his own Guard?

We have his general.

Owen drives our vehicle to the back of the mansion. I told Mother I knew a way in. The First Lady's handprint. It unlocks an opening.

I told Mother I am not weak. She told me she knows that.

I am a survivor. I am strong.

She makes me strong.

I was born into this fight. She knows I will not stay apart from her now.

"You're going to get everyone killed, not just me!" the First Lady shouts from the seat next to me. I keep hold of her wrist.

I squeeze. She quiets down.

"Stop here," Mother says. She sits beside Owen. She's calm. Ready.

We all look like CGs. Bulletproof vests. Heavy boots.

Yellow marks across our chests and Goodwin masks separate us from the enemy.

No more sirens or calls for the Common's surrender. Speakers are shot down. No one watches. Cameras are in pieces on the ground.

The vehicle doors open. We exit into the crowd. Two Guards from a second vehicle stand with us.

Guards, Common members, civilians. Everybody moves aside.

They know who we are and why we are here.

I make sure the mask still covers the First Lady's face. If she's recognized, we lose our way in.

The civilians would finish what they started in the streets.

"We stay together," Mother says. "Fire on my command."

The skyscrapers all light up at the same time.

"Badass!" Owen shouts. "Ava's plan worked!"

Screens on the buildings' sides show the Governor's Mansion. Thousands of women and men on its roof. In the trees. On top of the wall.

Swallowing the mansion whole.

All around us the Dallas civilians cheer.

"It's a digital world," Mother tries to explain to me.

"You're killing it, man," Owen says into his mouthpiece. He speaks to Blaise. Back at the Last Stage.

"But where do they come from?" I don't understand.

"They come from everywhere," Owen answers, a big smile on his face. "From cities all over the US. It's a virtual-reality protest."

"The entire country storms the mansion with the Common tonight," Mother says.

A Scream Gun goes off. It's too far away to send us to the ground. Was it ours or theirs?

"Please! We can still turn back!" the First Lady begs.

"We got it the first time. You don't want to go home," Owen says. "Just accept that it no longer matters what the hell you say. You're only here for your prints."

Mother turns her eyes on the mansion. I see only a dark mass. Sections of the lawn lit blue by the screens.

"We move quick and clean," Mother says.

I take the lead.

I go thirty feet to the left of an empty Guard tower. The place where I saw the First Lady exit. The spot is set in my mind.

I still have hold of the First Lady's wrist. I slam her right hand against the see-through wall. Her palm lights up.

A shoulder-width hole slides open.

"Leave it open," Mother says. She crawls to the other side.

"No!" the First Lady whispers. Too scared to scream. "The people will loot my house!"

"You lived here at the pleasure of the people," the tall Common Guard says. He backs her into the wall. "Down."

The First Lady shakes her head, holds on to the wall. Tries to close it.

I force her to the ground and push her through.

Then I follow. Hand on her ankle. We stand. I grab hold of the back of her neck.

Her mask fell off her face in the struggle.

No time to go back for it.

No shots fired yet. But I'm prepared to shoot.

Gun in my left hand, the First Lady in the other. Pushing her forward.

A Common Guard signals. We are on the move again.

There's a clear line for twenty-five feet. Then a zigzag path through a garden for the next fifty. Blaise talks Owen through it, and we follow his path.

I can't make out the shapes we pass. A final left.

Bodies. Five soldiers without the yellow mark.

"Hold your fire!" two of the enemy soldiers shout at the same time.

They have no weapons. Their arms are up in the air.

Mother shines a light in their faces.

"We do not want to die for Roth!"

"We surrender!"

In the Camps, if you yielded, you died anyway.

"Cowards!" the First Lady cries.

How does it feel to have nobody fight for you?

"Tranquilize them!" Mother shouts.

Our two Common Guards fire. The enemy soldiers drop where they stand. Red sticks poke out of their necks.

"Asleep, not dead," Owen says to me. We keep moving.

The mansion is in full sight now.

"Movement up ahead," Mother says.

A flood of civilians leaves the dark building. They run into the garden, hands up. Screaming.

"It's the governor's staff! Don't shoot!" Mother shouts. "Let them pass!"

The First Lady tries and fails to free herself from my hold. "I took you through the wall. Now let me go!" she cries.

"If I were you, lady, I'd keep my voice down," Owen says. "Some disgruntled staffers of yours might recognize you, and well . . . your best bet is with us."

The First Lady goes quiet. We reach the massive back doors. They're already wide open.

"Keep moving!" Mother shouts. "Haven, Owen, stay close."

"All eyes," a Common Guard says.

We are inside a hall of mirrors. Glass and gold all around. A portrait of Governor Roth hangs at the end of the long passageway. The walls mirror his face at us a hundred times over. He is everywhere.

Owen jumps. The First Lady cries out.

"Five of them!" Owen shouts. "Ten o'clock!"

"Fire!" Mother yells.

A shot is fired from the left. Shatters a panel of glass. Another, then another. Roth's face explodes into a thousand pieces on the floor.

"Get down!" a Common Guard shouts.

I throw the First Lady behind a table knocked on its side. Lift my gun to a Guard with no yellow mark. The soldier falls before I pull the trigger. Mother.

A bullet shoots by my head. Sparks spray the gold wall behind me.

"Guards in back!" Mother shouts. Her gun is aimed over my shoulder.

The Common taught me to shoot at the safe house. *Protect yourself,* they said. *You can shoot back now.*

Our enemies are shooting to kill. I return fire until my bullets run out.

I hit a body.

"All clear!" a Common Guard shouts.

Six Guards down, one of our own.

All goes still. Without the flash of gunfire, it's all black. Like my eyes are closed.

I move for the table that covers the First Lady. Mother is behind me. Glass crunches beneath our feet.

The First Lady is gone. But where?

"Blaise says somebody is running up the hall, opposite the Governor's Quarters!" Owen shouts.

Our remaining Common Guard leads. Mother stays behind me. We step over the broken portrait of Roth, full of bullet holes.

We turn left into another dark passageway. It's silent.

There are no windows in this hall. The First Lady could be hiding right in front of me. I wouldn't see.

Every door is locked. I get to the end of the hall. Nothing opens. I kick the wall. It moves. It's a door.

The First Lady must be on the other side.

Gun up, I lift my hand in a signal to the others. The way Mother taught me.

I can see more now. My eyes are used to the dark. I don't scream. It's not a body in front of me. It's a portrait. Massive. Covered behind glass.

I know that face. What is his name?

"Halton Roth," Mother whispers. She sounds angry. She spits on the floor.

The Common Guard pushes open the door with his boot. Mother charges in.

The room is large. Made for a Camp Warden.

It's empty.

"Lights on," Owen says.

The room stays black. Something moves in the left corner. A bright-blue light. Halton. In uniform. The kind the governor wears. I can see through him.

"It's a hologram," Owen says.

The hologram walks up and down the room. Marching like the CGs at inspection. Is he guarding the room?

"Super creepy," Owen says.

Mother walks right through it. "Under the bed," she says.

We find the First Lady on the floor. Still. Quiet. She doesn't fight when I pull her out from under the bed of her dead grandson. Halton. Her failed family.

She's tired. All the fight has left her. She looks like an Inmate who has failed her final Assessment Checkup. An expired body.

I zip-tie her wrist to mine. We need her prints for the locks. I will take zero chances now.

No Guards are on the short run to the Governor's Quarters. The door there is steel. Closed. Locked.

"Blaise gives the thumbs-up. All clear on the other side," Owen says.

Mother takes off her mask. Everybody follows her lead. She looks at me. Smiles just for me. Like I passed my own Checkup.

"I've spent the majority of my life fighting for this moment. I'm thankful you're here with me," she says. "But stay back when we get to the bunker entrance. I won't let a governor take you from me again." She squeezes my free hand.

"Unlock the door!" the Common Guard shouts at the First Lady.

"You're killing all of us," the First Lady whispers. I lift my left arm. Force her right hand onto the scanner.

It lights up green under her finger.

The door opens. Shots sound.

Not all clear.

There's a hailstorm of bullets.

AVA

I'm back at Strake University.

The campus is devoid of students. Unless you count Mira and me. *But we aren't students anymore.* Our uniforms are black, not pure white, our royal-purple ranks renounced. We're renegades with yellow slashed across our chests.

"*That's* a college football stadium?" Theo asks, incredulous. Governor Roth's east tunnel exits next to Strake's stadium, the largest in the country. Probably the world. A twelve-thousand-square-foot scoreboard was approved for the state budget while untold numbers of citizens die from hunger all across Texas. But it's more than just a football stadium, I realize now.

It's one of Roth's emergency escape plans. A giant field makes for a perfect helicopter pad in a megacity otherwise clogged with buildings. It's ingenious.

But Roth won't be making it out of the tunnels a free man. Common members block every entrance: east, west, north, south, and center. The only way he's getting out of this is if he's in handcuffs or dead. *I'll take either.*

What's left of Mira's and my teams have combined to attack the bunker from the east: Pawel, Theo, and Alexander. Barend and Ciro chose a different team. *We needed strong members to lead the north entrance,* they said. I keep telling myself they want to be close to each other, just as I want Mira by my side, but we still have an unknown betrayer among us.

We all sit in the back of our escort SUV, waiting for Blaise to hack open the tunnel entrance. Before I left the safe house, I told Blaise about the virtual-reality protest I encountered in Calgary. His eyes lit up when I asked if we could use the VR technology to the Common's advantage during our siege of Dallas.

I've waited my entire career for an opportunity like this, he assured me. *Consider it done.*

It must be happening right now. The largest protest Dallas has ever seen.

The double doors of the armored vehicle are open, and I stare out at Guardian Tower looming high and bright behind campus. *Is that where my father died?* Kano is there now. The only Common member from headquarters in Roth's custody. *Or did he get caught on purpose?*

Kano could be our betrayer.

Focus on the mission. What's done is done. I can't get distracted from the goal of taking down Roth. *He's so close now.*

A Common Guard with a yellow slash across his chest approaches. He signals the tunnel has been unlocked.

It's time to go underground. *It wouldn't be a proper homecoming if we didn't.*

As we file out of the vehicle, I hear Mira murmuring with Theo. He brings out a knife from his pocket, and my stomach twists. *Mira gave him her knife? Father's knife?* They've grown close; it's irritatingly clear how protective of him she feels. One look at his face and I know a Scream Gun couldn't keep him away from her.

Battle bonds, Rayla calls them. Or is it something more?

The Common Guard takes us to the entranceway of the secret passage, which lies beneath the statue of Governor Roth's grandmother, the founder of Strake.

Alexander points to the lifelike statue. "Your great-great-grandmother, Theo."

Theo responds with an unimpressed grunt. *A Roth not enamored with his own pedigree.* Definitely not like Halton. Same father, different environments. The nature versus nurture debate resolved.

Alexander surveys the shoulder-width hatch opening. "I'll go in first," he says, holding up his gun. He's wearing full Texas Guard riot gear, and I have a flashback to the night Roth's soldiers raided our house in Trinity Heights.

I've come to return the favor.

Pawel had offered to stay aboveground and will help us from here, protecting the tunnel entrance and acting as our mission's eyes. A tablet's in his hands, the tunnel map displayed on his screen. The communication devices I have on make me feel like an agent, but they're necessary.

"I'm glad there will be someone topside that I can trust," I tell him as we get ready to go into the tunnel.

"You can always trust me," Pawel says. He clasps my shoulder. "I know you don't believe in luck . . . but good luck down there. I'll be watching out for you."

I smile, placing my hand on top of his. "I know you will." He always does.

Alexander vanishes down the ladder, followed by Theo, then Mira and me.

Immediately it's clear the thermal-sensor map General Pierce's drone picked up didn't show us the whole story. It's a labyrinth down here—many, many more passageways and potential exit points than we planned for.

There are more people than we anticipated too.

I catch sudden movement twenty yards ahead—and the sound of someone in flight. "It's the Family Planning Director!" Theo shouts. Without warning, he takes off running.

"Theo, wait!" Alexander calls out to his son.

Separating was not part of the plan.

"Get Roth," Mira says to me. She quickly turns to Alexander. "I'll get Theo." A look passes between them. He trusts her.

Mira takes off after him, leaving me alone with Alexander.

MIRA

"Theo!" I yell, but he can't hear me. I can barely hear myself over the echoing sounds of six boots hitting the pavement on a dead-sprint foot chase.

"Theo, forget her!" I scream as loud as I can, to no effect. He hits a new speed, hurtling us through the twisting maze of tunnels, away from the bunker.

I try to remember our path so we can find our way back, but I'm terrified I'll lose sight of the back of his golden-brown head.

I can't lose him.

Theo's hell-bent on a savior's path to right the wrongs of his family. But he doesn't truly know what evil can do. He's a product of Canada. A halcyon childhood, safe from Guards, governors, the constant threat of death.

He thinks good automatically wins. It doesn't. Not here.

If the Director finds him first . . .

I turn left, nearly spraining my ankle again. I ignore the pain and run faster. I've almost caught up.

"Theo, stop!"

Theo makes another hard left. His guiding light vanishes. Shoving my sweaty bangs from my eyes, I push my legs past their limit, tearing after him, knowing I've lost track of the turns. *We'll never find our way back.*

The governor. He's all that matters.

"We're wasting time!" I yell, but the threat of losing Theo keeps pulling me forward.

The tunnel walls change as abruptly as my direction. They're wider, smoother, the floor lined with a polished stone tile embellished with a lone Texas star.

The passageway's a dead end. Ten yards ahead, Theo pounds on a steel slab that looks to be a door.

"The Director went through here!" Theo shouts at me, slamming his shoulder against the unyielding metal, sweat-slick hands searching for a way in. "But it's locked!"

"Do you remember the way back?" I say, hands on my knees. More than half my energy is drained. I need to restore it quick. I need it all for Roth.

I suddenly see the huge symbol etched into the door. A shiny albatross, its wide wings in flight. My father's words thrust to the forefront of my mind: *"Instead of the cross, the albatross about my neck was hung."* The poem . . . the one he would read to Ava and me about penance and guilt—

"We can't just let the Director get away!" Theo says, kicking at the door over and over, like if he only keeps knocking, someone will finally answer it.

Locked between the albatross's curved, sharp beak, a scanning device flashes red.

"It requires a microchip to gain access," I say, suddenly consumed with my own need to find a way in.

Desperate, Theo looks at me. "She would have killed you, Mira! We can't let people like her get away with what they've done. I mean . . . she's separated families!"

Dr. Darren Goodwin, merely a few weeks prior, was also a Family Planning Director.

"My father—" I begin to say, but Theo stops me, abandoning his hammering.

"Mira, I didn't mean your dad—"

I shake my head, waving away his concerns. "No, I mean my father's microchip . . ."

Tossing my rucksack to the floor, I dig into an inner pocket, finding a compact bag filled with tools. I pluck out the tweezers, then lift up the grimy, scarred band of my wristwatch. From inside a thin slit above the tarnished buckle, tucked safe inside the vegan leather, I pull out my father's microchip.

I've forgotten all about it until this moment. I've carried it with me since the day they told me he died.

Like most citizens, I have no clue what happens to a deceased person's microchip. But with the pointed tip of the tweezers, I press a button the size of a pinprick, and the tiny capsule thrums with a single, long hum of life.

"Does that mean it works?" Theo asks.

In the palm of my hand, I raise the microchip below the scanner. "There's little chance his security clearance is still—"

The scanning device emits a loud *ping*. Approved.

As the door slides open, Theo and I press ourselves against either side of the wall, weapons at the ready. He holds my knife. I grip my new gun. We nod, two second-borns determined to take down the Director together.

We step into a laboratory lit by the strobing yellow flashes of emergency lights. A medical or research lab, ransacked and deserted.

"It looks like they've cleaned house already," Theo whispers.

I don't like it in here. It feels sterile. It feels heavy.

I want to leave.

Rows of bare steel workbenches fill the space, along with empty, smashed refrigerators. Capsized convection ovens, gutted cabinets, and an upended surgical table also lie scattered about.

Everything incriminating is gone. Including the Director.

There's not a single clue left to verify what the government did down here. Just a leftover, haunted energy that chills my very core.

Then, "We both want the same thing," the Director says from somewhere in front of us, concealed behind a mess of open cabinets. Slowly, Theo and I move side by side toward the sound of her voice.

"We both want to save humanity," she continues, composed and confident like she's behind a podium. "I, too, strive to safeguard our country and work hard to see its citizens flourish."

"A modern-day humanitarian," Theo spits.

Don't get distracted. Don't listen.

"Our society was insatiable, our population gluttonous and unstable. The Family Planning Division rescued America from extinction."

One Child, One Nation.

"It's not personal, Mira, Theo. It's for the greater good."

The Director steps out from behind the unhinged door of a medical cabinet. She holds no weapon; her holster is empty. So are her eyes.

She must have dropped her gun in the chase. "You wouldn't shoot an unarmed official," the Director tells me, walking toward us like she's in control.

"What is this place?" I say, without expecting any answers.

A maniacal smile distorts her mouth, a steel trap where no real truth could ever escape.

"If you won't answer me, then you'll answer to the people." With my left hand I grab the taser gun off Theo's belt. I aim and shoot without hesitation.

The short woman goes rigid, then falls to the floor, her head slamming against a steel countertop on her way down. I roll her seizing body onto her back with my boot. The high-voltage barbs pierce through her cloth uniform below her shiny row of medals.

I look her right in the eyes as she convulses. I hope it hurts. Even if it's only a trace, the slightest sting, compared to the amount of hurt she's afflicted on others.

"The Family Planning Division is dead," I say. "You were the last Director of Texas."

Theo unfastens the taser cartridge from the gun and pockets it. He lifts the Director by the underarms and slings her over his shoulder with a grunt. "Let's get her into the cabinet before she can move again," he says.

As I help Theo shove her deadweight into the storage space, her lips begin to twitch.

"How can the world survive . . . ," the Director's stiff voice manages to rasp out, "if Gluts . . . like the both of you get to live?"

I don't have an answer. Neither does Theo. He closes the door with a bang and zip-ties the handles shut, locking her and her stinging question inside.

"You won't win," the Director keeps talking, her voice now muffled. "The Rule of One and Project Albatross have already spread. It's global."

I stop listening. I hear the muted blast of a lone gunshot from somewhere in the tunnels.

"Ava," I say automatically. Theo looks as concerned as I feel.

The bunker. *Roth.*

Oh God, I shouldn't have left her.

AVA

My team made it to the bunker first.

The solid steel and concrete door is sealed shut—the five-spoke gilded handle will not budge an inch—and there's no one else in sight. "The thermal sensor says there's only one person inside," Pawel assures me from topside.

It's just the governor, Alexander, and me.

I'm about to face Roth with only his son by my side. If it comes down to blood loyalty, I'm outnumbered. *No . . . Roth ordered Halton's death.* We're competing on who gets to have their vengeance first.

But first we have to get the bunker open.

I've already shot at the door. I knew it wouldn't work, but I tried anyway. General Pierce told us the governor's underground shelter is fire, blast, radiation, and impact resistant, able to withstand a nuclear or chemical attack. There's no forcing our way through.

"Are you sure you don't see the combination dial or thumb scan to gain entry?" Pawel asks me again. I scour the door for the fourth time, still finding nothing. Then—

"Yes, I see it!" I say into my mouthpiece.

"Does Alexander's right thumbprint have a whorl or loop pattern?" Pawel asks, coolheaded and focused.

I grab Alexander's hand. "Whorl," I say, immediately seeing his plan. He's going to create an artificial, digitally produced "master print" that can imitate a range of fingerprints accurately enough to con the sensor into thinking it's Governor Roth's.

In our old life, Mira had to put on synthetic strips with my prints every time she left the basement. *The only part of me she didn't have too.*

"Done," Pawel says in my ear, startling me out of my memory. A flash of green light beside the scanner. *We're in.*

Alexander looks both impressed and mildly horrified. "I never thought I'd see a hacker break through my father's security."

"Roth is in the center of the room, directly facing the door," Pawel informs me. I relay the intel to Alexander, the former officer in the Texas State Guard. Instantly he springs into action, a soldier once more, turning the spoke handle on the door, barking out orders to me.

"We'll stack on the left side of the door. I'll take point. You take the number-two position. When I squeeze your leg, we will immediately enter the room, no hesitation. Never lower the barrel of your gun. Only fire if fired upon first."

"I know," I say, bristling at having to take commands from a Roth. But Alexander's trained for moments like this—I need to check myself. *We both have the same objective.*

"Lots of luck," Pawel breathes, his voice now tense, as we line up in position.

Alexander throws the steel door wide open, reaches back to firmly press my leg, and then we both burst into the bunker, guns raised. "On the ground *now*!" Alexander shouts.

But it's not Governor Roth we find hiding inside.

It's Skye Lin.

"You're dead," I say stupidly, half lowering my gun, at a complete loss. *What is going on?*

Her two French braids disheveled, Skye sits on an ornate wingback chair in the center of the plush carpeted room, looking perfectly calm, as if the Common finding her in Roth's bunker was part of the plan all along.

She's not handcuffed. There are no cuts or bruises or signs of a struggle. *Skye is here willingly.*

Our betrayer.

"Where is the governor?!" Alexander shouts at Skye. He scans the extravagant room, a safe house outfitted for nobility—four-poster bed and all—but Roth isn't here.

"She's a decoy," I snap. "Governor Roth was never here."

A microchipless red herring, focusing the Common's assault away from where Roth is actually concealed.

I scream and fire my gun into the ceiling, allowing my anger to let loose from the cage I've kept it locked inside. *If we don't have Roth, we have nothing.*

Pouncing on the traitor—one of our own—I point my gun directly between her eyes. "Why?" I demand. "You spent years locked in a prison cell for the Common's cause. You killed people for it. And then you betray us. *Why?*"

"We need to leave now," Alexander urges me. "We don't have time for this—we need to find Theo and Mira. We need to find the governor!"

I press the barrel of my gun deeper into the turncoat's forehead. I'm razor sharp again, ready and able to cut through anything.

Why shouldn't I be the one doing the hurting this time? This girl's treachery has caused so much of it. Mira's and my imprisonment, Roth's state invasions, multiple Common members' deaths . . . *Payback.* Not the primary revenge I desire, but a taste of it.

Rayla said an eye for an eye makes for a blind world, but I'm filled with so much hate that half my sight is already gone.

If my world goes dark in consequence, so be it.

"Your father's the one who told me it was possible," Skye finally speaks. She lifts her dark eyes to stare into mine, and I see my pain cast back at me.

"That what is possible?" I ask, my stomach twisting at the mention of my father.

"Three strikes, and a state governor has the power to do what they will with you." She holds up her hand, counting them off with her fingers. "A low-ranking thief, marked a juvenile criminal, strike one. An inherited genetic disorder I would continue to pass on to future generations, strike two. Displayed sexual interest in the same sex, strike three," Skye tells me, never breaking eye contact. Her tone's detached, void of emotion, like she's talking about someone else's life. "I was labeled an 'undesirable candidate' to bring a child into this used-up nation. I was sterilized, prevented from passing on my bloodline."

She lowers her three raised fingers, and I lower my gun, my head spinning.

"My cell was next to Darren's for a week. He talked to me about his love for his twin daughters, and I told him why I wanted to take down the Family Planning Division," Skye continues. "Darren understood. He told me that my tubal sterilization could be reversed."

Tubal ligation reversal. It's tricky and not a guarantee, but Father's right; it's possible.

"Governor Roth promised you the surgery?" Alexander asks, her motives for double-crossing the Common plain as day. She wants what the government tells her she can't have: a child. A family. A right to choose.

"After five years locked in prison holes, Roth comes into my cell, offering a trade: intel for surgery," she says, bitterness in her low voice. "And I took the traitor's deal."

"We're finished here," Alexander presses. "We came here for the governor." *Where is Roth now? Where is Mira?* But I have to know . . . did Skye succeed?

"Did you get what you wanted in exchange for handing your country over to a man who will destroy it?" I ask.

"I did not," Skye spits, staring daggers at Alexander. "Every Roth is a liar."

The edges of Skye's lips lift into a shadow of a smile. "But your father should be careful what he touches."

What does that mean? Did she poison Governor Roth, an assassin once more?

"Ava, there are bodies headed your way, from the north and west," Pawel says, urgent in my ear, bringing me back to my current dire reality inside this bunker.

The sound of boots charging in our direction causes Alexander to turn his weapon toward the door. "Flash!" Alexander challenges. If it's our side, they should respond, *Thunder!*

No response.

Skye lifts the barrel of my gun back to her forehead. "Please. Shoot me. I can't go back to Guardian Tower."

"Flash!" a voice challenges from the tunnelway. *Emery.*

"Thunder!" Alexander answers. All at once, Emery's and Xavier's teams charge into the bunker, out of breath and weapons raised. *They didn't find Roth either.* Emery takes one look at Skye and assesses the situation in a heartbeat, pulling out a pair of handcuffs, biting down on the inside of her cheeks, hard.

"Where's Mira?" I shout, heart sinking. She and Theo should be here by now.

"We haven't seen her," Kipling says, suited up in dark tactical gear and a ball cap. He looks like a stranger without his cowboy hat on. I pull my gun away from Skye's forehead and rush out into the passage.

Empty. All clear.

"The thermal drone's picking up two bodies close to the east tunnel entrance," Pawel says in my ear. Relief crashes through me in a giant wave. *Theo and Mira.*

But then all the hairs on my body stand on end.

Ashley Saunders & Leslie Saunders

Where are Rayla and Haven?

Did they run into trouble in the mansion? Theirs was the shortest path to the bunker.

"Ava, the drone's been shot down," Pawel warns, fear slipping into his voice. "We're sightless!"

We're on our own now.

I hear more pounding boots round the east corner, the direction my team entered the tunnel from. But it's not Mira and Theo—it's Ciro and Barend. *How the hell did they end up to the east?*

Roth created a tangled web beneath his lair.

"Is the target captured?" Barend shouts, a pistol in each hand.

I battled my way across the country for the second time in two months to face off with Governor Roth, to take my revenge against the man who shattered my whole life, but right now the only faces I want to see are my family's. The need to find them suddenly overwhelms me, overpowering my urge to find Roth.

I have to get to my family before he does.

OWEN

The First Lady won't stop shrieking.

"Is anyone shot?" Rayla shouts, checking on Haven and me.

"No . . . just the bad guys . . . ," I mumble in my I-just-survived-a-shoot-out stupor.

Those are four *very* real dead bodies on the floor. I've seen my share of dead bodies before tonight, but I wasn't ever the one *responsible* for making "people" turn into "dead bodies."

If we're keeping tallies, it's probably two for me. In the span of two hours. I shove that score aside and focus my eye line above the ground.

"Someone put a lid on the First Lady," Blaise grumbles in my ear.

Haven hauls Mrs. Roth after her by their zip-tied wrists. "More screaming, more Guards," Haven warns, clipped and to the point.

This shuts the First Lady up. The second she does I almost hanker for her to howl again. It's way too quiet in here. Like, we-could-be-in-the-center-of-a-deep-cave quiet. And it's definitely as dark as one. Visibility is zilch.

The windows are sealed—the walls must be ultra soundproof. Half the capital's citizens and half the Texas Guard are out there unleashing Armageddon, and all I hear is my heartbeat. And Blaise.

"Two rooms down to the right," Blaise instructs, as calm as a Zen master. "Then it's all clear for the tunnel entrance."

"All clear," I whisper to Rayla and our Common Guard.

Rayla leads the way.

Another fingerprint lock. *Bullshit!* We'll be the last to get to the bunker!

Haven slams Mrs. Roth's forefinger against the panel. Nothing.

"Working on it!" Blaise says before I even ask what the hell the malfunction is.

Our Common Guard turns on Mrs. Roth. "Get us through this door immediately, or we will throw you to the mob!"

Threatening his First Lady. A scant two hours ago, a comment like that would have landed him years of hard labor. In the present moment, the soldier smirks. *Bet that felt good.*

"It requires a voice command to unlock," Mrs. Roth finally fesses up.

"Do it!" Rayla shouts.

Haven presses Mrs. Roth's narrow lips to the speaker.

"Hail to the chief," the First Lady spits out like acid.

Rayla scoffs. "That will never happen."

"He's going to kill us all," Mrs. Roth mutters. She looks like a wraith. One foot in her grave next to Halton's.

Great pep talk.

Rayla shoves open the crazy-heavy door, and one by one we file into the bedroom.

"We're in," I whisper into my mouthpiece. "Blaise—man, do you copy? We're almost to the tunnel opening."

Radio silence. Dead air.

It's like we just stepped into a black hole.

"We lost Blaise," I tell our Guard, who updates Rayla.

We'll have to be our own eyes, then.

We're midway to the closet when something moves in the corner. Some*one*.

In the bed. There's someone in the bed.

Governor Roth speaks so low it's subterranean. "Agent Trace, when I give a goddamn order, I expect to be *obeyed*. Where is my medication, you useless half-wit?"

Our renegade train stops in its tracks.

Can he not see us? And why is he practically whispering?

"The governor is in residence," I hiss, crossing all fingers, toes, and eyes in hopes that Blaise can hear. "Send. Backup. *Now.*"

"Medication—really, Howard?" Rayla says all cool and conversational. "What ails you can never be cured."

Oh, to have night vision and see the dumb shock hit the governor's face when he hears Rayla Cadwell's voice in his bedroom.

I point my gun at the unmoving black shadow on the bed.

"You're surrounded, Roth," Rayla tells the man. "Put your hands up, and we can end this clean."

The shadow doesn't shift or stir. Zero signs of surrender.

"Full lights on!" the Common Guard commands.

The room brightens like it's high noon. We're only twenty feet from the governor. The ogre of a man looks like he's been dunked in a sweat bath. Chunks of his latest meal dangle from his lower lip. His vulture eyes squint like they can't stand the light.

Governor Roth looks sick. Like he's on his deathbed.

At a signal from Rayla, our line fans out, fencing in the governor.

Don't poke the beast. But I can't help it—the once-in-a-lifetime rush of staring down the most powerful leader in our country is too strong. *Just a small poke.*

"I bet you never thought low rankers could break into your fortress. Well, *ding dong.* The Common's here, and we've taken over."

Showing the first real signs of life, Roth rotates his thick neck, his focus bypassing me to land on his wife cowering at the foot of her old bed. Haven keeps Mrs. Roth's tiny body standing.

"You let them inside, Victoria?" the governor growls. "You've aligned yourself with the matriarch of *Gluts*?"

There's sudden movement under the sheets.

"You can die with her too!" Roth yells before firing a pistol.

There are so many screams, but mine's the loudest. *"Rayla!"*

But the bullet's not for Rayla. It's for his wife.

Mrs. Roth drops to the carpet, taking Haven down with her.

"Haven!" Rayla cries out, seeing the blood splattered on her daughter's face and chest.

"Not hers!" I shout. "Mrs. Roth's!"

All in slow motion, I see the governor go for a panic button on the side of the bed frame. "Bullshit!" I shout, dive-bombing toward Roth. Rayla's flying at him from the opposite side—double-team style.

The second I land on the bed—I swear right on top of a pile of vomit—the golden mattress folds into itself like a trunk, and a lid slides over the top, sealing the panic chamber shut. I howl bloody murder as all three of us drop down into a hidden compartment below the bed frame.

Next thing I know, a light turns on, and a lot of things happen at once: Roth bulldozes his way through an escape hole in a corner of the coffin-like box—does that lead into the tunnels?!—while Rayla reaches for her gun, which has become lodged between a stash of emergency water jugs, and someone lands on top of the abduction-proof bed above us and starts pounding.

"We're okay, Haven!" I scream, wondering if she can hear me, but I've got no time to worry about that, because I'm busy discharging bullets toward Roth's backside.

Empty clicks. Whoops, I'm out of bullets. And Roth made it out. Not good.

"Rayla, do we follow?" No answer.

I turn my head in the cramped space to find Rayla sort of panting. She must've landed wrong—her wounded arm looks bad. Like, she just dislocated her shoulder bad. And her stitches—they've busted open again. She groans, getting herself onto her one hand and both knees, ready to crawl out after Roth, injured arm be damned.

Out of nowhere I get a flashback of Mrs. Roth's dead body crumpling onto the fancy white carpet like a rag doll. I better shut *that* terrible image out of my mind *real* quick.

Rayla drags herself out of the small opening, and I follow.

Yep, we're definitely underground in the tunnels.

Wasting no time, Rayla gets to her feet and charges left down the passage.

"Roth!" she screams. His name bounces off the walls, leaving zero doubt he hears us coming. It sounds like an army is after him.

Maybe the rest of the Common is close.

"Roth!" Rayla screams again, louder. *"Do not run away!"* I don't know how *she's* running, let alone breathing. Her blood is everywhere. She's bone white, drowning in sweat. Her slumped body races down the tunnel almost at a diagonal, her good side dragging her wounded side after her.

"Coward!" Rayla shouts, trying to antagonize the governor into stopping and facing us—facing *her*.

"Coward!" I scream too. *"Coward!"*

The barrage of insults ricochets against the tunnel's concrete walls, finding him before we do.

Governor Roth waits for us at the next turn. His pistol at his side, Roth stands in the center of the passageway like he's bulletproof. I remember that I am too.

No one shoots. We linger in a face-off.

Roth suddenly teeters. Even in the pitch-black tunnel, I can make out how pale he is. Almost as pale as Rayla. He's like a sinister full moon.

Roth's sick. A psycho, yes, but he's also physically ill. *We can end this quick.*

"You have nowhere to run!" I shout. "The Common owns the tunnels!"

I shut my mouth. Rayla must have a million things to say to him. Rayla must get the final word.

"It's over" is all she says. It's all she needs to.

"Yes. It is over," Roth agrees. His gaze shifts over my shoulder. Is the governor smiling?

I hear the *pop* a millisecond before I feel it.

"I'm shot," I say stupidly.

Four more rounds are fired, two of the bullets connecting with my spinal cord.

The pain is mind melting. I face-plant onto the pavement. It's the fight of my life to suck in a breath.

How am I even breathing?

Bulletproof.

It's all coming back to me. I'm wearing a bulletproof vest. A real one. Barend. He handed them out at the theater.

Rayla's up against the wall, trying to lift her gun. Her shooting arm is shot up and disabled.

I twist my neck, scraping my cheek along the jagged concrete to look at what we didn't see coming.

Guards.

Roth's backup, not ours.

The governor takes his time coming for us—coming for Rayla.

The gun drops from my leader's hand.

Her strength is seeping out of her.

I'm in a virtual game, a dream, a fucking nightmare. I can't move. I can't scream. All I can do is watch.

The governor stands toe-to-toe with Rayla. He says everything he needs to with the bullet he sends straight between her eyes.

When Rayla hits the floor, I have an out-of-body experience. I look for her soul floating up here with me. I can't find her.

Don't die! I tell it—her—me.

I'm doing a really great job at playing dead. The Guards step on and over me to flank their governor.

I think I black out for a while after that.

When I come to, I'm alone.

I spend the next twenty seconds staring into Rayla's eyes. They never blink.

Don't die; don't die; don't die.

"Rayla! Don't die!" I shout.

Shout as loud as you want. She'll never hear you again.

That life-stopping fact powers me up to my feet. I grab Rayla's gun and sprint down the tunnel like an injured bat out of goddamn hell.

I fall to the ground. Pretty sure my ribs cracked from the bullets hitting the vest. *Too bad. Get the hell back up.*

"Rayla's dead, Blaise," I pant through gritted teeth to no one. Blaise can't hear me. I lost my mouthpiece somewhere in Roth's escape bed. I'm on my own down here.

And Roth's getting away. He's going to get away with everything if I don't catch him.

Stop him.

Shoot him.

Back on my feet, I drag one foot after the other. Left, right, left, right. One tunnel after the next.

Then the tail end of the governor's Guard is in my sights.

Bullets fly, but not toward me. Up ahead, into the left side of a crossroads.

"Grab the boy! Shoot the rest!" Roth's orders reach me down the passage.

Am I "the boy"?

"No! Theo—" Someone's rage-filled cry gets cut off by gunfire. *Was that Mira?*

Theo. He's the one Roth wants. I catch sight of his heir tossed over a Guard's shoulder. Needle to the neck, Theo's out like a light.

The governor's taking another one of us. And I can't do jack to stop him.

"Roth!" I scream, hoping Rayla's words will work a second time. *"Do not run away, coward!"*

But when I reach the junction, it's Mira I find this time, not Roth. She's lying flat on the ground at the entrance of a side passage.

The instant I spot her bulletproof vest, she comes to, gasping for air. I help her to her feet as our reinforcements finally storm down the tunnel.

Too late.

"He took Theo," Mira chokes out the words.

He took Rayla too.

We race up an exit ladder, no idea what we'll find on the surface.

Two of our Guards hang out the side of the van, dead.

Pawel is on the ground. A helicopter's in the air.

"The governor is escaping!" Alexander shouts at the top of his lungs.

The emerging Common members shoot at the military chopper, but it flies away until it's a pinprick in the sky.

I bet Alexander doesn't know yet that his son's in there too.

Ava's bent over Pawel's body. Her slippery hands cover a hole in his neck. Her screams sound like alarms. But we'll all never wake up from this nightmare.

"Rayla's last words were *it's over*," I mutter out loud.

"Last words?" Mira asks, her voice all raspy and broken. "What do you mean?"

I stand there quiet, delaying the truth.

It all definitely feels over.

PART IV

THE WILDFIRE

AVA

We've come to bury our dead in a cemetery full of trees instead of gray tombstones. A vibrant woodland on the outskirts of Dallas, where our fallen can rest in peace and beauty, creating new life out of death.

I lead the funeral march flanked by Mira and Haven. We're gripping each other's hands tight so we don't fall to our knees, holding up the honor procession with our insurmountable grief. Rayla would want her family to walk tall and proud. She would want us to show unity and strength as we honor those who have sacrificed themselves for the rebellion.

I'm utterly empty. My heart is so broken I can't feel it anymore; it's disappeared from its cage inside my chest. *That's what happens when your heart shatters into millions of little pieces.* It can escape.

Now I am heartless.

When we reach the base of a certain eighteen-year-old live oak tree, we stop our march. My mother, Lynn, was buried underneath this tree. Its long, sprawling branches reaching down toward the earth are her new limbs. Its simple, narrow green leaves are her new strands of hair, its thick, scaly barked trunk her new body. My mother lives on, growing inside this tree each year.

Rayla and my father will take their places beside her, surrounded by a yellow field of wild black-eyed Susans.

The pallbearers, Xavier and Owen, step forward with Rayla's body, encapsulated inside a biodegradable burial pod. Emery and Barend make their way to the front with Pawel's pod.

I couldn't save him. All his youthful vibrancy and intelligence, stolen with a single brutal bullet. If I still had a heart, it would ache in one long, continuous pang until the day it stopped beating.

Our father's body is lost to us—Mira and I have nothing to bury except the small, empty oval casket that I hold in my hands. I refused to let his microchip serve as a replacement—he will not be tracked even in death—and I couldn't bear to part with our family photograph. *His spirit will be buried as a seed in the earth. He will grow tall next to our mother,* Mira promised me. We will return to visit living memorials, not gravestones.

Together, the pallbearers place the egg-shaped capsules into holes in the ground, where saplings will then be planted directly above. Father is laid to rest on my mother's right, Rayla on her left, and Pawel a short distance away. Ellie, his adopted sister, gave her blessing. Her hologram is watching in the funeral congregation somewhere, but I'm not ready to face her. *The Common will look after her,* I vow to Pawel, wherever he is now.

The Common Guard shields the cemetery in a protective ring. Surveillance drones patrol the perimeter. Both sides have agreed to a temporary cease-fire, allowing twenty-four hours to bury the dead. But we're still at war. No armistice will allow me to forget that. The cruelest side effects of warfare are lying in the ground beneath my feet.

All the Texas Guard still loyal to Roth are retreating back to Texas at this very moment, abandoning the other states they invaded, assembling and plotting to take back Dallas.

Last night we won the battle to turn Texas yellow. Right now, Dallas is ours. How long will that hold true?

We survived, Father. We survived for you and for Mother. Just like you asked us to. What now?

We will have to figure that out for ourselves.

Mira, Haven, and I cast fistfuls of earth into each burial hole, then turn to face the hundreds of mourners who have gathered throughout the wooded Eden to pay their respects. We stand apart from the others, the Common multitude looking to us, the last of the Goodwins and Cadwells, tears and questions in every anguished eye.

It's strange having my aunt here with us now. This woman, a complete stranger, is a part of Mira and me. She's in our DNA.

Haven *is* our DNA. She shares identical genes with our mother.

Biologically, she's our mother too.

I'm so desolate inside that thought doesn't penetrate. Maybe someday that miracle will form a foundation for my heart's return.

Birdsong cuts through the heavy silence.

Mira and I were songbirds once, in another life.

No grand speeches are given. The dearly departed cannot hear our words. No soft murmurs of condolences are said. The surviving family has no use for sympathy.

Instead, one by one, Common members approach us, offering a nod or a clasp on the shoulder. Then they grab a handful of earth to help us bury our own.

Emery first, free of her signature long coat; then Barend, his arm wrapped around Ciro, whose honey-blonde locks have been shaved. Next Xavier, weeping, holding on to his freed son, Malik; then Kano, his long dark hair loose around his shoulders, and Owen, his eyes swollen with sorrow. He carried Rayla's body out of the tunnel himself, her ruined face covered in a yellow cloth.

The line of people goes on and on, wending its way deep into the woodland. We will be here all day. *Look, Father, Mother, Rayla. The people of Dallas have come.* They are recognizing the Common. They support us.

It's the wildfire Rayla promised could happen. The rebellion has spread farther than even I thought possible.

I squeeze my sister's hand.

A song bursts out of me, an inadequate tribute, but it's all I have to give. It was our mother's favorite.

Mira joins her voice with mine, a two-part harmony, singing to celebrate the valorous lives of Rayla Cadwell, Darren Goodwin, and Pawel Porter.

May they rest in peace. And may we remain unrested.

HAVEN

6:11 p.m.

That's the time I met Mother. I made it my tattoo. The reason I fight.

The needle hurt. Not as much as my heart does now.

I fall to my knees in front of the small hill of dirt. Reach out and touch the young tree. Mira said Mother will make it grow. Big. Strong. Alive.

Her body failed. I failed her. A governor took her from me again.

"I will fight for you, Mother," I say. Tears in my eyes. I put down six black-eyed Susans. One for every member of my family.

Even one for Father. Where is he? Who is he? No one has said.

Now is not the time for questions. There are too many. But one question keeps shouting in my head.

Why?

Why did Mother die?

Why did Governor Roth get away?

Why is Cleo still missing?

Why am I still here? Why not Lynn?

I move to the oak tree. Lynn is there. I sit under her shade. She blocks me from the Texas sun.

The Common leader sits there too. Emery smiles at me. "You look so much like your sister."

All my years, I felt alone. Like a part of me was gone. Missing. I thought it was just being an Inmate. But it was something more. I was a twin. A bond formed in a mother's womb.

"You knew Lynn?" I ask.

"She was like my own sister. We were friends for twenty years."

"Was Lynn happy?"

She pauses. "Yes. Until she found out that you existed. That you were taken away after you both were born."

I look up at Lynn's branches. At the leaves that make noises in the wind.

"Mother named me Haven," I say. "She told me it means a safe place. I will be that for Lynn's daughters."

Ava. Mira.

Emery nods. She looks sad. "They will need you now. And for what's to come."

I need them.

I will be their Haven.

"I want to fight," I say.

"Then you will fight," Emery says. "The war begins tomorrow."

OWEN

There's an after-service gathering at the Last Stage in Rayla's honor. The whole theater is full. As it should be.

I think Rayla's murder converted every person in Dallas into a Common member. The whole capital came out this morning.

Rayla would like that—her body being the vessel that turned Roth's own people against him. I knew her for way too brief a time, but I know well enough that she would gladly offer herself to save the cause. Again, and again, which she did.

The woman was a tank. I never thought she'd ever actually be stopped. It took a bullet between her eyes to do it.

Right now, the growing Common numbers mean nothing to me.

Rayla Cadwell's life meant more to the cause than the entire population of Texas joining its ranks.

Without her, how can we win?

Without her, I don't know what to do.

My whole useless net-junkie life, I never had anything to lose because I never cared about anything enough to really value it. Now I feel like I just lost my family. The most important thing I ever had.

Rayla stole into my boring Cog life and woke me the hell up. She forever changed me. Now she's just . . . gone.

After the funeral I found Malik—he was freed from Guardian Tower by his dad—and told him I'm ready for my rebellion tattoo. I figured out why I resist.

So that the "good guys" can stop being called criminals.

So that good people like Rayla can live.

We sit together at a table backstage—I wanted some privacy for this moment. The tattooing distracts me from the crazy pain the Guard's bullets left behind—cracked ribs and bruising all over my back.

Blaise hangs close. At least he tells me he's Blaise. He ditched his fiery bandana for the funeral and never put it back on again. Blaise is a looker. Who knew? Rayla never will. Rayla must've pictured Blaise just as pasty and stereotypically nerdy as I did. It's a lot of change to take in at once.

"What do you think?" Malik says. He lifts his needle and sits back. I stare down at my deflowered wrist.

An openmouthed rattlesnake uncoils itself out of a ridged cog. A symbol of my old self transforming into the new. It's got a silver diamond-shaped head and a rattler vibrating in warning. I asked Malik to make half the scales yellow, just like Rayla's. My homage.

I inked two red fang marks with my own hand in the spot where my microchip used to be. A reminder of how close death is—and how much it hurts.

I can't stop the waterworks. Don't think I even want to. In the past, I've always been one to check my emotions just fine, but here I am, my feelings spilling out of me on full display.

I can't work up the nerve to look at Ava and Mira. I failed them both. The sound the sisters made when they saw their grandmother's body . . . I'll never forget it.

Darren, Rayla, Pawel. They've had so many people taken from their lives in such a short time. A wink and suddenly everyone's gone.

Theo might as well be counted as one of them. There's no telling what Governor Roth will do with him—I mean, he had his other grandson, Halton, killed. If Theo's still alive, who knows how long it will stay that way.

Alexander blames the twins—especially Mira—for his son's abduction. He didn't even show up for the funeral, and now Alexander refuses to be in the same room with them. After the service I heard him locked in a screaming match with Emery, vowing to get Theo back, the oncoming Common war be damned.

That game plan is fine with me. I'll join forces with him—my only focus is to find Roth. I have my own war with the governor. The others can fight the Texas Guard.

I have to end what Rayla started.

I catch eyes with Ava—she stands close to her sister at the front of the stage. We go on staring at each other for a good thirty seconds, neither of us uncomfortable.

With my fingers bunched up like I'm ready to throw a punch, I hold out my wrist and salute her. My first official act as a full-fledged member. Ava uncrosses her arms and holds out her tatted wrist right back at me.

Her rebellion mark is a snake too. It's an Ouroboros, a tail-eating serpent, twisted into an infinity symbol.

"Death and rebirth," I say out loud.

Rayla will live on.

Governor Roth made her a hero. He cut off one snake's head, and millions more grew back in its place. Half the country's Common now.

The man could be on the moon, and we will still get him.

He doesn't stand a chance.

MIRA

We speed through the haze at eighty miles per hour.

Ava wraps her arms around my waist as I turn into our old neighborhood in Trinity Heights.

With one shared look, Ava and I had made our silent way to our Triumph motorcycle after the service. No one from the Common or the Common Guard tried to stop us. Not that they could. I had to get away.

We had to go home.

I flip up my helmet's visor, wanting no barrier between my eyes and what's become of our childhood streets. At first glance I could almost be tricked into believing we're riding into our past and that everything will be as it was. Our home will be intact and whole. Father will be waiting for us in the basement, ready to ask his usual question: What was your favorite part of your day?

Nothing, Father. Absolutely nothing.

I wipe the windswept tears from my eyes to see more clearly. Nothing is the same. Abandoned, looted houses are all that's left. We're the only ones here.

I wonder where our neighbors went. Did they flee the night we were caught, afraid to be accused of aiding the Traitorous Twins?

Ava releases her grip on me and points to the greenhouse—the place I'd spend my allotted weekends, gardening and reading and dreaming. The building's glass walls and roof are completely gone, its metal bones the only parts left standing. I imagine a mourner like me, keening out a death wail, hitting the perfect frequency to shatter the structure clean of glass.

I ease the clutch and stop the bike in the center of the road. But it doesn't feel like the world has slowed around me. It still races past, just like time. Never stopping. Always changing.

I used to dream of change. Now I know change just means losing something.

Ava leans the bike on the side stand, and I pull off my helmet. Even though there might be surveillance. Even though people might recognize us.

"Screw it," Ava says, ripping off her own helmet.

Those are the first words she's spoken to me since they showed us Rayla's body in the tunnels.

We move to the sidewalk and look down at the gaping cavity that was once our home.

I don't know what I expected to find: "Keep Out" warnings, "Exterminate the Gluts" signs, rubble, remains, anything that proved the Goodwin family was here.

The night we ran, our father detonated the basement, trying to destroy all evidence of our secret. In the aftermath, the Guard took everything, down to the last crumble of concrete.

All that's left is dirt and memories.

Ava sets her helmet next to mine, and we slide into the empty pit, making for the front corner where our basement would have been. I lie down. Ava lies beside me. We both gaze up at the changing sky.

We stay like this for a while, my thoughts flittering by with no real shape or fluidity.

"We keep failing, Ava," I finally admit now that no one else is around to hear.

I feel so desolate and numb in my misery. The fire that's kept me going is flickering and fading.

How much loss is worth the gain?

What if we keep losing?

"We have no idea where Governor Roth is," I say. General Pierce told us he sent out every drone in his arsenal to hunt down the governor.

We took his city, but the country's still not ours.

Our nation is so vast it makes my head spin. Roth could be hiding anywhere.

Ava squeezes her fingers into a fist, her knuckles white and sharp. "He was poisoned by Skye. He could be dying out there."

"Or he's getting stronger," I argue. "Regrouping. Calling every State Guard to his side."

The dirt crunches under Ava as she sits up, wrapping her arms around her knees. She hasn't cried yet, at least not in my presence. I want to tell her it's okay, that she can release her inconsolable, heartsick grief, that there's no one here to see but me.

"You can talk about him if you want," Ava says, quiet as the still evening.

Him?

She turns to me. "Theo."

I've muted Theo from my mind, out of guilt and shame of thinking about anyone else but Rayla and Pawel and Father.

They just grabbed him. Took him. I couldn't do a thing about it. My chest aches where a Guard's bullet hit my vest, right over my heart.

"Theo could still be alive," I say, trying to convince us both. "If we find Roth, we find Theo."

"And we win," Ava asserts, fanning a new spark of hope.

Finding Roth. Freeing Theo. Taking on the Guard. It all sounds impossible.

But then again, so were counterfeit chips and twins only a few weeks ago.

I look around at the raw earthen walls that surround us. *We can rebuild.*

We can still fight and make our future.

"It's not over," I tell my sister.

"No, it's not."

We will get him back. I renew our old promise. We'll get Governor Roth back for what he did.

I glance at my watch: 9:00 p.m.

Nine more hours until the cease-fire ends.

The night's still young, and there's much to plan.

Ava rises to her feet and holds out her hand to help me stand. We pull ourselves out of the hole, tug on our helmets, and tear through the darkening Dallas streets like a moving flame.

ACKNOWLEDGMENTS

To our editor, Jason Kirk, thank you for your endless encouragement and enthusiasm for Ava and Mira's story. We can't imagine this publishing journey without you by our side. It continues to be a dream come true.

To Ginger Sledge, the woman who made all of this happen. Before we met you, we were just dreamers; we built castles in the air, and you came and put foundations under them. You made it all real. Thank you for everything, from the bottom of our hearts. We love you.

To our developmental editor, Amara Holstein, thank you for returning to Ava and Mira's world with us. Throughout the entire editing process, your thoughtful insight and understanding of our story made all the difference. Thank you also to our copyeditor, Laura Petrella, and our proofreader, Amanda Mininger.

Our entire Amazon Publishing and Skyscape team, you are the best in the business. Our PR squad, Brittany Russell and Colleen Lindsay, we can't thank you enough for all that you have done for us and this series. Eternally grateful to you both for making this publishing experience once in a lifetime. Our marketing squad, Kyla Pigoni and Haley Reinke, you both have been fantastic, with boundless ideas. And to our favorite Hufflepuff, Sarah Shaw, you have been such an incredible addition to our team.

David Curtis, thank you again and again for designing our beautiful and badass covers. We *love* them. To everyone at Wunderkind PR, especially Elena Stokes and Brianna Robinson, it has been an absolute pleasure working with you amazing ladies.

To our CAA team, Wilhelmina Ross, a.k.a. Mina Ren, thank you for taking on our story and joining us on our adventure to adapt *The Rule of One* into television. You are the perfect agent for us, and you have our deepest gratitude. Tracy Brennan and Angela Dallas, we are endlessly thankful to you both. To our lawyer, Ashley Silver, otherwise known simply and affectionately as Silver, thank you for your guidance and skills.

To our dad and mom, Bill and Jerri Saunders, "thank you" in the back of a book will never be enough to repay what you have given to us. But everything we do is for you. Always. We love you more than the prettiest, most heartfelt words can express.

To Brandon Mckay, you were there from the beginning. Your continued belief in this story kept us going when we thought we couldn't. Thank you for reading every word we write. To our sister-in-law Shelly Saunders, thank you for the Spanish translations we used for our books. *Te queremos.* To Allen Ho, Trey Brown, Sinead Daly, and Mallory Rosenthal, thank you all for your genuine, unflagging support while we wrote this novel. All four of you were a light for us while we were in the writer's cave. Thank you for still being there on the other end when we crawled back out.

Lastly we would like to thank our dogs, Winston and Wyatt. They were with us for every page no matter the ungodly hour. The two best writing partners in town. (They're available for hire—just contact our agent.)

ABOUT THE AUTHORS

Photo © 2017 Shayan Asgharnia

Hailing from the suburbs of Dallas, Texas, Ashley Saunders and Leslie Saunders are award-winning filmmakers and twin sisters who honed their love of storytelling at the University of Texas at Austin. While researching the Rule of One series, they fell in love with America's national parks, traveling Ava and Mira's path. Currently, the sisters can be found with their Boston terriers in sunny Los Angeles, exploring hiking trails and drinking entirely too much yerba maté. Visit them at www.thesaunderssisters.com, or follow them on Instagram @saunderssisters.